EVER
Blue

Solis Lake Academy
Book One

K.D. SMALLS

Ever Blue: Solis Lake Academy Book One

First Edition published 2024

Copyright © 2024 by K.D. Smalls

Edited by C. Eileen Editing

Proofread by Under the Sea Editing

Cover Design by Maree Rose

SOLIS LAKE ACADEMY

Dedication

To Ms. Estabrook:
Thank you for being such
an incredible teacher
and for instilling in me
that my words matter.
This is for you.
But please,
for the love of god,
never **<u>EVER</u>** read this.

Note from the Author

If you, or someone you know, has been a victim of sexual assault, please reach out for help. You can call the National Sexual Assault Hotline through RAINN at 1-800-656-4673. You can also chat online with a trained staff member who can provide you with confidential crisis support at <u>online.RAINN.org</u>.

Trigger & Content Warnings

Sexually Explicit Content
Adult Language
Sexual Assault
Arranged/Forced Relationship
Toxic Relationship
Death of a Parent
Manipulation
Blackmail
Coercion

Please reach out to K.D. Smalls with any
questions or comments at kdsmallsauthor@gmail.com

Prologue

Everly

I stood, rain dripping down the sides of the black umbrella covering my body. Apparently the weather decided to give life to my emotions today. I stared down at my black heels, unable to drag my eyes to the scene in front of me. I knew what was happening, but my brain kept telling me that if I didn't look, it wasn't real. *If I can't see you, you can't see me.* Wasn't that what we thought as children?

Feeling a hand slide into mine, I peeked up through my lashes at Evan, his face a stony mask. He had shifted the umbrella we were sharing to his right hand, his left now secured with mine. His light green eyes– *Mom's eyes*– met my blue ones, tears glistening at the surface. He was trying so hard to be strong for me, trying to keep it together, so I didn't lose my shit. Someone had to be strong in this family. Dad had been basically catatonic, only speaking when absolutely necessary since Mom had... my mind couldn't wrap around the word. Evan and I essentially planned the entire service. I didn't know what would happen when we met with the lawyers later for the will reading.

"Everly, it's time." Startling at Evan's voice, I looked up quickly, realizing everyone was waiting for me to throw the white rose in my hand into the hole before me. The hole where my mother's casket was being lowered. Shit.

I sucked in a gasping breath, then another. I could feel the panic tightening in my chest, fingers wrapping around my broken heart. The tears in my eyes finally spilled over, and a sob wrenched itself from deep in my body. My gaze was drawn to the stone on the top of the grave.

Margaret "Maggie" Blackwell. Beloved Wife and Mother. Seven simple words etched into the dark gray granite Evan and I had picked out. It would have been beautiful if it didn't symbolize my mother's death.

Evan gently tugged the flower from my hand, tossing it onto Mom's casket. His lanky arm quickly encircled my shoulders, folding me into his side. I burrowed my face into the front of his black suit jacket, the tears now freely rolling down my cheeks. God, my heart wasn't just breaking, it was completely obliterated. Evan held me close, and I could feel his body shaking with his own grief. I pulled away, looking around, needing the comfort of my dad, needing him here with us. I found him, sitting on a folding chair, drenched by the rain, holding his head in his hands. Mom had been the love of his life. He was so lost, almost as if half of him had died with her that day.

"Evan, we need to get Dad," I choked out, tugging on his lapel. He quickly nodded, ushering me to Dad's side so we could all go home. Home. It didn't feel like home anymore. Not without Mom there. It felt like a shell, somewhere we existed but didn't live. Evan put his hand on Dad's shoulder, and I knelt in front of him, pulling his hands from his head. "Daddy, we need to go," I whispered. The other mourners had all dispersed, leaving the three of us alone. It had mostly been friends of our family; Mom had been an only child, and both of my grandparents had been gone for years. He lifted his head to look at me, pain etched into his features, his blue eyes filled with grief staring back at my own. "Daddy, come on, let's go."

My father stared at me for another moment before looking up at Evan. Devastation flashed across his face, no doubt from seeing my mom's eyes on my brother's face. He pulled one hand from where I had them clasped in mine and placed it over Evan's on his shoulder. He looked between the two of us, his face morphing from absolute grief to something else, something I couldn't name. His features hardened into a determined, almost angry mask, and he squeezed my hand in his.

"I promise you, I will do whatever it takes to keep this family going. I *will not* lose you. Either of you. I will make sure that we always have one another, do you hear me? Whatever it takes, I will make sure we are ok. I will take care of you," Dad said, his voice cracking on the last few words.

"Oh, Dad," I leaned up, throwing my arms around his wet shoulders. Evan leaned down, wrapping us both in his long arms. We stayed like that for a long time, the rain drops hitting the top of the umbrella creating a symphony with our tears. After what could have been hours, we all finally stood, wiping at our blotchy, red faces. With my dad on one side and Evan on the other, we made our way to the black limo waiting on the narrow asphalt strip that ran through the cemetery. Finally realizing just how waterlogged we all were, Dad snapped his fingers in mine and Evan's direction, using his magic to remove the water from our clothes. I hadn't realized just how uncomfortable I had been in the soaked garment until I was dry.

No one said a word on the drive home, each of us lost in our thoughts. Dad moved to one side of the limo while Evan and I sat side by side, our hands still clasped together. Once we reached the house, we filed inside. As soon as I stepped through the doorway, I could feel the emptiness. I knew I still had my dad and my brother. But I felt alone. While Evan and I were close in a way only twins could be, my mom had been one of my best friends. We had always been a close family, but we were fractured now, broken in an irreparable way.

I shuffled from the foyer down the hall, pausing to gaze at the many family photos that adorned our walls. A shuddering gasp slipped through my lips when my eyes found a picture of the four of us, taken last summer when we vacationed at the beach. Dad used his magic to swirl my hair above my head, Mom laughing at my side, and Evan holding the camera out with his freakishly long arms to capture all of us. We were so happy. I reached out, stroking my fingers gently over my mother's cheek, tears filling my eyes yet again. God, would they ever stop? There had to be a limit, right? Like your body could only produce so many tears in a lifetime? If there were, I was sure I was there. I pulled myself away from the memory, shuffling past my dad's office toward the staircase.

As I walked by, I could hear my father's voice from inside the room. Was he on the phone? Who on earth was he talking to? His door was ajar, and I stopped just shy of the frame, able to see somewhat inside.

"I swear, Maggie, I'll figure out a way. I'll do whatever it takes," Dad muttered as he paced through the office, weaving around the small sofa and two chairs in an almost manic state. He continued murmuring, his voice lower now, so I was only able to catch snippets of his words. "Find a way... figure out who... powers." Jesus, what the hell was he talking about? Unable to just stand there, I knocked on Dad's door, alerting him to my presence.

"Dad?" I said louder than necessary, wanting to make sure he could hear me. His head shot up, an almost deranged look in his eyes. His salt and pepper hair was in disarray, his tie hanging loosely around his neck. He instantly softened when he saw me, though.

"Everly," he rasped, "what do you need, baby?"

"Just wanted to check on you."

"I'm ok, my little artist. Or, well, at least I will be." Hearing the endearment he and Mom called me since I was old enough to hold a paintbrush caused the air to catch in my lungs. *Mom will never call me that again.* Shaking my head and focusing on my dad, I moved into the room. "Dad, do you need anything? You hungry? We've got about three dozen casseroles in the fridge and freezer from all the ladies at Mom's work."

"Maybe later, baby. I've got some work to do, some things I need to look into." He looked distracted, sitting down behind his desk, jotting notes down on a legal pad. Dad was a successful accountant, his office full of spreadsheets, files, and bookkeeping materials. "Ok Dad, let me know if you need something. I'll leave a plate for you in the microwave." He didn't even look up at my words, clearly engrossed in whatever thoughts took over his mind. He started muttering to himself again, but I couldn't make out any distinct words, so I backed out of the room, closing the door fully.

Finally making it up the stairs, I dragged myself towards my bedroom. Evan's door, directly across from my own, was closed. Maybe he decided to lay down for a while, after all, it had been the shittiest of shit days. Not wanting to disturb him, I turned to the right and opened my own door, ready to take off this dress and burn it. I'd never wear it again. It was too tainted with the memories of burying my mom. Stepping through the frame, my eyes immediately went to the lanky body currently curled up on the right side of my bed, facing the middle. I walked to the opposite side and stared at my brother, tears blurring my vision. He lay there, gripping our mother's pillow between his arms like a life raft, silent tears running down his face.

Without a second thought, I kicked off my heels and climbed onto the bed, facing Evan. Tucking myself in as close as humanly possible, we wrapped our arms around one another and grieved. Grieved for our mother. For the things she was going to miss in our lives. For our dad; even if he was still alive, he was gone, never to be the same man we knew. But mostly for each other and the pain we knew consumed us both. And this pain was like a tidal wave, a tsunami that just wouldn't stop. I knew, deep in my soul, nothing would ever be the same.

One

Everly

This was bullshit. Complete and utter bullshit. Staring at my packed suitcases, my anger continued to rise. What the fuck was Dad thinking, selling the house and enrolling Evan and I at Solis Lake Academy? And at the beginning of fourth year? What the actual fuck!? My bestie, Celeste, was standing in the middle of my now empty bedroom—correction, my *old* bedroom—looking around the bare space.

"Explain to me again why you're moving?" Celeste asked, annoyance clear in her voice. "It's fourth year, and your dad is yanking you out of school to go live in the damn woods at that stupid prep school? What the actual fuck, Eves? This is bullshit." And that ladies and gentlemen, was why she's my bestie for life. Celeste had been my ride or die since second grade when she shoved Parker Stanley flat on his ass for pulling my hair and pushing me off a swing on the playground. We'd been inseparable ever since.

Traditional education in our state ended at age eighteen. Magical beings—or casters, as the humans called us—like Evan, me, my parents, and Celeste, continued on for another four years to help hone our magical abilities. I attended Staunton High with Evan and Celeste for my regular schooling, then had moved on to Staunton Prep with them at my side for year's one, two, and three. We were supposed to finish out strong for year four and celebrate turning twenty one together this fall, but my dad fucked up that plan when he gave Evan and I our Solis Lake acceptance letters.

Rubbing my temples, I attempted to stave off the headache I felt creeping in. "I don't know, C. And yes, it is bullshit. Trust me, I've asked Dad a thousand times why I can't just stay at Staunton High with you. He told me, and I quote, 'Everly, this is an amazing opportunity for you and your brother. And with my new job, it is expected that my children will attend school with my colleagues' children.'" I rolled my eyes, repeating the same two sentences my father had been spewing since he told Evan and I we would be leaving our old school behind and attending Solis Lake instead.

"What does Evan think?" Celeste asked as she pushed one of the rolling suitcases my way. She tried to hide it, but she was as sad about Evan leaving as she was about losing me. She'd never admit it, but I knew her feelings for him ran deeper than friendship. They'd be perfect together, except for the fact my brother was an idiot and had absolutely no idea Celeste was into him. I knew it hurt her every time he went out with a new girl, but she put on a brave face, having no shortage of male suitors. The boys at Staunton flocked to her with her thin frame and long honey-blonde hair that gave her a pixie-like look. Celeste was gorgeous, knew it, and used it. She took what she wanted and gave zero fucks what other people thought.

"Honestly, I think he's kind of excited. He knows that the classes there will help him expand his magic way beyond what he could have learned at Staunton High. And I think he's interested in their elemental programs," I explained, feeling irritated that my brother was so comfortable leaving our whole life behind.

"Evan, how can you be ok with this? Leaving school? Leaving our home?"

"Everly, I need this change. I feel stuck here, stuck in the past. I think a fresh start will be good for us. Help us move on." He squeezed my bicep gently, his green eyes imploring me to understand. He wanted us to move past the pain of losing Mom. But I knew he'd never go if I said no. Looking at my twin's face, I realized I couldn't hold him back like that.

"Fine," I huffed out. *"We'll go... but I won't be happy about it."*

He pulled me in for a hug, messing with the bun on top of my head. "I'd expect nothing less, Eves."

"Hmmph..." Celeste grunted, still obviously unhappy about the whole thing. *Join the club, sister.*

We made quick work of bringing my suitcases and art supplies downstairs to my dad's new car, the bags and boxes floating behind me as I used my telekinesis to move them. The shiny, black monstrosity was enormous, and according to Dad, the safest SUV on the market. Evan was ready to go, bouncing on the balls of his feet near the passenger door. Jesus, how could he be so excited? We were leaving our childhood home *forever.* The home we grew up in, where we each lost our first tooth, where we both fell down the stairs at the same time while racing to the bathroom. Evan broke his leg, and I had been in a cast with a broken arm for six weeks. We thought for sure Mom and Dad would be pissed, but they were more relieved we were ok than anything else.

"I'm so thankful it was only your arm and leg, guys," Mom said as she hugged us both. *"It could have been so much worse."*

Celeste pulled me in for a hug so tight I could barely breathe. I wanted to stay wrapped in her arms forever. "Think I'd fit in a suitcase?" she whispered, the words cracking with her tears.

I squeezed her even harder. "If only, C. I'd take you in a heartbeat. This is gonna suck without you." My own tears were threatening to spill over, but I held them back. I hadn't cried since the day of Mom's funeral.

"Everly, we need to get going if we're going to make it for your orientation tour," my dad's voice carried from the driver's side. I looked over Celeste's shoulder at him, and he gave me a soft smile. I knew whining and throwing a temper tantrum would do me no good, as much as my inner five year old wanted to. Giving Celeste one final squeeze, I pulled away, glancing at Evan and catching his eye. Celeste began walking to her cute little lime green hatchback; I shot Evan a look that said *you better give her a hug goodbye, or I'm going to gouge out your eyeball with one of my paint brushes.* He rolled said eyes but yelled out, "Celeste!" My bestie spun around, startled out of her misery by his voice. "Don't I get a goodbye hug too?" he asked, flashing her his lopsided grin. Even from my spot, I could see the tears threatening to spill over in her eyes. She strode over swifty, wrapping her arms around Evan's waist.

"Bye, Celly," Evan whispered into her hair, pulling her into a tight embrace. She melted into him, her body absorbing every second she was in his arms. God my bestie had it bad. How was it possible my brother was this big of an idiot? Suddenly, Celeste pulled back from Evan and looked up at him, staring into his green eyes. After hesitating for just a moment, she grabbed each side of his face, arched up on her tiptoes, and laid a kiss right on my brother's lips.

My jaw dropped open while Evan's eyebrows nearly crawled into his hairline, his hands still resting on her sides from their hug. Before the shock of what was happening could even fully register, Celeste jumped back and sprinted to her car like her ass was on fire. Evan just stood there staring at her, stunned into silence. My head whipped around to look at my friend, a giant grin spread across my lips. "Whoo hoo!! Yeah Celeste!" I shouted, jumping up and down, pumping my fists into the air. We made eye contact, and I gave her an air high five, something we had done since we were kids. Her face was flushed, and she was quickly approaching tomato territory, but a smile crossed her face as she air fived me back, then quickly hopped into her car and sped off.

I turned back to Dad's SUV, opening the rear passenger door. Evan continued to stand stock still, frozen like a statue. I chuckled, slapping my hand to my brother's cheek, "Bout damn time." I could hear Dad laughing from his side of the car, and I could swear I heard him murmur, "I knew she had it in her." Well shit, even *Dad* knew Celeste was crushing on Evan. Jesus, my brother was fucking blind.

I climbed into the back and pulled my seatbelt tight across my body, Evan and Dad getting settled into the front. I looked out the window at my childhood home, the "SOLD" sign placed squarely on our front lawn. Memories flooded me. Sitting with mom on the front porch, sipping coffee while wrapped in blankets on a cool morning. Evan and I building a snowman during the winter. Celeste and I trying to inconspicuously watch Mrs. Murphy's college-aged nephew mow her lawn in the summer with no shirt.

Not only was I being shipped off to a new school, but I wouldn't even have my home to come back to. The thought sat heavy in my stomach and resentment flooded my veins. Dad bought a condo in Emporia, the city where his new job was located, and apparently it was "fuckin' sweet" according to my brother. Neither of us had even seen it; Dad only showed us pictures from the realtor's website. It *was* pretty fancy looking, and Dad had promised it had enough rooms, so I could have an art studio. But my heart still ached for my bedroom upstairs with the window seat and my makeshift studio in the garage loft with paint splattered everywhere. The last six months had been spent reminding myself that I wouldn't see Mom in the kitchen making breakfast every morning. She wouldn't be curled up on the small sofa in Dad's office during the evenings, reading while he worked. I finally began to wrap my head around those devastating changes when Dad suddenly ripped the carpet out from under my feet again.

Not much I can do about it now. I turned my attention to the seat in front of me, the act a defense mechanism meant to keep the tears at bay. Evan must have felt my gaze because he spun around, locking eyes with me. "Yes, I knew," I answered him before he even got the words out. I knew what he was going to ask without him even speaking. Another one of those weird twin things. I sat back in my seat, crossing my arms over my chest.

"But how—you knew—did I..." he sputtered, clearly at a loss.

Shaking my head, I cut him off. "Evan you're a fucking idiot if you didn't realize Celeste has been in love with you for years."

"Everly Margaret, language," Dad scolded.

"Sorry. But seriously Ev, are you blind?"

"No, I'm not blind, Everly," Evan grumbled, "I just... she's always going out with different guys. Didn't seem like she was into me, that's all."

"Yeah, dumbass," I started.

"Everly Margaret! Watch your mouth young lady!" Dad interrupted angrily.

"Sorry dad," I apologized quickly. "Ev, yes, C likes to date. But she did that because you always seem to have a new girl hanging off you every five minutes. She wasn't just going to wait around until you noticed her. You know Celeste better than that."

"I don't think I know Celeste at all..." Evan muttered, looking out the window.

Forty-five minutes later we were pulling up to the wrought-iron gates of Solis Lake Academy. Once we left the highway, a scenic two lane road took us to the private drive that led to the Academy's entrance. Woods surrounded us on three sides, the main drive cutting through the dense trees. There was a large building straight ahead, its beautiful architecture stealing a small gasp from my lips.

Wide stone steps led up to heavy wooden doors. The building itself was made of stone and reminded me of a small castle, turrets adorning each side with lead glass windows throughout. Deep blue shingles topped off each slope of the building, and I half expected a damn Disney princess to burst out of one of the windows, woodland creatures and all.

Dad pulled the SUV along the circular drive and around a large fountain that sat smack dab in the middle. It was stunning. Atop a tall metal pole sat a golden globe, small jets of water coming out on all sides. Surrounding the post, more water shot out from beautiful golden rocks, the effect making the globe almost glow. I was so completely lost staring at the fountain, I didn't even notice Dad turn off the car and begin to climb out. I quickly followed suit, clambering out and walking around the front to where Evan was waiting. Dad used his telekinesis to unload our luggage, quickly stacking it off to the side of the vehicle.

A noise to my right caught my attention, and I turned just in time to see a stout man with a salt-and-pepper beard walk through the doors. With a flick of his wrist, the doors closed behind him, and he made his way down the stairs towards us.

"Mr. Blackwell, how nice to see you. And this must be Evan and Everly," he said, extending his hand towards Dad.

"Headmaster Charles, good to see you. Yes, these are my children. Evan, Everly, this is Mr. Charles. He's the headmaster here at Solis Lake." Dad shook the headmaster's hand firmly, then took a step back. He quirked a brow at me. "Everly, why don't you introduce yourself?"

Oh, shit. "Hi Headmaster." I smiled politely, holding out my hand. "It's nice to meet you." He shook my hand gently, a warm smile showing beneath his bushy beard.

"It's wonderful to meet you, Everly. We're so very happy to have you joining us for your final year. Your dad tells me you enjoy the arts. We have an excellent program here that I think you'll really enjoy."

Well damn, how was I supposed to hate it here when he was being all nice and talking about their art programs? "Yeah, it sounds great," was all I could think to say in response. I darted my eyes at Evan. *Help!*

Evan saw my plea and jumped into action. He had always been the more social twin. Friends with everyone, a never-ending trail of girls following him, popular but not quite the king of campus. Now, that's not to say I was unpopular. I had friends; I went to parties, but my favorite pastime was blasting rock music while I painted in my studio. I dated, having had one serious boyfriend, and I engaged in my fair share of drunken makeout sessions, even throwing the occasional party hook up into the mix. I was no stranger to having a good time. But my brother lived for the social scene.

"Hi Headmaster Charles!" Evan said brightly. "I'm Evan. I've heard you guys have a sweet Elements' program, is that true?" I sent Evan a grateful smile. My brother, the white knight. He shook Charles' hand while they discussed the Elemental classes Evan could take this year. My attention shifted back to my surroundings. This really was a beautiful place. I could just imagine sitting on the edge of the fountain with my sketchpad, drawing the nearby trees with my charcoals....

"Everly?"

"Sorry, what?" I spaced completely out of the conversation. Great. Charles was going to think I was some kind of airhead who didn't pay attention.

"I was just saying that we have a student coming to give you and Evan an orientation tour and to show you to your rooms. Our buildings are co-ed, and as you and Evan are siblings, we placed you in a suite together. You will each have your own bedroom and bathroom but will share a common space and kitchenette. The staff agreed that as new students it felt important to keep you together," the headmaster explained.

"The buildings are co-ed?" Dad asked, concern etched in his tone. Of course that would be the part he focused on.

"Yes, Mr. Blackwell. We believe the students must learn to interact socially with members of the opposite sex. Rooms are not co-ed, but some suites, like Everly's and Evan's, are. Typically they are separated by gender, but males and females do reside in the dorms together."

"Don't know how much I like that," Dad mumbled under his breath.

"Ah, here's your tour guide now." Charles gestured behind where Evan and I stood. I spun on the heel of my sandal, my short blue sundress flaring around my thighs.

Holy. Shit.

Two

Griffin

I quickly checked the time on my smartwatch as I dug around for my favorite navy blue SLA t-shirt. *Shit, I'm gonna be late.* I always liked to wear it when I gave orientation tours. I found it made the newbies a bit more comfortable. Lifting a throw pillow on the couch and striking out again, I spotted Chase's gray rowing shirt. Snatching it up, I threw it over my head, taking a moment to make sure it wasn't wrinkled to hell. Deciding it looked passable, I made the quick decision to teleport over to Solis Hall, knowing I'd be late otherwise. I snapped my fingers, my caster power depositing me just around the corner of the old brick building.

What I was not prepared for was the girl in the sexy blue sundress standing in front of the fountain who came into view as I entered the main courtyard. Tanned legs extended from the hem, not long but toned and lean. She was on the petite side, that was for sure. I slowed to a walk to take in the sight before me. Standing in front of the fountain, the late morning sun behind her, she looked almost ethereal, as if she were glowing. Letting my gaze move up her legs, I found a perfectly round ass, the dress clinging in all the right places. Long, dark hair hung down her back in a fancy braid—*what's it called? A*

French braid? Spanish? Oh, who the fuck cares—and I could see tendrils that had fallen out along her hair line.

"Ah, here's your tour guide now."

The sexy blue dress spun around, and holy shit, I think I died and went to heaven. This girl was beautiful. No, scratch that. This girl was fucking stunning. The tendrils that had come out of the braid framed her gorgeous face. She had soft, pink lips that were turned down in a slight frown, but it did nothing to detract from her beauty. My gaze moved up to her eyes, and I momentarily froze. The bluest eyes I had ever seen stared back at me, a vivid shade of tropical water, lined by dark lashes.

Her cheeks began to turn a rosy shade of pink as she realized I was completely checking her out. Shaking myself from my stupor, I continued towards the group, which included Headmaster Charles, an older man who I assumed was the girl's father, and a guy around my age. *Please don't let this be the boyfriend.*

I came up next to Charles, slinging an arm around his shoulders. The old man, who stood a good five or six inches shorter than my 6'3" frame, turned to look up, a smile appearing on his face.

"Evan, Everly, this is Griffin Cardarette. He'll be your orientation guide. Griffin, this is Evan and Everly Blackwell. They'll be living in the Bliss Hall dorms and are fourth years, same as you," Charles introduced us. *Hmm, not the boyfriend, then. Must be the brother?*

The older man stepped forward, extending his hand. "Mr. Blackwell, Evan's and Everly's dad. Nice to meet you, Griffin, was it?"

"Yes, sir," I shook his hand, then turned to the younger guy. "Evan, I'm guessing?"

"Yep!" A wide grin split across his face. I reached out and gave him a patented dude-bro-handshake-backslap. "Nice to meet you, man!"

"Yeah, you too! So if you're Evan," I said, spinning slightly to finally engage the blue-eyed beauty, "then you must be..."

"This is my sister, Everly," Evan threw out helpfully. *Sister, yes!*

"Everly," I repeated her name, loving the way it rolled off my tongue. I held out my hand and waited to see what she would do. This close to her, I could see the light dusting of freckles across her cheeks and nose, her smooth skin kissed by the summer sun.

Everly gave me a sweeping look from head to toe, biting her lip as her eyes perused my body, and after a moment she extended her hand to mine, apparently liking what she saw. Her hand was tiny in mine, and I squeezed gently, staring into her blue eyes. "It's really nice to meet you."

"Likewise," she responded simply, her voice soft but with a husky quality. My cock stirred in my shorts when she spoke. I could imagine her moaning my name, those tanned legs wrapped around...

"Griffin will show you around the rest of campus," Charles' voice shook me out of my dirty fantasy. "Your bags will be taken to your suite, and your father was kind enough to have bedding and other supplies delivered earlier today, so you should be all set. Your textbooks and tablets will also be there. Any questions?"

"No, sir," the siblings answered in unison. Were they twins? Charles said they were both fourth years. I briefly wondered if they had any freaky twin mind powers?

"Excellent!" The headmaster clapped his hands. Then, with a snap of his fingers, the pile of luggage standing off to the side of their car disappeared, presumably finding its new home in Bliss Hall. Charles was a telekinetic and a teleporter, making him a powerful Caster, but he was actually a pretty down to earth guy, even if he did have to be a hardass from time to time. He tried to make sure we got the best education money could buy while also ensuring we had a good social scene on campus. There were lots of clubs and sports to choose from, and he was also known to turn a blind eye to our monthly parties out in the forest. Chase, Knox, and I were typically the hosts at these events, and as long as no one got hurt, Charles didn't seem to care.

Turning to the twins, I looked them both over. I could see their similarities. Same dark brown hair, an almost chocolate color. Everly's was obviously long, while Evan's was cut in a short, cropped style. Both siblings had straight noses that turned up ever so slightly at the tips. Everly had more freckles than Evan, and god did they make her that much more sexy.

Their faces were where the similarities ended, however. Where Everly was petite, but curvy in a hot as hell way, her brother was tall and lanky. He looked like he had some muscle, not nearly the bulk me or the guys had, but definitely some definition.

"Alright, Evan, Everly, Mr. Cardarette and I will give you a moment to say your goodbyes, and then I will turn you over to Griffin for your tour. Classes begin Monday, but if you have any questions regarding your schedules, you can make an appointment with your counselor." Headmaster Charles gestured to the large building behind us. It housed his office, as well as the business offices, counselors, and a whole bunch of other offices I didn't give a shit about. The old man reached out, shaking Mr. Blackwell's hand one more time in goodbye, then turned back to the twins. "Enjoy your tour, and welcome to Solis Lake!"

With those parting words, Charles headed back into the administration building, leaving me to awkwardly witness the goodbyes between father and children. I stood off to the side, checking my phone while they chatted quietly.

As I mindlessly scrolled through social media, I tried to think up ways I could get Everly alone, so I could get to know her better. Damn, Chase and

Knox were going to lose their minds when they saw her. I'd have to find out if she had any special interests, anything that she might do *without* her brother. They seemed tight, and he seemed cool and would probably make a good friend. But damn, it was going to be hard to get close to this girl if her brother turned into a permanent cockblock.

Hearing the engine of the SUV turn over, I looked up to see Evan walking towards me, Everly trailing slightly behind. I noticed the sexy sway of her hips, and her blue eyes lit up as she looked at me.

Showtime.

Three

Everly

He had to be the best looking guy I'd ever seen, and I kept trying to subtly check him out without my dad or Evan noticing. He was tall, easily 6'3", and muscular, the Solis Lake rowing shirt tight across his broad chest. His tanned arms strained the sleeves, the muscles flexing as he played on his phone.

Letting my gaze roam down his body, I took in his trim waist and toned legs. Working out must be an everyday thing for this guy. His gray shirt hit just at the waistband of his khaki shorts, the hem sitting atop a black belt. I imagined if he raised his arms at all that I would be treated to some well-defined abs, maybe even that sexy V that made my mouth water. I was suddenly pulled back into the conversation by Headmaster Charles. *Jesus, I hope I don't have any drool on my chin.*

"Enjoy your tour, and welcome to Solis Lake!" Charles said as he departed.

Shit, that meant it was time for Dad to go. And I would be stuck here. Although, getting to admire Griffin didn't seem like such a bad way to start my stay. He had moved off to the side, clearly giving us a moment to say goodbye.

Dad quickly hugged Evan, giving him a firm slap on the back. He whispered to my brother, but not soft enough for me not to hear. "Watch out for her, Evan. Take care of each other." My brother gave a firm nod and squeezed my dad one more time before releasing him.

I stepped into Evan's place, and my dad's arms enveloped me in a tight embrace. I looped my arms around his back, nuzzling my head into his chest.

"Do you really have to go, Daddy?" I pleaded uselessly.

"You know I do, sweetheart. I've gotta get the new condo set up and get settled into my new job."

"Okay. I love you, Daddy. Please take care of yourself. Eat dinner. You always forget to eat," I started to ramble, not ready to let him go.

"I will, Everly. You and your brother take care of one another. I love you both very much." He squeezed me a bit tighter and planted a kiss to the top of my head before pulling away. "Alright, go take your tour. I'll call in a few days, give you a chance to settle in. Sound good?"

"Sure, Daddy," I replied at the same time Evan answered, "Yeah, Dad, we'll talk to you soon."

Dad climbed back into the SUV and pulled away, taking with him any hope I had of leaving. *Well, if you can't beat 'em, join 'em.* I squared my shoulders and turned to face Griffin. Putting a little sway in my hips, I followed Evan. Guess we'd see if the attraction was mutual, although judging by the smile spreading across his face when he looked up, I'd say I was on the right track.

Placing his phone in his pocket, Griffin moved toward us. "Okay, so first, I think I'll walk you guys to Voxina Hall. It's the academics building where all of your classes will be held. Then we'll hit the dining hall, and then Bliss, the dorm. Sound good?"

Evan and I both nodded our agreement, falling in step with Griffin as we strode down the sidewalk around, what was it again, Solis Hall? Shit, I wasn't going to be able to keep these damn names straight.

The campus was beautiful, the grounds a lush green with the last of summer's warm weather. There were garden beds with vibrant flowers along the sides of the buildings and tall trees that offered shady study areas. I could see students milling about, catching up after being away all summer. Voxina Hall sat between the administration building and the lake, a large courtyard spanning the open space. In the distance to the right sat a large, modern facility that almost looked out of place with the rest of Solis Lake's historical buildings. I noticed a few students walking that direction holding gym bags, so I assumed it was the sports complex. In the opposite direction, set some distance from where we stood, were a cluster of buildings that I concluded must be the dorms.

As we walked, Evan fell behind, leaving Griff and I side by side. I tried to slyly glance at him, but he caught me, a panty-melting grin gracing his handsome face. Luckily, he didn't call me out on my obvious gawking, instead steering the conversation into more neutral territory.

"So Blue, how'd you end up here at SLA? We don't get many students transferring in their fourth year," he questioned, his hazel eyes finding mine. Beautiful, long lashes framed them, the greens around his pupils giving way to beautiful ambers and golds that resembled starbursts. Damn it, why did boys always get such perfect lashes? I had to curl the hell out of mine and add mascara just to look awake most days.

"Our dad took a new job, sold our house, and bought a place in Emporia. I guess some of his coworkers' kids go here, so here we are, "I explained quickly, gesturing around me.

"Oh yeah? Where does he work? I bet I know some of the people you're talking about."

"Umm, I think it's called Thorpe and Stone Investments? Something like that?"

"Shit, seriously?" he asked, his eyes growing wide.

"Uh, I think so. Is that a bad thing?"

The grin from before made a reappearance. His cheeks had to hurt from how big his smile was. And Jesus, was it a nice smile. I felt butterflies in my stomach when he turned that grin on me and my panties dampened. *Jesus Everly, get it together, you just met the guy.* "Nah, that's awesome actually! My buddy Chase, his dad is one of the owners. So I mean, I guess technically his dad is one of your dad's bosses."

My jaw dropped in shock, as I swung to look at him. In my surprised state, I failed to notice a small chunk of stone missing from the sidewalk in front of me. I felt the front of my sandal catch the rough edge, and suddenly I was falling. Until I wasn't. A strong arm banded around my waist, keeping me from eating asphalt. Griff's hand splayed around my side, damn near taking up my whole rib cage as he pulled me into his chest.

I gasped at our sudden proximity. Griff's hazel eyes searched my face, looking for any sign of injury. We were only inches apart, a feat considering his tall frame. I could feel his warm breath fan across my lips, heat pooling in my lower belly. Jesus, I never thought of myself as a damsel in distress, but if Griffin wanted to play my knight in shining armor, I'd certainly let him.

"You ok, Blue?" he asked, still studying my face.

"Yeah," I replied, my voice breathy, but still having its signature husky sound. Celeste had told me once that if art didn't work out, I could always get a job as a phone sex operator. I thought Evan was going to throw up when the words had come out of her mouth. "Jeez, sorry, I'm such a klutz sometimes."

Neither of us made any attempt to move, Griffin's hand still firmly around my waist. He used his free hand to tuck a loose piece of hair behind my ear, a lopsided grin crossing his face. It felt like a scene straight out of a movie and god help me, I swooned at the gesture. *Goddamn, he's smooth.*

"Hey! You guys ok? Eves, you alright?" My brother's voice shattered the moment. Evan came running over, his super speed putting him next to us a second later. He had been distracted while reading a placard in front of one of the buildings; most days he was like a raccoon that had spotted something shiny. Concern marred his face, and he looked warily at Griffin's hands on my body.

"Yeah bro, we're good," Griff started to explain. "Everly just tripped, and I managed to catch her before the ground broke her fall."

"Eves?" Evan questioned, needing confirmation from me.

"Yeah, Ev, I'm good. Just tripped over my own feet. Let's keep going," I reassured him. Feeling my face growing red, I reluctantly stood, pulling myself away from Griffin. Maybe it was just wishful thinking, but it seemed to take him an extra few seconds to remove his hands from my waist.

Once I regained my bearings, we continued on our way. I made sure to pay attention to the path in front of me, not wanting to embarrass myself further. Replaying my near catastrophe, a thought sprang into my mind.

"Blue. You called me Blue. Twice. Why?" I swung to look at him once more, stopping dead in my tracks.

Griff paused just in front of me, turning when the question left my lips. He stared at me for a moment, his gaze roaming over my face before answering.

"It's your eyes, Everly. They are the most beautiful shade of blue I've ever seen."

An almost inaudible gasp escaped my lips, my eyes searching his for the lie. But all I saw was sincerity and truth staring back at me.

27

Leaving me stunned, Griffin turned and continued walking, as if the exchange had never taken place. We rounded a bend, and another stone building came into view. It was similar to the administration building, but on a much larger scale. It was five stories tall, with old leaded windows lining the brick exterior.

"This is Voxina Hall, but most of us just call it Vox. It's where all of your classes will take place with the exception of any PE or defense courses. Those are in the sports complex down near the lake. If you guys want, I can take a look at your schedules and see if we have any classes together, might help you out til you get the lay of the land," Griff explained. "What are you majoring in?"

"Yeah man, thanks. I'm planning to go into Elemental Sciences. I'm a fire elemental, so maybe research in that field." Evan chuckled, nudging me in the shoulder. "And it'd be cool to know at least one person besides my sister, too." I gasped, my hand covering my chest in faux shock.

"I don't know, your sister seems pretty cool," Griffin replied to Evan, but his eyes locked on mine as he said the words. I felt my cheeks flush at the compliment and bit my lower lip to keep from smiling. Evan didn't seem to hear, already moving down the path again toward the back of the building. We stared at one another for a few moments before he gestured toward where Evan had gone.

"What about you, Blue? What are you studying?"

"Art. I've been painting for a long time, so it was kind of a no brainer," I replied.

"Cool. We have a great art program here. One of my roommates is a double architecture and art major; I'll have to introduce you," he said, and as we started walking, his hand landed lightly on my lower back. I peeked at him through my lashes, a cocky grin on his face. Thinking maybe he was a bit too cocky, I decided to have a little fun.

"Awfully presumptuous, don't you think?" I asked, knowing full well he understood the meaning behind my words.

"Is it?" he teased. "Because I think it's just presumptuous enough. But I can move if you..."

"No, no," I interjected quickly, not actually wanting him to move his hand. I turned my face to look up at him. He really was stupidly handsome with a playful smile on his lips. *Damn, I bet he's a good kisser.* Because there was no way Griffin Cardarette wasn't a good kisser.

We rounded the building, and my breath caught in my lungs. About fifty feet or so in front me was the lake Griff mentioned before. But this wasn't just a lake. It was... perfect. Trees dotted the lawn leading up to a golden, sandy beach. The water was a beautiful turquoise blue, unusual for freshwater. It had most likely been enchanted that color, but honestly, I didn't care. It was the most beautiful thing I had ever seen. Suddenly, I could see myself, easel and paints in hand, creating art here in nature. It was the perfect spot.

"This is Solis Lake," Griff's voice shook me from my art filled day-dream. "It's two miles long and runs east to west on the grounds. The name comes from the fact that you can see the sun both rise and set on the water. The rowing team uses it for practices and competitions. Actually, they're out there now." He pointed toward the lake, where I could see a long row boat with about eight guys on board.

Griff stuck his middle finger and thumb into his mouth and let out a high-pitched whistle. Evan whirled around to see what was going on, but Griff was waving at the boat. I could see a blonde guy waving back, a long muscular arm extended over his head.

"That's Chase, the guy I was telling you about earlier. I'll have to introduce you later."

"Yeah, that sounds good," Evan answered for me. He was all over the place, checking out every little thing on campus, running around like an overexcited five-year-old let loose in a toy store. As much as I hated to admit it, Solis Lake seemed like it actually might be an okay place.

Feeling Griff's hand on my lower back again, I gave him a sly smile. Yeah, maybe Solis Lake wouldn't be so bad after all.

Four

Chase

I was in the middle of row practice when I heard Griff's signature whistle coming from the shoreline. Looking up from my spot as the stroke, I saw him standing with a girl in a blue sundress. Scratch that. A fucking gorgeous girl in a sexy little dress. Luckily we weren't rowing at the moment, so I raised an arm to wave. I was definitely going to be asking about the hottie he was with later at our dorm.

Just a few minutes later, Alex called practice from his position at the stern and we rowed back to the dock. After hopping out and making sure all of our equipment was stowed away, I grabbed my gym bag from the boathouse and headed back to Bliss to shower. Since classes hadn't started, we had double practices each day. Thank god that would be changing tomorrow since our coach gave us Sundays off.

I was going to need all the time I could get to study this semester. My dad convinced my counselor, Mrs. Bryan, to put bullshit classes like Mathematical Formulations in the Magical World on my schedule to help prepare me for work at his investment firm. Every time I brought up the fact that I had zero desire to sit behind a desk all day, Carrick Stone just laughed.

"As if you won't take over one day," he chuckled, slapping a hand on my shoulder.

"Dad, I really don't want to work at the firm. Seriously."

"Chase, it's not really up to you. You'll do what's expected. Now come on, let's open the bottle of bourbon your mother got me for our anniversary."

Just thinking about working at Thorpe & Stone made my skin itch and my heart rate pick up, anxiety creeping in. The thought of being stuck in an office all day everyday was legitimately my worst nightmare. I loved being outside, in nature, and especially on the water. Rowing crew was the one thing I felt I was really good at. The one thing I felt made my parents proud of me. It sure as shit wasn't my grades.

Taking the steps up to my dorm two at a time, I swiped my key fob at the pad, unlocking the door. I made my way up the stairs to the suite I shared with Griff and Knox. We had the largest suite on campus, my father making sure his only heir was in suitable housing; it was essentially a penthouse with only three or four other suites on our floor. Using my fob once more to open our door, I pushed inside and went straight to my room. I knew Griff wasn't home– asshole was with that hot girl– and I could hear Knox's music blasting from his room. *Jesus, I hope he's not in another mood, I really don't want to spend the night cleaning up paint splatter when he finally emerges.*

Stripping out of my clothes, I turned on the shower in my private bathroom. Luckily the hot water in the dorms never ran out—thank you magic—so I stepped directly under the warm spray. As I washed the sweat and grime from my body, my mind drifted to Griff and the girl in the blue dress.

She had been about fifty feet from the shore, but I could still tell she was gorgeous. And Griff totally had his hand on her back, which wouldn't have happened if she wasn't at least cute. He and the she-devil must be broken up again if he was making moves on this girl. Jesus, Morgan would lose her shit if she found out he was interested in someone else. Not like she had room to talk though. She was the one always breaking up with him so she could go spread her legs for some dick who would kick her to the curb the next morning. Then without fail, she'd come running back when she realized she had it made with Griff. Poor guy. Either he ignored her behavior or he really was booty blinded.

As far as I knew, Morgan had been Griff's first and only girlfriend. They met at the beginning of first year, and the bitch strung him along all the way through until the start of third year before she finally put him out of his misery and said she'd be his girlfriend. I don't know why he wasted so much time chasing after one girl, not when there were dozens willing to wet his dick but whatever. Dude was hot and girls would line up around the block for a chance with him if he'd just break up with Morgan for good. I was never in short supply if I needed a girl in my bed, so I guess I didn't understand the allure of having a girlfriend. To each their own, I guess.

My brain shifted back to the mystery girl as my hand found my dick. I pumped it a few times, the slide making it grow harder with each stroke. I pictured her little blue sundress pushed down around her waist, perky tits spilling over her bra, down on her knees for me. I rubbed the head of my dick across her lips, coating them with precum. She parted her pretty pink pout and took my cock deep into her mouth, the tip bumping the back of her throat. My hand shuttled up and down quickly as my fantasy pushed me closer to the edge. With one final thrust into my palm I exploded, ropes of white cum hitting the tile wall and covering my hand.

I heaved out a breath, my forehead pressed against the cool tiles. After a moment, I cleaned myself and the wall, then turned off the shower. Stepping out, I dried off quickly, wrapping the towel around my waist before walking into my room. I snagged an old rowing t-shirt and a pair of athletic shorts, and made quick work of getting dressed.

Dumping my dirty clothes in the hamper, I made my way out to the small kitchen we all shared, pulling a beer from the fridge. The guys and I all turned twenty-one over the summer, so we were finally allowed to keep beer in our suite. Not that it stopped us before we were legal. Were we supposed to have alcohol on campus before twenty-one? No. Was Headmaster Charles going to write us up, knowing that my dad was one of the school's biggest donors? Also, no. As long as we weren't complete idiots, Charles left us alone. He even ignored the once a month forest parties we started throwing during our second year.

I dropped down onto the sofa just as the front door swung open. Tilting my head, I saw Griff come strolling in, a shit eating grin on his face. Oh he had it *bad*.

"Yo," I called from the couch, raising my beer over my head in greeting.

"'Sup?" Griff responded. I could hear him rummaging in the fridge and then the distinct sound of a bottle being opened. His tall form came into the living room, and he dropped down on the opposite end of the sofa. Propping his feet up on the coffee table, he took a long pull from his beer. I stared at him for a moment, then figured, what the hell?

"So who's the girl?"

Nothing. Crickets.

"Yo, Griff!" I said louder, waving my bottle in his periphery.

Griff startled, clearly having been daydreaming. *About my mystery girl, perhaps?* Whoa, wait, why was she *my* mystery girl? I didn't even know this chick. Sure, I'd used her in my mind to get off, but that was it.

"What's up?" Griffin finally responded.

"Who's the girl?" I repeated.

That shit eating grin spread across Griff's face once more, and I could tell my buddy was already in deep. *Oh shit.*

"The girl is a new fourth year. Everly Blackwell. She and her brother just got to campus today. I was giving them a tour when we saw you rowing. Dude, she's gorgeous. Like, holy shit beautiful," he explained, his eyes lighting up at the thought of her. "And her voice, oh man, it's like husky, sexy, just... Gah, man you're gonna lose it when you meet her."

"She looked hot from what I could see," I said, taking a pull from my bottle. "So I take it you and Morgan are on the outs then?" I cocked my head to the side, studying my friend.

"Yeah, she and I are done. Like, done done." His voice grew quiet and his cheeks flushed red. Whoa, I had definitely missed something.

"What happened? Not that I'm not ecstatic that you're finally rid of her, but I mean, let's be honest, man. You're usually waiting for her to come back with open arms. What changed?"

"I actually caught her for once." *Oh fuck.*

"Ah shit, Griff, I'm sor—"

"Nah man, it's okay. I knew what she was doing. But she usually had the decency to break up with me before jumping in bed with someone else. This time, apparently, she couldn't wait. Caught her a few days ago, bent over a table in one of the study rooms in the library. I was making sure I signed up for the one I wanted this semester for my tutoring sessions. I guess she forgot which room I used."

I cringed at his blasé attitude. I knew catching her had to have hurt him. "Okay, so who's ass do we need to kick?"

"No ass kicking necessary. And it was Caleb Donovan, the prick I tutored last year for Magical Philosophies. Asshole can have her, I'm done." He took a long drink, a crease appearing on his forehead as he frowned.

35

"Cheers to that," I said, clinking my bottle to his, earning me a slow smile. "Trust me, Knox and I will be happy to never see her skanky ass in our suite again."

"Amen brother." He grinned. "Actually, how would you feel about me inviting Everly over? And her brother, Evan. Their suite is right down the hall from us. Thought they might want to hang out after dinner. Introduce them to Knox."

"You wanna introduce your new girl to us? What if she decides she likes us better?" I winked, teasing him.

Griffin's smile faltered for a moment.

"Too soon?" I asked with a wince.

He recovered quickly, shooting me a grin. "Nah, I'm not worried about you guys. You've got girls falling at your feet. And Knox is too big of an asshole for me to worry that Everly would be interested in him."

"The fuck?" Griff and I both about jumped off the sofa at Knox's deep voice. I swiveled around to look at him, and yep, sure enough the surly bastard was covered in paint. Standing in his doorway in nothing but his black painting sweats, he crossed his paint splattered arms across his broad chest. "I'm not an asshole, asshole."

Griff and I looked at one another for a beat, then burst out laughing.

"Whatever, dickbags," Knox mumbled before going back into his room. The loud rock music that I hadn't noticed had disappeared turned back on just as his door slammed shut. I took a few deep breaths, calming myself after my laughing fit.

"So is that cool with you, then? If Everly and Evan come over?" Griff asked after a few minutes.

"Uh, yeah man, go for it. Can't wait to meet them."

I definitely couldn't wait to meet the girl who had my friend all tied up in knots. Who knew, if things didn't work out with Griff, maybe she'd let me live out my shower fantasy.

Five

Everly

After Griffin finished showing us around, we walked to Bliss Hall—AKA my new home. It was situated on the far side of campus, clustered with three other buildings that housed students. Each one had the same historic look as Solis Hall, brick making up the main structure and the signature blue tiled roof of the other buildings on campus. He swiped a small key fob on a pad near the door, a distinct clicking sound coming from the lock. Griff pulled open the heavy-looking door, ushering us inside. I let Evan go first, and as I stepped through the doorway, I could feel Griff close at my back.

He leaned down near my ear, his breath tickling my neck.

"Welcome to Bliss Hall, Blue," he whispered, his fingers trailing lightly down my right arm. Goosebumps erupted on my skin, and I sucked in a quick breath.

Not waiting for my response, Griffin moved past me into the foyer. The building was beautiful, a common theme I was finding across the Solis Lake campus. Hardwood floors and wood paneling lined the room, while stunning stained glass windows followed the massive staircase to the upper floors. I spun around in a slow circle, taking in the dorm's decor. You could tell the building was old but well cared for. Original fixtures in place but with updated amenities. Instead of candles, beautiful wall sconces provided light down a hall, while a large chandelier hung in the entryway. It felt warm and historic, and I had to admit, I didn't completely hate it.

"It's beautiful," I stated softly.

"Yeah, all of the buildings on campus are pretty cool. I personally love the library. Sorry it wasn't open, or I would have showed you around. It's closed on the weekends before the semester starts. Maybe we can get together there later in the week to study?" Griff explained, his casual invitation peaking my interest.

"Yeah, that could be cool," I answered noncommittally. I had to at least make him work for it a little, right? Celeste would be so proud.

"Cool," Griff looked at me, his hazel eyes glinting in the afternoon sun that streamed in through the windows nearby. "Why don't we get you upstairs, and I'll show you your suite? You're on the fourth floor, same as me."

"I'm sorry, did you say the *fourth* floor?" Evan asked in disbelief. He had suddenly appeared at my right side, startling me. *Where the fuck had he disappeared to?*

"Yeah, it's actually not that bad, and there is an elevator if you don't wanna take the stairs. Besides, the top floor has the nicest rooms." Griffin had already started to make his way to the bottom of the staircase.

"We can do the stairs, it's not a big deal," I said, looking straight at my brother, waiting for him to argue. "Besides, you have super speed, so stop being lazy."

He looked back at me in defiance for a moment before letting out a long, dramatic sigh. "Fine. We can do the stairs."

Evan made quite a show of how strenuous the stairs had been, saying repeatedly that this would be the one and only time he used them. I walked quietly next to Griff, admiring the stained glass windows and paintings that lined the stairwell. Every so often, Griff's hand would brush mine, our pinkies making contact. With every touch, little bolts of electricity zapped up my arm, sending the butterflies in my stomach into a frenzy. I kept sneaking glances at his handsome profile, taking note of the mischievous smile on his lips. *Was he touching me on purpose?*

Making our way down a long hall, we came to a large wooden door with the number 612 hanging on it. There was a key pad above the knob, similar to the one at the entrance of the building. Shit, how were we supposed to get in? Evan and I hadn't been given a key.

As if he could read my mind, Griff pulled another fob from his pocket and swiped it over the pad. The door clicked open, and he twisted the knob. Looking over his shoulder at me, he grinned. "Tour guides are given master keys. Yours and Evan's will be inside with your stuff."

Ah, clever.

I made my way inside, and holy shit was this place nice. A small living area sat to my right, while a little kitchenette took up most of the left. Moving to the living space, I noted two cushioned chairs, a small sofa, a coffee table, and... was that a goddamn *fireplace?* I looked around, stunned by the room before me. Two more wooden doors stood opposite one another, leading to what I assumed were mine and Evan's bedrooms.

"Eves, this place is sweet!" I heard Evan say from behind me. He made his way into the kitchen area and was moving toward one of the closed doors. Twisting the knob, he pushed it open and disappeared inside. I heard a muffled, *"Holy shit..."* before I strode toward the door leading to my own room.

I stepped inside, spinning as I entered. *Damn.* Coming back to my original spot, my eyes ping ponged around the room, taking in the incredible space.

Set squarely on one wall stood a large bed, a soft gray duvet on top with a mountain of pillows. It took every ounce of willpower I had not to take a running leap into the middle of it. Another wall was covered in windows, the light from the afternoon sun filtering in, warming the space. I moved toward them, already picturing my easels set up in the corner. Stepping closer, I looked outside, noting a large oak tree, one of its branches only about three feet from my window. I was able to catch a glimpse of the lake down to the left while the dense forest backed up to the building.

Glancing around, I spotted a dresser, two nightstands, all of my luggage, a small desk that had a stack of books on top, and several more boxes that I didn't recognize. I pulled one open to reveal a shit ton of brand new painting materials, along with a bunch of other art supplies. My eyes stung with tears, knowing that my dad made sure I had all the things I would need to do the one thing I loved.

"What do you think?" I whirled around at Griff's voice. He was leaning against the door frame, arms crossed across his broad chest, his t-shirt pulled tightly around his muscular arms. I took a moment to drink in his sexy form before responding. "It's ok, I guess," I said nonchalantly, shrugging my shoulders in an attempt to hide how impressed I was with the space.

Griff barked out a laugh, his smile crinkling the corners of his hazel eyes. The sound settled warmly in my chest. He had a great laugh, and I found myself wanting to hear more of it.

"Seriously though, it's great, Griff. Thank you for showing us around today. It was a lot of fun." I smiled at him.

"It was my pleasure, Blue," he replied, moving toward me, his long legs eating up the distance quickly. He was standing directly in front of me, so close that I had to tip my head to look at him.

Looking down at me, Griff reached up a hand, tucking a stray hair behind my ear. His green and gold eyes searched mine, and I couldn't help but feel like he saw straight into my soul.

"Would you like to have dinner with me tonight? Me and the guys, I mean. Well, it'll actually just be me and Chase." The words tumbled from his mouth, and I could tell he was nervous.

Just as I went to answer, Evan burst into my room, bouncing up and down like he had springs in his shoes. *Leave it to my brother to completely kill the moment.* "Eves, this place is awesome! Our own bathrooms? Now I don't have to deal with all your girly shit every morning when I get ready. This is awesome!" Not waiting for a reply, he zipped back out into the living room, leaving Griff and I alone once more.

"So what do you say, Blue? Dinner later?" Griff asked again. While I had been busy watching my brother's ridiculous antics, Griff had moved even closer, our bodies now only inches apart. I craned my neck to look at him, and his hand landed gently on my hip.

"Yeah, yeah, dinner sounds great," I stammered, my voice almost a whisper. My hip blazed from the heat of his hand, and my blood heated from his proximity.

"Great. I'll pick you up at six." He leaned in and gave me a gentle kiss on the cheek before pulling back, a cocksure grin on his face. "Bye, Blue."

He spun on his heel and was out the door before I could process what had happened. He *kissed* me. It was probably the sweetest kiss I'd ever had. And I agreed to dinner. Ok Everly, calm down. It's dinner with him *and* his friends. And Evan, obviously I'd bring Evan. Shit. Did I just agree to a date on my first day here? My thoughts were spiraling inside my head.

Taking a deep breath, I closed my eyes, willing my nerves to calm the fuck down. It was just dinner in the dining hall. Blowing out the breath, I opened my eyes and took in my room again. I needed a distraction before my mind overloaded with thoughts of Griffin. Griffin's smile. His stunning green-gold eyes. The way his t-shirt clung.... *Stop it Everly!* Shaking my head, I focused on my suitcases. Okay, unpacking, that's what I would focus on.

Checking my watch, I saw it was only a little after three. That would give me plenty of time to get my clothes unpacked, my painting stuff set up, and get settled in before it was time to go eat. With that thought, I got to work.

I moved about half of my clothes into the walk-in closet off of my bathroom. And holy shit was my bathroom nice. A beautiful white tile walk-in shower stall took up one side, while a toilet and small vanity sat on the other. Soft, fluffy gray towels sat folded on the vanity, along with my favorite peony and jasmine scented shampoo and body wash. A narrow door stood off to the side of the vanity, housing my closet.

Taking my clothes inside, I began sorting and hanging. A perk of being telekinetic, I could simply point to where I wanted my clothes, moving them with ease. I lined up my shoes on the floor and folded all of my sweaters, placing them on the built-in shelves. Looking over my wardrobe, I decided I'd need to make a trip to the campus store and grab a Solis Lake sweatshirt. Maybe if he was nice, I'd get one for Evan, too...

A few hours later, all of my clothes had been unpacked and put away, pictures had been hung, and I was figuring out where exactly I wanted to place all of my paints and other art supplies. Standing in front of my floor to ceiling windows, drumming my fingertips on my chin, I didn't hear the knock on my door.

"Eves?" Evan's voice carried from the doorway, startling me from my thoughts.

"Hey Ev." I spun around. "What's up?"

"You settled in? Looks good in here," he commented, looking around my room. His eyes drifted to my desk, a photo of mom and I sitting on top. He stared at it, sadness creeping into his eyes. He closed them, taking a deep breath, and refocused on me when he opened them once more, the green color making my heart clench.

"Yeah, I'm good. Got everything put away. Just trying to figure out my studio area. How're you doing? You like your room?" I asked him.

"All unpacked. It's pretty sweet, I like the living room too. Kitchen's nice. Small, but it'll hold what we need. Speaking of... you hungry?"

Shit. "Uh, yeah, I forgot to tell you, Griff invited me, well us, to have dinner with him and his friends. You good with that?" I looked at him, silently praying he'd say yes.

"Hell yeah, that sounds awesome!" He smiled. I could always count on my brother to be Mr. Social Butterfly. He'd never turn down hanging out, especially if there was food involved.

Glancing at my phone, I realized it was already almost six. Shit, Griff would be here with his friends soon. Thankful I didn't get all hot and sweaty while unpacking, I smoothed my hands down the front of my dress, making sure I still looked semi-presentable.

"Griff said they'd be here at six, I'm just going to take a few minutes to freshen up. If they get here before I'm ready, will you come let me know?"

Trying and failing to hide his smirk, Evan teased, "Sure, Eves, you go get ready for your boyfriend. I'll let you know when he arrives." I picked up one of the thousand throw pillows on my bed and heaved it at his head, laughing. He ducked, the pillow hitting the door behind him. He stood up chuckling but caught my eye when his face turned serious.

"Seriously though, Eves, Griff seems nice, but if he gives you a hard time or anything, you let me know, okay?" My brother, the protector.

I crossed the room, wrapping my big, little brother up in a hug. "I thought as your older sister I was supposed to look out for you," I joked. Looking up, I saw Evan roll his eyes.

"You are literally a minute older than I am, you do know that right?" He cocked his eyebrow at me.

"Still means I'm older."

"Go get yourself ready, you look like shit." He ruffled the top of my head, tugging a bunch of hair out of my braid. I quickly pulled away from him, swatting his hands as I moved back.

"You dick!"

Evan was already out of the room before I could take my revenge, his laughter carrying through the suite. *He's lucky he's so fast. Bastard.*

I walked quickly into my bathroom, taking a seat at the small vanity where I set up all my makeup. Looking in the mirror, I was able to survey the mess that Evan made of my hair, deciding the whole braid was going to have to come out. Reaching around, I pulled out the elastic band and began combing my fingers through my long brown hair. It fell down my back in gentle waves, and I fussed with it for a few more minutes until I was happy with how it looked.

After applying a little bit of mascara and a quick swipe of pink lip gloss, I could hear Evan talking in the other room. *Oh shit, they're here!* Capping my gloss, I fluffed my hair a little more, then got up to go to the living room. I opened the door, seeing my brother, Griff, and a sexy blonde guy standing by the sofa. Griff and the mystery guy's eyes darted to me when I entered the room. Evan, god bless him, didn't even acknowledge my presence, just kept right on talking.

"Hey, Blue. Long time no see." Griff's smile stretched across his handsome face, and he was next to me in three long strides. He threw his arm casually around my shoulders, as if we were old friends, and looked over at the mystery man.

"Chase, this is Everly. Everly, this is Chase. He's the one who we saw rowing earlier."

Green eyes, the color of freshly cut grass, stared at me from across the room. He was beautiful. Shaggy blond hair fell over his forehead, providing a nice contrast against his tanned skin. My gaze roamed down, taking in the tight black t-shirt that stretched across his bulky upper body. His arms were corded with muscle. He had a lean waist, leading down to a pair of gray shorts sheathed around muscular legs. *Goddamn, they looked like they could break stone.*

Realizing that I was simultaneously staring and holding my breath, I tried to silently drag some air in between my slightly parted lips. When I refocused on his face, I could see Chase staring at me too. He was rubbing his stubbled chin, a dangerous smile playing on his lips. His eyes darted to Griffin's arm around my shoulders, and I could see the moment the challenge crossed his mind. *Well shit.*

Six

Chase

G riff wasn't kidding. This girl was a total smoke show. Petite and curvy in all the right places. Her long, dark hair hung down past her shoulders, framing her gorgeous face, while stunning blue eyes stared back at me. Her tits were a good size; not too big but definitely enough for a handful. My eyes drank in every inch of her tanned skin, and my dick sprang to life. She was gorgeous, soft and delicate like a flower waiting to be plucked.

I was vaguely aware of her brother still talking at my side, but I couldn't make out what he was saying; all of my attention was on the beautiful creature in front of me.

"Chase, this is Everly. Everly, this is Chase. He's the one who we saw rowing earlier."

She stared at me, her blue-eyed gaze blazing a trail over my body. I gave her a smirk, running my hand over my chin, feeling the stubble there. *Shit, I need to shave.* I briefly wondered if she'd like it scratching along her inner thighs.

As she took me in, I could see the interest growing in the bluest eyes I had ever seen. My own eyes shifted to Griffin's arm around her shoulders, noting his unconscious claim on her. I knew he was seriously into this girl, and I didn't want to be an asshole, but *damn*, I didn't know if my dick was going to let me stay away.

I shifted forward, extending a hand toward Everly. "Hi, Chase Stone. Nice to meet you." She placed her tiny hand in mine, and I swore I could feel sparks fly between us. Shit, this was not good. Griff and I could not want the same chick. Morgan had fucked him over too many times for me to hurt him like that. But could I really resist this girl?

"Hi Chase. It's nice to meet you. Griff said you guys are roommates?" Her husky voice had all my blood shooting straight to my dick, and all I could think about was how sexy it would sound when she moaned my name.

Fuck.

I swallowed roughly at the dirty thoughts. Turning my charm up to ten, I answered. "Yup, been friends with Griff since we started here at Solis." I leaned in, my voice a stage whisper, "Although, between the two of us, I'm clearly the better looking friend." I grinned at her, proud of the smile my joke earned.

"Hey!" Griff squeezed her closer to him, causing my hand to dislodge from hers. She laughed—god, now that was a beautiful sound. Without further acknowledging my joke, she looked at her brother.

"Ev, you ready to go?" she asked him.

"Yeah, we were just waiting on you, Eves. I know it takes a while for you to get ready to be seen in public." He was clearly teasing her. Everly had natural beauty. Sure, she had on a touch of makeup, but her skin was bare and her summer freckles adorned the bridge of her nose and the apples of her cheeks.

"Don't be a dick, Evan!" she said defensively, although I had a feeling she knew he was just kidding. Even as she tried to give him a death glare, her affection for him was obvious in her eyes.

"Alright, let's head out, then. Griff, lead the way," I said as I extended my arm toward the door. Griffin walked by, his hand on Everly's lower back. I smiled to myself. *One point to Griff.* Strolling with Evan at my side, I had the perfect opportunity to check out Everly from behind. The blue sundress she was wearing clung to the globes of her perfect ass, her hips swaying with each step. At this rate, I was going to have a raging hard on by the time we reached the dining hall. Jesus, this was gonna be a long dinner.

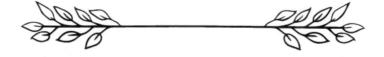

Solis Lake's dining hall was on the opposite side of Voxina from the dorms. The large structure had a similar style to the other buildings on campus, with its old brick and blue tile roof. Inside, large leaded windows lined the three walls of the dining area, interspersed with beautiful stained glass. Solid wood tables of varying sizes filled the space, ranging from square four seaters, all the way up to long, rectangular ones that could easily seat ten. Banners with the Solis Lake crest hung on the walls between the large windows, the tassels at the bottom brushing the old wood paneling.

The kitchen and food stations were all modern, the staff using only the latest and greatest for the academy's students. The serving area was set up in a U shape, with a multitude of stations offering a wide variety of dishes. Plates and silverware were set up at each station, with the beverage and dessert stations near the end on the right.

We showed Evan and Everly around, pointing out our favorite dishes before settling at a small four person table. The wooden chairs were large, and I had to stop myself from laughing when I noticed Everly's feet barely brushing the floor.

Griff and I took turns telling stories about our time at Solis. On my last turn, I decided to explain to them the time I convinced Griff to come swimming in Solis Lake, while I made off with his clothes, so he had to walk across campus in nothing but his wet underwear during our first year. We were all laughing when it dawned on me that Griff and I had done all the talking. I hadn't learned a single thing about either twin.

"So, Blackwell twins, what brings you to Solis Lake for year four?" I asked, looking between the two. I plucked a french fry from my plate, swiping it through some ketchup before tossing it in my mouth.

Evan and Everly both looked at me and then at each other, neither speaking but seeming to have a silent conversation. Griffin, unaware of the non-verbal twin talk, answered for them.

"Mr. Blackwell, their dad, got a job with Thorpe & Stone."

"Oh, really?" That surprised me. Dad hadn't mentioned any new employees or that said employee's kids would be going here. Seemed like something he would've mentioned. *Maybe he was finally getting the hint that I didn't care about the damn company and figured it wasn't worth telling me.*

"Uh yeah, he got hired over the summer," Evan answered vaguely.

"What does he do? Is he an investor?" I prodded, wanting more info.

Everly answered this time. "No, he's an accountant. He sold our house shortly after he got hired and bought a place in Emporia to be closer to work and enrolled us here."

Well, that didn't really track with what I knew of my dad's company. They already had a full team of accountants, and I knew for a fact none of them made enough money to buy a condo in Emporia and pay for two students to attend Solis Lake. Weird.

Figuring it wasn't really any of my business what their dad did for Thorpe & Stone, I let it go. Moving on, I fired off my next question.

"What's your mom do?"

Evan and Everly both froze, her spoon full of chocolate pudding halfway to her mouth. She set the spoon down gently, her eyes trained on her brother. There was a silent plea on her beautiful face, as if she was begging him for something. Evan looked down at the table, staring at his plate.

"Our mom was a nurse. She worked in a pediatrician's office," he said quietly.

My mind was processing his words when Griffin asked the question I was thinking.

"Was?"

I could see the immediate shift in Everly's demeanor. Her shoulders hunched forward, almost as if she were curling in on herself. I couldn't see her expressive blue eyes, but I could tell we stepped in a massive pile of shit.

"She died six months ago. She was mugged leaving work one night...." Everly's soft voice barely reached my ears.

Fuck. *How's that size 12 taste Chase?*

"Oh shit, guys, I'm so sorry," Griff apologized. He stared between the twins, putting his arm around Everly, giving her a small squeeze.

"That's terrible. I'm really sorry," I said, not quite sure how to respond. I still had both my parents. Granted, we weren't close, but I couldn't imagine losing one of them. I knew Griff was on his own, so I figured I would defer to him on this one.

"Thanks guys," Evan said. He took a deep breath before blowing the air out slowly. "Ok, enough with the heavy. You guys ready to head back to the dorm?" I could tell he was putting on a brave face for his sister, and it made me like the guy even more.

"Sure man, let's head out. You guys wanna come over to our place? Hang out, maybe watch a movie or something?" I asked, eyeing Griff for approval. He nodded his head at me. I knew he was planning to ask Everly to come over anyway, so I figured, what the hell?

"Yeah that sounds great," Everly finally spoke, her voice wavering slightly. She drew herself up, squaring her shoulders and looking around at us. "Do you guys mind if we swing by our place first? I just want to change into some comfier clothes."

"Sure, Blue," Griff smiled down at her, complete and absolute adoration on his face. Dude was in *deep.* Although the more I thought about it, the more I realized I was in the same damn boat. There was just something about this girl... she was like the blue Larkspur flowers that grew in the woods surrounding campus, beautiful and rare.

We all got up, clearing our trays before making our way out of the building. Griff was walking with Evan, leaving Everly to walk next to me just behind them. I could hear them discussing different magical elements. Sounded like Griff had finally found someone to rival his own nerdiness. Not that I would ever complain about how smart Griffin Cardarette was. It was because of him that I passed all of my stupid business classes last year. He was so good about tutoring me and not making me feel like a complete dumbass.

I watched Everly as we strolled back to Bliss Hall, noting each time her gaze drifted between Griffin and I. Did she like us both? I was certainly interested in getting to know her better. Maybe if Griff was into it, we could get to know her together...

We reached the dorm before too many dirty thoughts could infiltrate my mind. Griff pulled out his fob and unlocked the door, and we filed inside one at a time, Griff first, then Evan, followed by me, with Everly coming in last. I turned around halfway through the entrance, stopping her. She looked up at me, confusion in her pretty eyes.

"Little Larkspur," I said, my voice low. "Don't take too long getting changed." I pushed her dark hair over her shoulder, gently running my fingertips over her collarbone. Staring into her sapphire eyes, I saw desire flare in their blue depths. *Oh yeah, this definitely isn't one sided.* I smirked at the goosebumps my voice left along her arms.

Without another word, I pushed the door open wider, allowing her through. She walked quickly by, peeking up through her thick lashes, her cheeks a perfect shade of pink. Quite thrilled with myself, I shoved my hands in my pockets and followed her in. I knew she was interested; now I just had to figure out a way to convince Griff to share her.

Seven

Everly

I leaned against my bedroom door with my eyes closed and my mind racing. Holy shit. I hadn't imagined that, right? Chase had definitely been flirting with me when we got to the dorm; I was sure of it. I liked having his eyes on me during dinner, although, judging from the looks we were getting, it seemed he was *quite* popular with the female population here at Solis. There had been several girls blatantly staring and more than a few who tried to get his attention during our meal. To his credit, though, Chase's gaze never strayed from our table.

I could tell he felt bad when he asked about Mom. It was the first time someone we didn't know brought her up, forcing us to confront the memory of her loss. Hearing Evan's answer had been a gut punch, the fragile sutures holding my heart together pulling precariously. Luckily we had all recovered from the awkward moment quickly.

I realized I had been standing against my door for several minutes, lost in my thoughts, when Chase's words rang in my head.

"Little Larkspur, don't take too long getting changed."

His deep, low voice wrapped around my skin like velvet, and I had to hold in a shiver as his fingertips ran across my collarbone. Reaching up unconsciously, I touched the spot where his skin had met mine, heat still scorching through my veins.

Jesus, what was I doing? Griff made it incredibly clear that he was interested in me. He *kissed* me for Christ's sake. But I couldn't deny that both guys made my heart race in a way I'd never felt before. I couldn't be interested in two guys, *best friends*, at the same time... could I?

Shaking my head and pushing those thoughts aside, I moved to my dresser. The air had turned cooler on our walk back from the dining hall, and I didn't want to get cold, so I pulled out a cropped, gray sweatshirt and a pair of black leggings. I quickly discarded the blue sundress into my hamper, threw on my new clothes, and tossed my hair into a loose, messy bun on top of my head. Slipping my feet into a pair of flip-flops, I threw open my door and made my way into the living room.

"Evan, you ready?" I knocked on his door.

It opened a moment later, and Evan appeared before me, juggling a gaming system and controllers. He nearly dropped a controller, so I took some and helped carry them to the couch.

"What are you doing? We're supposed to be going to Griff and Chase's place." I looked at him in confusion.

"Yeah, about that. I'm not going. They're just going to flirt with you all night, and frankly, I'd rather not throw up the great dinner I just had," he replied casually while he situated his gaming crap all over the coffee table.

"I'm sorry, what?" I asked, because there was no way he was ditching me for fucking video games.

"You heard me. I don't feel like watching two guys who I'm hoping to be friends with drool over my sister all night. Plus, Kade and Jax just called. I'm gonna hop on here and game with them for a while. Once classes start I'm not gonna get a ton of time to talk to them." He looked up at me, giving me ridiculous green puppy dog eyes.

"Ugh, fine." I finally conceded after several long seconds spent glaring at him, because honestly, how could I tell him he couldn't play his stupid game with his stupid friends? I knew he missed them just like I missed Celeste.

I'd shot her a couple of texts throughout the day, filling her in on things. She begged for a picture of Griff, but I told her no. There was no way I'd be able to get one without him noticing. I promised to call her tomorrow and give her all the details.

I grabbed my key ring off the counter, making sure my new fob was securely attached. Evan was already booting up his gaming system connected to the flat screen hanging above the fireplace and had chips and a soda lined up on the table. *Jesus, we just ate, how can he possibly be hungry again?* During his exploration earlier, he discovered that our cupboards and fridge had been fully stocked with all of our favorite foods. Dad had really gone all out to make sure we were comfortable here.

"I probably won't be too late. We're just going to hang out for a while," I called to Evan. It was pointless though, he already had on his headset and was starting up his game. "*Be safe, Everly.* Oh, don't worry Ev, I will be. *I love you Everly, you're the best sister ever.* Why thank you Evan, I am the best sister ever," I muttered under my breath as I opened the door.

"Be safe, Eves! I love you!" Evan shouted from the sofa.

I stopped in my tracks, a smile breaking across my face. Damn him.

"Love you too, Ev."

I closed the door behind me and made my way down the hall to Griff and Chase's room, number 614. Their suite was at the end of the hall because as Chase explained, it was bigger. Instead of just two, there were three people who lived there. Neither Griff nor Chase really mentioned the third in their trio, except to say his name was Knox. I was curious if I would meet him or not tonight, although with my luck he'd be just as ridiculously good looking as the other two, and I'd be even more fucked than I already was.

Raising my hand, I knocked softly on the door. I heard footsteps on the other side just before the door swung open, presenting me with a smiling Griffin. He had changed into a pair of low slung gray joggers and a navy blue Solis Lake t-shirt, and *goddamn* did those pants do little to hide what was underneath. Trying not to gawk, I made sure to keep my eyes on Griffin's face.

"Come on in." He gestured into the suite, pulling the door fully open. The place looked like a typical bachelor pad. A large TV hung on the far wall, a sofa and several chairs in front of it. On their coffee table sat a few beer bottles and several gaming controllers. I'd have to mention to the guys that Evan liked video games too. As I looked around, Chase came out of what I assumed was his bedroom. He still had on his black tee but had also traded out his shorts for a pair of light gray sweats. *Were these men trying to kill me? Gray sweats were like my kryptonite.*

"Hey pretty girl," Chase said as he walked into the kitchen. He opened the fridge, then glanced back to where I was standing with Griff. "You guys want a beer?"

"Yeah, grab me one. Blue?"

"Umm, sure. But are we allowed to have booze on campus? I mean, are you guys old enough? I'm not twenty-one yet," I replied, looking around as if a teacher were going to jump out and write us all up.

Chase barked out a laugh, reaching into the fridge and snagging three bottles. "Yeah, we're all twenty-one. And don't worry about Headmaster Charles, as long as my dad's donation checks keep rolling in, I think we'll be okay if you want a beer." He popped the tops and handed out the cold bottles.

Griff nodded in agreement before clinking his bottle to Chase's. He turned to me, tapping the top of his beer to mine, smiling down at me. "Cheers, Blue. So, what do you wanna do?" *Well, that was a loaded question.*

I looked between him and Chase. I had these two hot guys standing before me, both of whom had made it very obvious they were more than interested in getting to know me. I decided to channel my inner Celeste and take what I wanted. "Let's play a game," I said coyly.

Chase's eyes lit up. *Of course.* "What kind of game, little Larkspur?"

Griff's brows furrowed at the nickname. I didn't know what it meant, but now didn't seem like the time to ask. Taking a long pull from my beer, I soldiered on, determined to see where this would go.

I closed my eyes and swallowed my beer, a low moan slipping out as the cool drink made its way down my throat. When I opened them, two sets of eyes stared back at me, both blazing with lust.

"Everly…" Griff growled in a deep voice.

"What?" I asked, my eyes rounding in surprise. What had I done?

"You can't make noises like that, little Larkspur. I don't think Griff's or my self-control can handle it," Chase answered for him, grinding out the words. Griff had turned away, but not before I caught him adjusting himself in his sweats.

Oh shit. The air in the room suddenly felt thick, charged with sexual tension. Had I really turned these two on with just a moan? Risking a glance at Chase, I could see a noticeable bulge in his gray joggers. My eyes darted back up to his face, my cheeks blazing at the sight of his arousal. Chase knew, and judging by the smirk on his face, he didn't care one bit that I had seen his erection.

"Umm," I stammered, embarrassment threatening to make me lose my nerve. "Let's play something easy. Truth or dare?"

A Cheshire cat grin spread across Chase's face. "Oh, little Larkspur, this should be fun."

Uh-oh.

Eight

Griffin

I was positive Everly was trying to kill me. If I thought she looked gorgeous in the sundress earlier today, then I was dead wrong, because it had nothing on the outfit she wore now.

Black leggings that made her ass look so good I wanted to spank it and a gray cropped sweatshirt that hung off one shoulder had my dick hard the moment I opened the door. Her stomach was soft, but toned, and her leggings sat right at the flare of her hip. She was barefoot, her flip-flops showing off her bright pink toenails. She had her long, dark locks up on top of her head in one of those messy buns that girls wear, leaving the long column of her neck on display.

I knew she spotted the situation in my pants when I answered the door, but she hadn't let her gaze linger. I knew I was packing in the dick department, and the sweats I wore did nothing to hide it. Wearing them may or may not have been a purposeful decision. After she let out that sexy moan while downing her beer, there was no way she could miss the hard on I was sporting. I tried to turn away to adjust myself, knowing she saw it. Chase stood proudly in front of her, not giving a damn that his erection was clear in his sweats.

Her cheeks were flushed when she stammered out her game idea. Truth or dare. With Chase. *Fuck*. I was screwed. The second he made a move on her, it was over for me.

Or was it? She seemed into me all day and even at dinner after she met Chase. I could tell that he was interested in her, I mean, honestly, what guy wouldn't be? And why should I assume she'd pick Chase? I was a good looking guy, a nice guy. I knew how to treat a girl well; just ask my shitty ex-girlfriend. My resolve strengthened, and I turned back around. "Alright, let's play."

We moved over to the living room, Chase and I each taking a chair, while Everly sat in the middle of the sofa, all three of us surrounding the coffee table. Chase set his beer on the table, and before anyone could get a word out, he started the game. "Okay, me first." His eyes gleamed with mischief, and I knew we were in for a wild night. "Everly, truth or dare?"

Everly took a sip of her beer, contemplating her choice for a moment. "Truth."

Not missing a beat, Chase asked his question. "Do you have a boyfriend? Someone you left sad and alone back home, someone who's pining for that beautiful smile and bangin' ass?"

Everly snorted and choked on her beer, while I did everything in my power not to spit mine out all over the table. "What the fuck, Chase?" I growled once I'd managed to swallow.

"What? She doesn't have to answer if she doesn't want to, but then she'll have to take a dare," Chase taunted while lifting his hands innocently.

"No, it's ok Griff," Everly interjected before I could deck my best friend. "I'll answer. No, Chase, there's no boyfriend. I'm pretty certain no boys back home are pining after me or my ass."

"Now, little Larkspur, I find that hard to believe," he said, a slight tease to his voice. "I bet all the boys were sad when you moved away. But their loss is certainly our gain." His eyes slowly perused her body, and a devilish smile sat on his lips. *Fucker.*

Everly let out a small snort of disbelief. "Yeah, no. No guys, I promise. Okay, moving on. Umm Griff, truth or dare?" Everly swung her pretty blue eyes to me.

Figuring I'd take the safe route, I answered, "Truth."

Chase coughed out the word *lame* as he mocked my choice. I flipped him off, turning my focus back to Everly. She chuckled at Chase's immaturity. At least one of us found him funny.

"Griff, do you have a girlfriend?"

"Nope," I responded confidently, the 'p' sound popping as I spoke. A wide smile broke across Everly's face at my answer. Feeling emboldened, I decided to take a leap of faith. "Okay, Blue, my turn. Truth or dare?"

Mischief flashed in her eyes. "Dare."

Yes!

Staring directly at her, I watched as her eyes grew wide in anticipation. She had a flush to her cheeks, and she darted her gaze between Chase and me. Pretending to think on it for a moment, I leaned back in my chair, taking a long drink from my beer. Finally, I jumped off the proverbial cliff.

"I dare you to kiss me."

From the corner of my eye, I caught Chase's lips tip up in a sly smirk. He knew what game I was playing, but he seemed inclined to join in rather than play against me. I pushed that thought to the back of my mind as I watched the beautiful flush staining her cheeks creep ever so slowly down her neck. But she hadn't moved a muscle. I was just getting ready to tell her it was ok if she didn't want to, when suddenly she set her beer on the table and stood.

My eyes tracked her every move as she made her way over to me. Bending at the waist, and I'm sure giving Chase an eyeful of her perfect ass, Everly slowly leaned over me. The top she wore gaped at the neck, and I caught a glimpse of her lace-covered breasts. Her eyes stayed trained on mine until her lips were a breath away. She closed them, pressing forward until the softness of her full lips met mine. A soft moan fell from her mouth, and my dick stood straight to attention while my eyes fell closed.

I reached up, wrapping my hand around the side of her neck, deepening the kiss. Licking the seam of her lips, I coaxed her mouth open, tangling my tongue with hers. I was so completely lost in the kiss, I barely heard Chase's muttered *holy fuck* from across the room.

At the sound of Chase's voice, Everly pulled away from the kiss, seeming to remember that we had an audience. Her pupils had blown so wide, the stunning blue color was nothing but a small ring, and her lips were slightly swollen. All I wanted was to keep kissing her, but before I could, she stood up and made her way back to the sofa. While her back was turned, I reached down and readjusted my dick in my sweatpants. Jesus, I was hard as steel from just a kiss. This girl was something else.

Everly sat back down, her cheeks pink with desire. She peeked at Chase and I, and I could see the embarrassment filtering into her face. Just as I opened my mouth to reassure her that the kiss was fucking amazing, Chase jumped in.

"Jesus, Larkspur, that was fucking hot," he told her, biting his bottom lip between his teeth, the tent in his pants showing just how much he'd enjoyed watching us. The bad feelings from before fled from her face at his words.

Blowing out a breath, Everly trained her gaze on Chase. "Okay, Chase, truth or dare?"

Leaning forward in his chair, Chase smirked at her question. "Oh, little Larkspur, dare all day long."

Without hesitation, she echoed my words from moments ago.

"I dare you to kiss me."

Chase shifted his eyes from Everly to me, silently asking for permission. He knew how much I liked her, but I could see the desire in his eyes too. I searched myself for any feelings of jealousy but came up empty. I knew from our kiss that Blue wanted me. If she wanted my best friend, too, who was I to say no? I gave him a small nod, and that was all he needed.

Jumping up from his chair, he stalked over to where Everly sat on the sofa. Wasting no time, he sat down next to her, cupped both sides of her face, and kissed the hell out of her. I could see her mouth open as he deepened the kiss, and she reached up to place her hands on his forearms. They kissed for a moment longer before Chase pulled away, planting one more soft kiss against her lips.

Chase got up and moved back to his chair. Just as he was sitting down, a loud knock sounded at our door. Chase stood again to open the door. "I got it."

Seeing Everly's confused face, I explained. "It's probably just Knox. He was going to the studio to do some work. Probably forgot his key. Chase'll grab it."

She relaxed back onto the sofa just as Chase reached the door. As he pulled it open, a piercing voice cut through the room, freezing me in place.

"Where the fuck is he, Chase?" *Oh fuck, no, no, no.*

"He's busy, Morgan. Why don't you go let Caleb Donovan bend you over a table again?" Chase bit back. *Shit.*

My ex-girlfriend shoved through the doorway, pushing Chase out of the way. Her eyes lasered in on me, not noticing Everly on the sofa.

"What the actual fuck, Griff? I've been messaging and calling you for the last four days!" Morgan strode to stand directly in front of me, crossing her arms over her chest and thrusting her tits upward with a huff. Her bleach blonde hair was pulled back in a tight ponytail, and her face was done up with about ten pounds of makeup. She was wearing tiny booty shorts and a cropped tank, despite the cooler evening temperatures, most likely in a bid to draw my attention. News flash, it wasn't gonna work. Not this time. Remembering Everly's beautifully simple, casual look, I couldn't help but wonder what I had ever seen in Morgan.

"Morgan, what do you want? I didn't answer your texts or calls because I don't want to talk to you," I answered her, keeping my face and voice purposefully neutral. I was still hurt over all of Morgan's betrayals, but I had zero desire to take her back.

"Baby," she started, her lips puckered in a ridiculous pout, "I'm so sorry about Caleb. It meant nothing. It was an accident," she pleaded. She reached forward, placing a hand on my bicep and squeezing. I stared down at it before pushing the offending appendage off my arm.

"What, like you tripped and he fell?" Everly's voice cut through Morgan's bullshit.

"Who the fuck are you?" Her words came out on a snarl as Morgan whipped around, looking ready to commit murder.

Before I could step in, Everly squared her shoulders and gave Morgan a look that bordered somewhere between indifference and disgust. "I'm the girl that just kissed him a few minutes ago. Who the fuck are *you*?"

"I'm his girlfriend, you bitch." Morgan smirked when Everly's eyes widened, shock marring her pretty face before she could school her features. Everly turned to look at me, her eyes searching my face. I knew exactly where her mind had gone. She thought I lied to her.

"You're my *ex*-girlfriend, Morgan. Emphasis on the *ex*."

"Griff, baby, it was a mistake. Please, let's talk about this." Morgan was begging now. I had never been the one to end things in the past; those had always come from her. Understanding dawned on her face that I had been serious about our breakup, and suddenly, I felt her attempt to push forgiveness and lust at me using her caster magic. Morgan was a pathokinetic and had the ability to push emotions on others, though she wasn't very good, never wanting to take the time to study and truly hone her ability. The only times it worked were if her target was either already emotionally invested or if they were in a heightened state of a particular feeling.

"There's nothing to talk about, Morgan. You fucked around, I found out. End of story. Now, please leave. We have company," I said cooly, gesturing toward the door with my beer.

"Company?! What, are you fucking the new girl now?" she asked, anger seeping into her voice. She spun to face Everly again, looking her up and down in that judgey, mean girl way. "Listen, Griff and I are just having a disagreement. He's still very much taken, so why don't you scamper off? I'm sure Chase would love to entertain you. He's been with half the girls on campus, after all. Although, I did see him with Heather Stevens just yesterday, so you may want to double check that he's available," she sneered, making sure to take jabs at both my girl and my best friend.

To her credit, Everly didn't take the bait. Instead, she cocked her head to the side and took a long pull from her beer. After a moment, she stood up, placing the empty bottle on the table. She fixed Morgan with a hard glare before moving to the door. Oh shit, was she gonna leave? Morgan seemed to think so, a victorious grin spreading across her made up face.

"Blue, I—"

Before I could get the words out, Everly opened the door but didn't step out. "I'm pretty sure Griff told you to leave." She held the door wide, gesturing for Morgan to get the fuck out. My mouth dropped open, and I could see Chase press his fist to his mouth, trying to stifle his grin.

"You heard the lady." Chase choked on his laughter. "Get the fuck out, Morgan."

"GRIFF!" she shrieked, making me wince. Jesus, we were lucky she hadn't shattered any glass. I shook my head and stood. Gently grabbing her by the elbow, I led her to the door. She looked at me in shock, unintelligible gibberish coming from her mouth.

"Out, Morgan, and don't come back. Lose my number. I don't want to see you again." I guided her through the doorway gently—I might not like her, but I didn't want to hurt her—releasing her once she was in the hall. I strode back into the room, Everly closing the door behind me.

I blew out a large breath. "Thank you Blue—" I started, turning to look at her. The sentence died on my lips when I saw the look on her face. Anger and hurt clouded her beautiful features, her blue eyes turned down toward the floor.

"Is it true? Is she your girlfriend?" she asked, the words a whisper.

"She was. I broke up with her a couple days ago. I caught her cheating on me," I explained, moving slowly toward her. I could see her thinking over my words. She turned to face Chase who was standing in the kitchen with another beer. "And you? Have you been with all those girls? Were you just with someone yesterday?"

Chase, to his credit, blanched at her words. He opened and closed his mouth several times before any words came out. He looked down at his beer bottle. "Yes," he said quietly, "but she's not my girlfriend. She's just a girl I hooked up with."

Everly sucked in a sharp breath, looking between the two of us before shaking her head.

"I think I should go..." she said, turning toward the door, and before either of us could respond, she was gone.

Fuck.

Nine

Everly

After hearing the bombs Morgan dropped at Griff and Chase's place, I quickly left, heading back to my suite. I went to grab my fob from my pocket once I'd reached my door, but it was empty. I knocked loudly, wanting to make sure Evan heard me over his stupid headset. He pulled the door open after a few seconds, his controller still in his hands. I mumbled something about being tired, avoiding having to explain my sudden arrival, and walked straight to my room, flicking my fingers at my door and slamming it shut. I flung myself on my bed and immediately called Celeste.

"Wait, so he does *have a girlfriend? Or he doesn't? I'm confused."*

"He said they broke up a few days ago. But it didn't seem like she was done, so who the fuck knows."

"And the other guy? Chase? He's a manwhore?"

"Apparently. When I asked him about what Morgan said, he confirmed he had just been with a girl like yesterday."

"Okay... I mean, if he doesn't have a girlfriend, he's free to hook up with whomever he likes, right?"

"Yes," I sighed. *"But that doesn't mean I want to be some booty call, C."*

"I know babe," she said. Silence filled the line for a few moments, and I could tell she was dying to say more.

"Go ahead, spit it out."

"I just think you owe them a conversation, that's all. Get everything out on the table before you decide to cut them off completely. From all your messages earlier, it seemed you really liked this Griff guy, at least."

Damn it, she was right. I *did* like Griff. And Chase. But I also didn't want to deal with any ex-girlfriend drama or be another notch in Chase's bedpost. I had a lot to think about.

Sunday morning came bright and early with Evan knocking on my door. "Eves, you wanna get breakfast?" I had been up for awhile, thoughts of my evening with Griff and Chase keeping me from a restful night's sleep.

"Yeah, Ev, just let me get up. Give me thirty?"

"If you're not ready in exactly thirty minutes, I'll leave without you."

I jumped out of bed, sprinted to my bathroom, and took the world's fastest shower. I washed my hair quickly, planning to let it air dry into my natural waves. Just as I was stepping out, I heard Evan's voice in my bedroom.

"Eves, I'm gonna head downstairs. I'll meet you out front!"

"Okay, just don't leave without me!"

I quickly dried off and moved into my room. Snagging a lacy pair of lavender panties and matching bra from my dresser, I put them on. I grabbed a pair of cutoffs from the next drawer down and threw on a faded v-neck band

74

tee to complete my outfit. Sitting down at my vanity, I figured I had a few seconds to spare. Swiping on some mascara and dabbing a little gloss on my lips, I sprang up and jogged out into the living room.

Moving to the counter to grab my keys, I looked around but couldn't find them. *Fuck*. I looked up at the ceiling and closed my eyes, remembering my empty pocket last night. I must have left them at Griff and Chase's place. I was so hell bent on getting out of there, I completely forgot them on the coffee table. Shit.

Well, I was going to have to talk to them anyway. Maybe I could catch up with them after breakfast. Recognizing that I was minutes away from Evan leaving my ass, I shoved my feet into my flip-flops, flinging open the door, and darting out. Only instead of continuing down the hall, I ran straight into a solid wall of muscle.

"Oooph." The air whooshed out of my lungs, and my body bounced backward. Before my ass could hit the hardwood floor, I felt a big hand grip my upper arm and another land on my waist, suspending me in mid air.

I looked up and was met with dark, chocolate colored eyes. He had a look of complete surprise on his face as held me up, those deep eyes searching my face. When he spoke, his voice was a deep, gravelly baritone, with just a hint of a southern accent.

"Jesus Christ woman, you okay? You came flyin' out of there like your ass was on fire."

"Uh, yeah, I'm fine. Just running late."

We both just stared at each other for another moment before realizing his hands were still on me. He stood me up, suddenly pulling his hands away like I'd burned him. My arm and hip felt branded from his touch.

Straightening up, I took in the handsome stranger, noting his broad shoulders and muscular, ink covered arms. His sharp jawline looked like it was carved from stone and was covered in scruff that was several days old, bordering on a beard. He had a dark and broody look about him, and it felt like his eyes could see straight into my soul. Smudges of paint were splattered across his gray t-shirt. Taking a closer look, I realized it was the men's version of the same one I was wearing.

"Thanks for the save, stranger." I smiled. Damn, he was hot. "And nice shirt. Diary of Jane is a great album. Gotta go!" I gave him a quick wave then darted down the hallway, praying Evan hadn't left me.

I reached the main floor in record time, my feet barely touching the steps on my down. I burst through the doors and spotted Evan leaning against a lamp post a few feet away.

"Hey Ev!" I called out, jogging over to him.

"There you are," he huffed. "I was getting ready to leave without you. I'm starving. Where are Chase and Griff? Figured that was what was taking you so long."

"No, I ran into some guy in our hall. Like literally ran into him," I answered, purposely avoiding his comment about the two men who lived down the hall from us. "Come on, let's get you fed. You turn into a cranky monster when you're hangry."

"Hey, I do not!" Evan protested but followed me down the path anyway.

We made our way into the dining hall, made our breakfast selections, and found a table near some beautiful stained glass windows. Evan and I dug into our food, eating in comfortable silence, when a shadow fell over our table. I looked up at a tall, lanky guy with messy brown hair smiling at us, something about him raising the hairs on the back of my neck.

"Can we help you, dude?" Evan asked, immediately going on the defensive. We had no idea who this guy was, and the way he was leering put me instantly on edge. As if he could sense my discomfort, Evan puffed up his chest, a clear challenge to this stranger's attention.

"I'm Austin. Just thought I'd introduce myself. Heard we had a couple of new fourth years and figured I'd say hi. Mind if I sit?" Without waiting for an answer, he pulled out the chair next to me and plopped down.

"Uh, sure, I guess," I answered, shocked at the balls on this guy.

"So, like I said, I'm Austin. Austin Thorpe. And you are?" He looked at Evan, briefly dismissing him, before turning all of his attention to me.

Wonderful.

"She's not interested, Thorpe, so back the fuck off."

I spun around in my seat. I hadn't noticed them come in, but a few feet behind my chair stood Griff and Chase, each with their arms crossed over their chests, matching looks of annoyance on their equally handsome faces.

"Griff, Stone. I think the lady can answer for herself, right gorgeous?" Austin glared at my guys—*my guys?*—before turning to me, that lecherous look back as his gaze traveled from my face to my chest. I held back a shudder, trying to be polite in hopes that he would leave quickly.

"I'm Everly, and this is my brother Evan. We were just waiting for Griff and Chase to join us for breakfast." I darted my eyes to the guys, hoping they'd play along.

"Damn straight," Chase said, grinning. "So you can fuck off Thorpe, you're in my seat."

Austin's cocky look fell from his face, and he stood reluctantly. Griff and Chase both moved to my back as Austin backed away, but not before he leaned down to my whisper in my ear. "I'll see you soon, *pet.*"

My jaw dropped, but Austin took his leave before I could respond. *What the fuck?* I shook my head as Chase dropped into the spot Austin just vacated, Griff taking a chair next to Evan.

"You okay, Blue?"

"Yeah, he was just weird. Gave me the heebie jeebies. I'm fine."

"He's a dick," Chase grunted. "He's my dad's business partner's son. I've known him since we were kids. He's always been a fucking creep. You tell me if he gives you any more trouble, yeah little Larkspur?" Chase looked between my eyes, a serious look on his face, and I nodded my agreement.

Picking up my coffee, I took a sip as Evan rose from his spot. "I'm gonna grab some more eggs," he said, walking away from the table.

With just the three of us at the table, tension filled the air. I looked down at my plate, pushing my eggs around with my fork for a few minutes, my appetite suddenly gone.

"Hey, Blue, can we talk after breakfast?" Griffin asked from across the table, breaking the silence.

I looked up at him, seeing the desperation in his eyes. Taking pity on him, I responded, "Sure, Griff."

I could see him visibly relax, a deep exhale leaving his chest. Evan returned to the table, and Griff and Chase got up to grab some food as well. The boys and I ate in relative quiet, with Evan pretty much single-handedly carrying the conversation. He was going on and on about his plans for the day, which included scoping out Voxina Hall some more, as well as the sports complex down by the lake.

When we were all finished, we made our way back outside. Evan left after a quick goodbye, leaving me alone with Griff and Chase. Chase gave Griff a quick nod, then turned to look at me.

"Larkspur, I know Griff wants to talk to you alone, so I'm gonna head back to the dorms. But know that you and I are going to have a conversation as well, okay? There are some things I need to explain." Without waiting for a response, he leaned down, giving me a soft kiss on the cheek, then turned and made his way back to Bliss Hall.

Left with just Griff, I shuffled my feet on the concrete steps, looking anywhere but at the man standing in front of me.

Suddenly, I felt fingers at my chin, and my face was being tilted up. Griff's handsome face came into view, and those damn butterflies were back at it again. Griff looked at me with soft eyes full of remorse. We stared at each other for a few moments, his fingers moving up to stroke my cheek.

"Blue, I'm so sorry about last night. But please believe me when I tell you that Morgan and I are done. She was way out of line last night, and I'm so sorry if she hurt you at all." The words rushed out of Griffin's mouth on a single breath. His hand cupped the side of my face, and I turned into it. I could hear the sincerity in his voice, and my anger from last night disappeared.

"Thank you, Griffin," I breathed out. "I believe you. She just took me by surprise is all."

"Well surprise again then, bitch." I closed my eyes, anger surging through me as Morgan's voice sounded out in the airy space. Griff's eyes widened as he looked over my shoulder, his cheeks flushing a bright red. I turned in his arms to see Morgan moving down the stairs to where we stood. A sneer was plastered on her face as she approached, no doubt at seeing Griff and I together. He moved his hands to my hips, his fingers digging into my denim clad skin. Before I could respond, shock ripped through my body as Morgan's hand struck my cheek in a sharp slap.

"What the fuck, Morgan?!" Griff roared from behind me. My cheek stung from the impact of her hand, and I reached up to touch the sore spot. Griff spun me to face him, inspecting my face for any damage.

Looking into his hazel eyes, a fury I'd never experienced roiled through my body. Who the *fuck* did this chick think she was?! I put a hand on Griff's chest, feeling his heart ready to burst through his rib cage.

"I'm fine, Griff," I told him, my voice a deadly calm. I balled my hand into a fist at my side, my rage making me shake ever so slightly. "The same can't be said about Morgan though." He raised an eyebrow at my statement, cocking his head slightly in question.

Without another word, I turned, staring Morgan down for a good three seconds before I launched my fist into her face. I felt my hand connect with the hard bone of her cheek, pain lancing through my fingers and up my arm. She screeched, stumbling backward, her ass landing on the stone steps.

"YOU BITCH!" She screamed the words at me, cupping her rapidly bruising cheek. I shrugged, masking the adrenaline erupting in my veins.

"Play stupid games, win stupid prizes," I tossed out before turning toward Griff. "You ready?"

Griff gaped at me, his jaw hanging slack on his handsome face. I'd obviously shocked him. Hell, I'd shocked myself. I'd never hit anyone before, the pain in my hand reminding me of that fact. Although a few broken bones were worth the look on Morgan's face when I'd punched her. I flexed my fingers, looking them over. I didn't see any swelling, so they were most likely just going to be sore.

I looped my arm through Griff's, pulling him away from his still-shrieking ex and down the rest of the steps. We walked in silence for a few moments before Griff finally found his voice.

"Holy shit, Blue." The words whooshed from his lips on a breath. I leaned my head against his bicep, doubt about my actions making my stomach clench.

"Are you mad?" I asked quietly.

He jerked us to a stop, pulling me around to face him. I stared down at my feet, unable to make eye contact. I wasn't a violent person by nature, but between the way she treated Griff and the slap, I just lost it. Anger had taken over and I saw red.

Griff ducked down so we were at eye level, his green-gold eyes shimmering in the morning light.

"Everly, look at me." He spoke with a soft command, forcing my eyes to meet his. "I am not mad. I'm shocked, pretty goddamn proud, and turned the fuck on, but I most definitely am NOT mad."

My eyebrows scrunched together in confusion before he continued.

"You standing up for yourself, standing up for me? That was hot as fuck. Morgan had no right to hit you like that. She's a bitch, and I'm glad you put her in her place." He gently picked up my sore hand, turning it over as he inspected my knuckles. "You're lucky you didn't break anything. It's probably gonna be sore for a few days. First punch?"

I nodded my head in confirmation, my cheeks flushing from his previous words. *Me hitting Morgan turned him on?*

"Gotta make sure you don't tuck your thumb next time." He chuckled, kissing each knuckle before twining our fingers together. He paused for a moment, seeming to contemplate his next words. "I like you, Blue, like *a lot*. I don't want this to screw up any chance I might have with you."

I'm pretty sure in that moment, if his hand hadn't been touching my body, I would have melted into a puddle. "We're good, Griff," I said to him with a smile. "And just for the record, I like you too." I leaned up on my tiptoes and placed a soft kiss on his lips.

When we got to our dorm, he slipped my keys out of his pocket, handing them to me. "Figured you'd want these back. Although, I had considered holding them hostage if you wouldn't talk to me." A playful grin spread across his face. Rolling my eyes while I laughed, I shoved his chest, and we entered the building. When we made it to our floor, I spotted Chase waiting in the hall, leaning against my door.

"Okay, little Larkspur, my turn."

Ten

Knox

Her eyes were the most stunning shade of blue I had ever seen. As soon as I got to my room—after nearly plowing her over—I immediately started painting. I looked at the canvas, and a large pair of blue eyes stared back at me. Lined by thick, dark lashes, I added in the outline of my body in the reflection of her sapphire orbs. Lost in my work, I didn't hear Griff when he came in.

"Hey Knox," he called, startling me from my painting. I spun around, palette and brush still in hand. "What's going on man? Haven't seen you around much."

Setting my supplies down, I ran a hand through my wavy hair. It was getting long on top, and I'd have to make sure I cut it before going home for the holidays, lest I incur the wrath of my mother and her judgment.

"Yeah, sorry. I've been in a funk. Been spending a lot of time in the studio."

Griffin moved further into my room. Our suite was situated at the end of the hall, with my room in particular having one of the building's original turrets. I had my painting space set up there, the curved windows giving me a ton of natural light to work with. My drop cloths covered the old hardwood floors, and I had a perfect view of the lake. I couldn't count the number

83

of hours I'd spent standing here, staring at the tropical blue water while working. My entire room was a mess of art materials, canvases strewn about and sketches hanging on my walls. My bed was centered in the space, a large king with blankets thrown haphazardly on top and matching nightstands on either side. A desk was pushed into the corner, covered in sketch pads and charcoals, with several paint-stained shirts hanging off the back of my chair.

Typically, I didn't like anyone in my space. I kept a lot of my art in here, but I knew Griff would never judge my stuff. He and I had been friends since our first year when we'd been roomed together, with Chase joining our little duo once Griff started tutoring him. We'd lived together ever since. They were my best friends, even if Chase was a pain in the ass most of the time.

"Whatcha working on?" he asked, stepping up next to me. I heard him suck in a breath when he saw my latest piece. "Wow," the word was a whisper. He turned to face me, confusion on his face. "Is that...? That looks like... but you haven't... have you?"

"Griff, what the fuck are you talking about? Are you having a stroke?"

"Your painting, the eyes in your painting..."

"Yeah, I ran into this girl in the hall. Well, she ran into me, actually. But her eyes, man, they were unreal. Like the perfect mix of sky blue and tropical turquoise," I said reverently, looking at the painting and remembering how she felt in my arms. Where the hell had she come from? Did she live on our floor? Was she visiting someone? And most importantly, would I see her again?

"Those are Everly's eyes." Griff seemed to be talking more to himself than to me.

"Who's Everly?" I asked, needing more information about this mystery girl.

"She's a new student. Fourth year. She and her brother live down the hall. Chase and I have been hanging out with her. She was actually here last night before Morgan scared her off."

"Why the fuck was Morgan here?" Disgust filled my voice. I couldn't stand the girl. She was a grade A bitch, and she'd fucked Griff over more times than I could count. When she found out how much Chase and I hated her, she'd tried that emotional pushing bullshit with us, but we'd just laughed off her attempts. "I thought you kicked her ass to the curb. Dude, don't tell me you took her back, please." Jesus, if he took that skanky ass bitch back, even after catching her cheating, I was going to kick his ass myself.

"No, man." He put his hands up in defense. "She came over last night, asking me to forgive her. I told her to fuck off. Well actually, Chase, Everly, and I all told her to fuck off." He chuckled at the memory.

"Thank Christ," I mumbled, relieved that Griff finally stood his ground.

"Anyway," he said, rolling his eyes, clearly not wanting to talk about Morgan anymore. "Where'd you say you ran into her?" He gestured at the painting on my easel.

"Out in the hall. I was coming home from the studio, and she came flying out of a doorway. She ran straight into my chest, would've ended up on the floor if I hadn't grabbed onto her." The memory of my hands on her skin had my cock twitching in my jeans. She had been so small in my arms. She couldn't have been more than 5'2" on a good day, probably less. My 6'2" frame nearly obliterated her.

Silence fell over us both as we stared at my painting. I had been able to match the blue hue of her irises perfectly, the color branded into my memory from our less than minute long encounter. I ran through our quick conversation in my head up to the moment she ran off down the hall. A laugh burst from my lips and I smiled.

"What's funny?" Griff asked, giving me a side eye. I wasn't exactly known for my humor, so to hear me laugh was probably throwing him off.

"My shirt," I said, looking down at the Breaking Benjamin tee I was wearing. "She complimented it." I tugged on the front of my shirt. "She was wearing the same one, albeit a lot smaller."

"Huh..." Griff said, a smile creeping onto his face.

I looked around, confused. Did I say something funny?

"What?"

"Nothing man, nothing." But that smirk stayed put, and now I was getting annoyed.

"What the fuck are you smiling about, Griff?" I demanded. He chuckled, rubbing his fingertips along his freshly-shaved chin. Nodding toward my painting, his next words landed in my brain like a bomb.

"It would appear that Everly Blackwell has gotten under your skin as well, my friend."

Griff left my room, that goofy smile still on his face as his words repeated in my head. I literally spent less than a minute with the girl. Hell, I didn't even know her name until two *seconds* ago.

But I couldn't deny the feeling that sat in my chest everytime I looked at my painting. It was like I could see into her heart, her soul. I wanted to know everything about the girl with the most beautiful blue eyes I had ever seen. I was drawn to her, and I couldn't explain why.

I worked for a while longer on a different piece before emerging for some food. I worked straight through breakfast, having come home early this morning after spending the night at the studio painting. It was midday now, and my stomach started to growl. I needed to eat before crashing for a few hours.

Pulling some food from the fridge, I set out making myself some lunch. Turkey, provolone, lettuce, a bit of spicy mustard, and voila` the perfect sandwich. Growing up, our housekeeper, Helen, always made them for me, knowing they were my favorite. It wasn't like my mother could be bothered to cook.

"That's what we have staff for, darling."

Just as I took my first bite, my phone started buzzing. Looking down at the screen, I rolled my eyes. *Think of the devil and she shall appear.* I set my sandwich down, took a deep breath, and answered.

"Hello Mother."

"Knox. Did you get settled at school?" She complained when I said I wanted to come back a few weeks early. I had to lie and say it was for my advanced art classes. Not that she really gave a shit. It was just one more thing for her to try and control.

"Yes, Mother, I'm all settled in. Was that why you called?"

"What, I can't just want to speak to my only son?" I rolled my eyes again, so hard this time that I worried they might get stuck in the back of my skull.

"Of course you can, Mother. Did you need anything else? I was in the middle of lunch." I wanted to end this torture as soon as possible and get back to my sandwich.

"Actually yes, there was something else. Ginny Monclair was over yesterday for cocktails and happened to see one of your *paintings*." Mother said the last word as if it personally offended her. "She was quite intrigued and asked if you wanted to submit a few items for the charity auction next month. I tried to tell her she should contact an actual reputable artist, but she insisted she needed one of your pieces."

Well, shit, that was unexpected. It must really be eating my mother up inside, having to ask for one of my paintings. She despised the fact that I loved art, loved creating and making something out of nothing. The fact it was one of her friends who had been trying to bed me since I turned eighteen that was asking for a painting was just the cherry on top.

My art was the reason I planned to go into architecture once I graduated from SLA. Painting was my passion, but I also knew it wasn't a sustainable source of income. When I turned twenty-two, I would get the inheritance my father left when he died. I planned to use the money to start an architecture firm, and hopefully open an art gallery where I could sell my paintings.

Pushing my dreams for the future aside, I answered my mother, "Of course, Mother. Should I have them shipped over? Or would you like to come pick them up?" I smirked, knowing full well she wouldn't deign to set foot on campus. It would infringe upon her tea times and cocktail parties.

"Heavens no, Knox! Please just box up what pieces you want to donate and have them shipped to Ginny. She can sort out what she thinks would be worth putting in the auction, if anything." The last dig at the end didn't escape me, but I chose to ignore it in favor of ending the call faster.

I closed my eyes, pinching the bridge of my nose. This woman could induce a migraine in a goddamn corpse.

"Is that all, Mother?"

"Yes, darling. Please send that out to Ginny by the end of the week. I'll call you again soon." And with that she hung up the phone.

Thank Christ.

Finishing up my sandwich, I moved back into my bedroom and began surveying my completed paintings. I set aside two landscapes I had done down by the lake and one of Solis Hall. My gaze fell back to this morning's work, still sitting on my easel. It was easily my favorite piece I had ever done. It would probably go for quite a bit to the right buyer.

As quickly as the thought entered my mind, I squashed it. No way in hell was someone else going to be staring at Everly's eyes. Not when I hadn't even scratched the surface of what lay beneath.

Eleven

Everly

C hase stood in the hallway, his broad back leaning against the wall, a foot kicked up so the sole of his shoe sat on the molding at the bottom. I met his eyes as we approached, noting his trademark smirk was missing from his handsome face. In its place was a serious look I hadn't really seen, and it made me nervous for our conversation. All thoughts of my confrontation with Morgan flew from my mind as my nerves kicked into overdrive.

"Okay, little Larkspur. My turn."

I turned to Griff, who stopped at my side, his hand still firmly held in mine. "We're good, Blue?"

"Yeah, we're good." I smiled at him. "Why don't you text me later, and we can hang out?" Slipping my phone from my pocket, I handed it to him. He quickly shot off a message to his number.

"I'll get a hold of you later. See you soon, Blue." He leaned down and planted a soft kiss on my lips. Straightening out, he fist bumped Chase. "I'll catch you later man. Good luck." And with that, he proceeded down the hall to his own suite.

Turning my attention to Chase, I unlocked my door. I knew Evan was going to be out for a while, so I figured this was as good a place as any to have this conversation. Pushing the door open, I gestured for Chase to enter. He strode in first, and I shut the door behind us.

Chase moved to the living room area, one hand on his hip, the other pushing his shaggy blond hair off his forehead. I loved the messy look he sported, like he'd just rolled out of bed... *Or had been rolling around in one...*

Shaking that visual from my brain, I focused on the task at hand. Walking deeper into my suite, I schooled my face into one of neutral indifference. I was not about to let this man see me get upset when he inevitably told me he was only interested in a good time.

"What did you want to talk about, Chase?" I kept a safe distance between us, not wanting to get swept up in the sexual tension I could already feel building.

Chase looked up at me, an almost pained expression stretched over his features. I held my breath, ready to hear him say he wasn't interested in anything serious.

"Everly, I'm so sorry. I really fucked up last night."

Wow, well that certainly hadn't been what I was expecting. But I was still wary of his intentions.

"Okay," I responded cautiously. "What did you fuck up? I mean, you don't owe me an explanation of who you're sleeping with. It's not like we're dating. You're free to sleep with whomever you want." The words hurt my heart as I spoke them.

"Fuck, Everly." He ran his fingers through his hair again, frustration obvious in his voice. But why was he frustrated? I was growing more confused by the second. "I... I guess you could say I have a... reputation. I've, umm, *been* with a lot of girls on campus. I've never really been a relationship kind of guy."

"Look, Chase, if you—" My words were suddenly cut off when Chase's hands cupped the sides of my face, and his lips slammed down onto mine.

The kiss was brutal, all consuming. I had never been kissed with such fire before. He licked into my mouth, forcing me to part my lips and let him in. My hands came up to rest on his chest, my fingers gripping the thin t-shirt he was wearing and grazing over the hard muscles underneath. I could feel every ounce of his frustration and passion with each stroke of his tongue.

Finally, when I felt like I was about to run out of air, Chase broke the kiss, pulling back slightly and staring into my eyes.

"Larkspur," he said softly. "I am so sorry if you thought..." He let out a large sigh, closing his eyes and leaning his forehead to mine, before continuing, "I don't want you to think you're just another girl to me. You're more than that. Okay, yeah, do I want to do naughty, dirty things to you? Yes, I mean have you seen yourself? You're smokin'." He opened his eyes and gave me a little smirk. "But I also want to learn everything there is about what makes you, *you.*"

"So this isn't just, I don't know, a booty call type thing for you? I mean what about Heather, whatever her name is?" I needed to be crystal clear about what he was saying.

"Everly." He pulled back some, staring directly into my eyes. "Please hear me when I say, the *only* girl I am interested in is you. Have I been with" He trailed off and swallowed roughly, his Adam's apple bobbing. "A lot of girls? Yes. But you are the only one who has made me want to look below the surface. I know that sounds shallow, but Larkspur, you have no idea the things you do to me, and I've only known you a day."

Looking into his green eyes, all I could see was the truth behind his words.

"Okay," I said hesitantly. "But Chase, I refuse to be some casual hook up who you sleep with and never speak to again. If that's where this is headed, we should just cut our losses now."

"Larkspur, I have zero intentions of never speaking to you again. In fact, I want to talk to you everyday, from here on out. In fact, multiple times a day. I insist on it." That trademark, panty-melting smile was firmly back on his face.

Another thought niggled at my mind, and I figured I might as well lay all the cards on the table.

"What about Griff?" I asked.

"What about Griff?" Chase repeated my question.

"Well, I like you, but I like Griff too." And as I said the words out loud, I realized how hypocritical I was being. Here I was telling Chase that he couldn't go around hooking up with other girls if he was with me, while I was kissing his best friend right in front of him.

Shocking me yet again, Chase replied, "So?"

"So? I mean, that's not really fair to you, either of you."

"Look, Griff and I know the score here, and we're both okay with it. I'll take being with you in whatever way I can. If that means sharing you with Griff, then so be it. I'd rather it be him than some asshole like that prick Thorpe."

"Really?" I asked in disbelief.

"Yes, Larkspur, really. Now, if you'll let me, I'll show you just how much I'd like to get to know you." A sultry grin graced his lips. *Lord this man could ruin my panties with just a look.*

Chase's hands moved from my jaw down to my waist, his fingers splaying out across my hip bones. He tugged me closer to his body until we were nearly flush against one another. I could feel how hard he was, his erection pushing against my abdomen. Holy shit, he was *big*. He leaned in close to my ear, his warm breath fanning my cheek.

"Little Larkspur, let me make you feel good." His lips found the sensitive spot just below my ear, sending shivers down my spine. I instinctively arched my back, my breasts pushing into his chest.

"Mmmm," was all I could manage to get out as Chase trailed featherlight kisses down the column of my neck. His hands moved back, cupping my ass through my denim shorts. In the next instant, he was lifting me up, my legs wrapping around his trim waist. My hands found the nape of his neck, my fingers digging into the long hair at the back of his head.

I pulled his face from my neck, so our lips met in a blazing kiss. I could feel us moving through the room, and the next thing I knew, I was flying through the air. I landed in the middle of my plush bed, sending throw pillows off the sides. I heard my bedroom door shut and the lock click. I looked up at Chase standing at the foot of my bed, the pupils of his green eyes blown with desire. In one swift move, he reached behind his head and yanked off the t-shirt he had been wearing.

I'm fairly certain I stopped breathing at the sight of him. He was all tanned skin, muscles, and a patchwork of black ink. Looking closer, I could see leaves and trees tattooed across his tanned flesh, the images creating a beautiful nature scene, while a set of crossed oars sat on his left pec. His chest looked as if it had been carved from stone, his hard abs on full display leading down to that sexy-as-fuck V that I loved so much. He had a dusting of blond hair that led into the waistband of his athletic shorts, which were doing nothing to hide his arousal.

"See something you like, little Larkspur?" he teased, running a hand down his stomach.

"You're fucking right I do." My voice came out in a raspy husk.

His grin widened as he climbed up the bed toward me. He reached for the waistband of my shorts, his eyes meeting mine, seeking permission. I nodded, and he made quick work of popping the button and drawing the zipper down. Chase slowly pulled them down my legs, while I quickly discarded my shirt, leaving me in my lavender panties and matching bra.

"Jesus, fuck," Chase said under his breath, his eyes taking in every inch of my body. I could feel his gaze burning into my skin, and I don't think I'd ever felt more sexy or wanted in my life. "You're perfect, Everly. My perfect Larkspur."

I could feel the blush on my cheeks from his words, my face growing warm. He moved further up the bed, so he was hovering over my body.

"Baby, as much as I love the purple panties, they're gonna need to go for what I have planned for you."

Twelve

Chase

I could barely contain the raging hard-on in my pants at the sight of Everly on her bed in nothing but her tiny purple bra and panties. I hooked my fingers into the sides of the lacy material and drew it slowly down her tanned legs.

As I pulled it away, her thighs fell closed, and I could see the shyness on her face.

"Oh no, little Larkspur, you don't get to hide from me." I smiled at her, sliding my calloused palms up her thighs, pushing her legs apart.

Holy Jesus Fucking Christ. I have died and this is heaven.

I stared down at her, taking in every delicious inch of her glistening pussy. I moved one hand toward her center, swiping my thumb over her clit. She arched her back in response, and a moan escaped her lips, making my grin spread and my cock jump.

"So wet for me, Larkspur. Do you want me to touch you?"

"Yes, Chase, please," she answered, the words breathy and sounding sexy as fuck with her husky voice.

I knelt between her thighs and leaned down. I started at her knee and left a trail of soft kisses along her inner thigh, stopping just shy of her pussy. When

I finished with one leg, I immediately started on the other. Everly began to squirm on the bed at my touch.

"Chase, plea—" she began to whine but then cut off when I flattened my tongue, licking her dripping cunt. She tasted divine, sweet, but with a little tang, and it was instantly my new favorite flavor. I lapped at her arousal, coating my lips and chin.

"Oooh!" she cried out, her hands clenching the duvet.

"What was that, little Larkspur? Were you saying something?" I teased, speaking the words against her core, my breath making her wiggle. I licked her again and still got no verbal response. Chuckling, I moved my tongue up to play with her clit. I flicked it back and forth, teasing the sensitive nub.

"Oh my god, Chase..." Everly moaned. One of her hands found my shaggy hair, and she threaded her fingers through it. While holding on, she thrust her hips upward, pushing my face even deeper. Shit, I could live here forever, eating her pussy twenty-four seven.

As I kept toying with her clit, I slowly pushed one finger inside her entrance. *Holy. Fuck.* She was so wet and warm, and my dick wept at the thought of how she would feel when I was buried balls deep inside of her.

But that wouldn't happen today. I was going to prove to Everly that this was about more than just me getting laid. I was going to make her come until she begged me to stop, but that would be the extent of our fun, for now.

I pumped my finger inside her a few more times before adding a second, giving her a moment to adjust to the stretch. She continued to make all manner of sexy noises, each one going straight to my dick. Jesus, I was going to have one hell of a jerk off session later, remembering all the sounds she made and the mental pictures my brain filed away. It would be like my own personal porn reel.

I looked up her body, her chest and face flushed with her arousal, my fingers still working her over. Her tits were encased in her lavender bra, so reaching up with my free hand, I pulled down one of the cups, her breast falling free. I grabbed a handful, squeezing the perfectly sized mound before my fingers found her taut nipple. I pinched and rolled the hardened peak between my fingertips while continuing to thrust my fingers into her warm cunt.

I could feel her body begin to quiver, her pussy tightening around my fingers. I knew she was close, so I went back to working her clit with my tongue.

After another minute, her pussy clenched around my fingers so tightly I could barely move them. Her back arched off the bed, and her thighs squeezed against the sides of my head like a vise. Her small fingers twisted in my hair so much it bordered on painful, but I didn't give two shits. In this moment, all I cared about was giving Everly every ounce of pleasure I could.

"Oh, God! Chase! Oh, fuck, I'm coming!" Music to my fucking ears.

I continued to lick and stroke her through her orgasm, only stopping once she tried to close her legs, her oversensitive flesh still pulsing from her release.

I sat up from between her legs, her arousal all over my lips and chin, and grinned down at her, loving the gorgeous flush of her skin. One of her breasts was still hanging out of her bra, and god damn was she stunning.

"Little Larkspur, you taste so good. That's a meal I could eat for breakfast, lunch, and dinner," I said, my voice low and gravelly. I was so goddamn hard that I was sure a single brush of her hand would set me off like a rocket.

Seeing the tent in my shorts, Everly sat up from her position, reaching for my waistband. I caught her wrist in my hand, and she looked up at me in confusion.

"Nope. Not today, Larkspur." She opened her mouth to protest, but I continued. "This was all about you, your pleasure. I want to *earn* your touch."

Everly's face softened at my words, and she instead reached up to stroke my cheek.

"Chase," she murmured, leaning forward to plant a kiss on my lips, not caring in the least that they were coated with her cum. She stroked my lips with her tongue, seeking entrance and deepening the kiss. I palmed the back of her head, letting her taste herself.

Knowing I was edging toward the point of no return, I pulled away from her perfect mouth. Her pupils were blown so wide the blue was nothing but a slim ring, and lust filled her eyes once again.

"Larkspur, I'm trying to be a gentleman here, but goddamn you make it hard."

She smirked and pulled me toward her. We settled on her bed, pulling the gray duvet over our bodies. Everly snuggled herself into my side, and I wrapped an arm around her, tucking her in even further. We lay like that for several minutes, just enjoying the quiet, listening to one another breathe.

I felt her body jerk next to me. Startled, I leaned up so I could see her better, but she had her face buried into my side.

"Everly, are you okay?"

"Mmhmm," was her muffled reply.

"Are you sure? Can you look at me?"

Her shoulders were shaking now, and oh shit, did I hurt her? Oh fuck, what did I do? I sat up quickly, pushing her onto her back, scanning her body and face for injuries.

It took me a moment to realize that the convulsions I was feeling were actually from Everly *laughing*. She was laughing, well, she was trying to hold in her laughter but was doing a shit job at it. When she finally made eye contact with me, she lost it, her laughs erupting from her chest.

"What? What are you laughing at?" What in the ever loving fuck was going on?

Everly held a finger up to my face while she caught her breath. After about thirty seconds she calmed down, finally regaining the ability to speak.

"When we were lying there snuggling," she finally answered, still giggling like a little kid, "all I kept thinking was, 'Damn, that was one hell of an apology!'"

I fell back on the bed, a loud laugh coming from deep in my chest. Jesus, this girl. I snagged her arm, pulling her closer to me again. "Come here, you."

Settling in once again, Everly snapped her fingers, and rock music began playing at a low volume from a Bluetooth speaker near her windows. *Ah, so she's telekinetic.* Looking over at the sound, I noticed several easels, canvases, and various paints scattered about and a large drop cloth on the floor.

"You paint, little Larkspur?" Obviously she did, but I wanted to know more about her, so I asked anyway.

"Yeah," she sighed. "I don't remember a time when I *didn't* paint. I had a studio above our garage at my old house." Her blue eyes turned momentarily sad, and part of me wondered how much of her art was tied up with her mom. "I haven't really gotten a chance to do anything since I got here. My time has been a bit preoccupied." She raised a brow and gave me a lopsided grin.

"I'll occupy all your time, baby." I waggled my eyebrows at her, earning me a snort of laughter. "But seriously, Solis has some really great art classes," I told her. "Or, well, at least that's what Knox has told me. He's an artist too. I'll have to introduce you two, he could show you the studios and all that."

"Yeah, that would be cool. Griff had mentioned introducing us." Her smile broadened, and I internally high fived myself at the fact I'd made her happy.

We lay there, content in each other's arms for a while longer, neither of us in any hurry to move. I was just starting to doze off when I heard the front door open and then close.

"Oh, shit! That must be Evan. Umm, we should probably get up, and I should get dressed." Everly started to climb out of the bed, but I snagged her around the waist, pulling her back down. I gave her a deep, soul scorching kiss, hoping she could feel how much I cared for her already. It was crazy how quickly I'd fallen under my little Larkspur's spell.

When I released her from the kiss, she looked at me, fire dancing in her eyes. My erection had returned and was currently poking her in the thigh.

"You want me to take care of that?" She smirked, glancing down at my crotch.

I lay back on the bed and covered my eyes with my arm. "As much as I want to say yes, I'm going to politely decline. Why don't you go out and see what your brother is doing, cause baby, if you stay in here with me nearly naked, this boner is never going away."

Everly chuckled but climbed out of bed, throwing her clothes back on. She gave me one more gentle kiss before leaving the room, the door closing behind her with a snap of her fingers. I could hear her and Evan's voices softly through the door as I lay in her bed, thinking about the last two days.

I knew there was still a lot I didn't know about Everly, but I could already feel the stretch of my heart as it made room for her. With my little Larkspur in my life, I was certain my last year at Solis Lake was going to be one I'd never forget.

Thirteen

Everly

Slipping out of my room, I attempted to smooth my hair and clothes. I didn't want it to be obvious to my brother that I just had one of the best orgasms of my life a few minutes ago. Jesus, the things that Chase had done with his tongue should be illegal. Any orgasms I'd had in the past were from me and my trusty pink vibrator that Celeste gave me for my eighteenth birthday. Guys I'd been with in the past had either not cared enough to get me off, or just didn't know what the hell they were doing. Chase, on the other hand, was a master at his craft. *If he sticks around, I don't think I'll be needing the vibrator very often....*

The thought twisted in my gut. He clearly had a reputation and the skills to back it up. I hoped he was serious when he said he wasn't interested in anyone else. I really liked Chase, a lot, and the fear that he was only looking for his next conquest still plagued me.

Surveying the living room, I found Evan seated in the middle of the sofa, a game controller in his hand.

"Hey Eves," he called from his spot.

"Hey Ev," I replied, plopping myself down next to him. I was trying to think of a way to tell him that Chase was in my room when the man himself appeared, as if summoned by my thoughts.

"Yo, Evan, what's up man?" He walked over, giving my brother a fist bump in greeting. "You got another controller?"

"Yeah man!" I swear my brother's eyes lit up like Christmas morning at the thought of Chase playing video games with him.

Chase launched himself over the back of the sofa on Evan's other side. I stared at them both, my mouth hanging open. I wasn't sure what I thought would happen when he came out of my room, but playing video games with my brother was definitely not on the list. He looked over, shooting me a quick wink.

The game had begun to load when Chase leaned back, looking at me from behind Evan. "Larkspur, Griff texted me a few minutes ago. He and Knox are gonna stop by in a little bit, if that's okay with you."

"Uh, sure." I shrugged my shoulders. What the hell else was I going to do today? The urge to paint wasn't niggling me like usual; I was struggling to find inspiration, and it was beginning to bother me. Typically I could pick up a paintbrush or my charcoals and have no trouble bringing the images in my mind to life. But ever since Dad told us about the move, it was like my well of creativity dried up.

I curled up on the couch, scrolling through social media and listening to my brother and Chase shoot each other for about thirty minutes when I heard a knock on the door. Glancing at them both and realizing neither was moving an inch, I climbed up from my spot.

"Oh, don't worry boys, I'll answer the door."

"Thanks Eves! You're the best!" Evan didn't even look away from the screen. I rolled my eyes, crossing the room to open the door.

On the other side, I found Griff, a wide smile gracing his handsome face when he spotted me. His hazel eyes crinkled at the corners in a way that I loved, and he leaned down to give me a kiss on the cheek. I noticed he did that a lot, the chivalrous act making me melt into a puddle each time.

"Hey Blue," he said when he straightened back up, happiness clear in his voice.

"Hey Chase said you were gonna stop by with..." My words trailed off when I spotted the guy from earlier standing behind him in the hall.

He stepped forward, an intense look on his face. He stared into my eyes like they held the answers to all the world's secrets, and I could feel myself blush under his gaze. He still wore the Breaking Benjamin t-shirt from earlier, but I noticed now how his muscular arms filled out the sleeves. Colorful tattoos ran down the lengths of both arms, stopping just shy of his wrists. The art was beautiful, and I had to restrain myself from grabbing his hand, so I could get a better look.

Chase's chipper voice broke through my thoughts, suddenly at my back, "Knoxy!"

Knox snorted, coming forward to stand next to Griffin. Both men stared at me for a moment, and I realized I was still standing in the doorway.

"Shit," I mumbled to myself. "Sorry, come on in."

Griffin chuckled to himself, moving past me into the suite. Knox followed, and when I turned around after closing the door, my breath caught in my throat. Standing before me like a goddamn buffet of sexiness were three of the most attractive men I had ever seen in my life. I felt my cheeks flush further, and Chase grinned at my obvious embarrassment. He had his hands shoved in his pockets and was leaning against the back of the couch.

Griff walked toward me, circling his arms around my waist and tugging me close to his body. "Hi," he said softly, leaning in to give me a soft kiss on the lips. My hands found their way to his chest as I returned the kiss, momentarily forgetting that Knox, Chase, and Evan were all privy to our moment.

"Come on!" Evan's voice startled me from the kiss, and I peaked around Griff's body, ready to incur my brother's wrath at making out in front of him. "Can't you at least, like, go in your room or something? You didn't make me watch you suck face with Chase earlier," he huffed out.

My face had to be the shade of a tomato. I looked up at Griff, expecting to see anger at hearing about Chase and I, but he just grinned down at me. He pecked me on the nose and released me, stepping back toward the kitchen counter. I looked between the guys, my gaze landing first on Chase, a shit eating grin on his face, then to Griff, who happily looked around the room, and finally landed on Knox.

Knox looked between his two best friends, his confusion clear. Obviously Griff and Chase hadn't filled their roommate in on the dynamic between the three of us.

"Umm, okay, so... Chase and I... but I like Griff too..." I stammered, trying to explain.

"Little Larkspur, Griff and I both know the score here, but we're not looking to compete. In fact, I think we're both prepared to put some points on the board together," Chase said smugly, cutting off my rambling.

"Really?" I asked, Knox echoing the question at the same time. I swung my face toward his, taking in his scruffy jaw and dark eyes. *Damn, he's good looking... Fuck! Stop it, Everly!*

"Seriously, Chase and I are good with this. Honestly, Blue, I'll take however much of you you want to give me. If it were anyone else, I wouldn't even entertain the idea, but Chase is one of my best friends, and I know how he feels about you. It's the exact same way I feel." Griff explained our little triangle with such simplicity, and I knew he meant every word.

"Okay, hold up a second," I heard my brother from the sofa again. "So you're *both* going to date my sister? Dude, I don't know about this. I don't want Everly getting hurt, or rumors starting about her or some shit." Evan stood, his long arms crossed over his chest in full brother bear mode. He always had my best interests at heart, and as much as I didn't want him dictating my dating life, I couldn't help but smile at his protective nature.

"I absolutely agree, Evan," Griff responded. "I have zero intentions of hurting your sister. And I feel confident in saying that I don't think Chase will hurt her either, right Chase?"

"Right." Chase nodded his head in agreement.

Griffin continued, "And if Everly is okay with dating both of us, I don't think we should let other people's opinions determine our relationship." *Our relationship, oh I liked the sound of that.*

"Eves?"

"I'm good, Evan. This is what I want." I gave him a reassuring smile.

Evan stared at both men for a moment, before blowing out a deep breath. "Okay, if this is what Everly wants, then I'm good. But just know, I'm a fire elemental, and my magic is fucking strong. I will burn you both to ashes and bury your bones without a second thought if you hurt my sister."

All three men shared a look, Griff and Chase each giving my brother a nod.

"Okay then, who wants to get their ass whooped on the Playstation?" Evan gestured to the flat screen. Not needing anymore than that, Griff and Chase each moved to the sofa and grabbed a controller. I gaped at the three of them, ribbing each other's gaming skills, as if the last few minutes had never happened.

"What the fuck just happened?" I heard the deep voice behind me ask. I completely forgot Knox was here, my brain consumed by Griff and Chase's declarations.

I turned toward him, those dark eyes searching my face once again. I could feel the scrutiny from his gaze, and my mind started swirling. *God, he probably thinks I'm some sort of slut, dating both of his friends.* I shut those thoughts down as soon as they entered my head. *Fuck that, I can date whomever I want.* I squared my shoulders and moved toward where he stood, sucking in a deep breath.

"Hi, I'm Everly."

Fourteen

Knox

"Hi, I'm Everly."

All I could do was stare into her electric blue eyes. Those eyes had occupied my mind for the better part of the day, and now here they were, in front of me once again. While she talked with Griff, Chase, and who I gathered was her brother, I took the time to study her delicate features. She was a tiny thing, petite but curvy in all the right places. She was tanned, probably from spending the summer outside, and her hair had a certain "just fucked" look. Chase had already been here when we arrived... That thought sent an unexpected pang of jealousy into my chest.

Shaking my head in an attempt to dislodge those thoughts, I extended my hand toward her. "Hey, I'm Knox." Short and sweet. I wasn't a big talker. I expressed myself through my art. The guys knew how I was feeling based on how much paint ended up on my body.

She accepted the gesture, her tiny hand dwarfed by my larger one. "Acrylics?"

Huh? Cocking my head to the side, I stared at her, confused. "What?"

"Acrylics?" she repeated as she looked down at where our hands were linked. "You have paint on your hands. It looks like acrylic. Is that your preferred medium?"

Ooooh. Damn, she noticed that? Shit, I thought I had washed most of it off, but it would appear that I missed some. "Uh, yeah, I like acrylics... I dabble in water colors too. Not a huge fan of oils. They smell too much."

"I agree. I prefer watercolors for painting and charcoal for sketching." I blinked at her in surprise. Who the hell was this chick?

"Oh, uh, that's cool. Griff didn't say you were into art." Griff didn't say much at all, asshole.

"That's my major. Art, I mean. Chase and Griff both mentioned you're an artist. I'm not sure what I want to do with it yet, but yeah, it's always been art for me. I thought about going into illustrating, but I don't know." She shook her head, pulling her hand from mine to gesture around herself. "I just want to paint, ya know? I know I can't really do much with it, career wise. It's probably dumb," she rambled, and I could see the doubt creeping onto her face, but I found myself unable to look away. Not even thinking, the words tumbled out of my mouth.

"Can I see some of your work?"

She froze, shocked eyes locking onto mine. "You want to see my paintings?"

"Yeah," I breathed out. What the hell was happening to me? It felt like a lock in my chest was opening, one mechanism at a time. I was inexplicably drawn to this girl. I took a step toward her. "I'd love to see your paintings."

"O—okay," she stammered. "I have some boxed up in my room. It's this way." She motioned toward a closed door off to the right. She turned and moved toward the bedroom, with me following just a step behind. This close, I could smell her shampoo, an intoxicating blend of jasmine and peonies. It took everything I had not to shove my nose into the back of her head as we walked into her bedroom.

"They're just over here," she said, making her way over to what was obviously her painting area. She had several drop cloths laid on the floor, two easels set up with blank canvases, and a plethora of brushes and paints. I noticed a closed sketchpad and a small leather satchel on top, most likely full of her charcoals. She began rummaging through a tall cardboard box, until she finally pulled out a midsize canvas.

"This is one of my favorites. I painted it after we went to my cousin's wedding last year." Her beautiful face pulled down into a frown, and I could see sadness spreading through her features. Her blue eyes glistened with unshed tears. This piece was special to her; it evoked emotion, but I hated to see her hurting. My desire to console her, to hold her, raged even though we had met only minutes ago. She stood still, gazing at the painting, lost in thought, seeming to forget that I was in the room.

"Can I see it?" I asked softly, drawing her attention back to me.

"Oh, yeah." She shook her head, taking a deep breath. "Sorry. Umm, it's a painting of my mom. She... she died six months ago. So, yeah, this one is my favorite."

She slowly turned the canvas toward me, and my world stopped. It was perfect. Large peonies surrounded the edges of the painting, each one done in various shades of pink and purple. Green leaves and stems peaked between the flowers. In the middle of the canvas was the face of a woman, looking away from the audience, only her profile visible. She was beautiful and looked like an older version of Everly. The dark brown watercolors that created her hair were astonishing. It had to be the most beautiful painting I'd ever seen.

"I know, it's not that great, but I think it'll always be my favorite. Peonies were both my mom's and my favorite flow—" she began rambling before I cut her off.

"Everly," I breathed out, moving closer to the painting. "It's perfect." Unconsciously, I stroked my fingers over the delicate blooms, noting the variations in color, the soft lines in each petal. I drew my gaze up to her face, her blue eyes wide.

"Knox, you don't hav—" she said, but I cut her off once more.

"Everly, believe me when I say: This. Is. Perfect."

Her cheeks flushed, the pink nearly the same shade as the peonies. Not wanting to embarrass her further, I decided to shift the conversation.

"So what made you choose watercolors?" I turned around slightly, spotting her desk chair. I pulled it out and planted myself in the seat, my upper body bent forward, my elbows on my knees. Everly placed the painting back in its box and moved to sit at the foot of her bed. Looking behind her, I noticed the duvet was rumpled and the pillows slightly crushed. Yup, Chase must have been with her earlier. *Damn it.* Hopefully he'd take it well when I told him and Griff I was throwing my hat in the proverbial ring as well, because there was no way in hell Everly wasn't going to be a part of my life.

Everly stared at her easels for a moment, seeming to contemplate her response. Finally, she put those gorgeous blue eyes on me and answered.

"When I was about five, my parents took Evan and I to an art exhibit. Everything was incredible, but when I saw Monet's *Water Lilies,* I just knew. It was so beautiful. The way Monet blended the colors so seamlessly on the canvas. The way they moved, almost like they were their own type of magic, the paint choosing its path. On the way home, I begged my parents for an art set. Luckily mine and Evan's birthday was just a few weeks after. I've been painting ever since."

"Your parents encouraged your art?" *Fuck, wouldn't that be nice? To have a parent that appreciated your passion?*

"Oh god, my parents were so supportive. I mean, my dad still is, but yeah, my mom even helped me set up a studio above our garage for my sixteenth birthday. Most kids get a car, I got an art studio." She laughed, and my heart skipped a beat. Her husky voice coupled with that laugh had my dick thickening in my jeans. Was it possible to fall in love with someone this fast? Because my brain was telling me this girl was the other half of my soul. I felt a pull to her that I couldn't explain. I just knew I needed to know her, needed to be near her.

Everly cleared her throat, and I realized that I had been staring like a total creep for the last thirty seconds.

"Sorry," I tried to explain. "My mother... She doesn't appreciate my passion for art. She thinks it's a hobby that shouldn't be encouraged. Art to her is just something that you hang in your home. It serves no purpose other than decor for your walls."

"That's terrible," Everly whispered. She looked at me, her eyes widening in horror as she covered her mouth with her hands. "Oh my god! I'm so sorry, I didn't mean to say that your mom is terrible. Shit, I'm so sor—"

I barked out a loud laugh, startling her enough that her words were interrupted. "Don't be sorry. My mother *is* terrible. I'm jealous that you had such supportive parents."

"What about your dad?"

"My father died when I was two," I stated matter of factly, shrugging my shoulders.

"Jesus! Knox, I am SO sorry! Damn it, I just keep sticking my foot in my mouth." Everly covered her face with her hands.

I got up from my spot and crossed the room in two strides. Crouching in front of her, I gently pulled her hands away from her beautiful face. This close, I could see the freckles across her nose and cheeks, like stars in the night sky.

"Everly," I started softly, "it's okay, little Monet. I don't even remember my father. I've never known a life with him. Do I mourn the idea of him? Of course. But I don't mourn the man himself. He's nothing more than a man in pictures that my mother keeps in her home."

"Still Knox, I'm sorry. I know what it feels like to lose a parent. It's a really shitty club to be in." I squeezed her hands, giving her a sad smile.

"You're right, it is shitty. And I'm really sorry about your mom. I bet she was amazing, given you're her daughter." That beautiful pink filled her cheeks once again at my compliment. I stared into her blue eyes, and I swore I could feel my soul trying to entangle itself with hers. Unable to help myself, I slowly leaned forward, my eyes darting to her lips. I flicked my gaze back to her eyes, silently asking permission.

Everly parted her lips, a small gasp breaking free. I felt her body lean toward mine, and I took that as the go ahead, slanting my lips against hers. Her mouth was soft, the kiss delicate, yet powerful. In that moment, I knew this girl would be a part of my life forever.

Suddenly, Everly pulled away, breaking our perfect moment.

"Knox," she whispered, "I'm, umm... I'm... *involved* with Chase... and Griff."

"I know, little Monet, but now you're involved with me, too."

Fifteen

Everly

After his declaration, Knox tugged me back into the living room. He made his way to one of our cushioned arm chairs and plopped down heavily, pulling me onto his lap. I gasped at the sudden movement, grabbing his shoulders to brace myself. Looking at him in surprise, I was met with a smug grin.

Feeling eyes on me, I looked over at the sofa to find both Griff and Chase staring, matching grins stretched across their faces.

"So I see you two are getting along well," Chase quipped, earning a low growl from Knox.

"Shut it, Chase," Knox bit back, but there was no heat behind his words.

My brother, finally looking away from the flat screen, groaned loudly. "Really, Everly? Knox, too?"

Griff put his arm around my brother's shoulder. "Remember our conversation earlier? All of that applies to Knox as well. Everly can date the three of us if she wishes. We're all cool with it, right Knox?" Griff asked as he looked over at his friend, the question hanging in the air.

Knox was quiet for a moment, one hand wrapped firmly around my waist, the other planted on my bare thigh. He looked between his best friends, then gave a silent nod of approval.

Chase whooped and jumped off the sofa in his excitement. He was like a golden retriever, bouncing around excitedly. "Everly, we're gonna date the fuck out of you!"

"And that's my cue," my brother huffed out. Standing from the couch, he made his way to the counter, grabbing his keys. "I'm gonna go check out the sports complex and maybe take a walk around the lake. I'll be back later." Before anyone could respond, he was out the door.

"Shit," I said softly. I didn't want my brother to be angry with me, or worse, disappointed. But I also couldn't help the intense feelings I already had for the three men sitting in my living room. Silence blanketed the room for a moment before Griff leaned forward, placing a large hand on my exposed knee.

"Blue, he'll come around." He sounded so sure, but unease still filled my stomach.

"Yeah, Larkspur, he's probably just having a hard time imagining his little sister with three boyfriends," Chase chimed in.

A small chuckle fell from my lips. "Actually, I'm his big sister. I was born a full minute before him."

"He just wants the best for you, little Monet," Knox reassured me, his big hand squeezing my thigh above Griff's.

I turned to look at him. "Monet, huh?"

"Yep," he replied with a grin, popping the 'p' at the end.

I rolled my eyes, smiling. Pushing thoughts of my brother to the back of my mind, I tried to focus on my... wait a minute...

"Chase, did you say *boyfriends*?"

"Yeah, Larkspur, that's what we are, right? I mean, I sure as fuck wanna be your boyfriend, and I'm assuming these assholes do too," he explained, looking at his friends.

"Damn right," Knox mumbled from behind me.

"Hell yeah," Griff added, grinning. "So what do you say, Blue, you wanna be our girlfriend? Wanna be *ours?*"

I looked at each of the men, taking in their handsome yet different features. Chase, who always seemed to make me laugh with his easy grin and carefree attitude. Griff, who I was still getting to know, but I enjoyed the time we'd spent together so far, while Knox and I seemed to have connected over our love of art. Did I want to be theirs?

A playful smile stretched across my face.

"Abso-fuckin-lutely."

We spent the rest of the day lounging around, watching movies and just getting to know one another. I now knew that Griff's favorite color was blue (I rolled my eyes playfully when he'd answered), Chase had been rowing for about ten years, and Knox's favorite food was a turkey, provolone, lettuce, and spicy mustard sandwich. Oddly specific, but whatever.

When dinner time rolled around, I texted Evan to meet us at the dining hall. I needed to make sure things were going to be okay between the two of us, especially if the guys were going to be a part of my life for the foreseeable future. My brother was one of the most important people in my life; I couldn't bear the thought of anything coming between us.

Evan met us just outside the doors to the dining hall. He had his hands shoved in his pockets and looked at us all warily. *Oh shit.* I was hoping the afternoon by himself would have helped to settle any worries he had, but judging by the look on his face, it hadn't helped a bit.

As if he could sense the tension brewing, Chase sidled up next to Ev, throwing his arm around his shoulder and giving him a megawatt grin. "Sup bro?"

Evan stared at him for a moment before breaking out into his own smile. A whoosh of air left my lungs, and I realized I had been holding my breath, waiting for the fallout. Griff slapped Evan's hand in greeting in that weird way guys do, while Knox gave him a silent head nod.

"Hey guys, ready to head in?" Evan asked, gesturing with his head toward the building.

We headed inside and settled at a table. After a drama free dinner where we stuffed ourselves—well, Chase mostly, I guess being an athlete meant he ate enough for three people—we made our way back to Bliss Hall. Griff intertwined his fingers with mine while Knox had an arm around my shoulders, tucking me into his side. Chase walked ahead of us with Evan, the two chatting about Solis Lake's sports programs and the athletic facilities on campus. Every so often he would turn and throw me a quick wink or smile, making my heart flutter in my chest.

When we reached the fourth floor, and after listening to Evan whine about all the stairs, Griff squeezed my hand, drawing my attention to his handsome face. I smiled up at him, hardly able to believe that this man, let alone all three, wanted me.

"Blue, would you like to hang out for a bit? With just me, I mean?"

"Uh, sure. I mean, is that okay with everyone else?" I turned to look at Chase and Knox. This was all new territory for me. I'd only had one serious boyfriend, and that had been toward the end of high school. It had ended in disaster when I found him getting a blowjob in the parking lot of Staunton High. He had been human, as was the girl I caught him with. She had been chasing him forever and was vocal about her dislike of casters. I'd knocked on the window, flipped them both off, and left without saying a word.

Chase gave me a sly smile. "Sure, Larkspur. Nothing saying we can't all spend time with you one on one. We can always add in group activities later." He waggled his eyebrows at me, my face turning at least eighteen shades of red. Jesus, the things out of this guy's mouth...

Evan promptly plugged his ears and began singing, loudly and off key, causing Chase to burst out laughing.

"Seriously though, go spend some time with Griff. Knox, you cool?" Chase asked.

I stared at Knox for a moment, his eyes boring into my own. The dark orbs felt like they penetrated my soul whenever he looked at me. It made me feel equal parts nervous and turned on. He gave me a brief nod, his blessing to spend the evening with Griffin. He ducked his head, bringing his lips close to mine.

"I get you tomorrow then, little Monet." His breath rolled across my lips before he planted a soft kiss against my mouth. He pulled away, giving Griff a nod and releasing me from his arm. "I'm gonna head to the studio for a while. Everly, I can show you the studios and the art department tomorrow, if you want. I'm assuming you'll be in that wing of Vox for classes?"

"Yeah, that would be great Knox, thank you!" I was so excited to start my classes. Everything felt like it was finally coming together, and the urge to create was slowly coming back.

"Shit, I don't have your cell number. Actually, Chase, I don't have yours either," I said as I realized.

"All good, Blue," Griff said as he pulled out his phone. He shot off a text, and my phone vibrated in my back pocket a moment later. "I made a group chat for the four of us. That way you can save Chase and Knox's numbers from it."

"Good call, Griff." Chase slapped him on the back. "Obviously, I'm the face of this little operation, and he's the brains. I'm not quite sure what Knoxy's role is yet, though..."

Knox punched Chase in the shoulder, earning him a haughty, "Oww!"

"Chase you wanna play some more Playstation?" my brother asked.

"Yeah, man, as long as my arm isn't broken." Chase dramatically rubbed the spot Knox hit. "Larkspur, will you kiss it better?" He pouted his full lips and turned the puppy dog eyes up to ten.

I laughed, reaching up to give him a peck on the cheek. "Go shoot each other and have fun. I'll text you later." Flashing me a grin, Chase followed Evan into our suite. Knox pulled me into his arms for another kiss once they were gone.

One hand gripped the side of my neck while the other held my waist, my body flush against his. He quickly deepened the kiss to the point where my toes were curling in my flip flops. I could feel his erection pressing into my stomach as he finally broke the kiss, and god damn was this man big. Knox stared into my eyes for a moment before stepping away.

"What time is your first class, little Monet? I can pick you up, and we can grab breakfast beforehand."

"Eight-thirty, I think. I can check my schedule and let you know later for sure."

"Okay." He nodded at me. "I'm going to head to my room and work for a while. I'll see you later." He gave me one last gentle kiss on the forehead. Knox turned to Griff, giving him a quick nod goodbye, then made his way down the hall, disappearing into the guys' suite.

"Looks like it's just you and me, Blue. Wanna take a walk?"

"Sure." I grinned at Griff, threading my fingers with his. "Lead the way."

Sixteen

Griffin

I held Everly's hand on our way down to Solis Lake. I planned to take her out to sit on the dock and watch the sunset. She was quiet on our walk, her eyes soaking in the beauty of the campus as the sun began its slow descent behind the trees. The sky was turning a beautiful myriad of colors as reds, oranges, and pinks streaked across the horizon.

I loved coming to the lake; it was always so peaceful, and I enjoyed finding a quiet spot to study until the weather got too cold to sit outside. There were several docks scattered along the two mile shoreline, so I steered us to one set away from the more trafficked areas. We made it to the end, and Everly sat down, her legs dangling off the edge. I followed suit, sitting next to her and leaning back on my arms.

Everly stared out at the water, and I took advantage of the moment to admire her beauty. She was truly stunning. I still couldn't believe that she was interested in dating me—hell, I couldn't believe she was willing to date all three of us, but I'd be damned if I made her choose. After a few minutes, as if she could feel my eyes drinking her in, she turned to face me.

"So, Griff, since you're my boyfriend now—well, one of my boyfriends," she said and laughed, "I feel like I should know more about you." She nudged my arm with her shoulder. "You've known Chase and Knox for a long time, you give campus tours, your favorite color is blue." Cue her eye roll. "And you obviously had terrible taste in women before you met me."

I barked out a laugh, her jab at Morgan perfect. She smiled at my response.

"But seriously, I want to know everything about you." Her small hand landed on my thigh, the warmth heating my skin. My cock stirred, but I willed it to behave so I could answer her.

"Well, Blue, I came to Solis Lake at the beginning of my first year. I'm on an academic scholarship. I tutor other students, including Chase. That's how we met actually. Knox and I were roommates, and Chase moved in with us during year two."

"Where are you from?" she asked, then hesitated. "Family?"

I took a fortifying breath. My childhood, for lack of a better word, sucked. It wasn't something I enjoyed talking about, but it fueled my reasons for being at Solis Lake, and I didn't want to hide any part of me from Everly.

"I'm originally from Emporia. I never knew my dad; he took off before I was even born. My mom..." I hesitated. I already hated the pity I knew I would see in her eyes.

As if she could read my mind, Everly squeezed my leg and gave me a soft smile.

"No judgment, Griff. You don't have to tell me if you don't want to. Either way, it won't make me think any less of you. You'll still be Griffin Cardarette, the sexiest campus tour guide I've ever met." She winked at me, putting the ball firmly in my court.

I inhaled deeply through my nose, catching hints of her peony and jasmine scent, letting the smell wash over me. It somehow soothed my nerves and gave me the strength to continue.

"My mom, well, let's just say I would've been better off if she'd left me too. She was a drug addict, which led to her selling herself for her next high. We lived in a shitty one-bedroom apartment, paper-thin walls. I could hear everything."

To her credit, Everly's face remained neutral. Her forehead scrunched a tiny bit at my last statement, but I didn't see the typical pity that usually accompanied my story.

"When I was about ten," I continued, "my mom had run out of money and couldn't pay her dealer. I had stolen some of her cash to pay for food, so she was short when he came around. She thought I was sleeping in the bedroom, but I had only been pretending." My mind was slipping back to that night, a tightness taking hold in my chest.

I heard Stan come in a few minutes ago, his beefy fist banging on our door. Mom let him in, and I tucked the blanket up closer to my chin. It was thin and scratchy, but I pulled it tighter anyway, pretending it was a shield that would hide me. The bedroom door was ajar, so I could hear their voices clearly. And Stan was mad.

"I don't care, Viv, I want my money."

"I know, Stan, I'm sorry. I can—I can work it off. Right? Like before?"

Ugh, gross. Even at ten, I had heard and seen enough to know exactly what that meant. I didn't know which I hated more: that my mom let men have sex with her for drugs or that my mom loved drugs more than she loved me.

"Not this time, you dumb cunt," Stan spit back at her. "You owe too much. Plus, you're not worth nearly what you owe. You'd have to blow me every hour for the next two months to come close."

"What the fuck, Stan! You know—" her voice was cut off by a sharp smack, and I knew he had slapped her. Silence filled the space for a moment before he spoke again.

"Listen you bitch, I want my money. You better figure it out, and figure it out fast, because now I'm fucking pissed." Anger was clear in his words. He really was fucking pissed, way more than I had ever heard him before. Typically, he'd yell at my mom, slap her a few times, maybe even beat her, then use her body however he wanted. This time, though, seemed different.

Scared but needing to see what was happening, I silently climbed out of bed and crept to the door. They were in the middle of our dirty shoebox apartment, making it easy to see them both.

Mom had her hand on her cheek, a red mark blooming from the hit. The vein on Stan's forehead bulged, and he fisted her skimpy top.

"I. Want. My. Money." He ground out each word, pulling her up until she was on her tiptoes. "You have about three seconds before I fucking kill you." His hands moved to her neck, and I could see her face turning red.

"Griffin!" she choked out. At first, I thought she was calling me for help, and I nearly stepped into the room but stopped short when she spoke again.

"Take Griffin! You can have him!"

My heart thundered in my chest. She... she was giving me to him?

Stan's voice cut through my thoughts.

"Keep talking."

"Sell him. Or keep him and pimp him out. Use him to run drugs. Do whatever you want. He'll bring in good money, and it'll get him out of my hair. Win, win, right?"

I knew my mom didn't want me. I knew she wished she'd never had me—she'd told me enough times—but I couldn't believe she would hand me over to be abused. My breaths came in short bursts, and my heart thundered in my chest. She hated me so much that she'd give me to Stan?

Their voices faded from my mind while tears blurred my vision. I needed to get out of here and fast. I moved deeper into the room, crossing to the window.

Outside was an old rusty fire escape that I'd shimmied down before when Mom had men over, and there'd been nowhere to hide. I pushed the window open and climbed out...

"That was the last time I saw my mom."

We sat in silence for a minute, Everly resting her head on my bicep. Her hand had moved from my thigh, so her fingers were now entwined with mine. I felt her take a deep breath and prepared myself for the inevitable pity I knew was coming.

"Griff—" she started softly.

"Please, Blue, please don't say you're sorry. I don't need your pity. It all happened a long time ago. I've moved on." I stiffened as I said the words, shoring up my armor from years of reliving that particular story.

She sat up and looked at me, the anger in her blue eyes taking me by surprise.

"Griffin, please listen to my words very carefully," she said evenly, her hand slightly trembling in mine. "I *do not* pity you. Do I feel bad that you had a piece of shit for a mom, if you can even call her that? Yes. But I don't pity you. Pity would imply that I thought your past had damaged you, held you back in some way, when it is so obvious that you have thrived *in spite* of your childhood." She paused for a moment, her tiny body trembling. "What I am, is angry. I am fucking furious that the bitch who gave birth to you thought she could just sell you, get rid of you, like you were garbage. I know I've only known you for a short time, but I can't imagine ever thinking you were anything less than fucking perfect."

Her chest heaved with emotion when she finished, while all I could do was stare. Her blue eyes danced with fury, like she would storm my mom's old apartment and tear her limb from limb if given the chance.

We stared at each other for another moment before I was able to find my voice again.

"I was on the street for a couple days before the cops picked me up. I wouldn't give them my mom's name, and since she hadn't reported me missing, they dumped me in the foster system. I bounced around for a few years, so many homes that I lost count. When I was fifteen, a guidance counselor helped me apply to Solis Lake Prep. It's the high school version of the academy. I got in on an academic scholarship. Once I'd gotten away from my mom and went to school consistently, I actually did really well. I have a photographic memory, so I always had good grades, even when I was moved from home to home. It's part of the reason I tutor, it's a requirement of my scholarship. That and I just like helping others."

Everly looked at me with such intensity, her blue gaze seared into my soul. She leaned into my side again, but this time I wrapped my arm around her waist, tucking her in even more. We stared out over the lake, watching the sun sink closer to the trees that lined the west shore. The sky was a beautiful mix of oranges, yellows, and reds.

"What happened to your mom?" Everly's soft voice broke the silence that had surrounded us.

"She overdosed about a year after I ran. CPS figured out she was my mom while I was in the system, but she never showed for any of the court dates, so the judge terminated her parental rights. My caseworker came to one of the homes I was in to tell me."

"Good. Fucking piece of shit," Everly said under her breath.

I gave her a squeeze. Jesus, she was amazing. When I tried to explain to Morgan about my upbringing, she looked equal parts disgusted and horrified, saying she didn't really need or want to know. Super supportive, that one.

"I think that's part of the reason I let Morgan treat me like shit for so long. I—I just wanted her to love me, just wanted to feel wanted, I guess." I had never really explored the inner workings of my relationship with Morgan, or why I put up with her cheating for as long as I did. I had been so wrapped up in the idea that someone might actually care about me, I ignored all the shitty things she did.

"Ah, so she's always been terrible, then? The other night and today weren't just flukes?" Everly teased, although there was still a tinge of anger to her voice.

"Yeah, she was always terrible," I laughed. "I'm pretty sure the guys wanted to kill me the last few years. Chase used to joke that I was the only guy he knew who had a steady girlfriend while also maintaining a steady case of blue balls."

"What do you mean?" Everly's eyebrows furrowed in confusion, her nose wrinkling in an adorable way.

"Umm…"

"Griff, what do you mean?" Her voice was a bit more firm this time, the question dancing in her eyes.

I swallowed thickly, not wanting to share the information sitting heavy on my tongue, but judging the look on my Blue's face, I knew she wasn't gonna let this go. I could feel my face turning red, embarrassment creeping in.

"Umm… Morgan, she umm… she wasn't the most… *generous* girlfriend," I stammered out the words.

Everly looked at me intently, trying to work through my answer. She chewed on her bottom lip, her eyes looking down at the water. Suddenly she straightened, her mouth falling slightly open, and her beautiful blue eyes going round. She slowly turned her head toward me.

She stared at me for a moment, realization on her face. Then, a slow, mischievous smile spread across her plump lips.

"Griffin," she purred, "did Morgan not *satisfy* you?"

I opened and closed my mouth several times before speaking.

"Uh, I mean, we slept together, sure," I sputtered. Her nose scrunched up at my mention of having sex with Morgan. "But she always acted like it was a chore. And god help me if I asked for a blow job. Pretty sure I could count on one hand the number I got while we dated. Honestly, I don't know why she dated me. Half the time it seemed like she didn't even want me around."

Everly huffed out a breath. "What a dumb bitch. Was she fucking blind? Not only are you absolutely gorgeous, but you're one of the sweetest guys I've ever met. The fuck is wrong with her?" She shook her head, her irritation with Morgan obvious. My heart ached from her sweet words. It felt strange to have someone besides Chase or Knox so concerned with my well being. She turned to face me once again, the last remaining rays of sunlight dancing across her freckled nose. "But I guess her loss is my gain."

I reached up and cupped her jaw gently. I didn't know how it happened so fast, but Everly was quickly becoming the center of my universe. She had blown in like a hurricane, tearing the way I viewed myself to shreds and replacing it with her honest and caring nature.

A sly smirk crept up her lips, and her eyes lit up with desire. "Griff, can you take me somewhere more... *private*? I want to show you how generous of a girlfriend I can be."

Oh, fuck yes.

Seventeen

Everly

Griffin stared at me for a moment, shock written across his attractive face. *Shit, did I break him?* A husky laugh escaped my lips, and I reached up to touch the hand he had resting on my cheek. The contact seemed to shake him out of his trance. Suddenly both of his hands were on my waist, and I was being tugged into his lap. I squealed, gripping him tightly, so I didn't end up in the lake.

"Hang on, Blue," he said. It was the only warning I got before we were suddenly moving through space at an indescribable speed. It felt like my body was liquid, and I was being sucked through a tube at lightspeed. In the next second, I was back in Griff's lap, but instead of on the dock, we were in a large wooden shed. I could hear water, and looking around, I realized we were in a boat house. Long row boats were tied to posts, and oars lined the walls.

I twisted around to see Griffin's face, a wide grin in place.

"You can teleport." The words tumbled from my mouth, not a question but a statement of fact. Because, yeah, he just teleported us.

"Yeah, pretty cool, huh? When my caster ability manifested at sixteen, I found out I was a teleporter. I've gotten pretty good at it since then. I have

131

to be able to picture the location I'm porting to in my head. It has to be somewhere I've been before."

"You've been to the boat house? Do I even want to know why?"

He barked out a laugh.

"Yeah, I've only been here to help Chase with the boats a few times. But I knew it would be empty at this time of day."

As we both climbed to our feet, I felt myself sway as though I was tipsy. Griff reached out, lightly gripping my elbow with one hand, the other landing on the swell of my hip. "Teleporting for the first time can make you feel a little unsteady. You okay?" His question was laced with concern as he studied my face for any signs of distress, but I was fine.

Besides, I had way more important things to worry about. Like showing Griffin Cardarette exactly how his girlfriend should treat him.

I looped my arms around his neck, causing me to stretch onto my tiptoes and push my chest into his abdomen.

"Well, Griff," I purred, my voice coming out low and husky, "I wanted to show you what generosity looks like."

I could feel his hard dick pressing into my belly through his shorts. Both of his hands had fallen to my hips, and his fingers slipped under the hem of my shirt, gently rubbing my soft skin.

"Blue, you don't—" he started, but I cut him off, gripping his face in my hands and bringing his lips to mine. I stroked my tongue into his mouth, tangling it with his. I would show this perfect man exactly what he deserved in a girlfriend and exactly how he should be treated.

Griff's hands slid down to my ass, and he gripped my flesh tightly, digging his fingers into my denim shorts. Suddenly, I was hoisted into the air, my legs automatically wrapping around his toned waist. Griff walked us straight to the wall behind me, my back hitting it with enough force to momentarily break our kiss. I sucked in a breath before his lips found mine again.

I took my hands from Griffin's face, dragging my nails down his chest before reaching for the hem of his Solis Lake tee. I grasped it and began tugging it upward. Griffin thrust his pelvis into me, pinning me to the wall and making me cry out as his dick rubbed my clit through our clothes. He leaned his upper body back an inch, so I could tug the shirt upward.

I finished stripping him of his top and looked at his muscular chest, trailing my fingertips slowly down his pecs and across the ridges of his abdomen while he kissed along the side of my neck. A shudder escaped me when his lips touched the sensitive flesh where my shoulder and neck met.

My fingers finally found the waistband of his athletic shorts, and I slid my hand inside, under his boxer briefs. I wrapped my fingers around his hard length, and *holy fuck*. He was fucking huge. Jesus. I stroked him from balls to tip for a minute, my tongue tangling with his in a slow dance.

I broke from our kiss but continued planting soft ones across his chest as I spoke.

"Set me down." I whispered the words softly between kisses, removing my hand from his shorts. He pulled his body back by an inch and slid my feet down to the floor. Concern flashed in his eyes like he was worried I'd leave him hanging. Not a fucking chance.

Once my feet hit the decking, I continued to slide down until I was on my knees before him. I sat back on my heels, and he stared down at me with so much adoration and affection. It was intoxicating.

"What do you want me to do, Griff?" I'd give him whatever he wanted, but I wanted him to tell me exactly what that was.

He was silent for a moment, not seeming to understand my question.

"Griff," I spoke softly, but firmly. "You're going to have to tell me what you want me to do. I want to know *exactly* how to make you feel good."

I watched as those words sunk in, and a moment later a sexy as fuck smile spread across his face.

"Up on your knees, Blue." His voice had gone deep, the words gravelly and low. My panties were soaked, and my lower belly tingled with anticipation.

"Yes sir," I said as I raised up on my knees. The sir was a gamble, but when I saw the heat flare in his eyes, I knew it was the right choice. Griff needed to be in control, needed to dominate me, and I was fucking here for it.

"Take out my cock."

I ran my hands up his legs, feeling the muscles bunch under my palms. Tucking my fingers into the waistband of his shorts and boxers, I tugged them down to his mid thigh. His thick cock sprang out, slapping his abs before standing proudly at attention. He was long, the head red and dripping with precum. I looked up at Griff through my eyelashes.

"What now, sir?"

Griff growled, the sound rumbling from deep in his chest. I could feel my own arousal coating my thighs, my underwear absolutely ruined. His large hand landed on the top of my head, his fingers tangling in my long strands.

"Let me fill that beautiful mouth, Blue." The words were choked as he thrust forward into my waiting lips. He slid about halfway in, my tongue stroking his steel shaft teasingly. Griff sucked in a breath through his teeth, his entire body going rigid. I began bobbing my head on his dick, licking and slurping his delicious length.

Griff dropped his head back between his shoulders, tilting his face up toward the ceiling, a moan escaping his lips.

"Fuck, yes, Everly, just like that."

He used his hand to guide my head, making me take him even deeper, until he was nudging the back of my throat. I fought not to gag, tears spilling from the corners of my eyes. I swallowed around him, my throat tightening around his cock.

"Fuck Blue, goddamn you feel so good." He tilted his head so he could gaze down at me. He watched with rapt attention as his cock slid in and out of my mouth, my saliva coating him. He was salty but with a hint of sweetness, and my god, I couldn't wait to swallow every last drop.

I continued to suck him, hollowing out my cheeks and running my tongue up the underside of his shaft. Using one free hand, I cupped his balls, rolling them between my fingers. Griff moaned loudly, and I internally preened at how much he seemed to be enjoying this.

I was so turned on from blowing him, I was ready to combust. Using my other hand, I popped the button on my shorts, lowering the zipper before diving beneath my panties. His cock in my mouth had me so wet, I was easily able to glide two fingers directly to my clit.

Griff began to fuck my face, but when he saw my hand disappear into my shorts, he let out an animalistic growl. He picked up his pace, thrusting in until his dick threatened to cut off my air supply. I tried to circle my clit to his rhythm, but I was so close, it was nearly impossible. With his dick down my throat, I came, my vision darkening at the edges. My eyes rolled closed, and it took everything I had to keep sucking him through my orgasm.

As I began to come back to earth, I could feel Griff's dick thicken on my tongue, his release close.

"Fuck, Blue, I'm close. I'm gonna—"

Before he could get the words out, hot ropes of cum shot down my throat. I tried to swallow it all, but there was so much, and his dick was so large that some spilled out the corners of my mouth. When he gave one final shudder,

I pulled off and gave the head a soft kiss. Making a point of catching his eye as I looked up, I used a finger to wipe his cum off my chin. When I gathered it all, I popped the finger in my mouth, sucking it clean.

Griff's face and neck were flushed from his orgasm, and his chest heaved. His pupils were blown so wide I could barely see the hazel and he looked absolutely feral. I loved that I made him feel so wild and wanted.

Pulling his fingers from my hair, his hands found my shoulders and the next thing I knew, I was on my feet in front of him, my hand still in my shorts. Griffin yanked it free, sucking my fingers into his mouth.

"Mmmm..." he groaned, his eyes closing. "You taste so sweet."

His beautiful eyes opened as he released my fingers. We stared at each other for what seemed like forever. Slowly, a smug grin spread across his face.

"Well Blue, what do you say?"

"For what?" I cocked my head at him, confused by his question.

His hazel eyes danced in amusement. He paused, kissing the tips of my fingers before answering.

"I gave you my cum, and you swallowed it all down like a good girl. Now, what do you say?"

Momentarily stunned by his words, I pondered them for a moment, noticing the mischievous glint in his eyes. Realization dawned on me, and I returned his smirk with one of my own.

"Thank you... sir," I purred. Griffin let out a growl from deep in his chest before slamming his lips down on mine in a bruising kiss.

New kink level unlocked.

Eighteen

Knox

Monday morning rolled around and with it the first day of classes. They were going to seriously cut into my studio time, but luckily half of my credits this semester were for my independent art study. I was focusing on the use of the water element in art and architecture, which worked out well, considering water was my elemental skill. I was still required to take other classes during my fourth year as well, including some elemental magic courses, magical defense, and a course for shifters.

My shifter ability manifested at sixteen, along with my water power. Casters who were shifters weren't super common, and it was surprising I had that ability given that neither of my parents were shifters. Mother was a telekinetic, and according to her, my father had been as well. To say she was disappointed to find out I was a shifter was putting it mildly. The idea that her son would shift into an animal, *in her home*, disturbed her on a number of levels. I had made sure to run through the house as a pig each time she had gone out of town once I learned how.

Personally, I loved shifting. As long as I had seen the animal, or at least a picture, I could typically shift into it. It did have drawbacks though; the bigger the animal or the more unfamiliar, the more magic the shift used. Could I shift into an elephant? Probably. Would it drain all of my magic quickly? Absolutely.

I had a couple animals that were my go to's. My snow leopard was a stunning beast, his white coat incredibly soft and his claws razor sharp. My other top choice was a red-tailed hawk. Flying was one of the few things I enjoyed as much as painting, although I didn't get to do it as often as I would like with school.

I grabbed my bag, looping the long strap over my head, so it rested against my chest. Everly texted me last night after Griffin took her home, confirming our breakfast plans. Asshole came home with a big dopey grin on his face after their impromptu date. When I asked him what was up, he just smiled even bigger and mumbled something about the boat house being his new favorite place. Whatever.

Shoving my keys into my pocket, I made my way out the door and down the hall to Everly's suite. Chase and Griff were going to meet up with Evan for breakfast a little later. None of them had class until ten, and I knew Chase was already gone for the morning; he had early row practice everyday at the ass crack of dawn. I was excited to finally spend some time alone with my little Monet, learning exactly what made her tick. My steps brought me to her door, and I raised my hand, knocking softly.

The door swung open a moment later, and my breath caught in my lungs. The sunlight shone behind her, framing her silhouette. Everly wore tight blue jeans and a soft, rose colored tank. The top had a deep vee, showcasing the swell of her tanned breasts. My dick was instantly at attention, images of my handprints all over her tits in acrylic flashing through my mind. She would be stunning, naked and covered in my paints. The perfect masterpiece.

"Morning, Knox," she said softly, gesturing for me to enter. I stepped into the suite while she moved to the sofa, grabbing her bag. Evan's door was still closed, and I didn't hear anything, so I assumed he was still asleep. "You ready?"

I nodded at her, stepping back into the hallway first. She followed, checking the door to make sure it was locked. I pulled her backpack from her hands, slinging it over my shoulder. Everly gave me a soft smile.

"You don't have to carry that. I can do it."

"I know, little Monet, but I want to. The southern gentleman in me dictates that I should carry any and all bags for you. Blame it on my debutante mother's etiquette lessons."

She giggled but didn't try to take the bag back. I snagged her hand, linking our fingers while we descended the stairs. After a quick walk across the quad, we reached the dining hall. I loved coming at this time of day; most students were still sleeping, so the lines were shorter, and it was quieter.

We found a table near the windows, leaving our bags and grabbing our breakfast. Everly brought back a small bowl of granola and yogurt, some orange juice, and a piece of toast, while I loaded up my tray with scrambled eggs, bacon, toast, and a small bowl of sausage and gravy. My appetite required me to hit the gym nearly every day, but god damn was it worth it. The food at Solis Lake was top notch.

We ate in comfortable silence for a few minutes before I noticed Everly slightly bouncing in her seat.

"Everly?" I asked, dragging out her name.

She startled slightly as if she had forgotten I was there. "Yeah?"

"You okay? You seem, I don't know, nervous maybe?"

Her beautiful cheeks flushed pink, and a shy smile played across her lips. She bit her bottom lip, and I couldn't help but want to replace her teeth with my own. It blew my mind how gorgeous she could look in just a simple tank top and jeans. Her dark brown hair was down and swept over her shoulder, hanging over her right breast.

"You'll do great. You've got Water Magic with me first, right? What's after that?"

She pulled her schedule out of her bag, her eyes scanning the worn piece of paper. From the looks of it, she'd probably double, triple, and quadruple checked it since she arrived.

"Yeah," she replied, still looking at the page. "Water Magic, then Caster Potions. I don't have Magical Defense until tomorrow."

"We'll probably be outside until the weather turns too cold for that."

"Oh, you're in that class too?" Her voice held a hopeful tone that made me smile. If I was being honest, I think I smiled more in the last two days, since meeting Everly, than I had in a long time.

"The guys and I are all in that class. Although, I think Evan said he was in a different section. And I'm pretty sure Griff and Chase are in Potions with you. Do you have any art classes this afternoon?"

"Uh, yeah, Elemental Magic in the Arts at one in Vox."

"Cool. After Water Magic, the rest of my day is blocked off for my independent study, so I'll be in my studio. I do have Advanced Shifter Studies at four, but I'm done before dinner."

"You're a shifter?" Her eyebrows lifted in surprise, her mouth forming a little 'o'.

"Uh, yeah. Sorry, I don't always think about mentioning it."

"That's so cool! I've never known someone who could shift before! There was an underclassman at Staunton who was a shifter, but I'd never met her," she rambled excitedly.

"Yeah, we're not super common. Solis is one of the few schools that offers Shifter Studies, so there are quite a few of us here. I think maybe ten or fifteen." It was one of the reasons I enrolled here after finishing my general studies at eighteen. That, and their art and architecture program. "What's your caster ability?" I asked her, realizing I only knew her elemental skill.

"Telekinesis," she said, sighing. "Boring." She stirred her granola and yogurt, a frown forming on her lips.

"That's not boring," I replied. "I wish I could move shit with a snap of my fingers." I snapped them for emphasis, knowing full well nothing would happen. "See, now that's boring." The corners of her mouth lifted, and a small giggle escaped. I smiled at her. "Show me. Move something, I wanna see."

"Knox, seriously, it's so boring. I'm sure you come across telekinetics all the time. It's the most common ability."

I shook my head and sat back in my chair, crossing my tattooed arms across my chest, fully intent on making her give me a show. "Nope, I wanna see. Come on, chop chop."

She stared at me for a moment, and when she realized I wasn't backing down, she rolled her eyes and looked around the room. Her gaze landed on the mountain of pastries at one of the food stations. Looking at the muffins, she raised her hand, her index finger extended in a come hither motion. I watched as a blueberry muffin lifted from the table and moved smoothly across the room, coming to rest on my empty plate.

I grinned at her as I took the wrapper off the muffin. "Now see, that's fucking awesome."

"It's boring," she pouted, her bottom lip jutting out. She rested her chin on her hand, leaning on the table.

"It's not," I told her as I ran the pad of my thumb along her lip. She surprised me when she pressed a soft kiss to it. Grinning, she sat back in her chair, crossing her arms across her chest. Her tanned breasts pushed upwards with the movement, and my eyes immediately zeroed in on her tantaliz-ing flesh.

"Okay, I showed you mine, now you have to show me yours"

My brows furrowed together. What did sh—

"I want to see you shift! Now come one, chop chop." She nodded her head, throwing my words back at me.

"We can arrange that," I told her. She began bouncing in her seat again, her excitement about my shifting clear. "But later. I don't think anyone would appreciate me stripping down in the dining hall."

"I mean, I'd be okay with it," she said so quietly, I almost didn't hear her. But I could tell from the blush on her cheeks that she had indeed said the words. I barked out a laugh, causing the mousey looking girl a few tables over to look up. Most people on campus weren't used to hearing me talk, let alone laugh. Everly caused me to do a lot of unexpected things.

"I'll shift for you later, when we have a little privacy."

"Promise?"

"Promise."

After breakfast, Everly and I made our way over to Vox hall for our morning classes. I noticed some students staring as we moved across campus, no doubt having heard through the grapevine that Everly was dating not one, but three of the most eligible bachelors on campus. I glared as we walked by, their whispers dying as we passed. I was not about to tolerate anyone bad mouthing my girl or our relationship.

We sat through Water Magic, each of us getting our syllabus and listening to the professor drone on about our assignments for the upcoming semester. I was bored to tears, and I could tell Everly was too. I moved my hand to her thigh, stroking her denim clad leg with my thumb. I could see the corner of her mouth twitch up as she fought a smile, but she continued staring at the front of the room. Not one to give up so easily, I leaned in, my lips grazing the shell of her ear.

"Bored, little Monet?"

A shiver rolled through her body, and goosebumps raised on her arm, but ever the obedient student, she remained silent.

"How about I make you a deal?"

She shifted her eyes to the side, giving me a quick glance. Now I had her attention.

"Come by my studio after your next class. I'll shift and show you some of my... other abilities."

I watched her throat bob in a nervous swallow as her cheeks darkened. She nodded her head quickly in agreement.

I smiled, knowing in just a few short hours, I'd have my little Monet all to myself.

Nineteen

Chase

I stood just outside the doorway to the Potion's Lab, waiting for Everly to arrive. All the science labs were housed on the top floor of Voxina, giving them easy access to the rooftop garden. Professor Moore kept a beautiful, state of the art greenhouse up there with all manner of plants, most of which we used in our labs. I was stoked to be taking this class, working with so many different herbs and flowers.

She rounded the corner from the stairwell, her long dark hair cascading over her shoulders. The rose colored top she wore matched her cheeks, slightly flushed from her trek up the three flights of stairs from the water classrooms on the second floor. I grinned when she came into view, my entire day made better simply from the sight of her.

"Hey there, little Larkspur." I pressed a kiss to her soft lips in greeting.

"Well, hi to you too." She grinned against my mouth. Even though I knew it had been less than twelve hours since the last time I saw her, my heart still raced in her presence.

"You ready for Potions? Griff's taking this with us, too, but I haven't seen him yet," I said, looking over her head down the crowded hallway. Students were milling about, making their way in and out of the classrooms while Everly and I waited for my best friend. He wasn't typically late for—

"Boo!" Griff's voice whispered in my ear, and holy fuck did it scare the shit out of me. I jumped, nearly smashing into his face, which was situated just above my shoulder. Everly dissolved into a fit of laughter, doubling over at the waist. I turned quickly, punching Griff in the arm.

"Oww!" he cried out, holding his bicep. "Damn man, I was just joking; no need to go all super strength on me. Jesus." He winced, rubbing where I'd hit him.

"Sorry, but Jesus dude, could you not teleport directly behind me next time?"

He nodded, rubbing his arm gingerly but still giving me a lopsided grin.

Everly stood up, wiping a few stray tears from her eyes, still giggling to herself. "You boys ready to head in?"

Griff stepped around me and cupped her jaw in the palm of his hand. He leaned down, giving her a kiss that had my dick thickening in my jeans. Fuck. I never knew it could be so hot to watch my girl and my best friend, but damn did it turn me on.

Breaking apart, Griff ushered Everly into the lab, me following behind them. Long, rectangular tables with stainless steel countertops were situated in three rows facing the whiteboard at the front of the room. Professor Moore was already in place, books, beakers, and mixing bowls scattered across her desk. Shelves lined the walls, jars full of herbs and elixirs on display.

Everly, Griff, and I took a table in the middle row, setting our bags down before pulling out our textbooks and tablets. Griff sat on her left side, me on the right, putting her directly between us. As I settled onto my stool, I glanced over, admiring the way her tanned skin looked under the sunlight streaming in through the large windows on the far wall.

More students filed in, filling the tables around the room. I noticed Austin waltz in, taking a seat at an open table behind us. I turned as he walked by, glaring at his back. I hadn't liked the way he'd stared at Everly the other day at breakfast, something about the guy setting me on edge. I'd known him a long time through our dads' business, but I'd never liked him.

A loud clap drew my attention to the front of the room where Professor Moore was standing.

"Good morning, everyone!" She greeted us with a bright smile. Moore had been my favorite professor since coming to Solis Lake. She was the head of the Environmental Conservation department and my academic advisor, so I had worked closely with her over the last few years. She was always encouraging me to look for a career in conservation after I graduated, even though she knew all about the future my father had planned out for me.

"Morning Professor!" I called back, giving her a grin.

Everly turned to look at me before whispering, "Suck up."

I stuck my tongue out at her before focusing back on Professor Moore.

"Here are your syllabi," she said, handing out paper packets to each table. "You will have readings and chapter summaries due each week. We will have two lecture days and one day of lab work."

Over the next few minutes, Moore ran through the list of topics we would be covering this semester: a healing elixir for minor injuries, a sleeping potion, a powder meant to turn its taker into a living statue for a short time, and a size elixir meant to make objects larger or smaller. Each recipe called for a variety of items and had extensive brewing times with complicated directions.

"So," Moore continued. "You will be making each of these potions over the course of the semester with a partner." I raised my hand high in the air. "Yes, Mr. Stone, you have a question?"

"Yes, Professor. Are we allowed to work in groups of three?" I was crossing my fingers that she'd say yes. What better way to spend my favorite class than working in a group with one of my best friends and my girl?

"Unfortunately, Mr. Stone, you will be working in pairs. We have an even number of students, so everyone will be partnered with one other student. And to make it easier, I've partnered you up alphabetically."

I slouched in my seat, disappointed that I wouldn't be working with Everly or Griff for that matter. Both their last names were at the beginning of the alphabet, while I was toward the end.

Professor Moore began reading off the pairings, and I listened intently to see who Everly would be with. "Adams and Bernum, Blackwell and Cardarette, Clark and Franklin..." I stopped listening when I heard Everly and Griff's names paired together, instead turning to look at them.

Griff was smiling ear to ear, while Everly simply looked relieved. I stuck out my bottom lip, giving them both a dramatic pout. My Larkspur laughed, patting my cheek like I was a five-year-old, which I supposed I *was* acting like one. But come on! *I* wanted to work with Everly. My inner toddler stomped his feet.

"No fair," I whined. "How come you two get to work together?" I crossed my arms over my chest, huffing out a breath. Maybe if I laid it on thick enough, Griff would switch with me... Nah, who was I kidding, he'd never swap.

Just as I was about to start begging, I felt a hand on my bicep. Turning, I was met with a face I wished wasn't so familiar.

"Hi Chase," Heather said, batting her eyelashes. She was standing to my right, one hip popped against the lab table, tits nearly spilling out of her low-cut blue top. Her mousy brown hair was hanging around her make-up covered face, a single finger stroking my upper arm. I looked at it first, then to her face, lifting an eyebrow before pulling away from her roaming fingers.

"What do you need, Heather?" I internally rolled my eyes at her presence. Heather had been one of my regular hook ups before I'd met Everly, good in bed, always down to fuck. Unfortunately, she was also a stage-five clinger, never quite understanding that I wasn't a relationship kind of guy. Well, at least not until Everly.

"Didn't you hear the teacher?" she asked, twirling her hair around her finger. She leaned in closer, her breasts brushing my arm.

"Jesus, Heather! Personal space!" I barked, scooting my stool away from her. Not taking the obvious rejection, she stepped into the empty space. I was fairly certain she'd climb into my damn lap if I let her.

"You weren't looking for personal space on Friday. In fact, you were *all* up in my personal space, several times." She lowered her voice in what I think was an attempt to sound sexy, but it just came off as awkward.

"No, and do you need a cough drop? What's wrong with your voice?" I knew I was being a dick. But damn it, I also knew how this was going to look to Everly, and I was trying to prove to her that I wasn't that guy anymore.

Heather straightened up a bit, her eyes flicking over my shoulder briefly before landing on my face once more. I turned around to see my Larkspur and Griff. Everly had a frown on her pretty face, her eyebrows scrunched together. Her sapphire eyes kept darting to Heather behind me, and I knew I needed to smooth this over, and fast. I quickly turned back to the obnoxious girl.

"Heather, what the fuck do you want?" The words were harsh, but I needed her to understand she wasn't welcome.

Her bubblegum pink lips turned down in a pout as she crossed her arms, pushing her boobs even further out of her shirt. "Professor Moore said we're lab partners." She pointed between us. "Stevens and Stone. Almost like we're meant to be." She threw me a wink and I nearly gagged.

"Not fucking likely," Everly growled, the words low enough that Heather didn't hear. *Fuck fuck fuck*. I glanced over my shoulder at Griff, silently pleading for some assistance.

"Blue, why don't we go take that empty table back there?" He pointed toward the back corner, an empty lab table waiting for them. "We're supposed to sit with our partners anyway."

Everly stared at me for a moment before scooping up her materials. She stood, but before she followed Griff, she leaned in close to my ear.

"I'm trusting you here, Chase. Please don't make me regret it." She placed a small kiss on my cheek before meeting Griff at their new table. My shoulders sagged with disappointment. Fuck. I couldn't let Heather fuck this up.

As if my Larkspur had never been there, Heather slid her skinny ass onto the probably still warm seat. She started taking her book and tablet out of her bag, but I snatched it from her hands.

"Chase! What the fuck?" she snapped at me, leaning closer to grab it back, but I held it just out of reach. I looked around the room, knowing I only had about a minute before Professor Moore was going to start her lecture. She was still handing out the syllabus and answering questions, moving from table to table.

"Heather," I started, my voice low but firm. "Whatever we had going on, our hookups, they're over. We'll be lab partners because we have to be, but other than that, this"—I pointed between the two of us—"is done. Understand?"

Heather rolled her eyes, flicking her overly processed hair over her shoulder. "Chase, you know we're good together. Why are you acting like this? I was actually going to ask if you wanted to meet up after classes were over, pick up where we left off on Friday. What do you say?" She placed her hand on my thigh as she spoke. I quickly shoved her off, my eyes darting to Everly. She didn't appear to have noticed, but she still wore the same frown from earlier. I followed her line of sight to the table behind me where Morgan was now sitting with Austin. Jesus, that was a fucking match made in hell. The she-bitch was watching our exchange as if we were some kind of goddamn soap opera. She had a poorly covered bruise on her cheek, and I briefly wondered who else she must have pissed off before deciding I didn't give a fuck. I considered flipping her off, but her gaze flicked over to Griff before I could, shooting a glare in their direction.

"I mean it, Heather," I said through gritted teeth, turning my attention back to the girl next to me. "Stay the fuck away from me."

Twenty

Everly

Once my classes were over for the day, I began making my way to the basement of Voxina Hall. My mind was still a jumbled mess after our Potions class. I didn't like the idea of Chase working with Heather, especially after he admitted he'd slept with her only days ago. But since I couldn't change the pairings, I'd just have to trust that he'd keep his word and his hands to himself. Griff's attempts to distract me during class worked briefly, though now that I was on my own, doubt slithered into my brain once more.

Knox texted me with the room number of his studio after Water Magic ended, and I told him I'd meet him there. I could still feel the weight of his hand on my thigh, the heat of his skin still warming my leg. He wasn't much of a talker, especially when they were all together, instead sitting back and observing his environment. I didn't mind Knox's quiet nature, something deep inside tethering me to him in a way I didn't yet understand.

I quickly reached the basement level of the gigantic building, still distracted thinking about Chase and Heather. Taking a right out of the stairwell, I was met with multiple corridors. This place was like a damn maze. Shit, I would be lucky if I didn't get lost down here. Checking my phone for the studio number, I started down a hall, praying it was the right one.

About halfway down the hall, I realized the numbers weren't even close to what I needed. I turned down a second corridor but was still met with no luck. Stopping in a doorway, I pulled my phone out to text Knox.

"Lost, Everly?"

I shrieked, jumping about two feet in the air, my phone flying out of my hands. It landed a few feet away, skidding to a stop. Spinning around, my eyes landed on Austin Thorpe standing in the doorway.

"Jesus Christ, Austin, you scared the shit out of me." I placed a hand on my chest, my heart thundering against my ribs. Austin smirked. His dull, brown hair was pushed back from his face, and I could see a predator's glint in his pale blue eyes. He was tall but not as big and broad as my guys. I immediately retreated a few steps, my back hitting the wall on the opposite side of the corridor. Austin moved toward me, trapping me between his body and the wall.

"What's the matter, Everly? Scared?" He placed a hand on the wall next to my head, the other picking up a lock of my hair and playing with it. I batted his hand away, making him laugh, the sound deep and menacing.

I squared my shoulders, trying to exude way more confidence than I was feeling. I was *not* going to be intimidated by some asshole on a power trip.

"Austin, back up," I said through gritted teeth, praying he didn't hear the tremble in my voice. "Please." I tried to push him away using my telekinesis, but for some reason nothing happened.

I didn't have time to dwell on my malfunctioning magic as Austin leaned in closer, his long nose running up the side of my exposed neck. He inhaled, causing me to shudder. The hand that had been playing with my hair gripped my hip, his fingers digging in so hard I knew I'd have bruises. My stomach roiled in disgust at how close he was, real fear quickly setting in. I didn't know where the fuck I was, where the fuck Knox was, or what the fuck Austin was planning to do.

"Mmmm...." he hummed against my neck. Suddenly, I felt something wet against my skin and I fought the urge to vomit on his shoes when I realized he had licked me. Still pressed into me, his obvious—and obviously lacking—erection nudging my stomach, he grinned. "But only because you asked so nicely." I could feel my body shaking, but I couldn't make it stop.

"I'm looking forward to getting to know you, *pet*." Stepping back, he strode quickly down the hall, leaving me reeling from the encounter.

I sank down to the floor, taking a ragged breath. Snapping my fingers, my phone flew across the floor into my hand. *So glad it decided to work now.* With shaking hands, I pulled up Knox's contact, praying that he'd pick up. After the third ring, his deep voice came down the line.

"Everly? You here?"

"Knox." His name came out as a whispered sob.

"Everly? What's wrong? Where are you?" I could hear the sudden panic in his voice.

"I, I don't, I don't know," I stammered, looking up and down the empty corridor. I needed to get out of here before Austin came back. I sucked in breaths rapidly, my chest tightening. I could feel my vision tunneling...

"Everly," Knox's voice cut through my racing thoughts. "Listen to me, baby. Are you in Vox?"

"Yes," I rasped out.

"Good, good. That's good, baby. Are you in the basement?"

I nodded my head but realized he couldn't see me when I didn't get a response. "Yes, I'm in the basement. Knox, I'm scared." My voice broke on the last word.

"I know, Everly, I'm coming. Baby, look around. Are there numbers on any of the doors? Tell me what room you're near."

I stood up, moving down a few feet to the next doorway.

"1024."

"That's great, baby. I'm only a few halls away. I'll be there in twenty seconds."

As the seconds ticked by, I could hear footsteps quickly approaching. My breath caught in my throat when I saw Knox's large body round the corner. When he was only a few feet away, I flung myself at him, my arms wrapping around his neck.

His muscular arms enveloped me against his body, and I held on as he stroked my back and hair. He kissed the top of my head, whispering against my hair. I pressed my face into his chest, inhaling his scent of paint and cedar. We stood, wrapped around each other for several minutes while my heart rate returned to normal. Stepping back, Knox gripped my upper arms, ducking his head so he could look me in the eye. He moved one hand, his thumb swiping my cheek and coming away wet.

Oh my god, I was crying. I hadn't cried since the day of my mom's funeral. Swiping at my cheeks with my fingertips, I wiped the tears away, looking up at Knox's concerned face.

"Everly, what the fuck happened?"

I took a deep breath and told him everything from the last ten minutes; me getting lost in the basement, Austin basically assaulting me, my ensuing panic. By the time I was done, I was shaking again, and the tears were back.

Knox pulled me into his arms again. "You're safe Everly. I've got you. He can't get you."

I pulled back, still in his arms. Looking up into his face, I could see the truth in his words, but I needed to feel it on my skin. I pushed onto my tiptoes and pressed my lips to his. I must have shocked him because he took a half second to kiss me back.

He cupped my jaw with both hands, his tongue teasing the seam of my lips. I opened, letting him in, my tongue dancing with his. I got lost in his touch, my hands moving to rest on his broad chest. I needed him to make me feel safe.

I dug my fingers into his shirt, feeling spots of wet paint on the cotton. Tugging him toward me, I backed into the open doorway. Knox followed, still kissing me like I was going to disappear and kicking the door shut behind him. We broke apart a moment later. Knox's chest heaved, and his face was flushed with arousal. He looked at me with wild eyes, and I could feel his dick against my stomach.

"What do you need, Everly?"

"You, Knox," I whispered, leaning up to kiss the corner of his mouth. "I need you."

He looked around the room, my head swiveling to take in the space too. It was a classroom, but it didn't look like anyone had used it in quite some time. White sheets covered in dust were draped across old desks with a large table near the whiteboard at the front of the room. His gaze moved back to mine.

"Everly, are you sure? I don't want you to reg—"

"Knox," I said, moving back a few steps toward the table. I gripped the bottom of my tank top, pulling it over my head. "I'm sure. I want you to make me forget. I need your hands on my body. Take away his touch. Please," I pleaded.

Needing no more words, Knox moved quickly, his big paint-covered hands gripping the backs of my thighs. He picked me up, placing me on top of the table. Our mouths clashed in a fiery kiss, his tongue licking into mine with an intense ferocity. Once my ass was on the edge of the table, I tugged his paint-stained t-shirt over his head. I took a moment to admire his ink-covered chest, taking in his many tattoos. I made a mental note to explore each one later on... in great detail, preferably with my tongue.

After stripping off his shirt, I moved my hands to Knox's waistband, popping the button on his jeans and pushing them down his hips. He must have had the same idea because suddenly my own jeans were being tugged down my legs along with my lacy blue underwear. When they were off, he flung them over his shoulder. I leaned back on my elbows, my pussy completely bared to him.

Knox gazed at my core, hunger in his eyes. He ran a hand up the inside of my thigh, his other stroking his long cock. I stared at it, a glint of metal catching my attention. *Holy shit.* His dick was pierced with a Jacob's ladder, the metal barbells lining the underside of his shaft. Oh. My. God. I could feel myself get wetter the longer I looked.

"Everly."

My eyes raised, with some effort, from his dick up to meet his dark chocolate irises. He was still stroking himself, and the hand on my thigh gripped my skin tightly.

"Baby, I don't have any protection," he gritted out, his voice strained.

"It's okay. I take a birth control elixir every month, and I'm clean." The words quickly tumbled out of my mouth. Fuck, if I didn't get him inside me soon...

My statement must have been enough, because the next thing I knew, Knox leaned forward, lining up his dick with my entrance before thrusting all the way to the hilt. I gasped, his thick length stretching me. I could feel every piercing as they rubbed my inner walls. He pulled out slowly, nearly to the tip before pushing inside again, slower this time.

"Jesus fucking Christ, Everly," he ground out. "You feel so goddamn good. So fucking tight." He continued to hammer into me, moving one hand to my back and pulling me closer. His piercings felt amazing, and I moved my hips in rhythm with his. With every thrust, he grazed my clit, working me closer and closer to my release.

Knox moved his free hand to the space where our bodies met. He pressed his thumb to my clit and started rubbing firm circles. After a minute, I could feel my orgasm barreling down on me. My back arched, and I threw my head back.

"Knox!" I cried out his name as pleasure coursed through my body. I squeezed my eyes shut, bright spots dancing behind my lids. He continued his ministrations through my release until my body relaxed, held up solely by his large arm still wrapped around my back.

Once my own orgasm waned, Knox picked up his pace, pounding into my pussy with such force that my tits were bouncing in my bra, and I could feel his balls slapping against my ass. His thrusts became erratic, his own release close. He gripped my hips with his large hands, fingers digging into my flesh. I momentarily hoped he would leave bruises to cover those left by Austin.

"FUCK!" he roared, his hips stilling, his dick spurting ropes of cum deep inside me.

He leaned his forehead against mine, both of us breathing heavily. I reached a hand up, stroking the side of his face. He turned into my palm, leaving a gentle kiss.

"Are you okay?" he asked softly, his hands still firmly on my hips.

A giggle escaped my lips before I could stop it. He leaned back and quirked an eyebrow at me.

"Sorry," I giggled again. "But yes, I'm okay. Although, after that, I'm not sure 'okay' really covers it. I think you and your pierced dick broke my brain."

159

For the moment, the events in the hallway were a distant memory. Knox had done exactly what I needed; he made me forget, even if just for a little while.

Knox stared at me dumbfounded for a moment before a big grin broke across his face.

"Little Monet, me and my pierced dick will break your brain, and your pussy, whenever you ask."

Twenty-One

Chase

By the end of our first day of classes, I was exhausted. We had an early morning row practice to prepare for our upcoming regatta, and then I had back-to-back-to-back classes. This semester was going to kick my ass. Hard. I was going to need to set up a tutoring schedule with Griff before he got too booked up. Although, maybe my little Larkspur would want to study... I could think up all kinds of incentives she could give me for good grades....

On top of everything else, I was still pissed off about being paired with Heather for Potions. She spent the rest of the class trying in vain to get my attention, her bony little fingers touching me at every opportunity. It took every shred of patience I could muster to keep from using my caster strength to launch her out the window.

Shaking those thoughts from my brain, I made my way to the dining hall to meet up with Everly and the guys. I also had another item on my agenda that I planned to execute this coming weekend; I was going to surprise Everly with a picnic in the forest.

Besides being on the water, being in the woods was my favorite place to be. Fresh air, beautiful plants all around, it was like heaven. No, scratch that...

being between Everly's legs was heaven. But the forest was a close second. I remember trying to explain it to my dad once. He definitely did not see the appeal.

"Chase, you can't just keep disappearing off into the Solis woods. I need you to get your shit together and start doing better in your classes."

"I can study out there easier, Dad. I like being out in nature. It's calming to just sit out there sometimes."

He scoffed. "Calming. You can be calm and study in your very nice, very expensive room. Or better yet, the library that I have donated so much money to. Honestly, Chase, who the fuck goes out to the woods to just sit."

If my dad wasn't surrounded by every modern convenience, I don't think he'd know what to do with himself. Don't get me wrong; I fully enjoyed all the perks that came with being wealthy, but being out in nature most certainly didn't appeal to my dad's lap of luxury personality.

I secretly wanted to go into environmental conservation when I graduated. My counselor helped ensure I took all the core classes to have it as a major, alongside the business major my father demanded. It had been grueling, but I loved each of my conservation classes. It was like night and day looking at my grades. Barely scraping by in all my business courses, but top of the class in my conservation ones. Even my conservation advisor, Professor Moore, was willing to write me recommendations for after graduation. But I knew my dad; me not working at Thorpe & Stone would only happen if hell froze over.

Attempting to lighten my mood, I plastered a big smile on my face and made my way through the dining hall toward my best friends and my girl. Evan was sitting with our little group as well, talking animatedly about something. I noticed that Griff and Knox both wore serious expressions, neither really listening to Everly's brother. Weird. Probably just a stressful first day. I plopped down in an empty chair next to my Larkspur, slinging my arm over the back of her seat.

"'Sup guys!" I greeted my best friends and Evan. I got a round of 'heys' before Evan excused himself for an evening class, slapping each of our hands and giving Everly a quick squeeze before leaving. As he walked away, I fixed my gaze on the woman sitting next to me.

Beautiful blue eyes turned in my direction, and my breath caught in my throat. God, I'd never get used to how stunning she was.

"Hey Gorgeous," I said, leaning in to give her a kiss.

"Hey yourself. How was your first day?" She placed her hand on my thigh, her touch warm through my athletic shorts.

"Good, busy. It's gonna be a tough semester until rowing ends," I covered her hand with my own, giving it a squeeze. "How was yours?"

"Oh, umm... classes were okay," she murmured, looking down at her plate, avoiding my eyes.

"Just okay?" I prodded. Something wasn't right, and I'd be damned if I wasn't going to find out, crossing my fingers that it didn't have to do with Heather and our Potions class. I looked across the table to find Knox staring at us intently. I could tell by the look in his eyes that something was wrong.

Using my fingertips, I gently turned her face to mine.

"Everly," I said, my tone serious. "What happened?"

"This afternoon, I, umm... I ran into Austin... in the basement of Vox." Her voice was so soft I could barely hear her, but I could feel my blood pressure rising at the mention of that dickwad's name. I had noticed him staring at her during class the few times I'd glanced at his table.

"Okay," I started gently, not wanting her to see the anger bubbling just under the surface. I really hated that douche canoe. "What did he want? Did something happen?"

"Yeah, something fucking happened," Knox interjected, the words spit through gritted teeth, his palm hitting the wooden table. "He fucking scared her. *Touched her*."

What in the actual fuck?

I looked at Everly. She was quiet, hunched in on herself, like the day I stupidly asked about her mom. She had taken her hand off my thigh and was wringing both in her lap. She wasn't my happy, sassy Larkspur. I saw red.

Rage flowed through my veins like wildfire. I would kill that fucker. Looking at Knox and then Griffin, I could see my anger reflected in their faces. That asshole had touched our girl. I was going to break a rowing oar over his fucking skull.

"Where the fuck is he?" My voice came out low, deadly.

"We don't know. Haven't seen him. He's hiding out," Griff said, his voice soft so as not to carry to the neighboring tables. I, on the other hand, didn't give a fuck who heard me.

"Everly," I said, taking a deep breath to calm myself. I didn't need her thinking I was angry with her. "What happened?"

She quietly rehashed the afternoon's events for me. Judging by the look on Griff's face when I arrived, I assumed Knox or Everly had already told him what happened, and I could tell by the pained look he wore now that he was feeling as guilty as I was.

"He—he cornered me in one of the hallways, in the basement," she said softly, her voice shaking. "He started playing with my hair and had trapped me between him and the wall. I told him to move, but he got super close to me, and then—" her voice cut off, a small sob breaking loose.

I reached over and tugged her from her seat into my lap. She offered no resistance and curled herself into my body. Luckily, we were sitting at a table in the corner, so no one really noticed our new seating arrangement. I stroked the back of her head, pressing soft kisses to her temple.

"Little Larkspur," I said quietly into her ear. "None of this is your fault. At all. I know you don't want to talk about it, but baby, I need to know what happened. Can you do that for me?"

I could feel her small frame trembling, but she nodded her head before sucking in a deep breath. She exhaled, then continued.

"He got really close to me, his face was near my neck, and his hand was holding my hip really hard. I tried to push him away with my telekinesis, but it wouldn't work for some reason. Then, he—he *licked* me. It was so disgusting Chase, and I—I didn't know what to do! I froze." She buried her face in her hands at the last word, sobs wracking her body. After a few moments she calmed a bit and looked up, tears running down her beautiful cheeks.

"When he left, I called Knox. I had gotten lost in the basement, that was how Austin found me. Knox came, he rescued me."

Knox's cheeks turned a light shade of pink, but he scoffed under his breath. I knew what he was thinking. He hadn't gotten there in time. But it wasn't his fault either. It was that fucker Austin. I was going to end the little bastard.

Everly was calming down, the trembling of her body slowing. I kept my arms wrapped around her; not just to comfort her, but to keep me from jumping out of my chair to find Thorpe. When she squeaked out a breath, I loosened my grip a bit; with my caster ability being super strength, I'd have to make sure I was extra gentle with her while my anger raged.

Griff, who had been quiet this whole time, finally spoke. "I think it would be best if one of us walked Everly to all of her classes. Between the three of us, we should be able to manage it." He turned his attention directly to the girl in my lap. "Blue, do you have any classes with him?"

"So far, just Potions, but that's with you and Chase. I haven't had all of my classes yet either, so I'm not sure." She bit her bottom lip so hard that I was afraid she'd draw blood. Griff must have noticed, too, because he gently tugged it from between her teeth.

"Well," Griff spoke again. "I think it would be a good idea if one of us met you after every class and walked you to the next one. I know you have some classes without any of us, but since most are in Vox, we should be able to at least make sure you have an escort. Maybe Evan can pick up any slack."

"No!" Everly interrupted abruptly, her cheeks flushing at her outburst. "Sorry. I didn't mean to yell. But I don't want Evan knowing about this. He's super protective. I'm honestly surprised at how okay he is with all this." She gestured between the four of us. "He'll lose his shit if he finds out that Austin..." Her lower lip trembled. Jesus, he'd fucked her up so badly she couldn't even say the words.

"Okay, Blue, we won't say anything to Evan," Griff said, attempting to placate her.

"We won't say anything *yet*," Knox interjected. I looked over at him, his eyes full of the same rage I was feeling. I couldn't imagine how he felt, finding her scared and alone in that hallway. He stood up and moved around the table to kneel in front of our girl.

"But listen, little Monet, if Austin tries anything, *anything*, we *will* be telling Evan. Do you understand?"

Everly nodded her head in agreement. He had a paint-stained hand resting on her knee, his deep brown eyes fixed firmly on her face. There was a look there that I had never seen from Knox. He stared at her as if she hung the moon, stars, and every damn galaxy that ever was. Complete adoration filled his eyes, and it was almost as if he... no, that wasn't possible. Not after only a few days right? I knew I felt strongly for Everly, more so than for any girl before, but I didn't think we were in L-word territory yet. But looking at Knox looking at her, I suddenly began to wonder just how deeply my own feelings ran.

Twenty-Two

Griffin

Friday afternoon finally came, bringing an end to the first week of classes. The days had gone by in a blur of school work, time with Everly, and setting up my tutoring schedule. In the past, I had always taken on more tutoring sessions than my scholarship required. It was easy money, and I actually enjoyed the work. This year though, I found myself only scheduling the bare minimum to meet my requirement, so I would have more free time with Blue.

Sitting down on the sofa, I popped the top off my beer and took a long pull. Chase was in the shower after coming home from row practice. His first regatta of the season was tomorrow, and I knew he was excited to have Everly on the shore, cheering him on. Grabbing another beer from the fridge, I decided to see what Knox was up to; the loud rock music blasting from his room telling me he was home.

Not bothering to knock, I pushed his door open. He was in just his painting sweats, a canvas on his easel. I walked up behind him, tapping his shoulder with the top of the cold bottle. He spun around, obviously not having heard me enter. He tapped the bluetooth speaker sitting next to him, Crossfade's "Colors" lowering to a dull roar.

"What's up man?" he asked, shoving his wavy brown hair back from his face. I could see streaks of blue paint weaved into the brown strands from where he pushed it back while he painted. He reached out, snagging the beer I'd brought for him.

"Nothin', just figured I'd see what you were up to." I shrugged. "It's just you, me, and Chase for dinner. Everly said she and Evan are eating in their suite. I guess they're going to video chat with their dad, have some sort of family dinner."

"That's nice, I guess," he said, shrugging. I knew the relationship between Knox and his mom was strained at best. Mrs. Montgomery didn't understand his artistic aspirations, his need to express himself through creation. Knox hated going home during breaks, typically choosing to spend any time off from school here with me. Chase was usually called home to fulfill his Stone family obligations. I had no family, so I never had to worry about those types of things.

Shaking those depressing thoughts from my head, I moved to stand next to my friend. He had been working on some new pieces, and I was secretly dying to see them. I knew, after the painting of Everly's gorgeous blue eyes, that he'd likely have a whole collection dedicated to her. Looking at the easel, I knew I was right.

My Blue was there, her stunning likeness on the large canvas in a beautiful watercolor masterpiece. Her back was to me, her face turned over her left shoulder, giving me the perfect view of her stunning profile. Her left side was drawn in black ink, wispy lines making up her gorgeous form. Knox had painted peony blooms around her and had placed light streaks of blue through her hair, the color matching her eyes. Her hands were reaching up, cupping her slender neck.

"Knox," I said softly. "It's perfect."

Knox's cheeks tinged pink. He was an incredible artist, but had always been self conscious about his work from his mother's constant judgment. However, there was no denying the painting before me was one of his best works.

"*She's* perfect," he said affectionately. I'd noticed a change in Knox since meeting Everly, and particularly after that day with Austin in the basement of Vox. Art had been his passion for as long as I'd known him. His true love, one might say. But I had a sneaking suspicion it was about to move to number two.

We stood silently, staring at his painting for a few minutes, each taking sips from our beers until they were empty. I nudged Knox's arm with my own, tipping my head toward the door. He followed me out into the kitchen, where we found Chase, shirtless in just a pair of athletic shorts, his head stuck in the fridge.

"Hey!" He greeted us with a large grin. Chase was an all around happy guy, but he'd been smiling bigger ever since a certain brunette moved in down the hall. Straightening up, he pulled three beers from the fridge, handing off two to Knox and me.

"Cheers my dudes!" We clinked our bottles together, taking a long drink each. I had been debating earlier in the day how to bring up the subject of the three of us all dating Everly and what that was going to look like in the long term. Taking another sip from my beer, I decided now was as good a time as any.

"So guys," I started.

"I know, I'm sorry," Chase quickly interrupted. "I'll make sure I clean up my rowing bag and my workout clothes. Sorry. It's just been a hectic week."

I laughed, setting my beer on the counter. "While I appreciate the apology, because your gym shit stinks, I actually wanted to talk about Everly."

Panic mixed with rage erupted on Chase's face. "Did something happen? I swear to Christ, if that fucker Thorpe did anything…"

Knox held up a hand, cutting off Chase's tirade.

"Everly's fine. She's at her place with Evan, having a virtual family dinner with their dad."

Chase's shoulders sagged in relief. He knew better than any of us exactly what Austin Thorpe was capable of. They'd known each other since grade school, their fathers being business partners since before they were born. The fact that Chase was so worried about Austin put me on edge and gnawed at the back of my mind.

"Yes, she's fine. I wanted to talk about *us* and Everly." I leaned back against the counter, my hands holding the edge. I stared at my friends. Knox's brows furrowed while Chase moved across the kitchen, so we were standing in a makeshift triangle.

"What about us and Everly? I thought everything was good." That panicked look was back on Chase's face. His bare chest began rising quickly, his anxiety ratcheting up. "Is she having second thoughts? Are *you* having second thoughts?" God damn did he spiral quickly. I could see his grip on the beer bottle in his hand tightening. I needed to reel him in, and fast, before he broke the damn thing and shredded his hand.

"Chase, calm the fuck down." I used my stern tutor voice, the one that always got him to sit down and pay attention. I noted to myself belatedly that it was the same tone I'd used with Everly in the boathouse. I stifled a chuckle at the thought while Chase straightened his back, pulling himself together. "No one is having second thoughts. I just wanted to make sure we were all on the same page, that's all."

"Oh, okay." Chase released a deep breath. Damn, my friend had it bad. I'd never seen Chase so head over heels for a girl… Come to think of it, I don't think in all the time I'd known Chase, that he'd ever even had a girlfriend. There had been a revolving door of one or two night stands. Some girls came back for a repeat performance, and he had his "usuals" he could call at the drop of a hat. But Chase never kept a girl around for longer than a few days. Everly was under his skin, deep.

I looked over to where Knox was leaning against the fridge. He, too, had never had a steady girlfriend, but he wasn't the manwhore that Chase was. Knox definitely fucked around, but he wasn't as obvious about it. When he needed to get laid, he did, but he didn't need a woman to warm his bed every night... until Everly strolled into our lives.

"I know we all care a lot for Everly. And I know she agreed to date all of us, but I guess I want to clarify what that means, what it looks like."

Knox raked his fingers through his hair, a hum coming from his chest. He wasn't the type of guy to just start talking, but when he spoke, he meant every word.

"I don't know about you assholes, but to me, it looks like whatever Everly wants it to look like. I'll take whatever she wants to give.... I—I can't be without her."

I looked at Knox, stunned. He was never the type to need anyone, and he sure as fuck didn't talk about his feelings. He was one of my best friends, but some days I felt like he barely tolerated Chase and me. To hear him say he couldn't live without Everly... My friend was falling hard.

I glanced at Chase, gauging his reaction to Knox's admission. His jaw hung slack, and his green eyes were wide in surprise. He was clearly just as shocked by Knox's words as I was. We all stood in silence for a few moments before Chase spoke.

"Dude, same. Like, I can't imagine not having her in my life. It feels like she's always been here. She just *fits* with us." Chase spoke the words reverently, a serene look crossing his face. "I think I..." The sentence dropped off, but I had a feeling I knew where it had been headed.

Looking between them both, I spoke again. "Okay, so we're all in agreement, Everly is in charge of this thing?" They both nodded, so I decided to continue, not sure if my next question would be met with resistance... Or fists.

"I think we can all agree that Blue is gorgeous. I haven't been with her... like *that*, but we have definitely fooled around. Are we all okay with the fact that she will, most likely, be intimate with all of us at some point?"

Heat flared in Chase's eyes. I was ninety-nine percent sure he'd messed around with her too, especially after he'd had her alone the other day. I hadn't gotten specifics, but it was pretty clear something happened.

"I'm fine with that," he replied a little too casually, taking a pull from his beer. "Honestly, I'm fine with whatever she wants in the bedroom. Single, doubles, group action, I'm down with all of it. Her sweet pussy tastes—" Chase froze as the words left his mouth, realizing he had just admitted to eating Everly's pussy.

I laughed, patting him on the shoulder. "It's all good, man. Better we know how far we've all gotten, I suppose." I took a drink from my beer before setting it on the counter. "For the sake of transparency, she gave me the best blow job of my life down in the boathouse the other night."

I heard Knox mumble under his breath as Chase choked on his beer, laughing in between coughs.

"What was that, Knoxy?"

"Shut up asshole," Knox grumbled, shooting a glare in Chase's direction. "I just said 'no wonder he was so happy the other night.' Fucker had a big dopey grin on his face when he came home."

Chase and I laughed, but I quickly noticed Knox had gone silent again. I moved across the kitchen to where he was standing. He moved away from the fridge, his beer bottle dangling between his fingers.

"What's up man?" I nudged his shoulder with my own. I knew dragging anything out of Knox was like pulling teeth. If he didn't want to tell us, he wouldn't.

He stood silently for another minute, staring at a spot on the floor before lifting his gaze to Chase and me. He took a deep breath in through his nose, blowing it out slowly.

"So, the day Austin—" he started, a flash of anger crossing his face before he spoke again. "The day Everly got lost in Vox... after I found her, she was a mess. She was so scared, and she asked me to take away his touch. We started kissing in one of the empty classrooms..." His voice trailed off, and his cheeks flushed pink.

Chase spoke first. "Okay? So you what, made out with her? Dude, that's awesome! I mean, it's no blow job, but—"

"I fucked her." Knox's voice cut through the kitchen, and you could have heard a pin drop in the silence that followed. Chase and I stared at our friend, shocked silent by his admission.

"Well shit, Knoxy, way to go!" Chase finally chuckled before looking at me. "Seems like we've got some catching up to do, Griff."

Twenty-Three

Everly

Having dinner with Evan and Dad, even though it was virtual, was such a nice surprise. Evan called Dad earlier in the week and set the whole thing up. I missed seeing my guys, but after we finished eating, I had to call Celeste and fill her in on my first week at Solis. That particular conversation had taken up the rest of my evening.

"*Okay bitch, spill! What is going on with you and those sexy men?*"

"*Hi Eves. How's school? Are you settled in okay? I miss you,*" I snarked back at her.

"*Don't sass me! Spill! Now!*" I grinned at her obvious excitement over my love life. In the past, it was always her latest conquest at the center of our girl talks. My situation with Griff, Chase, and Knox was definitely new territory for the both of us.

"*Things are... good.*" My attempt at being coy was not going well.

"*EVES!*"

"*Okay, okay! Jesus, C, calm down!*" If I knew my best friend, she was pacing around her bedroom in her fuzzy, hot pink pajama pants, munching on a Twizzler. Putting her out of her misery, I continued.

"*I agreed to date all three of them.*"

"*Hell fucking yes!*" *she screamed over the phone. I could see her in my mind, fist pumping the air, dancing around. "And?*"

"*And what?*"

"*Everly Margaret, you are dating three of the hottest guys I have ever seen in my life—thank you for the pictures by the way.*"

"*You're welcome. Not like it's a hardship to take pictures of them.*" *A smile crept onto my face, my thoughts drifting to how sexy my guys were....*

"*Everly, focus. I need to know which one is the best in bed. Penis size to thrusting ratio. Oral skills. Details! Now!*" *I could hear her snap her fingers over the line.*

"*Who says I've slept with any of them yet?*" *She was going to blow a gasket at my cheekiness. Silence filled the line. Three, two, on—*

"*WHAT?!*" *Aaaand there it was.*

"*Oh, calm down, C.*" *I went on to explain exactly how far I had gone with each of the guys, purposefully leaving out the details of my encounter with Austin leading up to sleeping with Knox. Celeste would storm onto the Solis campus and hunt down Austin's creepy ass if she found out what he had done.*

"*God damn, Eves. I'm so happy for you, but I am so fucking jealous.*"

Grinning like the Cheshire cat, I teased her, "I mean, I could call Evan, if you wan—"

She cut me off before I could finish. "Whatsorrycanthearyougottagobye!" The line went dead, and I let out a loud laugh.

Now, it was Saturday morning, and I was just finishing getting ready for the day. Chase had his first regatta, and I was excited to finally see him in action. Griff and Knox would be with me; the guys made sure I was never alone all week. It was comforting to know they cared so much about my safety. They kept their promise of not telling Evan, too. I didn't like keeping secrets from him, but I didn't want to add more to his already full plate. I knew his course load was pretty heavy; he didn't need that extra stress, especially since Austin hadn't tried anything else.

I hadn't had any more encounters with him since the incident in Vox. I saw him a few times on campus, and when we had Potions together, but not much besides that. He caught my eye a few times, his lecherous gaze roaming over my body, making me sick to my stomach. I didn't know what his fascination with me was, but I hoped it ended quickly.

I was just finishing my double french braids when I heard Griff and Knox in the living room. I knew Evan wasn't awake yet, so Griff must have used his master key to get in. I threw on a soft, yellow sundress and a pair of white sandals, grateful that the weather was still warm. Jogging across my room, I opened my bedroom door, my breath catching in my lungs.

Griff and Knox stood before me looking sexy as fuck. Griff had on a pair of bright blue board shorts with a gray cut off, his muscular arms on full display. Knox was next to him, a tight black t-shirt stretched across his chest, his cargo shorts covered in his signature paint stains. The evidence of his art had a small smile tugging at my lips.

I crossed the living room to my guys, their eyes tracking my every move. I leaned up on my tiptoes, pressing a kiss to Griff's lips first, then moving over to Knox and giving him the same treatment. "Morning guys," I said against Knox's lips.

"Mmm," he moaned. "It's always a good morning when I get to kiss these lips little Monet." His arm snaked around my waist, and he dipped me backward. I squealed as his lips met mine again.

"Alright you two, come on," Griff teased. "We want to make sure we get a good spot to watch the race." He playfully tugged me out of Knox's hold, planting a gentle kiss on my lips before tangling our fingers together.

We made our way down to the shore, following a throng of students dressed in Solis Lake regalia. Lucky for me our school colors were blue and gold, so my dress fit in well. I didn't know much about rowing, other than there were eight guys and one long ass boat. As we got closer to the shore, I could see our rowing team gathered together. My eyes zeroed in on Chase and *holy fuck.*

He wore a tight, one piece unitard in blue and gold, the Solis Lake emblem stretched across his broad chest. The lycra material hugged every single muscle on Chase's body—and there were a lot—making my mouth water. He was the definition of sex on legs.

As if he could sense our arrival, Chase's head swung in our direction, his eyes immediately locking on mine. I could see his shimmering green irises in the morning light, and it took everything I had to keep from sprinting across the space into his arms.

He patted one of his teammates on the shoulder before jogging over to the three of us. Before I could even say hello, Chase scooped me up in his arms, twirling me around.

His mouth found mine as we stopped spinning, my arms twining around his neck, and my feet dangling in the air. Everything around us faded away, and the only thing I could feel were Chase's lips on mine, his arms around my body. He pulled away, just enough to speak.

"Morning, Larkspur. I missed you."

I pulled one hand from around his neck and cupped his cheek.

"I missed you too."

I could feel myself falling hard and fast for all three of these men, and while it scared the living daylights out of me, it also made me feel more alive than I ever had before. I'd even started painting again, creating more art in the last week than I had in months. Emotions I was still trying to understand were painted across my canvases, each brushstroke full of my feelings for Griff, Chase, and Knox.

Chase placed me back on my feet and quickly fist bumped Griff and Knox before rejoining his team. Feeling a little bold, I swatted his ass as he turned to go. He spun around, his mouth open in faux shock.

"Madam! Hands off the goods!"

Griff barked out a loud laugh while Knox just smiled and shook his head at my antics.

We meandered around for a few minutes as more and more of the student body arrived. I spotted a coffee cart across the quad, and seeing as I hadn't had my caffeine fix for the morning, I decided to go grab a cup.

"Griff," I tugged on his hand to get his attention, "I'm gonna go grab a coffee from the cart. You or Knox want one?"

"No, we're good. You want me to go with you?" He looked around, and I knew he was searching the crowd for Austin.

"No, I should be fine. Can you guys just stay here, though, so I don't lose you?" They had been chaperoning me all week, and while I appreciated the gesture, a girl did need a few minutes to herself. I was perfectly capable of walking a hundred feet by myself.

"You sure?" Knox's low voice sent a shiver down my spine. His hand was resting on my lower back, his thumb drawing circles on the fabric of my dress.

"Yeah, I'm good. I'll be right back." I gave them each a peck on the cheek before making my way over to the cart.

Standing in line, I scrolled through social media, waiting for my turn. I wasn't paying attention, until I heard an annoying voice from behind me.

"Well, if it isn't the bitch who stole my boyfriend and gave me a fucking black eye. I should return the favor." I closed my eyes, taking a deep breath through my nose. And my morning had been going so well.

A second voice, this one nasally and high pitched joined Morgan's. "Eww, this is the girl that Griffin is dating? Didn't you tell me she was fucking Chase too? What a slut."

Oh no, this bitch was not about to call *me* a slut, not when her bestie cheated on Griffin for two fucking years. I'd be damned if I'd let them slut shame me. I tipped my head to the side, speaking over my shoulder.

"Morgan, is there a guy on this campus you *haven't* slept with?" I drawled. "I mean, besides Knox and Chase, because I know they wouldn't touch your skanky ass. You also might want to invest in some better concealer." I made a show of pointing at my cheek, mocking her bruise.

"Chase might never have been with Morgan, but he damn sure found his way into my bed on a regular basis," bitchy girl number two, who I knew to be Heather from our Potions class, snarked.

Unwilling and unable to back down, I turned around to face off with dumb and dumber. "Not since I got to campus," I bit back, a smug smile playing on my lips.

"He was literally with Heather like twelve hours before he met you," Morgan huffed. Heather crossed her arms over her chest, a satisfied smirk on her overly made up face.

"He hasn't found his way back there though, has he?" I snarked, my anger getting the best of me. "I don't give a fuck who he was with before me. He's with me now, that's all I care about. Now if you'll excuse me, I want to get my coffee and go back to my *boyfriends*," I replied, making sure to emphasize the last word.

I moved up to the cart, giving the barista my order and making a show of ignoring the two douche canoes at my back. I could hear all their nasty insults, and when they realized they weren't going to get a reaction, they moved on to talking about my guys and all their *times* together. The urge to throat punch them both was at a near tipping point when my iced white chocolate mocha was finally placed in my hand.

As I turned to walk back to Griff and Knox, I heard Morgan call out, loud enough for everyone in the area to hear.

"Enjoy our sloppy seconds, Emberly. And don't worry, they'll come crawling back to us soon."

I paused, rage filling my body at the balls on this girl. I took a long sip of my drink, debating throwing it in her face for a moment before I decided that would be a complete waste of good coffee. Pushing away the urge to pummel her on the quad, I turned around slowly, taking deliberate steps until I was nearly on top of them both.

"My name is Everly, you twatwaffle. But don't worry, I'm sure you'll hear Griffin screaming it later when I'm making him come." I turned and looked at Heather. "Chase and Knox, too." I winked at her, my words low enough for only them to hear. Heather's jaw went slack in shock while Morgan's face turned a lovely shade of red, steam nearly pouring from her ears.

With those parting words, I turned and made my way back to where Griff and Knox were waiting. They were chatting with a few other students, but excused themselves as I walked up. Griffin gently took a hold of my elbow, steering me away from the crowd.

"You okay?"

I furrowed my brow at him. "Yeah, I'm fine. Why?" I took a sip of my coffee, admiring the way the morning light enhanced the gold in his hazel eyes.

Knox stepped up behind me, his deep voice in my ear. "We saw Morgan and Heather get in line behind you. Did they give you a hard time?"

A laugh bubbled up from my chest, even as my irritation still lingered from my encounter with tweedle dee and tweedle dum.

"Umm, yeah. They tried to get a rise out of me, making sure I knew that they knew exactly how good Griff and Chase were in bed and calling me a slut for dating all three of you. But it's okay. I let them know I didn't care what you had done before me." I could feel Knox's hands on my hips, noting how they squeezed a little tighter when I mentioned Heather's insult.

"How the fuck you dated that raging bitch for as long as you did is something I'll never understand, Griff." Knox was so close to my back, I could feel the words vibrate from his chest.

Griffin closed his eyes and heaved out a deep sigh. "I get it man, I don't know why I stayed with her either." Opening them again, he fixed his beautiful hazel gaze on me. "But damn if I'm not happy she ended up cheating on me. If she hadn't, I never would've met you, Blue."

Griff reached up to cup my jaw, leaning down to give me a scorching kiss. His tongue invaded my mouth, marking his territory and making damn sure everyone around us knew *exactly* who I belonged to. I could feel Knox's nose skim the column of my neck, his lips close to my ear.

"I love seeing you with my friends, little Monet. Love seeing how turned on they make you. I bet you're soaking."

Jesus, the mouth on this man. But I couldn't deny that my panties were indeed wet with desire. Breaking away from Griff, I inhaled deeply, the scents of both guys filling my lungs. As much as I wanted to drag them both off behind a tree, we needed to get to the shore to watch Chase.

I stepped away from them, my chest heaving, both looking at me with heat in their eyes. Knox's were nearly black, his dark brown irises barely visible with his dilated pupils. I grabbed Griff's hand while Knox kept his firmly on my hip.

"Before I start tearing your clothes off, we need to go watch the race." Knox huffed out a breath of displeasure, reaching down to subtly adjust his shorts, the outline of his erection pressing against the fabric. Sneaking a peak at Griff, I could see a tent forming in his shorts as well. He blushed when he caught me looking and quickly attempted to fix himself. Knowing how much I turned them on was a heady feeling, and my body hummed with desire.

Looking over Griff's shoulder, I spotted Morgan and Heather shooting daggers in our direction. If looks could kill, I would have been dead on the ground at Knox's feet. Feeling particularly smug, I blew them a kiss, then flipped them each the bird.

Checkmate, bitches.

Twenty-Four

Chase

Our rowing team crushed today's regatta, sweeping the competition. I was on a post-win high, my energy levels through the roof. You'd think after rowing two thousand meters, I'd be exhausted, but the thrill of winning, and knowing Everly was waiting for me on the shore, were enough to have me bouncing up and down after the race. My caster strength might have helped a little too, giving me a boost during my rowing.

Once our team was finished stowing our equipment and had wrapped up our post regatta meeting, I found Everly with Knox and Griff sitting on a bench. Knox had her on his lap, his inked up arms wrapped around her middle. She looked like sunshine and happiness sitting with my two best friends, a beautiful smile on her face as she laughed at something Griffin whispered in her ear. I jogged over to them, pulling Everly from Knox's lap before he could complain.

"Oh!" Everly let out a little shriek as I scooped her into my arms, bridal style. She was laughing, her head thrown back, and she had never looked more stunning. I began leaving soft kisses up the column of her neck, just light enough that they would tickle. She giggled, wriggling around in my arms. "Chase! Stop! Chase, that tickles!"

When she stopped squirming, I planted a possessive kiss on her plump lips. Her hand cupped my stubbly jaw as I deepened the kiss, my tongue tangling with hers. I got lost in her, but it was so easy to do. She felt like coming home after a long day, everything about her speaking to my soul.

A voice cleared behind us, breaking our moment. I let out a playful growl. "Griff, there better be a damn good reason why you're interrupting me kissing our girl."

"Just figured you'd rather take this somewhere more private."

"Let them watch," I said against Everly's lips, giving her another kiss, although this one was a bit more chaste. Setting her back on her feet, I grinned at my two best friends. Griff smiled back at me while Knox rolled his eyes. I was pretty sure I had seen the corners of his mouth lift in an almost-there smile, though. Knoxy loved me, he just didn't like to admit it.

"Let's head back to Bliss. I need a shower. And then you and I," I cupped Everly's face in my hands, "have a date."

"A date?" she squeaked. I could see the excitement on her face. She tried to school it quickly, appearing nonchalant. "Aren't you supposed to *ask* me if I want to go on a date? Pretty presumptuous to assume I'd just go." Goddamn I loved it when she got sassy.

I moved past her, swatting her ass like she'd done to me earlier. A gasp fell from her mouth as she turned, her hand moving to rub her butt cheek. "Move it, gorgeous, daylight's burnin'!"

Once I showered, I threw on some athletic shorts and a Solis Lake row team t-shirt. I quickly grabbed one of my neck ties from my closet and tucked it into my pocket before rushing out to the living room to find Everly perched in Griff's lap. They were so lost in each other; they didn't even hear me come in.

Rude.

I stealthily moved across the room until I was nearly on top of them, creeping up behind Griff. Everly must have sensed my presence, because her eyes flew open while she continued to kiss my best friend. I pressed a finger to my lips, telling her to stay silent. She winked, then closed her eyes again, sinking into Griff's kiss. Time for a little payback.

"Well, hey there, stud. Where're my kisses?" I whispered against Griff's ear. He jumped, startled, nearly knocking Everly off his lap.

"What the fuck Chase?!"

I fell over backward, my ass hitting the hardwood floor as I howled in laughter. Before I knew what was happening, Griff's body was on top of mine, playful punches landing in my midsection.

Still laughing, I managed to choke out, "Consider that payback for scaring the shit out of me before Potions the other day."

I could hear Everly snort from somewhere to my left, her husky giggles filling the room. After wrestling around for another minute with Griff, I made my way to my feet, extending a hand and pulling Griff's heavy ass up too.

Turning to face my girl, I pulled her into my chest. "You ready to go, little Larkspur?"

"And just where are we going, Mr. Rowing Champ?" Her sassiness made my cock twitch in my shorts. I gave him a firm mental rebuke, though, because now was not the time to get a hard on. We had places to go!

"It's a surprise!" I spun her around, giving her a gentle push toward the door. I grabbed my backpack off the floor and jogged into the kitchen. Opening the fridge, I pulled out a bottle of moscato and stuffed it in my bag on top of the blanket I had already stowed inside. Throwing in two Solo cups from the cupboard, I quickly zipped up my bag, slinging it over my shoulder. Snagging my keys from the bowl on the counter, I grabbed Everly's hand and pulled her out the door.

With our fingers intertwined, we made our way across campus, the afternoon sun highlighting the subtle chestnut strands in Everly's dark hair. I nearly tripped more than once because my eyes kept straying to her beautiful face. There was a light dusting of freckles on her shoulders, and I promised myself I would kiss each one before the day was over.

"We've gotta make one pit stop," I told her, pulling her to a stop next to the dining hall. "Wait right here. Don't move." She opened her mouth, a look of confusion on her face, but I jogged off before she could respond.

Making my way to the service door at the back of the dining hall, I knocked loudly three times. Martha, one of the cooks, opened the door a crack, peeking out. Once her aged gray eyes met mine, she swung the door open and squished me into a hug.

"Chase! Where've you been my boy?" She tutted at me. Martha had been like a surrogate grandmother to me since I came to Solis Lake. I liked to think it was because of my never-ending charm and dazzling wit. She said it was because I reminded her of her grandson, Derek. Tomato, tomato. I was just grateful for the amazing woman and the way she continuously kept me fed with all of my favorite foods.

"Hi Mama Martha," I said as I squeezed her back, my large frame engulfing her small body.

"Come to pick up your basket, then?" Martha moved across the kitchen and picked up a medium sized, soft sided cooler. Earlier in the week, after batting my eyelashes about a thousand times and giving her my best puppy dog eyes, I convinced her to put a picnic basket together for my outing with Everly.

"Martha, I swear, if it wasn't for Everly, you'd be the only woman for me." I shot her a wink before I wrapped an arm around her shoulders and dropped a kiss to the top of her gray-haired head.

"Oh now, none of that, you big flirt." She shooed me toward the door, hitting me with her dishtowel. "Go get your girl, and have a good time." I turned to give her one last hug. She reached up a hand, cupping my cheek. "I hope she knows how special you are, Chase, and how lucky she is."

"Nah, Mama, I'm the lucky one." I grinned widely at her. "Gotta go! Thank you!" I gave her a quick peck on the cheek and disappeared out the door.

A few seconds later, I was back at Everly's side, leading her down the path once more.

"And just where did you run off to, hmm? And what's that?" She tried to lean around me to see the cooler, but I kept her tucked firmly under my arm.

"That, my nosey little Larkspur, is part of your surprise. Now, one final thing." I stopped just at the edge of the forest, a footpath in front of us. Spinning her around so her back was to my front, I pulled the tie from my pocket. Not giving her a second to question what I was doing, I quickly tied the blindfold over her eyes.

"Chase, what the hell are you doing?" Everly laughed, the sound lighting up my insides. She spun around to face me, reaching up to tug the tie away, but I grabbed her hands.

"You trust me, Larkspur?" I whispered as I leaned in close. My breath ghosted along the shell of her ear, and I smiled when I saw goosebumps raise on her arm. I brushed my lips against the sensitive skin of her neck before pulling back.

"Yes, Chase, I trust you." The words were a whisper, a shiver running through her body. She was a thing of perfection. Her cheeks had a rosy flush that was slowly creeping down to her chest, and her tongue dipped out to wet her lips.

"Good girl." I pressed my lips to hers, having to restrain myself from taking it further. Taking her hand, we wordlessly headed down the path, an easy silence hanging between us. I navigated the forest with practiced ease, able to move off the main path to the area I had chosen for our picnic.

When the small clearing came into view, I took a deep breath, a moment of panic coming over me. What if she hated this? Maybe she wasn't a nature kind of girl. Anxiety swirled in my gut that she would think this was a stupid idea. I should have asked her first. Or better yet, I should have just taken her on a normal date...

"Chase?" Everly's soft voice startled me from my spiraling thoughts. "You okay? Why did we stop?"

"Oh, uh, we're here." I pulled the blindfold off her face, her beautiful blue eyes meeting mine the moment it was gone. She didn't look around, didn't check her surroundings; her sapphire orbs sought me out first. That thought sucker punched me, my chest getting tight.

Everly stepped back, slowly spinning and taking in the small meadow around us. Nestled deep in the forest was a clearing of long grass and beautiful Larkspur flowers. I knew as soon as she agreed to be mine that I had to bring her here, but doubt still sat heavy in my mind.

"Chase." My name on her lips was barely a whisper. I could hear the cicadas in the distance, and squirrels rustling around in the trees nearby. I'm pretty sure my heart stopped beating as I held my breath, waiting for her next words.

"It's beautiful." A bright smile graced her perfect face, and the air whooshed out of my lungs, relief coursing through me.

I gripped her hand and pulled her to the middle of the clearing. Silently, I pulled the blanket from my bag. Using my earth magic, I shortened the long grass around us and spread the blanket on the ground, dropping the cooler and my bag. In an over the top, sweeping gesture, I motioned for her to take a seat.

Everly dropped down, tucking her toned legs under her body. I sat next to her, opening the cooler and rummaging around to see what Martha had packed. I pulled out several containers of cut up fruit and a few deli sandwiches.

"You brought me on a picnic?" I looked up at her from the cooler, genuine surprise written across her face.

"Uh, yeah," I replied, but then that damn doubt crept back in. "Do you not like it? We can go. God, I'm sorry, Larkspur, I should have asked you first." I began putting everything back in the cooler when her small hand landed on my forearm, stopping my movements.

"Chase." My name on her lips sounded so perfect. I couldn't look at her though, couldn't bear to see the disappointment on her face. "Chase, look at me, please." Her pleading tone had me shifting my eyes slightly, just enough so I could see her profile.

With an annoyed huff, the next thing I knew, Everly had planted herself in my lap, her hands on either side of my face, tipping my head up to look at her.

"Chase Stone, listen to me right now," she said, the words firm. "This is the sweetest thing anyone has ever done for me. I have never had a guy plan a date for me, let alone a romantic picnic in the most beautiful place I've ever seen." She leaned forward and pressed her soft lips to my mouth. Still in a bit of shock at her admission, it took me a half second to return her kiss. My hesitation didn't last long, though.

Dropping what I was holding, I planted my hands firmly on Everly's hips, digging my fingers into her soft flesh. I lifted her slightly, and without words, she swung her legs over to straddle my lap. The feel of her lace covered core on my growing erection had me moaning into her mouth, my tongue pushing in even further.

Maybe this wasn't such a terrible idea after all.

Twenty-Five

Everly

I poured everything I was feeling into my kiss with Chase. I wanted to show him how much I loved our picnic, how much I... shit, just thinking about those three words scared the hell out of me. I had been jaded after catching my ex-boyfriend cheating, but I couldn't help being drawn deeper and deeper into the orbit Chase, and the three men who consumed all of my thoughts as of late.

Chase thrust his hips upward, grinding his hard cock against my core. Jesus, he had me soaking for him, and we were both still fully clothed. That was something I needed to remedy, and quickly. Shifting my hands down until I found the hem of his t-shirt, I gripped the edges and pulled upward, only breaking our kiss when the fabric lifted over his head.

My lips quickly found his again, my hands moving to his hard chest. I trailed kisses along his jawline and down his neck.

"Everly," Chase's grip tightened on my hips, and I relished in the slight bite of pain.

"Hmm?" I responded, continuing my assault on his neck. I trailed the tip of my tongue back up before I nipped his earlobe.

"What about our picnic?" He panted out the words, like it physically hurt him to speak.

I sat back, my hands still planted on his pecs. I cocked my head to the side, my eyebrows creeping up my forehead.

"Really, Chase? You want me to stop so we can eat some sandwiches?" I sassed him.

He stared at me for a moment, absolutely dumbfounded by my response. Shaking his head before a wolfish grin spread across his face.

In the next moment, Chase flipped us, my back landing gently on the soft blanket. His muscular frame hovered over mine, one hand still on my hip, the other supporting his weight next to my head.

"You're right. Besides, I can think of something else I'd like to eat." He waggled his eyebrows suggestively, making a laugh bubble up from my chest. His body slowly slid down mine until he was kneeling between my legs. Chase stared down at me, a look of absolute hunger on his face that had me squirming. I wasn't used to being the center of anyone's attention, and his laser focused eyes had my self-conscious mind working overtime.

"You're thinking awfully loud, little Larkspur," he commented, his emerald eyes locking on mine.

I felt myself blush, not wanting to admit what was on my mind. As if he could read my thoughts, Chase spoke again.

"Everly, you can tell me. Nothing you say will change how I see you, how I feel about you."

Hearing the sincerity in his words, I closed my eyes and leaned my head back against the blanket. Taking a deep breath, I spoke my doubts aloud.

"Sometimes, I look at you, and Griff, and Knox, and I can't help but wonder... Why me? I mean, shit, Chase, you look like you were carved from stone by the fucking gods. You guys are the sweetest, most attentive guys I've ever met. And I'm just... me." I snapped my mouth shut after rambling out the words, shame flushing my face a deep red.

Chase remained silent, and my doubts screamed louder. Of course, now that I'd laid it all out, he was probably wondering why the hell he was with me, too. Goddamn, I was so stupid...

Suddenly, Chase's face filled my vision as he brought us nose to nose. Anger flared in his green eyes, and I braced myself for a break up I knew would devastate me.

"Everly Blackwell," he started, his voice low, nearly a growl. "If I ever, and I mean *ever*, hear you talk about yourself like you are less than, like you are not a fucking goddess, I won't hesitate to take you over my knee and turn your fine little ass red. Then, I'll fuck every doubt you have about yourself, or us, out of you. Do you understand me?"

I blinked at him, shock rendering me speechless. Not giving me a moment to argue, Chase fused his lips to mine in a scorching kiss that made my toes curl in my sandals. My fingernails raked down his bare back, no doubt leaving long red lines across his tanned skin. I parted my lips, giving him unspoken permission to deepen the kiss. And my god, he did not disappoint.

Chase fucked his tongue into my mouth, tasting every inch while his hands roamed my body. I felt his hand at the hem of my short sundress, pushing the material higher up on my thighs. Fingers danced across my lace panties, no doubt feeling how wet he was making me.

Chase broke our kiss, moving down my neck. I tilted my head, giving him better access, and he planted soft kisses up and down, landing just below my ear. I heard him suck in a deep breath, his body going still.

"Chase," worry lacing my words, "what's wrong?"

"Nothing, sweet girl. I told myself that I wasn't going to rush this, that I was going to romance you, *woo* you. And all I want to do right now is strip us both down and bury my cock in your tight little cunt." He groaned into my neck.

I laughed, causing him to sit up and lean his weight on his forearm. He furrowed his eyebrows in confusion, not understanding why on earth I would be laughing, which in turn just made me laugh even harder.

"You know Everly, a lesser guy may be offended that his girlfriend had a giggle fit when he told her he wanted to fuck her." His tone was teasing with just a hint of a pout, so I decided to put him out of his misery.

"Chase, I want nothing more than for you to fuck me right now. And trust me, you have romanced me. Now, get naked and fuck me like you mean it." I knew my admission was bold, but damn it, I needed him inside me like yesterday.

Needing no further instruction, he stripped my dress from my body, leaving me in nothing but my yellow lace panties and matching strapless bra. Chase groaned as he took in my waiting body. "Jesus, Larkspur, your body was made for sin."

I reached down, pushing the waistband of his shorts past his hips. I couldn't get them much further—damn my short t-rex arms—but Chase took pity on me and pushed them the rest of the way down, along with his boxer briefs. Within a few seconds he was naked above me, his dick resting against my lace covered pussy.

"Well, little Larkspur, it seems that now you have on too many clothes. Let me help you fix that." Leaning back on his heels, Chase looped his fingers into the top of my panties, slowly peeling them down my thighs. Once they were off, he flung them to the side, his eyes taking in my soaking core. Sitting up slightly, I quickly unhooked my bra, leaving myself completely bare to him.

"Everly." My name was a prayer on his lips. He stared, heat flaring in his eyes as he drank in every inch of my body. I could feel his gaze everywhere, his green eyes burning a path across my skin. I did the same, eating up every toned, tanned muscle he had on display.

Movement over Chase's shoulder caught my eye, and I was suddenly very aware that we were naked, out in the open. An acorn landed at my side, nearly clipping Chase in the thigh, and an angry chittering noise erupted from a nearby tree. Realizing it was just a black squirrel, probably pissed that we were invading its space, I calmed slightly, but the fear that anyone could see us had me questioning what we were doing.

"Chase," I halted him. "Chase, anyone could see us right now."

He looked around the clearing, coming to the same realization. But just as quickly, a grin spread across his handsome face. He flicked his eyebrows up, his eyes twinkling with mischief.

"Trust me, Larkspur?"

I answered without hesitation.

"Always."

His smile broadened. Closing his eyes, he took a deep breath. Suddenly the grass and flowers around us began to grow toward the sky, weaving together, creating a thick wall and hiding us from the outside world. I stared up in wonder. I had never seen such beautiful earth magic before. Chase grew the wall to nearly six feet, leaving us hidden to the outside world. The grass was a vibrant green, nearly matching the shade of Chase's eyes, and there were pops of blue throughout, a scattering of a beautiful flower I had never seen before.

"They're Larkspurs." Chase's gravelly voice interrupted my thoughts. I swung my eyes to him, his lust pouring off him in waves.

"What?" The question came out in a whisper, my mind still wrapping around the amazing elemental magic Chase had just displayed.

"The flowers," he answered. "They're Larkspurs. They're a rare perennial." He leaned down until our faces were a breath apart. "And they are," he kissed my forehead, "the exact same shade," Another kiss, this time to my nose, "as your eyes." One last kiss to my lips.

My heart was thundering against my ribs, and I knew without a doubt. Even though it had only been a week, and maybe that was crazy. But I knew.

I was falling in love with Chase.

I reached up, stroking the side of his face with my fingertips. "Chase."

I spoke his name, but there were a million unspoken things behind it. He closed the distance between us, pressing his lips to mine in a soul stealing kiss. At the same time, he pushed into my core, until he was fully seated inside me.

Chase slowly stroked in and out of me, his pace languid, as though we had all the time in the world. And in a way, I guessed we did. Out here, in the safety of Chase's grass and flowered fortress, the world couldn't touch us.

He reached between our bodies, his fingers finding my clit soaked from my arousal. He began rubbing quick circles, building the impending release coursing through my body. Chase's face was nestled into the crook of my neck where he whispered against my skin.

"God Larkspur, I didn't know it could be this good." His praise speared straight through my heart. "Your pussy was made for me."

"Chase, I'm com—" I couldn't even get the words out before my orgasm barrelled through me. I clung to his body, my nails digging into his flesh. My walls clenched around his dick, squeezing him in a vice grip. I closed my eyes, and an explosion of colors danced behind my lids.

"Jesus, Everly, you're so fucking tight." Chase ground the words out, his hips still thrusting into me through my orgasm. As my release tapered off, he continued to power into me, setting a steady pace.

Suddenly, he pulled out. A whimper escaped my lips at the feeling of emptiness, but it didn't last long. I was flipped over on all fours, my forearms bearing my weight as my ass was lifted up in the air.

A growl rumbled from Chase's chest, his large hands splayed across my ass cheeks, spreading them apart. He hummed his approval at the view.

"Larkspur, your ass is so... mmm... I just wanna bite it." And he did just that.

I yelped as his teeth met my flesh, a sharp sting as he bit down hard. Then without another word, he thrust back into my pussy, his balls slapping my clit. Chase set a bruising pace, his hands gripping my hips to keep me from falling over. He felt so much deeper at this angle, hitting a spot inside that set my body, fuck my entire *soul*, on fire.

"Chase, god, yes, I'm close." I closed my eyes, relishing the feel of his skin on mine, a second orgasm building inside me.

His hands left my hips, one snaking around my front, tugging me upright, so my back was flush to his front. His fingers curled around the base of my throat, applying light pressure. His other hand wound around my body until he found my clit once more with his magical fingers.

"Come for me again, Everly. Come all over my cock one more time." He rubbed the sensitive bundle of nerves, sending me headfirst into another release. I shot off like a rocket, my body going rigid in his arms. This time he followed me over the edge, his hot cum painting my pulsing walls.

We stayed locked together, Chase's strong arms the only thing holding me up. My body had turned to jelly after the back-to-back, mind-blowing orgasms. He pressed his lips softly to my shoulder, once, twice, before I realized he was covering my shoulder in kisses. The feather light touches tickled my flesh, and I giggled.

"Chase," I said as I laughed, twisting to try and see him. "What are you doing?"

He continued layering kisses along my shoulders before answering.

"I told myself earlier that I would kiss each and every one of your freckles, Larkspur. Just making sure I kept that promise."

And with those words, I fell even deeper.

Twenty-Six

Everly

The rest of the weekend passed quickly. After our picnic—well, after we actually ate—Chase took me on a walk through the forest, pointing out all sorts of plants and animals along the way. He was incredibly knowledgeable when it came to all things nature, and I silently hoped that he would go into conservation like he wanted. I couldn't imagine Chase stuck behind a desk all day at his dad's investment firm.

Now it was Monday again, and I was just wrapping up my morning classes before heading out to have lunch with Griffin. I was trying to make it a point to spend time with each guy individually. Who would have thought juggling three boyfriends would be so hard? I had my date with Chase on Saturday, and on Sunday, Knox came over to watch me paint. It made me nervous at first, until he pulled out a sketch pad and started drawing. Several hours later, I had filled a canvas with a field full of Larkspur and grass the color of emeralds before I was wrapped up in Knox's arms, naked under my duvet.

My afternoon class had been canceled, and Griff's afternoon was free, so we decided to meet up for lunch and spend some time together. After our boathouse excursion, Griff and I hadn't had the opportunity to really be alone again. And if I was being completely honest, my body was aching for his dominant side to come out and play. Seeing Griffin take control of both of our pleasures was such a turn on, and an experience I was hoping to recreate.

Packing up my books and tablet, I stood from my desk when my phone pinged with a notification. Digging it out of my bag, I saw it was from Griff.

> Griff: Blue, I thought we could do lunch at my place… cause what I want to eat isn't available in the dining hall.

> Everly: Leaving class now. Be there soon… sir.

Well fuck, there went my panties.

Grinning at my reply, I threw my backpack over my shoulder and made a beeline for the door. As I entered the hall, I ran into a body, nearly falling on my ass before catching myself.

"Watch it, bitch!" Morgan screeched, her smoothie spilling down the front of her oversized Solis Lake tour guide shirt. It looked suspiciously like a lot of the ones Griff owned, and I'd bet my last ten dollars that it was his. As she twisted around, I was able to see *Cardarette* printed across the back in blue block lettering. *Fucking thief.*

"Oops!" I gasped dramatically, covering my mouth with my hand to hide my smile. "Sorry about your shirt," I feigned an apology. "Or well, should I say Griff's shirt. Guess you should have given it back when he dumped you."

"You fucking slu—" She started toward me, but I skipped away.

"Sorry, Morgan, gotta go! Griff is waiting! We're having a little afternoon delight!" I threw a wink over my shoulder, positively giddy that my accidental run-in with her had ended so totally in my favor. I shot off down the hall and out into the quad, mentally fist bumping myself as I ran.

Once I reached Bliss Hall, I slowed my steps. I didn't want to be a hot, sweaty mess until *after* I saw Griff. Opting to take the elevator to give myself a minute to calm my nerves, I took a couple of deep breaths, bringing my heart rate back to normal.

I was excited to be alone with Griff again, but I was nervous. Griff was the only one of my guys I hadn't slept with yet, and I wanted to make sure our first time together was perfect.

The doors to the elevator opened, and I strolled down the hall, past my door, and on to the guys'. Before I could even knock, the door opened, and Griff pulled me into the suite. Kicking the door shut with his foot, he spun me in his arms, so my back was pressed to the dark wood.

A devilish grin spread on his handsome face, his eyes glittering with heat.

"Hi Blue." He swooped in for an absolutely devastating kiss. It stole the breath from my lungs, his lips moving against mine with purpose.

Finally breaking apart, I sucked in a deep breath. I stared into his hazel eyes, watching the gold and green hues dance in the afternoon light.

"Hi Griff," I breathed out, my lips still millimeters from his.

Griff raised a brow, his eyes darkening. Big hands landed on my hips, squeezing my soft skin, holding me in place.

"What was that, Everly? Is that how you should greet me?" His voice was so deep, it wrapped around me like silk. I paused for a moment before a smirk grew on my face. I answered, dropping my voice to an even huskier tone than usual.

"Hello... sir."

"Much better." He smiled darkly. Suddenly, his right hand reached up, grasping my ponytail. He pulled down, hard, tilting my head toward the ceiling.

"I want you naked and on your knees in my room. Now." Releasing me, he stepped back, cool air brushing over my heated skin. My heart hammered in my chest, my panties slick from his words.

"Tick tock, Everly. I'd hate to have to punish you."

Holy shit. Dom Griff was fucking hot.

Not needing another reminder, I hurried off toward his bedroom. I didn't feel him at my back, so I knew he was giving me the opportunity to follow his directions. I pondered being a brat for a moment and ignoring his instructions, but decided we'd try that another day. I quickly shed my clothes, leaving them in a pile near the door, before releasing my hair from my ponytail. Looking around, I realized he hadn't told me where to kneel. Taking a chance, I folded my legs under my body on the floor at the foot of his bed. Then, I waited.

After what seemed like forever, Griff appeared in the doorway. His tanned, muscular chest was on display, and the ridges of his abs led down to the delicious V aimed straight into his gray sweatpants. I could see the tent his erection was creating, and I unconsciously licked my lips, the thought of tasting him again making my mouth water.

He strode over to me, his steps slow and measured. Once he was directly in front of me, I peered up through my eyelashes. I knew Griff would never hurt me, but he looked damn intimidating when he went into dom mode.

Griff reached down, gripping my chin tightly before tilting my head up, so I could fully see him.

"You look fucking beautiful down on your knees for me, Everly." Complete adoration showed in his eyes, and I knew he meant every word. A split second later, those same eyes grew dark, his feral desire taking over. "Now take out my cock, and show me how much you missed me."

I pulled his sweatpants down to his ankles, pleasantly surprised to find he was going commando underneath. Griff stepped out and kicked them to the side, leaving him as bare as me. I wasted no time, taking his thick length into my mouth.

I swirled my tongue around the head of his dick, lapping at the precum I found leaking there. Griff threaded his fingers through my hair, his hand guiding me deeper onto his cock. I made a mental note to breathe through my nose as I attempted to take him into my throat. Pushing through my gag reflex, I felt his balls hit my chin, confirming that I had taken every inch of his glorious length. And goddamn did he taste like heaven.

"Fuck," Griff groaned. "You take my dick so well. Such a good girl." He let me pull off some, enough to get a lung full of air, before I continued sucking him down. I ran my nails up and down his hips, leaving goosebumps in my wake.

"Your mouth feels so good, Blue. Fuck. I'm not going to last long if I don't stop now." I ignored his words, instead ramping up my efforts and hollowing out my cheeks as I ran my tongue over his dick.

A hard yank of my hair had me popping off his length, and I was met with hazel eyes blazing with desire.

"I said to stop, Everly." If I didn't know better, I would think he was angry with me. But I could see beneath his gritted teeth and clenched jaw. Griff was hanging on by a thread. A geyser ready to erupt at the slightest provocation.

"I'm sorry, sir. You just taste so good, I didn't want to stop." I gave him my best doe eyes, coupled with a solid attempt at sounding contrite, but the small smile that crept onto my face gave away my game.

"I think you're being naughty, Blue," he playfully scolded. My jaw fell open in fake shock. *Not me.* "Get your ass on the bed, on your back, knees spread. I want to see what's mine."

My core clenched in anticipation. Jesus, Griffin's words had me dripping and my clit throbbed. I needed his hands on me. Now.

I slowly climbed onto the bed on all fours, making sure to sway my ass in his direction. I rolled onto my back, planting my feet on the mattress, purposefully keeping my knees together. Maybe I'd decided to be a bit of a brat after all.

"Everly," he growled from the edge of the bed.

Smiling to myself, I slowly parted my thighs, giving him the view he was so desperate for. Griff placed a knee on the bed, moving himself between my legs, his eyes never leaving my pussy.

When his body was settled, he ran both hands up my legs from my ankles to my thighs.

"Little Blue... you weren't trying to tease me, were you?" I couldn't tell by the look on his face if he was hoping for a yes or no. Fuck, being punished by Griff sounded just as good as being rewarded.

"Sir, I would never tease you." My husky voice was soft, and I shook my head, a small smile playing on my lips.

"See, I don't think I believe you. I think you were trying to keep this pretty pussy from me." His fingers stroked over my wet lips, teasing my entrance. A gasp fell from my mouth. "And that just won't do." With those words, he thrust two thick fingers inside me, up to the knuckle, filling me up.

"Jesus, Griff! Fuck!" My fingers curled into his soft comforter, holding on for dear life. He began to move in and out, the heel of his hand grinding against my clit.

"Everly," he tutted. "What do you say when I give you something?"

Nearly lost in the feel of his fingers in my pussy, it took me a second to answer.

"Thank you, sir." The words came out in a rush, my body building up to what I could already tell would be a mind blowing release.

"Much better," he praised, and damn if I didn't preen under his approval. Closing my eyes, I let my body be carried away as he finger fucked me closer to my release.

Then, he stopped.

What the fuck?

I opened my eyes and lifted myself up onto my elbows, so I could look at Griff. He was licking his fingers—the ones that had just been inside me—and wearing a shit eating grin.

"But," he finally spoke after licking every trace of me off his long fingers. "You were quite naughty before. I don't know if you deserve to come yet."

Oh shit.

Twenty-Seven

Griffin

Having Everly laid out naked on my bed, her pussy glistening with her arousal, was like every fantasy I'd ever had come to life. I loved that she was so willing to let me explore my dom side, that she was so trusting in her role as my submissive. It was like Everly knew I needed the control, the sense of commanding both our pleasure. When she submitted in the boathouse, it was like a door unlocked in my brain, a release valve letting off a small amount of pressure.

I had gotten so used to Morgan dictating every aspect of our relationship—where we went, who we hung out with, if we were even dating or not—that I grew complacent in my passive role. I didn't even realize how restless I was feeling from my lack of control. Everly gave that back to me by trusting me with her body and her heart, and I was determined to show her just how much that meant to me.

How much *she* meant to me.

"I'm sorry, sir," Everly apologized, her eyes trained on my face. "I wasn't trying to tease. Please let me come, sir." The blue of her eyes was nearly eclipsed by the black of her pupils. "I want to come for you."

"Hmm…" I murmured, my gaze raking over her perfect body. "I suppose, if you behave, I can let you come. Would you like that, Everly?"

"Yes, sir," she answered immediately.

Smiling smugly, I trailed my fingers up her legs again. "That's my good girl. Now keep your eyes on me, Everly, no closing them. If you close them, I will stop. Do you understand?" My voice was firm and offered no room for negotiations.

She swallowed, her throat bobbing, reminding me how tightly it had squeezed my cock earlier. I reached down with my free hand, stroking my length and smearing my precum down my shaft. Everly licked her lips, her eyes fixed on my dick.

"Everly," I warned. "I need your words."

"Yes, sir. I understand. Now make me come, please?"

Needing to taste her properly, I didn't waste another second. I leaned forward, swiping the flat of my tongue from her entrance up and over her clit. Everly's body arched from the bed, her hips chasing my mouth. She was easily the best thing I had ever tasted, and while I wanted nothing more than to spend the rest of the afternoon lost in her pussy, I knew if I didn't get my dick inside her soon, I would explode.

"Don't worry, my good girl," I reassured her. "I'm going to fill that pretty pussy up."

Not giving her a second to respond, I lined up and thrust in fully in one go. Her velvet, soft heat wrapped around my cock, gripping me tightly. Fuck, I'd never felt something so perfect and right. It was like she was made for me.

"Fuck, Griff!" she cried out, her hands gripping my thighs, leaving tiny moon shaped indents from her fingernails. I watched her eyelids flutter, holding still, waiting to see if she closed them.

But she proved, yet again, how good of a girl she was for me when she kept them open. I leaned forward, hovering over her immaculate body while I slowly pumped into her, grinding against her clit with each thrust. Bracing on my forearms, I nudged her head back with my nose, so I had better access to her slender throat.

I nipped her skin, leaving little marks along the column of her neck, all while driving into her pussy at a steady rhythm. Needing to mark her all over, I moved so I could suck on her perky tits. I took one nipple into my mouth, sucking and licking until it was so hard it could cut glass. Once I lavished it with enough attention, I moved to the other side, giving that hard bud the same treatment.

Everly was moaning in pleasure, my name falling from her lips like a prayer. I always thought I wanted to work with the underserved, those pushed aside by society, but now I knew. My only job, my sole purpose for existing, was to give Everly every pleasure she could ever want.

"Griff, fuck, yes." Her words were nearly incoherent, her brain muddled with everything I was giving her. Needing to feel her come, I brushed my fingers down her abdomen until I found her clit, swollen and waiting. Using two fingers, I began to rub tight circles. Everly's entire body clenched, her cunt squeezing me like a vice. Her hips began to buck, meeting me thrust for thrust.

"Griff, I can't—I'm going to come. Please sir, let me come!" Her desperate plea sending me closer to the edge.

"Go ahead, baby. Come all over my cock," I commanded, the words a whisper in her ear.

She detonated around me. Her blue eyes disappeared behind her lids, and her mouth opened in a perfect 'O' while she screamed her release for all to hear. She was so tight I could barely move, but I continued to pump into her slick pussy and play with her clit until her orgasm subsided. Her eyes fluttered open, finding my face. A lazy smile spread across her kissable lips, and her eyes had a glassy look.

I grinned at her, feeling pretty smug about the orgasm I'd just delivered. "Everly," I prodded.

"Hmmm?" Apparently, I fucked all the words from her brain.

"You closed your eyes."

Her eyes, the ones she was supposed to keep on me, were suddenly a lot clearer, and lust flared in them.

"I'm sorry, sir. I couldn't help it."

"Well, now I'm going to have to punish you. Are you ready?" She bit her bottom lip, her cheeks flushed a beautiful red.

"I won't hurt you, Everly. I promise." I stopped pumping my hips for a moment, allowing the seriousness of my vow to hang in the air.

"I trust you, Griffin," she whispered, reaching up to cup my jaw.

Without another word, I began rutting into her. It was like a flip was switched, and all I could feel was the way her pussy enveloped me. I was rock hard and so fucking close. Everly's heels dug into my ass, urging me deeper, while her nails scraped down my back. Every single nerve in my body was on fire, lit up from the feel of her.

Giving a few final thrusts, I erupted inside her, ropes of cum shooting out of me. I yelled out my release, her name falling from my lips.

"Everly!"

We lay like that for several minutes, our bodies slick with sweat. My heart rate slowly returned to normal, and my breathing slowed. Moving to her side, I pulled Everly so she was lying half on top of me, her head tucked under my chin. I wrapped one arm around her back, pulling her in close. She pressed her lips to my pec, and I dropped a kiss to the top of her head in return. We stayed wrapped around each other for a while longer, enjoying just being together, before she broke the silence.

"Griff?" she whispered.

"Yeah, Blue?"

"That was amazing." I could feel her smile against my chest, and I gave her a squeeze.

"*You're* amazing. I'm so fucking happy I was assigned as your tour guide. Maybe I should send Headmaster Charles a gift as thanks." I kissed her again before moving to get out of bed.

"Where do you think you're going?" Everly pulled my comforter to cover her body as she sat up. She looked fucking perfect in my bed, naked and freshly fucked. It was a sight that would be forever seared into my memory.

I didn't answer her, instead walking into my bathroom. I grabbed a soft washcloth and ran it under some hot water. Moving back into my bedroom, I wordlessly pulled the comforter away from her body.

"Hey—" she began to protest. I pushed her backward, so she was flat on the bed again and knelt between her knees. Using the washcloth, I gently cleaned my release from her pussy—but not before pushing it back in with my fingers, pumping them a few times for good measure. Shooting her a cheeky grin and wink, I finished cleaning her up.

Sitting up on her elbows, her cheeks tinged pink. "Thank you," she whispered.

"I'd do anything for you, Blue." And I meant it. I was in deep. Just like Knox. Just like Chase.

I was falling in love with Everly.

I schooled my face quickly, not wanting her to see the emotions roiling inside me. I didn't want to scare her off, so I was going to have to keep this revelation to myself for a while.

Once we had redressed, Everly and I made our way back out to the kitchen. Apparently an afternoon of sex made my little Blue hungry because the first thing she did was demand I feed her. Wanting to show off a bit, I suggested ordering pizza.

"Griff, where are we going to get a pizza? You can't order a whole pie from the dining hall. Trust me, I've checked."

"Just trust me, Blue."

I pulled out my phone and placed an order for a cup and char pepperoni pizza from a place in the next town over.

"It'll be ready in twenty. You want a beer? Or I think Chase had some wine in here, too, if that sounds better?" I pulled the fridge open, grabbing a beer for myself. I stood up, glancing over my shoulder at her.

"Yeah, a beer sounds good. Although, for future reference, I'm more of a champagne kind of girl," she said and sniffed, her nose turned up in the air. I turned to look at her, shocked at her pouty attitude. I was met with a playful grin and bright blue eyes. I barked out a laugh at her teasing, reaching in to grab another beer. I popped the top, but when I made to hand it to her, I grabbed her hand instead, pulling her to me.

"Someone's feeling sassy," I purred in her ear. A shiver ran through her body, and since she hadn't put her bra back on, I could feel her nipples pebbling against my chest.

"You going to punish me again, sir? Because if it's going to be like my punishment earlier, sign me the fuck up." I leaned down and kissed her, my hands groping her ass.

We continued to make out in the kitchen like two fifteen year olds for the next twenty minutes until a notification went off on my phone. Pulling away, I checked it.

"Pizza's ready," I told her, moving toward the door. I slid my flip flops on before turning toward her.

"Griff, where the hell are you going to get pizza from? The nearest town is like fifteen miles away! It'll be cold by the time you get back," she looked at me in total confusion.

"Oh ye of little faith," I said before grinning. throwing her a wink and snapping my fingers.

In the blink of an eye, I was standing in the middle of Antonio's Pizzeria. I walked up to the counter, an older Italian man behind the register.

"Hi, pick up for Griffin?"

He grabbed the box labeled with my name from a shelf behind him. After ringing me up, I moved over to an empty spot in the shop. With the pizza in one hand, I snapped my fingers and was back in my suite.

Everly stood in shock, mouth hanging open and eyes the size of saucers.

"I told you I'd get us pizza," I said, shrugging, the words nonchalantly rolling out from my mouth.

She stared at me for another few seconds before letting out the most beautiful laugh I'd ever heard in my life. Shaking her head, she pulled out a couple plates from the cupboard, setting them on the counter.

"I don't think I'll ever get used to that. Alright, let's eat, Mr. Teleporter."

Twenty-Eight

Knox

"**K**nox, pleeeeeease?" Everly begged. I wished I could say she was begging for my dick, but we were sitting in the middle of the dining hall having dinner with the guys. And as much as I loved fucking her, there was no way in hell I'd let any of these motherfuckers see her like that. Except Chase and Griff. I guess they could watch. Maybe.

I let out a loud sigh, knowing there was no point in saying no. I couldn't deny her anything. The woman could have asked me for a damn kidney, and I'd have laid it on a silver platter, bleeding out at her feet with a smile on my face. Looking around the table, I found Griff and Chase both grinning. They knew exactly what I was thinking; both assholes felt the same way. We'd each give her the world. All she had to do was ask.

"Fine," I finally answered her.

"But Knox, plea—" she continued begging, until she registered my response. "Really!?" She squealed. "When?? After dinner? Oh please say after dinner." She clasped her hands together in front of her face in a begging motion.

Nodding my head, I tried to hide my smile at her excitement. "Yes, I can show you after dinner." Turning to Chase and Griff, I asked, "You guys mind if I shift in the suite? I promised Everly I'd show her my snow leopard."

Everly was bouncing in her seat like a five-year-old on their way to Disneyland. Her gaze ping ponged between my best friends, eagerly awaiting their answer. I already knew they'd say yes. None of us could tell her no.

Griff shrugged. "Fine with me. Chase?"

Chase grinned. Shit. He had that look on his face that said he was going to be a pain in the ass about this.

"It's fine with me," he started. I closed my eyes, waiting.

"But..." There it was. Jesus, he couldn't just let something be simple. I looked over at him, his shit eating grin even bigger. I titled my head toward the ceiling, closing my eyes and dragging in a deep breath through my nose, a piss poor attempt at controlling my irritation.

"What the fuck do you want Chase?" I snapped.

"I want snow leopard snuggles."

"No, no fucking way. Sorry, Everly." She immediately frowned.

"But Knox, please?" she begged with her perfect, pouty lips. In my mind, I could see those lips wrapped around my cock as I fucked her throat. Chase was going to pay for this later. Then the fucker decided to chime in with his own guilt trip.

"It's okay, Everly, he doesn't have to cuddle with me. He's just so soft, and I love the feel of his fur..." He released a ridiculously dramatic sigh. Everly looked from him to me, her tiny hands clutched in front of her chest. Jesus christ, the things I would do for this girl.

"Fine." The word came out through gritted teeth. I was going to bite Chase's fucking hand off if he so much as touched me when I shifted.

Everly squealed again, rushing to take care of her tray so we could leave. Luckily, we were all pretty much finished, Chase shoving the last of his hamburger into his big mouth before following her. I begrudgingly threw away my garbage and made my way to the door, Everly's arm wrapped around my waist. I knew she was excited, and I was happy she wanted to see me shift. I even wanted to cuddle with her. I just didn't want to fucking cuddle with Chase.

Once we had made it back to our suite, everyone settled into the living room, a round of beers being passed around. Everly found a spot in the corner of the sofa, her legs tucked under her perfect little body.

She looked so fucking sexy today, a pair of painted on jeans with rips up the front and back hugging her curves, paired with a distressed From Ashes to New band t-shirt and black converse. I loved that she was so into rock music. It was something we bonded over while we painted, spending Sunday afternoons rocking out and creating art. I had already filled one entire sketchbook just with drawings of her. Added bonus? We always ended up naked in her bed. Win-win in my book

"Okay, Knox, I'm ready," she called to me from her spot in the living room. I grabbed a bottle of water from the fridge, guzzling half of it in one go. Leaving it uncapped on the counter, I moved into the middle of the open space. Chase had helped Griff move the coffee table out of the way, so I'd have more room to move. My tail had been known to take out a lamp or two.

"Okay," I said, looking at the guys. "You guys know the drill. If you don't wanna see my dick, I suggest you close your eyes now." Without another word, I started stripping off my clothes. It wasn't that they would tear, at least not from shifting into my snow leopard. I just hated being all tangled up in them when I was down on four paws and furry.

A low moan of appreciation drew my eyes to Everly. She was staring at my near naked body, desire making her blue eyes glimmer. Her breathing had picked up, and her cheeks were tinged pink.

Wanting to mess with her, I pulled at the waistband of my black boxer briefs, trailing a finger down my abs. "I can shift later, if you want something else, little Monet..."

My voice shook her out of her lust fueled haze. Shaking her head, she pulled her eyes to my face, but not without some effort. Damn, I almost had her. Chase chuckled from his spot on the opposite end of the sofa, clearly onto my game.

"Not getting out of it that easy, Knoxy. Now strip! I need cuddles!" He clapped his hands twice, and it took every ounce of willpower in my body not to throttle his ass.

Shucking my boxer briefs to the floor, I kicked them to the side. I heard Everly suck in a breath, while Chase gave a low whistle.

"Now Knoxy, how does it work with your pierc—"

I shifted before he could finish his stupid question. Suddenly I was on all fours, my long tail brushing the floor behind me. I stretched out, my claws protruding from my large paws. Sitting back on my haunches, I swung my gaze around the room, looking from Griff, to Chase, and finally settling on Everly.

She stared at me in awe, frozen in her seat. Her eyes were round, the blue catching in the sun's setting rays. She slowly crept off the sofa, crawling toward me at a snail's pace. I stood up and padded across the floor to where she sat with her legs crossed and sniffed her. She smelled even better this way, her peony and jasmine scent invading my nose and shooting straight to my brain like a drug. I nuzzled my whiskered face into her neck, a loud purr beginning deep in my chest.

I continued to rub against her, nudging my head under her hand in a bid for pets. She must have understood my unspoken request because her fingers began to stroke my fur covered body from head to tail, over and over, until I was purring like a motorboat. Wanting to be closer, I climbed my big ass body up into her lap, making her laugh. I swished my tail around, flicking her ear and tickling her under her chin.

"Knox, you're so soft and soooo beautiful," she murmured the words low, and I was only able to hear them thanks to my heightened animal senses. She continued to pet me for a few minutes, each of us content, touching our mate. The thought was primal. My leopard mind told my human one that that's exactly what she was. Our mate. My leopard was completely smitten with my girl. There was no way he'd ever let her go now. He was in as deeply as I was. Nearly a month of being with Everly and I knew. She was the one.

In the next minute, Chase's voice broke through my thoughts. "Okay, Knoxy, my turn. Hop that fluffy ass up here."

I let out a low growl, making Everly giggle. She gave me one final scratch between my ears before I slinked off her lap and hopped up onto the sofa. Chase reached out his hand, which I promptly batted away, sans claws. Griff chuckled from his spot on the arm of the couch.

"Hey now! You promised cuddles!"

Huffing out a sigh, I moved closer until I was sitting right next to him. When he went to pet me again, a growl vibrated deep in my chest. I glared at him, and he slowly put his hand back on his lap, rolling his eyes. "Fine, no petting."

To show my agreement, I pushed my head into his shoulder, nuzzling him slightly. Deep down I really did like Chase. He was a good guy, and I knew he'd do anything for Griff, Everly, and me. He was just my polar opposite in every conceivable way, with his golden retriever attitude and sunny disposition. He listened to Olivia Rodrigo on repeat last year, for Christ's sake.

"Aww, Knoxy!" Chase tilted his head, so it met my furry one on his shoulder.

Having had enough cuddles for one day, I hopped down and moved back to my original position. Shifting quickly, I was back on two feet, my naked body chilled after being warmed by all the fur. I grabbed my clothes off the floor, throwing them on hastily. Once I was fully dressed again, I sat on the sofa between Everly and Chase. I snagged his bottle, taking a pull before he could object.

"So, little Monet, whatcha think?" I asked after swallowing the cold beer.

"Knox, that was amazing!" She was clearly a big fan of my shifting. I made a note to find out her favorite animal and practice for her as a surprise.

Chase grumbled from next to me. "Wasn't exactly the snuggles I was looking for."

"Shut the fuck up, Chase." I punched him lightly in the arm. "Be happy I didn't claw your ass to shreds." My lips tipped up at the corners, which he of course saw. Fucker knew I was just messing with him.

Satisfied with himself, Chase snagged back his beer, slinging an arm along the back of the couch. "I knew you loved me, Knoxy."

Yeah, I did love the asshole.

But I loved the girl sitting next to me more.

Twenty-Nine

Everly

The next few weeks passed in a flurry of school work, potions labs, time spent with my guys, and weekly virtual family dinners with Evan and my dad, followed by a phone call or video chat with Celeste. I kept her up to speed on my relationship status, and to say she was jealous as fuck was an understatement.

I was working up the nerve to tell my dad about Griff, Knox, and Chase, but I didn't know how to explain that his little girl was getting railed by the three hottest guys on campus on the regular. And that I was head over heels in love with each of them. I hadn't even told *them* that yet. I didn't imagine the conversation would go over well, at least not if that was my opening line.

My feelings for the three men who took up most of my time were undeniable, my heart and head both in agreement. I was in love with three different men. Now, the question that gnawed at my mind everyday, keeping me awake most nights: did they love me back? While every soft touch, every sweet whispered word brought me closer to that conclusion, doubt still reared its ugly head.

School was also stressing me out. Midterms were coming up in a couple weeks, and the guys were planning to throw a party in the woods tonight to help everyone take the edge off. The idea of cutting loose sounded heavenly. With school and studying occupying so much of my time lately, finding a spare second with the guys had become increasingly tricky. Some evenings were spent with my nose in a book on their sofa just so we could be in the same room.

Austin was another source of tension. I hadn't said anything to the guys, but I had noticed him lurking outside my classes more lately. Knox agreed to loosen up on escorting me everywhere, and I didn't want to overload them anymore than necessary. They were all crazy busy; Chase with rowing, Griff with tutoring, and Knox with his architecture project. It seemed silly to bother them, especially when Austin was keeping his distance. If he wanted to be a creeper and stare at me, whatever. As long as he stayed away, I could handle his stalkerish leering.

I stepped out of the shower, wrapping a fluffy towel around my body, twisting another around my hair. I mosied into my closet, flicking through my clothes in search of something to wear to tonight's party. The boys were busy getting everything set up; Griff was teleporting in kegs, while Chase used his caster strength to carry picnic tables and benches into the clearing where the parties were held. Knox made sure the clearing was dry, pulling any excess water with his elemental ability. He said he'd be by at 9 p.m. to pick me up, and it was currently 8:20 p.m., leaving me just forty minutes to get dressed and glam myself up.

This was one of those moments when I wished Celeste was here. Or that I at least had a female roommate. But seeing that it was just me, I decided to crank up some music and get to work. I put on my Rain City Drive playlist while I plucked out a pair of ripped jeans and a navy blue bustier top. I flicked my finger toward my clothes, floating them across the room and laying them on my bed before moving to shut my curtains. Movement outside caught my eye just before I snapped my fingers, and I spotted a small black squirrel perched on the tree outside. It looked at me for a moment before I drew the curtains closed. *Cute little critter.* Walking back to my bathroom, I dropped my towels and got to work on my hair and makeup. I quickly pulled most of the moisture from my hair, thankful for my water powers, leaving the rest to air dry.

Thirty-five minutes later, I was applying the finishing touches to my winged eyeliner when Evan knocked on my door, opening it a crack. My long hair hung down my back in loose waves and tickled my shoulders when I reached down to put on my black ankle boots.

"Jesus, Everly, what are you wearing? You aren't going out in that, are you?" Evan's scandalized tone made me laugh. My goal was to end the night in bed with one of my guys... or maybe more than one, if my outfit did its job. The idea of having more than one of them at a time made me nervous, but hot as hell at the same time.

"Don't worry, Dad," I sassed, grabbing my leather jacket. "I'll wear a coat." I brushed by him, his irritation at my clothing choice—or lack there of—clear.

"Knox!" he called out from my doorway. But Knox was already moving toward me, a hungry look on his face, his eyes tracking me like a predator.

My brother continued his crusade for my virtue. "Knox, you can't let her go out like that. Jesus, she's barely dressed. Please tell her she has to change. You're her boyfriend, she'll listen to you."

"The fuck I will," I murmured, as Knox's lips found mine.

"Mmmm..." Knox said against my lips, his hand palming the back of my head and deepening our kiss. "I think she looks perfect."

"Oh for fuck's sake!" My brother muttered, huffing his way across the suite. "Well, if you're not going to change, I guess we may as well get going. Jesus christ..."

Breaking away from Knox, I simply shrugged my shoulders. "Ready?"

Knox smiled at me, lacing our fingers together. "Let's go."

Two hours later, we were all buzzed and having a good time. Music was pumping from a bluetooth sound system set up around the clearing, and before everyone had arrived, Griff cast a roaring bonfire that warmed the cool night air, making shadows from the flames dance around the crowded space. Seats were scattered about, and students filled the makeshift dance floor to the right of the fire. Evan had stuck around for a few drinks with me and the guys before disappearing, most likely with a girl.

I swayed my hips to the music, dancing on a raised platform where Griff, Chase, and Knox had all taken up residence. Several girls from a few of my classes joined me, grinding their bodies together in hopes of attracting attention from the men sitting before us. I knew, without even looking, that three sets of eyes were permanently fixed on my body. I could feel their stares practically burning holes through my bustier.

As one song blurred into another, I felt large hands on my hips, tugging me back into a rock hard body. I smirked, glancing over my shoulder to see Knox's deep brown, lust filled eyes. The beat picked up and I started grinding my ass against his quickly hardening dick. Strong fingers dug into my flesh as we moved together, his body moving with mine to the sensual rhythm pouring from the speaker. I tipped my head back, leaning it against his chest, relishing in his possessive touch. The fact that any guys dancing close to me were miraculously now at least five feet away made a laugh tumble from my lips.

I was lost in the music, and when the song ended, my very full bladder reminded me that it was time for a break. Turning around, I mouthed the word bathroom, pointing towards the dark woods. Griff's brows furrowed together for a moment before he nodded. I rose up on my tiptoes, pressing my lips to his in a kiss that told everyone around us that he was mine. I pulled back slowly, looking into his dark chocolate eyes. Desire and affection stared back at me. He held me a moment longer before reluctantly letting go. The alcohol running through my blood had me throwing him a cheeky wink before I darted off the platform.

I bobbed and weaved through the mass of bodies, making my way towards the treeline where I had seen a couple other girls head. Leaving the clearing, I stumbled through the dark for a few minutes, my feet crunching across the overgrown terrain. The light from the party had faded significantly in the dense trees and even the music was muted among the thick foliage. Coming across a large tree, I ducked behind it and took care of business. When I was finished, I adjusted my top, pushed my hair from my face and started making my way back to the party.

I was about ten feet from the tree line when I was suddenly pushed hard from the right. My body landed roughly against a tree, and I yelped, the volume of the music drowning out my cry. My front was smashed up against the rough bark, and I turned my face in just enough time to keep my nose from being broken. One of my arms was pinned tightly behind my back, the angle making my shoulder scream, the other trapped beneath me.

Someone was pressed against my back, their hot breath washing over my ear, making vomit rise in my throat. I opened my mouth to scream, but his other hand came down quickly to cover it, stifling any noise I could have made. I tried to fling him off me with my caster power, but every time I tried, it was like my telekinesis shorted out. I couldn't make him move.

"Shhh, pet," Austin chuckled into my ear.

I froze, fear locking my body in place. *No no no no!*

"Now, be a good pet, and don't scream, so I can uncover your mouth." I couldn't move, and when I didn't answer him, he twisted my arm tighter. The added pain shook me out of my stupor, and I nodded vigorously. He slid his hand from my mouth, and I sucked in a breath. My first instinct was to scream at the top of my lungs, but I knew Austin would hurt me worse, so I kept my mouth shut.

"Good pet," he whispered in my ear, and I gagged at his proximity. Jesus, fuck. My guys were only forty, maybe fifty feet away, across the clearing. But the trees were so dense, and it was so dark, there was no way for them to see me.

Austin's disgusting hand slid from my neck and down my bare shoulder. He released a bit of his weight from my body, just enough so he could wedge his arm between me and the tree. Groping at the front of my bustier, he wrenched the fabric down just far enough so he could grab my breast. I cried out at his brutal touch. His grip felt hard enough to leave bruises on my sensitive flesh, and I whimpered in fear.

Tears streamed down my cheeks, and I cried into the rough bark, praying for his assault to end. He continued to paw at my breast, pinching my nipple painfully before twisting. I stayed frozen, even as my brain was begging me to yell, to scream, to call out for my men. Surely they had noticed I'd been gone for too long. Why weren't they coming?

"Please, Austin, please stop." I sobbed the words quietly, hoping they would have some effect. In the next second his hand stopped manhandling my sore breast, but he leaned in closer, crushing me to the tree, the bark digging into my skin.

"Oh, pet, are those tears? For me?" He brought his face to mine and licked my cheek, swiping his tongue over my skin. I closed my eyes, the beer in my stomach rising into my throat. Disgust ripped through my body, and I choked down the vomit threatening to break free. My cheek felt slimy, the wetness mingling with my tears. I tried once again to call on my caster powers, but it was like there was a wall blocking them.

"Everly!"

Chase's deep voice carried through the woods, bringing my fear-frozen body back to life. I started to buck against Austin, moving any part of my body I could. I tried to raise my legs to kick, but Austin had them pinned beneath his, so I arched my back, pushing my hips and ass back into his abdomen. When I heard him moan at the contact, I quickly tucked myself forward as far as I could, revulsion swirling in my gut.

Austin, not appearing rattled in the least as Chase's voice grew closer, mumbled, "Goddamn it, fucking Stone. Ruining all my fun." He pulled his hand from my front and gripped my hair, angling my head back. "Now pet, be a good girl, and don't tell anyone about our time together. I'd hate for Griffin to lose his scholarship. Or for your dad to lose his job."

I glared at him for a second before he smashed my head into the tree. The world tilted, and pain exploded from my left eyebrow. I slid down to my knees, Austin's weight no longer holding me in place. Reaching up, I could feel a sticky wetness on my fingers and the beginnings of what I was sure would be one hell of a knot. Twisting so I was against the base of the tree, I tipped my head back, my vision swirling.

"Everly!" Chase's voice cut through the night again. "Everly!" Now Griff's voice joined him.

Unable to stand, I stayed on the ground, mustering just enough strength to yell back. My voice trembled as the words left my mouth.

"Here! I'm here!"

Chase's big body appeared in the darkness, and he lumbered toward me. "Griff, she's here! Griff!" Dropping to his knees as he reached me, Chase scooped me up into his arms. "Larkspur, baby, are you okay? What happened?"

As soon as his arms were around me, I lost it. My body began to shake, and I sobbed uncontrollably into his chest. A hand brushed my hair from my face, causing me to flinch. I looked up into Griff's shadowed face, horror filling his eyes.

"Everly," he whispered. I couldn't answer. I was breathing, but I couldn't seem to get any air to my lungs. My vision began to tunnel. "Chase, fuck, Chase, she's hyperventilating! We need to slow her breathing." Griff's voice sounded so far away as panic set in again.

I was shifted in Chase's lap, my back to his front, and Griff's hands cupped my face.

"Everly, I need you to breathe with me, baby. Come on, Blue, breathe with me." He gently took my hand, placing it on his chest. He began to take deep breaths in through his nose, blowing the air out through his mouth. I could feel the rise of his chest with every inhale. I closed my eyes, trying to mimic his actions. After several minutes, my breathing had slowed, but my tears continued to fall.

"Good Larkspur, that's good. You're doing so good. Keep breathing. Just like that." Chase whispered words of encouragement in my ear, his arms banded around me protectively. "Griff, go get Knox, tell him we've gotta go."

Griff nodded, planting a gentle kiss to my forehead. I winced at the contact, my head throbbing. "You got her?" he asked Chase. Worried lines creased his forehead, his handsome face visible in the small slits of moonlight coming through the trees. The forest was so heavily wooded, that even with a full moon, it would still be difficult to see, let alone the crescent that was out tonight.

"Yeah, I'm good. I'll carry her back to Bliss. We'll meet you on the trail." Without another word, Griff ran off toward the party, leaving Chase and I in the quiet of the woods.

"Everly, I'm going to pick you up now. Is that okay? I don't want to hurt you, do you have any injuries?" His voice was soft, patient.

Licking my lips, I answered, my voice quiet and shaky. "My head. I hit my head. It hurts."

"Okay, baby, I'll be gentle. Just close your eyes. We'll be home soon." Chase shifted me again, tucking me into his chest and standing, lifting me as if I weighed nothing. He began to quickly move through the trees, staying to the outskirts of the clearing to avoid any of our classmates.

We came up to the path Knox and I used when we arrived just a few hours earlier, though it felt like a lifetime ago now. He and Griff were waiting, tension filling the cool night air. I closed my eyes, not able to look any of them in the face. Shame flooded through me, and a sob wracked through my bruised body. Even with them shut, my eyes could still make out the colors of the flames as they danced against the darkness. They warmed my cold skin as we walked by, and as we moved away, I snuggled closer to Chase's chest, missing the heat.

I listened to their hushed voices as we moved back toward campus.

"I don't know what the fuck happened, Knox. She was on the ground when we found her. She could barely speak, and she started hyperventilating," Griff whispered.

"Do you think she fell? She didn't have that much to drink," Chase asked. I wanted to explain, the words on the tip of my tongue, but it was as if my voice was frozen in my throat.

"No man. Did you see her face? She looked terrified," Griff responded.

"Fuck!" Knox said, the word coming through gritted teeth.

Not wanting to listen anymore, I squeezed my eyes shut, and I let the darkness consume me.

Thirty

Chase

E verly had been asleep on my bed for about an hour, the guys and I scattered around my room. My clothes were strewn about, some hanging half out of my hamper, others draped across the top of my dresser. Books on botany and magical plants were lined up on my desk side by side with my business textbooks, while three framed pictures sat on top of my dresser next to my rowing trophies.

One was a picture of Everly and I that Griff had taken a few weeks back. I had my arm slung over her shoulder while she smiled at the camera, my eyes trained on her beautiful face. The second was a group selfie of the four of us sprawled out in the living room. Everly had used her telekinesis to hover the camera so we could get everyone in the picture. And the last was a photo of me and my parents from my high school graduation.

Everly had finally stopped shivering after we'd made it back to the suite, and I'd cocooned the blanket around her tiny body. Knox wanted to change her clothes, but Griff talked him out of it. We didn't know what happened and didn't want to traumatize her further.

I sat on the bed next to her, gently wiping her forehead with a damp cloth, trying to clean off the dried blood and dirt. She had a cut over her left eyebrow and a big knot just above it. A nasty purple bruise was forming, too. She was going to have one hell of a headache when she woke up.

"What the fuck happened out there, Chase?" I looked over to see Knox sitting in one of my chairs, his body leaned forward, elbows on his knees, his leg bouncing. I could feel the anger radiating from him, nearly matching my own.

"I don't know man. It's like Griff and I told you. We found her on the ground. She was shaking, crying. I didn't even realize she was hurt until she told me, it was so dark. That was all she said, that her head was hurt. Then she passed out while I was carrying her," I said, repeating the same words I'd told him twice already. I knew he was frustrated, but it's not like the story was magically going to change.

Griff, ever the voice of reason, spoke up from his spot on the floor in front of my dresser. "We're just going to have to wait until she wakes up. But we can't just start interrogating her." He shot a pointed glare at Knox, who huffed before sitting back in his chair.

"Mmmm," Everly groaned softly from next to me. I adjusted my position on the bed, setting the wet rag on my nightstand. Knox and Griff were there in the blink of an eye, each placing a hand gently on her body, reassuring themselves that she was still here.

"Everly, baby, can you hear me?" I gently stroked her cheek, willing her to wake up. Slowly her beautiful blue eyes fluttered open, her disoriented gaze landing on my face. "Hi Larkspur. Damn, I missed those pretty eyes."

"Chase?" She sat up slowly, reaching to gingerly rub her bruised forehead, wincing as her fingertips brushed the large knot. A low hiss escaped her lips before she looked around the room, finally realizing where she was.

Using just my eyes, I tried to silently tell the guys that we needed to go slow. Knox scowled but kept his mouth shut. Griff nodded at me, giving me the go ahead.

"Larkspur?" My voice was gentle, wanting to tread lightly, so I didn't upset her. "Baby, can you tell me what happened in the woods? You left to go to the bathroom, and we realized you had been gone a long time." I paused for a moment to make sure she was following my words. When her eyebrows scrunched together, and she nodded, I continued. "Griff, Knox, and I went to look for you. We found you sitting against a tree. You were in rough shape. Do you remember what happened?" I spoke to her softly, almost like I would a scared child, not wanting to send her into another tailspin.

She sat silently, drawing her knees up to her chest. Griff snagged another blanket and draped it around her shoulders. She gave him a small, sad smile, pulling it tightly around herself. He snapped his fingers toward the small fireplace on the far side of my room, flames appearing instantly, immediately warming the space. The tension in my room was getting thicker by the minute. Her blue eyes glistened with tears, and I could see she was losing the battle against her emotions. Everly dragged in a shuddering breath, her quiet voice breaking the silence.

"I—I had to pee," she started. "I was done and trying to get back to the party, and—" She didn't finish, instead, a sob broke free. I grabbed a box of tissues, holding them out for her. She grabbed one, whispering "thanks" before wiping her eyes. She took a deep breath, keeping her eyes focused on her lap, her hands balling the tissue up.

"I was coming back to the party when I was pushed into a tree, hard." I heard Knox growl from his spot by her feet. I glared at him, shaking my head subtly, silently telling him to keep his shit together. The last thing Everly's fragile emotional state needed was for Knox to explode.

"I didn't know what was happening. Then, I was shoved up against the tree." Tears were running down her cheeks, dripping onto the blue blanket she was wrapped in. My anger was building by the second, and while I know I told Knox to keep it together, I was struggling with the rage I felt growing in my body.

"He—"

That one word. I knew it. That motherfucker. I would kill him. Blood rushed in my ears. I tried to focus on her next words, my nostrils flaring with wild breaths as I struggled to contain my rage.

"He twisted my arm behind my back," she whimpered. "It really hurt. He—he told me not to scream, and then, he...." her voice faded out, her eyes staring at her lap but unseeing.

"Then he what, Everly?" Griff asked softly, his hand rubbing her knee gently.

She took in a shuddering breath, closing her eyes. The rest spilled from her lips, while she kept her eyes scrunched shut.

"He pressed me into the tree, pulled down my shirt, and grabbed my breasts. He was really rough, mean. It hurt. I-I tried to push him away, but my powers wouldn't work against him. When he realized I was crying, he licked my face, my tears. Then we heard Chase yelling. I tried to fight back, but he smashed my head into the tree trunk." She was crying so hard, my heart was breaking with each tear that fell down her cheek. "I fell down. He must have left after that." She opened her red, tear-filled eyes, looking at Griff and me. "That's when you found me. You rescued me." Her tiny hand reached out and wound its way into mine.

Unable to control myself, I hauled her into my lap. It was either that, or I was going to storm out and commit murder. I was still contemplating it.

Judging by the look on Knox's face, he was teetering on the same edge. The only thing currently keeping me in the room was the girl in my arms.

"Everly." Griff's voice was gentle. He was so patient with her, making sure to stay calm. "Blue, I need you to tell me who hurt you. That way we can go to campus security, and they can call the police."

"No!" She sat straight up in my lap, and I felt her sway a bit from the sudden movement. She held her head for a moment before looking at each of us in turn. "No." Her voice was calmer this time, but I could still hear fear in the single word.

Knox had clearly had enough. He jumped off the bed, his fingers raking through his dark hair. "What the fuck do you mean 'no' Everly?! He *hurt* you. He fucking sexually assaulted you! He'll be lucky if I don't fucking rip his goddamn head off his shoulders!" Knox roared, his chest heaving with his rage.

Everly cowered into my chest, her small body trembling.

"The fuck Knox!?" I yelled, holding her tighter. I needed to keep myself in check, so I didn't hurt her. "Calm the fuck down, and let her talk or get the fuck out. You think fucking yelling at her is gonna help? Don't be a dick, man!"

Knox paced the room like a caged animal. I glanced at Griff, needing him to calm the fucker down before he scared Everly into another meltdown. Seeming to understand the look I threw him, he rose, walking over to where Knox was crossing my bedroom floor.

He placed his hand on our friend's shoulder, halting his movement. When Knox swung to look at him, Griff grabbed his other shoulder, catching his eye. "Knox, pull your shit together. She needs you." His voice was low, probably meant only for Knox, but I could hear his commanding words.

Knox scrubbed his hands down his face before coming back to sit on the bed. While I could still see his anger simmering just below the surface, he had it locked down for the time being. He looked from Everly's curled up body to me, regret swimming in his eyes. It was obvious what he wanted, needed.

But before I'd hand her over, I needed to be sure he wasn't going to flip the fuck out again. "You good? 'Cause if you pull that shit again, Knox, I'll knock your ass right out. I fucking mean it."

"I'm good, man. Just let me hold her." His voice was calmer, more even. "Please, Chase, I need to hold her." He let out a deep sigh, his eyes pleading with me to let him hold our girl.

Without a word, I transferred her into his lap, his arms immediately wrapping her in a tight hug. I could hear him whispering apologies in her ear, her head nodding with immediate forgiveness. Fuck, she was more than any of us deserved.

Griff sat down next to them, holding out his hand to her, a couple painkillers resting in his palm. She snatched them up before taking the water bottle he also had and swallowed them down. "Blue, why can't you tell us who hurt you? Did he threaten you? 'Cause baby, if we go to the police, he won't be able to hurt you anymore."

She sat silently for a minute or two. Honestly, it could have been hours for all I knew. I just stared at her beautiful face, marred by the damage that fucking asshole had done. Looking down her body, I could see bruises and scratches along her chest, no doubt from where she'd been pinned to the tree.

Before I let my rage boil over, I took a deep breath, closing my eyes and counting back from ten. Once I felt slightly calmer, I opened them to find Everly staring at me. Her beautiful blue eyes looked dull and sad, missing that mischievous spark that I loved so much. She looked so tired, and I wanted nothing more than to wrap her in my arms and let her sleep this nightmare away.

She turned her blue gaze to Griff, tears glinting at the surface, threatening to spill over again. She went to speak, but a small sob came out instead. Knox tightened his arms around her, rocking her slightly from side to side.

"It's okay, Monet, just tell us. We'll figure it out from there."

She blew out a breath before speaking again, so softly I could barely hear her.

"It was Austin."

I fucking knew it. Motherfucker was dead. I should have beat the shit out of him the last time he put his hands on her. But before I went and killed his ass, I knew I needed to make sure Everly was okay.

She was back to looking at her lap, my heart fracturing from her pain. I knew she was feeling guilty, like this was her fault. I would make it my life's mission to prove to her she didn't do a damn thing wrong... you know, if I managed to stay out of jail after I killed Austin Thorpe.

Griff, who at this point was probably the most patient human being on the planet, pushed her hair from her face, urging her on. "What did he say to you, Everly? Did he threaten you?"

She closed her eyes, shaking her head. "I mean, I guess technically, he threatened me. He said my dad would lose his job if I told anyone." *Motherfucker.* I'd make sure to call my dad in the morning, to ensure that Everly's dad stayed on at Thorpe & Stone.

"I can take care of that, Larkspur. I'll call my dad, get it all straightened out." I felt good being able to fix at least one thing for her.

She smiled weakly at me. "Thanks Chase," she said before the smile fell from her face.

"What's wrong?" Now that we knew what he was hanging over her head and had a solution, I expected her to be a tad more relieved.

"He didn't just threaten my dad," she whispered.

"Who else did he threaten, Everly? You? Evan?" Griff questioned. I could see him working through the possibilities with that big brain of his.

She looked straight at him, fear etched on her beautiful face.

"You, Griff. He threatened you."

Thirty-One

Griffin

A week had passed since Everly's attack, and she had been painfully withdrawn. She was still spending every waking moment with us and had even taken to sleeping in our suite most nights, sneaking out after Evan had gone to bed. None of us dared to touch her except when she cried in her sleep. Nightmares woke her nightly, and she was becoming a zombie from the lack of sleep.

She'd begged us to lie to Evan about her injuries, and in the end, we'd agreed. She told him she tripped and fell in the woods, hitting her head on a rock. He was pissed she didn't go to the medical building to get looked at, but she brushed off his concern saying she was fine. I knew better though. She didn't want to be touched by a stranger. She'd peddled the same story to her dad during their Friday dinner.

When she wasn't with us or in class, she was locked in her room, painting. Knox had seen some of her pieces, and according to him, they were dark and disturbing. Not her usual soft lines and warm colors. Instead, harsh edges and large swaths of reds and blacks filled her canvases. My heart ached at how badly she was hurting and how helpless I felt.

I knew she was scared. For her dad and for me. The guys and I argued about it after she fell back asleep that night. I wanted to go to campus security, fuck what Austin said. But Chase and Knox had been in agreement that we shouldn't be reckless. Austin was unpredictable, and he had the power to fuck with my scholarship if he wanted. I knew Chase's dad could help us out with Mr. Blackwell's job, so at least that was taken care of. And, as he'd pointed out, it was ultimately Everly's decision if the authorities got involved or not.

Another week of classes wrapped up, and I decided I needed to pull our girl out of her funk. She had been listlessly moving about campus, drifting from class to class like a ghost. It had been too long since I'd seen her beautiful smile light up the room, and I was determined to bring the spark back to her cobalt eyes. I let myself into her suite using my master key and knocked softly on her closed bedroom door.

"Everly," I called through the thick mahogany. "It's Griff, can I come in?"

A few seconds later the door opened, revealing my beautiful girl in a gray, paint splattered tank top and black sweatpants. If I didn't know any better, I'd think they were Knox's. Her hands were stained with paint and charcoal, and I had a hunch she'd been locked in here all day with her art.

She declined our invitation for breakfast this morning, saying she had PopTarts and coffee in her suite, and I was worried she wasn't eating. Taking in the way her top and sweats hung on her already petite frame, it appeared my suspicions were correct. Casually, I set a buttered croissant on top of her desk that I'd wrapped in a napkin and smuggled out of the dining hall, nudging it in her direction.

"Whatcha working on?" I asked, my eyes moving to her painting area.

She quickly shuffled across the room, turning her easels, so they were out of view. My chest tightened at the apparent lack of trust she had in showing me her paintings. "Nothing. What's up?"

My heart sank. But I wasn't going to be deterred that easily.

"Well, I wanted to see if you would go someplace with me."

She sighed heavily, and I knew I was going to have my work cut out for me today.

"I don't know Griff. I don't really feel like going—"

"Everly, I know you don't want to go anywhere. But baby, hiding in your room isn't going to help anything. It's not going to make you feel better, and it's not going to take away what he did to you." I cut her off, not letting her finish her brush offs and excuses. Her blue eyes narrowed in irritation, but I continued anyway.

"I want to help you, Blue, but you've got to let me in. You've got to let Knox and Chase in. We're going to start today. I'm going to take you down to the sports complex, and we're going to work on some simple self defense moves. I know part of the reason you're upset is because you said you froze when your magic didn't work, and you couldn't fight back. I want to help you with that. I want you to know how to defend yourself, so you never feel that powerless, ever again."

She glared at me silently, not moving an inch. But she hadn't kicked me out yet, so I was taking that as a win.

"Get changed, put on some comfy clothes and sneakers. I'll be in the living room." Not waiting for her answer, I left the room, closing the door behind me.

Ten minutes later, I was nearly convinced she wasn't going to come out when she finally emerged. She traded out her painting clothes for a pair of green leggings and a long-sleeved yellow t-shirt. I looked down at her sock covered feet and quirked an eyebrow.

"My sneakers are by the door," she answered, rolling her eyes. She silently put them on, tying the laces and standing. Her hair was swept back from her face in a high ponytail, highlighting her high cheekbones and the freckles that danced across her nose. Dark rings hung under her blue eyes, and though she'd lost weight and was obviously exhausted, she still took my breath away.

"Okay, let's go."

Twenty minutes later, we reached the sports complex. We walked into the main gym area where the sparring ring and mats were located. State of the art weight machines and bench presses lined one side, a mirror covered wall running the length of the space. A few guys I recognized from Chase's rowing team were lifting weights, alternating between spotting and lifting, strained grunts echoing off the walls. The school kept the facilities in tip top shape, small refrigerators stocked with bottled water scattered throughout, towels, and a myriad of other sports equipment for student use. I grabbed her a pair of fingerless gloves and a set of sparring pads for myself. First, we'd work on the basics, her ability to throw a punch.

Living on the streets and in some shitty foster homes, I learned to fight pretty early on. It wasn't something I liked to advertise, but I could definitely hold my own. Some of the guys I sparred with from time to time tried to get me to join some underground fighting rings. The allure of easy money tempted me, but I didn't want to chance fucking up my brain and not being able to pull the grades I needed to keep my scholarship.

Stepping onto the mats, I handed Everly the gloves. She looked at them, her eyebrows raised. "What am I supposed to do with these?" Damn, she was in a pissy mood.

Deciding I was done being nice, I snarked back, "You put them on your hands, smart ass. Then you hit me as hard as you can." I patted the sparring pads. "Right here."

Rolling her eyes, she stuck her tiny hands into the gloves, tightening the velcro at the wrists. She held them up in front of her, showing me she could at least follow those directions. Her sass and attitude were going to get her ass spanked right here in the gym if she wasn't careful.

"Okay, let's see what you've got." I got into position, my knees slightly bent and the pads in front of my chest.

She threw a half-assed jab at my left hand, my arm barely moving. I raised an eyebrow.

"Really, Everly? That's all you've got?" I knew I was being a dick, pushing her buttons and pissing her off. But I needed her to get mad. I needed her to feel something, anything. This scared version of Everly that was constantly hiding in her bedroom wasn't going to help her overcome what happened. She needed to know she was in control, that she had the power. And if it meant she was going to be angry with me, well then so be it. She couldn't go to the authorities, couldn't tell anyone what happened because she was protecting me. Now, it was my turn to protect her.

"Fuck you, Griff. You know Morgan is the only person I've ever hit." She spit the words at me, and I smiled, hitting the pads together.

"Yeah, and that was at least a halfway decent punch, unlike the one you just threw. Now, again." Her next hit landed with more force. "Again." Thump. "Again." Another punch. After several more mild digs from me, she didn't need further encouragement.

Everly began beating the shit out of my sparring pads, blindly throwing punch after punch. I could see tears building in her eyes, her breathing growing more ragged with each hit she landed. She was physically here with me, but I'd bet anything it wasn't sparring pads she was seeing right now. Which was what I wanted. I needed her to focus all that anger, that rage, that despair, and aim it at *him*.

"You motherfucker!" she screamed, wailing on my pads over and over. I had to adjust my stance as she continued her assault. "I hate you! I hate you!" With one last cry, she fell against my chest, sweat trickling down her forehead.

I dropped the pads, wrapping my arms around her. Fortunately the gym was empty except for a few guys bench pressing at the opposite end, so we had at least a modicum of privacy. I held her while she broke, her tears dampening my t-shirt. I didn't give a shit though, I'd let her drown me in her tears if it meant she was finally processing what Austin had done to her.

I stroked one hand down her back, holding her head to my chest with the other, planting soft kisses to her hair while I held her tight to my body. Her arms finally came up to wrap around my waist, and after a few minutes, I felt her sag against my chest, finally giving in to my comfort.

"Everly?" I asked quietly. She remained silent for another minute, but I'd hold her as long as it took for her to come back to me.

"Thank you." Her soft voice was muffled against my shirt. She pulled back, her arms still circled around me. Her cheeks were covered in tears, her eyes and nose red from crying. "Thank you, Griff," she repeated.

"Everly, you never have to thank me for loving you." Maybe this wasn't the right time to say those words, but I needed her to hear them anyway. She needed to know that what had happened to her would never make me love her any less. She sucked in a sharp breath, more tears filling her eyes. Burying her face in my chest once more, she cried, sobs shaking her tiny body.

"I love you, too, Griff." Her words were muffled, but I heard them as if they'd been blasted over a loudspeaker. She loved me. No one, with the exception of Chase—and Knox once when he was drunk—had ever said those words to me. Not even Morgan, in the entirety of our relationship, had ever said it. My heart nearly burst, and tears filled my eyes.

I held her tight to my body, never wanting to let her go. I would burn the world to ash for this girl. She was it for me, and I vowed then and there that I'd never let anyone hurt her ever again.

Eventually, Everly stepped back, slowly removing the sparring gloves, stretching and flexing her fingers. I grabbed her a bottle of water from the stocked cooler, and she downed half of it in one go. We sat on the edge of the gym, leaning back against the wall.

"You okay?" I asked her, knocking my knee into hers. She released a shuddering breath.

"No," she answered. "But I think I will be." She looked up at me from her spot on the floor, a smile *finally* making its way onto her face. It was the first genuine smile I'd seen from her in a week, and a wide grin broke out on my face.

"Hey, at least you didn't tuck your thumb this time." I nudged her again, and a laugh burst from her lips, sweet, but short lived. She leaned her head against my bicep as we fell back into silence.

We sat quietly for another minute before she spoke again.

"I meant what I said before, Griff. I love you." She swallowed, her voice shaking slightly. "Thank you for pulling me out of the darkness. I think I'm ready to move forward, to stop hiding."

"Good," I said, twisting to my knees, so I could face her. I leaned forward, cupping her cheek with my hand, bringing my lips to within a breath of hers. "And I love you, too, my Blue girl. Thank you for coming back to me."

Thirty-Two

Everly

Over the next two weeks, in between midterms, Griff worked with me on my self-defense skills. I was taking Magical Defenses, but Griff's lessons were about simple physical force. It would come in handy, especially since my magic had been faltering whenever Austin and I were alone.

He also helped me open up to Knox and Chase, explaining to them the darkness that had enveloped me. Hurt and anger had mixed with guilt, shame, and disgust to create a hurricane of emotions in the wake of Austin's attack, emotions that my brain couldn't process. After my breakdown with Griff at the gym, all of those feelings came flooding out, and I was finally able to work through them with the help of my guys.

All three were so incredibly supportive, and I realized I should have been leaning on them all along. Knox even offered to burn the paintings I created while I was drowning in my despair. As much as I considered it, I ultimately declined. Maybe someday in the future I might change my mind, but for now, I needed the reminder of how I felt that night and the promise I made to myself to never feel that way again.

Currently, it was Tuesday night, and we were all sitting around the guys' suite, Evan included. They'd just wrapped up some game on the console and were now discussing plans for the upcoming weekend. Apparently, the academy granted us a week off from classes after midterms, so I was looking forward to lounging around and recuperating from all our studying. My mind was absolutely fried, and having some time off sounded great.

"So, Eves, what do you wanna do?" Evan's voice cut through my thoughts.

"Hmm? Do for what?"

"Our birthday, dummy. We'll have Friday night dinner with Dad, but Saturday is our actual birthday. So what do you wanna do?"

Shit. I'd completely forgotten that my—our—birthday was this weekend. Cue the theatrics in three, two, one...

"Everly Blackwell! Your birthday is this weekend, and you didn't bother to tell us?!" Chase nearly shrieked from his spot on the couch, his eyebrows practically crawling into his hairline in shock. He was sitting forward in a flash, arms thrown dramatically in the air.

I glared at Evan, but he just grinned at me. Motherfucker knew exactly what he was doing. I'd never been one for big birthday blowouts. That was way more his style.

"Come on, Eves, we've gotta do *something*. We're turning twenty-one! What about another party in the woods?"

Three resounding "no's" echoed around the room, squashing any hopes Evan might have had. He sat back, a pout forming on his stupid face. "It was just an idea," he mumbled under his breath.

Knox leaned forward in his chair, rubbing his fingertips over his scruffy chin. I loved that he let it grow out for a few days before shaving. The way it tickled between my...

"What if we had a party here?"

"I'm sorry, what?" I looked at him in disbelief. Knox was the least social person I knew, only tolerating the presence of others because he had to. The idea that he wanted to throw a party was making my brain malfunction.

I twisted around from my perch on Griff's lap. "You, Knox Montgomery, want to throw a party? Here? Where anyone who comes would be all up in your shit? Chase, a little help?"

Knox just smirked at me, knowing there was no way I could talk my way out of this. I looked at Chase, but he was smiling, the gears already turning in his head.

"Let's do it," Chase replied. "Although, that only gives me a few days to coordinate food and decorations. I could probably have done more if *someone* had given me a little heads up." He gave me a pointed look before he sprawled himself back on the other end of the sofa, his long legs stretched out in front of him. He folded his arms behind his head, his black t-shirt riding up his abdomen. My mouth watered at the sliver of skin peeking out. The guys were all trying to take things slow since my attack, but I was hornier than a fifteen year old boy. He threw me a smirk, knowing exactly what he was doing to me. Well two could play that game.

I crossed one leg over the other from my spot on Griff's lap, making my cute little booty shorts ride further up my thighs. Chase's eyes zeroed in on the exposed flesh, his eyes flashing with hunger. I winked at him.

Returning to the conversation, I realized Griff had also agreed to host the party in their suite, making it four to one not in my favor. Deciding I would just let them have at it, I locked eyes with Chase again, subtly nodding at the door. A mischievous grin spread across his face, and he nodded. I stretched out on Griff's lap, making my way to my feet. I leaned down and gave him a sweet kiss.

"I think I'm gonna go paint for a while," I announced, grabbing my keys from the coffee table.

"You want some company, little Larkspur?" Chase called from his spot. I shrugged nonchalantly as he rose from the sofa, following me to the door.

"Blue," Griff's voice called out. I turned, meeting his heated gaze. "You want me to tag along? I can hang those paintings you were talking about the other day." There were no paintings to hang. He was on to my game, and I was here for it. Trying to keep up appearances, I shrugged again. But inside, I was a swirling mess of desire.

"As much as I'd like to help," Knox said disappointedly, knowing exactly what was happening, "I've gotta head to the studio to get some work done."

"And I have plans," Evan added as he rose from the sofa, stretching out his long arms, completely oblivious to our shenanigans. But him having plans was news to me.

"And just who do you have plans with?" I asked, my hands on my hips. He hadn't mentioned anyone to me, and sometimes my protective big sister side decided to come out to play. Besides, I was just kidding. Kinda.

"Just a girl from one of my classes," he answered cryptically. He looked at his watch, suddenly moving a lot faster than he was a moment ago. "And I'm gonna be late if I don't head out. I'll catch up with you guys later." He ruffled my hair as he walked past me out the door.

"Mmhmm, don't think this conversation is over, Evan Blackwell!" I leaned out the doorway, talking to his retreating form. He waved me off, taking a left down the stairs.

Knox was the next to go, slinging his bag over his head. He pulled me into his arms, his big hands resting on my ass, fingers playing with the hem of my shorts. "Have fun tonight, little Monet. I want all the details later." He waggled his eyebrows before slanting his mouth over mine, setting my body on fire as his tongue moved inside my mouth.

Breaking away and leaving me a little breathless, Knox leaned his forehead against mine.

"Fuck, I wish I didn't have to go work. Fucking senior project," he grumbled.

"I'll make it up to you, promise." I kissed the tip of his nose, sealing the deal.

"You better," he grumbled again. Stepping into the hall, he called out, "Have fun, you fuckers. You better make her come at least twice." And with those words, he was gone.

Chase shut the door, turning to look at Griff and I.

"Well, since everyone left, what do you say we just stay here? That way you don't have to worry about Evan coming back with any surprise guests and interrupting our fun," Chase reasoned, adding, "Besides, I have a California king sized bed." He flicked his eyebrows up, a sly smile lifting the corners of his mouth.

"Sounds good to me," I said as I whipped my slouchy gray t-shirt over my head, leaving me standing in my booty shorts and a lacy gray bra. It was as if time stopped for a moment, sexual tension crackling through the space like electricity in the air before a storm. Deciding to push my luck, I looked at Griff before adding, "What would you like me to do, sir?"

Chase's eyebrows rose in shock as he looked between me and Griff. I guess Griff hadn't shared how we liked to play in the bedroom. Well, he'd certainly be getting a crash course tonight.

"Sir, huh? Do I have to call you sir, too, Griff?" Chase grinned broadly.

Griff chuckled darkly before answering.

"No, but you will do what I say, Chase." To emphasize his point, Griff crossed his muscular arms across his chest, challenging Chase to disagree. "Now, go strip our girl down. I want her naked in your bedroom."

Chase wasted no time, striding across the room and flipping me over his shoulder. I squealed, my face suddenly staring at his lower back. I swatted his tight ass playfully, earning me one to my own.

Once we were in his bedroom, Chase sat me back on my feet. His hands stayed at my hips, fingers slipping into the waistband of my shorts. "Well, we don't want to make Daddy Griff mad, now do we?" He tugged my shorts and panties down my legs while I unhooked my bra, throwing it across the room.

"Very good, Chase." Griff's deep voice sounded from the doorway, drawing both our attention. "Everly, on the bed, ass up. I want to watch Chase lick that pretty pussy."

I shivered at Griff's words, hastily climbing onto Chase's big bed, assuming the position Griff ordered. I propped myself in the middle of the navy blue comforter, putting my weight on my forearms while I wiggled my ass in the air. A groan came from somewhere behind me, and I smiled smugly at the reaction.

"Bon appétit, Chase," Griff growled, lust lacing each word.

I gasped when Chase's tongue licked a long swipe from my clit to my taint. He moaned as he pulled away.

"Christ Larkspur, you taste so fucking good. Could eat you all fucking night."

He dove back in, spearing my pussy with his tongue before moving up to tease my clit. I felt him slide two fingers into my core, my walls tightening around him. He nipped and sucked my flesh, driving me closer and closer to the edge. Just as my orgasm was beginning to crest, I felt him pull away.

"That's enough, Chase," Griff ordered, his voice tight. I looked over my shoulder to see both men naked, their equally impressive erections standing at full mast. Griff was stroking his length, staring at my glistening pussy. "Fuck our girl while I fill her throat." My core clenched at his words.

I felt the bed dip as Chase knelt behind me. I could feel his dick notched at my entrance before he slid inside just an inch, his hands locked on my hips. I groaned as he teased me, my pussy begging to be filled. I tried to glance over my shoulder at him, but Griff's dick was suddenly shoved into my open mouth. He thrust in deeply, pushing me back fully onto Chase's thick cock. I gasped around him, my tongue licking the veiny underside.

"Fuuuck," Chase groaned out behind me, his dick seated fully inside. He began to thrust slowly, making me feel every inch of his impressive length. I tried to focus my attention on Griff, his cock nudging the back of my throat. I swirled my tongue around him, tasting his salty precum. I'd never been with two guys at the same time before, but fuck, this was heaven.

"That's right, Everly, take our cocks. Such a good girl." Griff's praise lit me up from the inside. "You like to be filled up, don't you, dirty girl? Next time, we'll get Knox in here too. We can each fill a hole." My god the mouth on this man. His dirty words pushed me closer to the edge once more.

Chase had picked up his pace, his thrusts coming faster as I bounced between his and Griff's dicks. I felt his hands leave my hips, spreading my ass cheeks apart, no doubt admiring the view of him disappearing inside me.

"Everly," Griff ground out, his hand tangling in my hair, controlling the speed of his thrusts into my mouth. "Have you ever had someone in your ass before, my Blue girl? Hmm?"

I felt myself flush at his question. *That* was not something I had ever done. But the thought had me tightening around Chase, my cunt dripping with arousal at the idea.

I must have taken too long to respond, because Griff tugged my hair roughly, pulling out of my mouth completely before speaking. "I expect an answer when I ask you a question, Everly."

"I'm sorry, sir. No, I've never had someone in my ass before. But I think I'd like to." I heard Chase moan loudly behind me at my answer. He was pounding into me at this point, my tits bouncing wildly. Each thrust had his balls slapping my clit, building me closer and closer to an orgasm.

"Well, my good girl," Griff said, his voice low and dangerous. "We'll have to see what we can do about that." Then he was pushing back into my mouth once more.

Oh fuck yes.

Thirty-Three

Chase

Fuck, I didn't realize that my mild-mannered, level-headed, calm-as-a-cucumber friend was a dom in the bedroom. I had a hard time picturing Griff and the she-bitch having that kind of relationship. I wondered if it was a new development since he started dating Everly. As curious as I was, I couldn't focus on those thoughts right now, not with Everly's tight pussy squeezing me in the most perfect way.

"Well, my good girl," Griff said to Everly. "We'll have to see what we can do about that."

Jesus, was he saying he wanted me to play with her ass? I locked eyes with him over her head as he thrust his dick back into her throat. She looked so fucking hot between the two of us, Griff filling her mouth while I pounded into her tight little cunt. He nodded at me, his instructions clear.

"Chase, why don't you show Everly how good it can feel with your dick in her pussy while you fuck her ass with your finger?"

Holy fuck. Somehow Griff telling me how to fuck Everly was seriously hot. Who knew?

"Larkspur, you good with that?" I needed to know without a doubt that she was okay with what I was about to do.

She moaned around Griff's dick, her head bobbing up and down. Good enough for me.

I spread her ass cheeks again, looking down at her tight little hole. I spit directly on it, my saliva glistening against her tanned flesh. Using my index finger, I swirled it around, teasing her rim. She tightened, her natural instinct to clench at the feeling of something probing her there.

I continued thrusting into her, letting her get used to the sensation of my finger on her tight ring. I picked up my pace, snapping my hips almost violently, my balls slapping her sensitive clit. She cried out around Griff, making him drop his head back on his shoulders.

Deciding it was now or never, I gently pushed in the tip of my finger, breaching her. It was a powerful feeling, knowing I was the first man to ever have her like this.

I slowly pressed in further before withdrawing, keeping a slow pace as I felt my balls tighten. Fuck, I was close. But I needed her to come before Griff and me. I picked up the tempo, fucking her ass with my index finger, and adding a bit more spit before burying it up to the knuckle. I felt her entire body tense before her orgasm burst through like a levy breaking. She went rigid, her pussy and ass clamping down around me.

She yelled her release, her pussy spasming in ecstasy. She was so fucking tight, I could barely move my cock. As she came down, I was able to begin thrusting harder, my own release close. I pulled my finger from her ass, earning myself a low groan, before looking at Griff.

I could tell by the tight set of his jaw that he was ready to come. He locked eyes with me and nodded. We both began to thrust in unison, filling Everly as much as possible. The tingle began at the base of my spine, and I felt my balls draw up before I emptied myself in her tight cunt.

"Fuck! Everly!" I roared, rope after rope of cum painting her inner walls.

Griff erupted a moment later, shooting down her throat. She swallowed him down greedily and holy shit. She looked like a goddamn goddess between the two of us, stuffed full of our cocks and cum.

We all stayed like that for a minute, connected through our love of the same girl. And that was how I felt. I knew; I loved Everly. Now I just needed to quit being a pussy and tell her.

I slowly eased out of her, my dick still half hard. I could probably go another round if she wanted, but I figured she needed a little recovery time after her first threesome. Griff left the bed, heading toward the bathroom before returning with a wet cloth and a small glass of water.

Everly rehydrated while Griff cleaned up the mess I made between her legs. The sight of my cum dripping from her pussy had me wanting to fuck her all over again, but I quickly jogged to the bathroom to wash my hands instead. I returned just as Griff was throwing the washcloth in my hamper. I hopped back on my bed, snuggling up next to my girl. I nuzzled my nose into her neck, earning myself a giggle as my stubble tickled her skin.

"And just where do you think you're running off to, Daddy Griff?" I teased when I noticed he was pulling on his clothes.

Griff's cheeks turned a light shade of pink before he answered.

"I'm gonna go grab a shower and order some food. What do you guys want? Pizza? Chinese?" he replied as he shoved his shirt over his head.

"Oooh! Can we get sushi?" Everly asked excitedly as she stretched across my bed like a cat. The sight of her perfect body had my dick hardening again.

"Sushi sounds good. Griff, you have a place you can 'port to?" I asked, tugging the comforter up over Everly and me.

"Yeah, there's a good spot in the next town over that I've been to a couple times. I'll call and order a couple rolls for each of us, then jump over to pick it up." He leaned down, giving her a sweet kiss on the forehead before shooting her a wink. "I already have an idea of what I want for dessert."

Her blue eyes darkened, and she bit her lip at his words. He grinned before striding across my bedroom and out the door.

"Make sure to order some for Knox!" Everly called out. I loved that she thought about us, even when we weren't around.

I realized, after Everly's attack, that I was completely in love with her. Shitty timing, I know. If I were being completely honest with myself, I probably knew before then, but I was a pussy who had never been in love before, and I was afraid of what that meant. Didn't make it right, but there it was.

Seeing her so hurt, so utterly broken had made something snap into place in my heart. I was devastated for her, and angry with myself for not protecting her better. She was my girlfriend, my whole fucking reason for existing it felt like most days, and I couldn't save her. I vowed that I would do everything physically possible to make sure she was never hurt like that again.

You know that feeling, when you look at someone and you don't know how you lived before them? How could you possibly live if they were ever gone? That was how I felt about Everly. She made everything better, made *me* better. I felt more like myself than ever before. That was how I looked at life now: before Everly, and after.

We hunkered down under my comforter, my little Larkspur snuggled into my side. She rested her head on my chest, her hand tracing over the ink that covered my skin. I let Knox start tattooing me a few years ago when we became roommates. He'd said the skin was just another canvas, the ink and tattoo gun just another medium. He was talented as fuck, so I figured, what the hell? He'd been tattooing me ever since.

She hummed softly while she tickled my skin with her fingertips. I pushed her dark hair off her face, in complete awe of her beauty. She was utterly perfect. Even beyond her physical beauty, her soul spoke to mine, fit with it as if they were puzzle pieces finally laid the correct way. I was a damn lucky bastard. Suddenly overwhelmed with my feelings for her, the words flew from my mouth before I could stop them.

"I love you," I blurted out.

My heart thundered against my ribs. There was no way in hell she couldn't feel it with her head lying flush on my chest. Not that I didn't mean what I said, but fuck, what if she didn't say it back? What if she didn't feel the same way? I didn't know if my heart could survive that type of devastation. She already owned every piece of it, and the thought she may not feel the same way threatened to shatter me into a million pieces. I held my breath, waiting for her next words.

She leaned up, resting her forearm on my chest, her sapphire eyes trained on my face. A sexy smile spread across her pouty lips before she responded.

"I love you, too."

Four words. That was all it took to turn my whole world inside out and upside down. She loved me. I suddenly had that feeling you get as a kid when a sugar rush hits. My body felt like a live wire, ready to bounce around the room, run a marathon, swim across Solis Lake, and back again. Every single atom felt as though it was waking from hibernation. But not a slow, Saturday morning, coffee in your pajamas kind of wake up. No. This one was electric, like being doused in cold water, but feeling like every molecule was on fire at the exact same moment. She. Fucking. Loved. *Me*.

I needed to feel her on my skin, my lips. Without another word, I dragged her on top of me, her legs straddling my large thighs. As she moved, I caught her lips with mine, pouring every ounce of love I felt for her into our kiss. My right hand palmed the back of her head, holding her to me, while my left stayed at her hip.

Everly gave as good as she got. Her tongue danced with mine while she braced her hands on my chest. Her warm pussy rubbed over my length, making me rock hard in an instant. Grinding up into her, I could feel her wetness coating me. I needed to be inside her like I needed my next breath.

Moving both hands to her hips, I picked up her tiny frame before bringing her back down on my cock. She let out a cry as I filled her, her head thrown back in pleasure.

"Fuck! Chase!" she cried out, her tits bouncing in my face. I leaned forward, taking one pink nipple into my mouth. I swirled my tongue around, sucking and licking, until it was a hardened peak. Switching to the other side, I lavished it with the same attention before releasing it with a pop.

I pounded into her from below, and she looked fucking divine riding me, her cheeks flushed a glorious rose and her hair falling around her shoulders. It was an image that would forever be imprinted into my memory.

We bucked against one another, taking pleasure from each other's bodies. She ground down against me, rubbing her clit in just the way she needed to get off, erupting with a yelp while I thrust into her. Her release set off my own, my hot seed filling her to the brim.

She slumped against me, my cock still deep inside her pussy. We lay like that for a long while, until we heard Griff return with our food. We slowly pulled apart, but not before Everly kissed me one last time.

"I love you, Chase Stone," she whispered against my lips.

"I love you, too, Larkspur. From now until always."

Thirty-Four

Everly

T he rest of the week went by as usual. Midterms were wrapping up, and I felt pretty confident that I was going to end up with decent grades. Griff organized some study sessions for Chase and I to help get us through, however, we had to move them from the suites to the library after the first one. We'd tried to work at the guys' place, but it ended with us all naked, so not much studying had gotten done. Well, at least no studying for exams. Griff and Chase had studied every inch of my body that night. My cheeks heated at the memory.

Friday rolled around, and I was getting ready for our weekly dinner with my dad. He had worked out a deal with the dining hall to have two dinners ready to go at five-thirty each Friday that Evan picked up on his way home from class. Dad would video chat with us, and we'd sit and pretend we were all at the table together. He hadn't shared much about his new job, except to say that he was super busy, but he always told us how much he missed us.

I was going to use tonight's birthday celebration as a way to tell my dad about my guys and our dating situation, crossing my fingers that it wouldn't blow up in my face. He'd never really had much of an opinion on my love life, save for the small comments here and there about some of my dates over the years, so I didn't see why this would warrant any sort of big reaction. Then again, I didn't know how any father would react to finding out his little girl was getting fucked by three different guys on a regular basis.

Evan propped the tablet up against the wall, putting the call through to Dad. He picked up quickly, his plate of food already in front of him.

"Hey guys!" A giant grin spread across his familiar face. I glanced at my brother, seeing the same nose and jawline as our dad, and it tugged at my heart, making me miss him even more.

"Hi Dad!" Evan and I called out in unison.

"How're things going? Midterms good?" He always started out the same, asking about school and if we were doing well in our classes. He was sitting at what looked like a bar top in his condo, a glass of amber colored liquor sitting next to him. His tie was loose and hanging around his neck, the top button of his dress shirt undone. He must have just gotten home from work right before we called.

Evan answered first. "School's good. I had a tough midterm in my fire elementals class, but I think I did pretty well on it."

"That's great, Evan! Everly, how about you? How's your Water Magic class? You said you had a friend that you were working with in there? Nate? Nash?"

I choked on the hamburger I had been chewing. *Well, I guess we're doing this now.* Trying to clear the food from my throat, I took a quick sip of my lemonade before answering.

"Uh, yeah, Knox. He's been helping me study, since he's a water elemental, too. Actually, there's a couple guys helping me study," I cautiously responded.

Evan snorted beside me. "Helping you study, right." He chuckled, trying to hide his smirk. I elbowed him in the ribs, praying he'd shut his fucking mouth. Just as I was getting ready to try to explain to my dad that my study partners were a little more than that, he spoke again.

"Oh! I completely forgot to tell you. Thorpe & Stone is hosting their annual Autumn Ball next Saturday night. You are both expected to attend. I've put money in both of your accounts, so you can go shopping. It's black tie, so you'll each need to pick up proper attire." The information dropped into my brain like a grenade, but my dad acted as if he was just letting us know we'd be having lasagna instead of chicken for dinner. I stared at the screen, dumbfounded, his words slowly sinking in.

"I'm sorry, we're going to what now?" Evan asked, his dislike for the idea as obvious as mine. I had no desire to spend an evening in a fancy dress and heels that were sure to hurt my feet.

"It's a big party that Thorpe & Stone throw every year," he reiterated.

"But dad, we—" I attempted to argue, hoping that I could come up with some excuse that would get us out of an evening rubbing elbows with Dad's rich coworkers, but he cut me off before I could finish my thought.

"Everly, it's not up for debate. It will be a good chance for you to meet some of my colleagues and their families, do some good networking for after graduation. I'll send a car to pick you both up at the academy, and text you the information regarding the times and locations. You're each allowed to bring a plus one, if you'd like." Well, shit, didn't look like we'd be getting out of this.

Slumping back in his seat, Evan crossed his long arms over his chest, mumbling about having to wear "a goddamn penguin suit."

My mind, however, was stuck on the fact that Chase hadn't mentioned anything about a ball, and it was his dad's freaking company. Did he know and just not tell me? Did he not want to take me? I was lost in my own thoughts, not particularly listening to the rest of the conversation as it continued.

As my mind swirled with those thoughts, a new and horrifying one gripped me. This was a *Thorpe* & Stone event. Meaning Austin would be invited, too. My stomach roiled, and my burger and fries threatened to make a reappearance at the thought of having to see him at the party.

Finally, after Dad took his last bite of chicken, he wiped his mouth and sat his napkin next to his plate. "Alright, kiddos, I've got to run. But please make arrangements to get your outfits for next weekend, and I'll see you then. I love and miss you both so much. And happy birthday!"

"We love you too, Dad," our voices combined as we answered, but while Evan's had a slightly pouty quality, mine was robotic, monotone.

My brother ended the call, and we sat in silence for a minute before I stood, gathering our take out containers and placing them in the trash, while Evan set our silverware in the sink to be washed. As he turned on the water and grabbed the sponge, I made my way to the door.

"I've gotta run out. I'll be back in a bit." I threw the words over my shoulder, my brain completely preoccupied with my need to talk to Chase and figure out why the hell he hadn't mentioned this ball to me. Did he already have someone he was planning to take? I knew he had a history, and the idea that he could potentially want to spend the evening with a past conquest was almost too much to bear. My brain got stuck on the fact that he had been working closely with Heather all semester for Potions, having to meet up at the lab to complete our assignments. She was obviously still interested in him... maybe he'd decided I wasn't enough.

Doubt and hurt swirled in my chest as I thought about the night I spent with him and Griff. He told me he loved me; had it just been a slip of the tongue? Did he truly mean those three words, or was he caught up in the emotion and lust of our threesome?

Marching the short distance down the hall, I knocked on the guys' door, tapping my foot while I waited for someone to answer. I wasn't left waiting long when Knox appeared, shirtless in his painting sweats. As much as I wanted to ogle his sexy, inked up body, I was far too anxious to appreciate the sight before me.

Giving him a quick kiss, I walked in, looking around the space for my green eyed boyfriend. "Is Chase here? I need to talk to him. Now." I knew I was being brusque, but the nerves twisting in my gut were putting me on edge.

"Yeah, little Monet, he's here," he answered, walking over to me. He rubbed my upper arms with his big hands before dipping his head to look at me. His deep brown eyes looked into mine, and his brow creased with worry. "What's going on, Everly? You seem upset."

"That's because I am upset. I need to talk to Chase," I snapped, feeling tears stinging my eyes. I swiped my hand over them, attempting to stem their flow.

Anger passed over Knox's face, and for a moment I thought he was pissed at my bitchy attitude. But then he swung around, heading toward Chase's bedroom door like his ass was on fire.

"You motherfucker! What did you do?" he bellowed as he burst into Chase's room. I quickly ran after him, not wanting a full on brawl to break out.

By the time my short legs brought me into the room, Knox had pulled Chase from his bed and was holding him up by the collar. To Chase's credit, he looked absolutely horrified, having no idea why his best friend was going all Hulk smash on his ass.

"What the fuck, man? The fuck are you yelling about? I didn't do shit!" Chase yelled back, obviously confused by Knox's behavior. Chase easily peeled Knox's fingers from his shirt, using his caster strength to free himself. He stepped back, both guys breathing heavily, glaring daggers at one another.

"Then why the fuck did Everly come in here, all upset and almost in tears, demanding to talk to *you*, motherfucker?" Knox snarled. He stabbed Chase in the chest with his finger as he spoke the words.

Worried fists were about to start flying, I sprinted across the room, inserting myself between my two boyfriends. Chase's gaze immediately swung to me at Knox's words, a perplexed look on his handsome face.

"Larkspur, what's he talking about? Why are you upset? Did I do something?" By the last word, his voice was barely above a whisper, and he was turning me to face him, panic etched across his features.

Those goddamn tears were back as I stared into his jewel-toned eyes. Eyes that looked at me in devastation and bewilderment. He really didn't seem to know why I was upset. He reached for me, his fingers brushing my arm before Knox interjected.

"You don't fucking touch her! Not until I know what the fuck you did and whether or not I have to kill you," Knox all but shouted, grabbing my arm and pulling me from Chase's hands. I tried to gently push him off, but he held on tightly.

"Knox, it's okay." My voice trembled when I spoke, my emotions barely in check. "I need to talk to Chase."

Knox grumbled but released me. "Fine, but I'm not fucking leaving." He strode over to Chase's desk and plopped himself down in the chair, his eyes never leaving Chase and I.

"Everly, I don't understand," Chase started, but I held up a hand, cutting him off.

"Did you know about the Autumn Ball that your dad's company is throwing next weekend?"

He straightened, his eyebrows furrowing, a frown appearing on his face. "Uh, yeah I guess, but I completely forgot that it was next week. I hate going to that shit, so I usually don't pay attention until my dad calls and demands my presence. Why?" He studied my tense posture, almost as if he were watching a wild animal in captivity.

"Because my dad just informed me that Evan and I are expected to attend. Were you not going to ask me to go, Chase?" My voice wobbled with emotion, the next question nearly getting stuck in my throat. "Were you going to take someone else?"

He was on me in a flash, his giant arms circling me, banding to his body. I was smashed into his chest, the air pushed from my lungs by his tight embrace. I let out a "ooph" but Chase didn't seem to notice.

"Oh Jesus, Everly, of course I would have taken you! Please believe me when I say, I really, truly, honestly had forgotten about it. I always take Griff as my plus one every year. I wouldn't dream of taking anyone but you, baby. You're it for me, from now until always." His voice shook at the end with obvious emotion.

I pulled back from him, not that he made it easy with the way he clung to my body. His green eyes swam with tears, and he looked at me with distress. I could see the truth in his eyes, my doubts shrinking with each passing second. But we still had one more thing to discuss. I swallowed thickly, my stomach in knots.

"Chase," I whispered. "Will Austin be there?"

His whole body tensed.

"Fuck!" Chase hissed, the realization hitting him. "Damn it." He squeezed me close again, as if trying to protect me from his next words. "His father is my dad's business partner, and they throw the damn thing together. He goes every year. Fuck!"

"Well, just tell your dad you're not going. Easy," Knox chimed in from his spot across the room.

"Not easy, dude," Chase threw back. At least they weren't at each other's throats anymore. I could tell Knox was still wound up, most likely from me dropping the bomb about Austin attending the party. "I don't really have a choice of not going. Everly, can you get out of it?"

I shook my head. "No. My dad made it very clear that Evan and I were expected to be there with fucking bells on. He said we needed to go shopping this week for outfits and that we were allowed to bring a plus one if we wanted."

Knox sprang up from the chair, closing the distance between the three of us.

"Well, we'll all go then."

"How do you figure?" Chase looked at him quizzically.

"Easy. Griff can still be your plus one, I'll be Everly's. Then we can make sure someone is with her the entire time so that dickwad can't come near her."

Mulling it over, Chase finally agreed. "That could work." I looked at each of them with hopeful eyes.

Chase chuckled, sweeping me into his arms again, this time planting a kiss on my forehead. I wrapped my arms around his waist, holding him tight. A moment later I felt heat at my back as Knox sandwiched me between them and all felt right in the world again.

"I'm sorry," I spoke into Chase's hard chest. "I was just scared."

"It's okay, little Larkspur. No blood, no foul. I am a little hurt you thought I wouldn't want to take you as my date. I want nothing more than to show you off to the whole world, tell everyone that you're fucking mine."

"Ours," Knox growled from behind me.

"Ours," Chase repeated. "I'm just grateful Knox didn't mess up my pretty face," he reassured me, a chuckle rumbling up from his chest.

"There's still time, motherfucker," Knox teased... Well, I'm pretty sure he was teasing.

Thirty-Five

Knox

Once Everly calmed down about the stupid fucking *ball* next weekend (that I was apparently going to have to go shopping for), we spent the rest of the evening cuddled up on the sofa, watching a movie. She had taken turns snuggling between me and Chase, neither of us letting our hands leave her body. Griff came home halfway through and sat on the floor at her feet, massaging her calves as the movie played. Eventually, she passed out on the sofa, and instead of waking her to go back to her place, I shot Evan a text telling him she was staying the night with us. I carried her to my bedroom and tucked her in next to me.

Holding her all night was fast becoming one of my favorite things. It ranked right up there with sinking balls deep into her pussy.

Now it was Saturday, and we spent the afternoon getting set up for Evan and Everly's party. The look of absolute shock on everyone's faces when I suggested we host it at our place was hilarious, but I knew we would be able to keep an eye on my little Monet better if we were here. With school on break, a large number of students left the dorms to go home, so we weren't expecting a ton of people anyway, unlike when we threw forest parties and half the school showed up. Although, ever since Everly's attack, the guys and

I had an unspoken agreement that we wouldn't be hosting anymore of those. At least not until that fuckwit Thorpe had been dealt with.

I still vibrated with rage every time I thought about what that fucker had done to my girl, how he hurt her. I tried to support her, holding her through her nightmares, watching her pour her fear and anger onto canvas after canvas, but it hadn't been enough, and that fact ate at me. I tried not to dwell on it, knowing that I connected with her in ways Griff and Chase didn't. Even still, it sat heavy at the back of my mind.

That was probably the reason I snagged her the moment we opened the door for the party, planting her on my lap, my arm banded across her thighs. I was nursing a beer, while Everly drank something mixed with orange juice that Chase created. I was keeping an eye on how much she drank, not wanting her to get too drunk. That would put a damper on the plans the guys and I had for later tonight.

We'd all been pretty open about the sexual side of our relationship with our girl. When Griff and Chase told me about their threesome... well, I'd be lying if I said I wasn't jealous as fuck. The thought of watching her between them made my cock hard in an instant, all my blood rushing south. Luckily, my little Monet was perched on my thigh, not able to feel the hard on I was sporting.

I'd nearly come in my jeans when Everly arrived earlier. She'd shown up in a pair of black leather pants that were practically painted on, the material hugging each gorgeous curve. A lacy white crop top showed off her tanned skin, the deep cut telling me she wasn't wearing a bra underneath. Dark wavy locks cascaded down her back, and she'd given herself what I think was called a smokey eye. Whatever it was looked sexy as hell, making her blue eyes appear brighter than normal. Her tiny feet were covered in little black boots, and she tapped her toes to the music while she surveyed the room.

Chase had gone all out. Streamers were hung throughout the room, and he had damn near filled the space with blue and black balloons. A large, silver inflatable number twenty-one sat in a corner while an assortment of food lined the countertop. He had sweet talked Martha into making several trays of Everly's favorites: brownies with peanut butter frosting, fruit with a whipped cream dip, and tiny bacon sliders. How that fucker got that sweet lady to do his bidding was beyond me. Griff had teleported to the next town over to pick up pizza, beer, and some liquor to round out our food and drink options for the evening.

They were seated on the sofa, each with a beer in hand. About twenty people had showed up, completely filling our suite, some spilling out into the hall, while a handful created a makeshift dance floor where our dining room table typically stood. Griff had teleported some of our furniture over to the twins' place so we'd have more room, which was definitely a good call considering how crowded it was. More guests were scattered throughout the space, drinking and enjoying the party. I was fairly certain that Everly didn't know a good chunk of the people present, but her brother seemed pretty well acquainted with most of the guests. Evan was a cool guy; definitely the more social twin, that was for sure.

I moved my hand to Everly's exposed hip, my thumb slowly stroking her soft skin. She turned those ocean eyes on me, a happy smile on her face.

"You having a good time, little Monet?"

"I am. Thank you, Knox. For suggesting the party, I mean, and for everything." She blushed, her cheeks turning that shade of pink I loved so much.

If I was being honest, there wasn't a thing about Everly that I didn't love. She was perfect. Her strength, her creativity, her passion for her art. She filled all the spaces in my heart that had been empty before she literally crashed into my life.

I'd overheard her say those three words to my best friends, and I knew those assholes were head over heels, just like me. I was hopelessly in love with her.

There was no rhyme or reason for why I hadn't told her yet; the moment just never felt *right*. I wanted to tell her after her attack, but I didn't want her to think I was saying it out of pity. And any other time the words were on the tip of my tongue, we were always interrupted. Either Chase would barrel through the door, or Griff would decide they needed to study... Hell, we were even interrupted by a damn black squirrel the other day, scratching and chittering at her window. She'd quickly sliced up a banana, and the little bastard had happily fucked off with its treat, leaving me to strip my girl down and worship her for the rest of the afternoon.

I made a decision in that moment that I would find a time tonight to tell her. Looping my fingers under the thin strap of her top, I pulled her to me, slanting my lips over hers in a heated kiss. Her small fingers curled into the fabric of my henley, clinging to me as I stroked my tongue into her mouth.

I broke away from her when Chase started to make cat calls from his place on the sofa. I grinned, flipping him off with the hand holding my beer, unwilling to remove the other from Everly's body. I found myself smiling more and more each day that Everly was in my life.

The party continued on for a few hours, people milling in and out until all the alcohol and food were gone. Everly made her way around the room, making small talk with some other fourth years. Evan ducked out about an hour before, saying he was "meeting up with someone." Obviously code for hooking up. He'd been sneaking off with some girl, but her identity remained a mystery. And although my little Monet hadn't said anything, I knew the fact Evan was keeping secrets bothered her.

Once we said good night to the last of the stragglers, I shut and locked the door. Turning around, I found Chase and Griff standing in the kitchen, bagging up some stray beer bottles. I locked eyes with Griff first, then Chase, an entire conversation passing silently between the three of us. Chase finished tying off the bag before quickly washing his hands. Both guys made their way to the living room where Everly was cleaning up.

I came up behind where she was bent over the coffee table, standing at her back, and as she straightened, her round ass pressed right into my already hard dick. I wrapped my hands around her hips, dipping my head to the crook of her neck.

"Everly," I breathed quietly against her skin. She shivered, goosebumps raising along her arms. Griff moved to her front, and I could see him trail a finger down her chest and over the beautiful line of her cleavage. I knew for a fact she wasn't wearing a bra, and I wondered if her nipples were hard against the white lace of her top.

Chase was at her side, one of his large hands splayed across her ribs, toying with the bottom of her crop top. Catching his eye, he gave me a subtle nod. Understanding, I moved my hands, gripping the fabric and pulling it up until she was forced to raise her arms. I stripped the top up and over her head, leaving her naked from the waist up. Her leather pants sat low on her hips, and the sight of her made my mouth water.

Griff gripped the sides of her face, kissing her like a man starved while Chase palmed one of her breasts. She moaned as he rolled her hardened nipple in his fingers. I worked my hands lower, popping the button on her pants before lowering the zipper. Sliding my hand inside, I groaned when my fingers met her slick folds under the leather. She. Wasn't. Wearing. Any. Panties.

"Everly," I growled, "where the fuck are your underwear?"

She pulled away from Griff, her breaths heavy and fast. Looking over her shoulder at me, she smirked, before shrugging her shoulders.

"I didn't want panty lines."

As if scripted, Griff, Chase, and I all groaned in unison.

"Little Larkspur, we need you naked. Now." In a flash, Chase knelt at her feet, pulling her little black boots off before dragging her pants down over her sexy curves. In the next instant, she was naked before us.

Stepping away, Everly moved toward the hall that led to all of our bedrooms. Her hips swayed as she walked, her pert ass bouncing with each step. My dick was painfully hard, and I almost wondered if it was going to bust through the zipper of my jeans. I couldn't take my eyes off of her tight body as she strutted away from us.

Just as I went to move in her direction, she turned, facing us. Then, in a moment that would forever live rent free in my head, Everly dipped her small fingers between her legs, the tips coming away shiny with her arousal. When she brought them to her mouth, her pink tongue peeking out to taste herself, I nearly came in my pants. Jesus fucking christ.

Griff, Chase, and I lunged forward at the same time. Everly squealed when I reached her first, flipping her naked ass over my shoulder, and giving her a swat before marching straight into my bedroom. I launched her onto the bed, the guys following us in. Within moments, we were all naked, our clothes discarded haphazardly around my room.

Everly lay on her back in the middle of my large bed, her upper body propped up on her elbows. I crawled up the foot of the bed, spreading her tanned legs. Her pussy glistened, so pretty and pink, just waiting for my tongue. I didn't waste another moment, diving in to feast like a man starved. Her taste exploded on my tongue, the slight tang making me moan in pleasure.

"Jesus, Knox! Fuck!" she cried out before Chase swallowed down her cries in a kiss. I continued lapping at her dripping cunt, alternating between spearing her with my tongue and flicking her clit. Peeking up her body, I could see Chase kissing her deeply while Griff licked and sucked her glorious tits. She was trembling below us, her perfect body writhing with the need to come.

I sucked on her clit before nipping it lightly with my teeth, her whole body jolting with pleasure. Knowing just how to push her over the edge, I thrusted two fingers into her tight channel. Crooking them up, I hit that sweet spot deep inside her. Her back instantly arched off the bed, her pussy gripping my fingers as she came.

"Fuck! Yes, oh yes!" She all but screamed her release, and I was grateful our suite was at the end of the hall. I didn't want anyone to know what my girl sounded like when she came.

Chase began to plant soft kisses along her neck, while Griff followed suit on her other side. I continued to lick her through her orgasm, only stopping once her body had fully relaxed, sinking into the mattress. I sat up, my hands on her knees, keeping her spread out like a fucking all-you-can-eat buffet. I stared at her gorgeous face, her eyes hooded and cheeks flushed.

After a moment, Everly spoke, her voice coming out raspy and sexy as hell. "Fucking christ. I think you guys short circuited my brain. I don't know if I can move." But her blue eyes told a different story as she looked between us, then down to the three hard dicks all pointed her way. She licked her lips, desire flashing in her eyes.

Trailing a finger over the sensitive flesh between her legs, I smirked when her body shuddered. Griff and Chase watched, hunger on their faces as I slowly rubbed light circles over her clit.

"Oh, little Monet. We're not done. Not even fucking close."

Thirty-Six

Everly

Holy fuck. My mind was still buzzing from the earth-shattering orgasm Knox, Griff, and Chase had wrung from my body. My skin tingled with every touch, my pussy still pulsing from Knox's tongue.

"Oh, little Monet. We're not done. Not even fucking close." A wicked gleam filled Knox's eyes as he spoke. My breath caught in my lungs, the implication of his words clear. Molten heat pooled in my lower belly at the thought of the four of us together.

All three men moved at once, the synchronicity of their movements a beautiful thing to watch. Griff lay himself on the bed next to me while Chase moved near the headboard.

"Come ride my cock, Everly," Griff's deep voice commanded. He wasn't going full dom tonight, but there was a clear tone of authority in his words. His thick length stood tall and proud between his legs, waiting for me.

I climbed over him, my legs straddling his waist. Bracing myself on his chest, I slowly sank down, each delicious inch disappearing into my body. I stilled for a moment once he was fully seated inside me, my pussy stretching to accommodate his size. None of my guys were small by any means, and I loved the tight fit they all created.

I began to move against Griff's body, swirling my hips, grinding my clit against his pelvis with each forward motion. As I fucked him, Chase moved so he was at Griff's side, his hand stroking his gorgeous dick. Precum was leaking from the tip, and my mouth watered with the need to taste him.

Griff's hands dug into my hips as he watched me bouncing on his cock.

"Everly, put that pretty mouth to good use. Suck Chase's dick." Maybe Daddy Griff was going to come out to play after all.

Not needing to be told twice, I opened my mouth and let Chase feed me his dick until he was hitting the back of my throat. My eyes watered as I swirled my tongue over his hard length. Chase weaved his fingers through my dark locks and began to pump himself in and out of my mouth. My eyes rolled back at his divine taste.

Griff had taken over fucking me, his thrusts pounding into my soaked pussy. Suddenly, I felt fingertips trailing down my spine, the movement setting my skin on fire. Knox's fingers reached the top of my ass before slowly running through my cheeks.

I popped off of Chase, moving my hand to stroke him while I looked over my shoulder at Knox. He was tugging on his dick, his eyes searing over my naked body.

"Everly..." His voice was deep and gravelly, the hint of a question coating my name.

I furrowed my brow, unsure what he was asking. My brain still hadn't come all the way back online since my orgasm, my body still riding that high.

I felt Griff's hand leave my hip before it gripped my jaw, turning me to face him.

"Everly, Knox wants to fuck your ass. Be a good girl and let him, yeah?"

I stared at his green and gold eyes, wrapping my head around his words. I turned to look at Knox again, pure lust written on his face. The thought of having all three of them inside me at the same time... my pussy clenched in anticipation, making Griff groan under me.

"I'll take that as a yes, my beautiful Blue," he said, his thrusts slowing some. "Why don't you show Chase some love, he's looking lonely over there. Knox and I will take care of you." And with those words, Knox pushed me slowly forward, so I was leaning over Griff's chest. Chase adjusted his position on the bed, bringing his cock back to my waiting mouth.

I licked the underside of his shaft, running my tongue up and down before hollowing out my cheeks. I brought him as deep as I could before I gagged while Griff continued his painfully slow thrusts into my pussy.

As I sucked on Chase, I felt a lubed up finger near my ass. Knox pressed against the tight ring of muscle, letting me get used to the sensation before he slowly pushed inside. I reminded myself of how good it had felt when Chase had done the same thing during our threesome with Griff. My body clenched at the memory.

"Relax, baby, let him in," Chase murmured as he maneuvered a hand between mine and Griff's bodies, his thumb finding my clit. Using the pad of his finger, he began to rub circles over the sensitive bundle, quickly pushing my body toward another release. "That's it, baby, let Knox make you feel good."

While Chase worked me over, Knox continued to stretch me, slipping his finger in and out before adding a second. The burn was still there, but I found it difficult to focus on with Chase playing my body like a goddamn instrument. Knox gently scissored his fingers inside me, and the pain slowly began to melt into pleasure.

"You look so beautiful with Knox's fingers in your ass, Larkspur. Griff pounding into that glorious pussy," Chase panted as he thrust into my mouth. His words heated my core, my body humming from the different sensations. "Knox, don't you have something you bought Everly for her birthday?"

Knox grunted behind me, and a wicked grin spread across Griff's face. I tensed, my body tightening around them both. What could he possibly have gotten for my birthday that we would need right now?

Moving away from my ass, Knox made his way to his dresser, opening and closing the top drawer. He came up to the head of the bed, standing next to Chase. Knox watched me take Chase's dick into my mouth for a few moments, his dark eyes like molten orbs. He stroked himself, his hand running over the barbells before twisting around the crown.

Something glinted in his other hand, and I pulled back from Chase to get a better look. A large blue jewel sat atop a metal cone shaped object, the light making the jewel shimmer.

"What's that?" I asked, my voice hoarse from deep throating Chase.

"Knoxy's going to use that to make sure your ass is ready to take him and his pierced cock," Chase crooned, his fingers running through my air. I looked up at him, my eyes wide.

"Will it hurt?" I whispered the words, scared, but wanting nothing more than to please my men.

"I'd never hurt you, Everly." Knox's growly voice washed over me, my skin erupting in goosebumps. Griff had slowed his thrusts, pumping in and out of my body at a measured rhythm. "It'll feel good, baby, I promise."

"Do you trust us, Blue?" Three sets of eyes set fire to my body, waiting with bated breath for my answer.

"Always." My answer came out on a gasp as Griff thrust roughly inside of me, hitting that perfect spot deep inside my pussy. He continued to stroke in and out while Knox moved behind me. I heard the bottle of lube opening again before I felt the liquid drizzled down over my hole.

A second later cold metal pressed against me, sliding in at an achingly slow pace. Knox had stretched me some, so I was able to accommodate the plug a bit easier, but it still burned as it entered my body. He pushed it in at small increments before pulling it out, just to repeat the process over and over until it was seated fully inside my ass.

The feeling of fullness in my ass, coupled with Griff's large cock filling my cunt, was nearly enough to send me over the edge. But I needed more. As if reading my mind, Chase began to play with my clit again, rubbing quick circles that sent me spiraling toward an orgasm. Pleasure ripped through my body, starbursts exploding behind my eyelids. My pussy gripped Griff like a vice while my ass clenched around the jeweled plug.

I gasped around Chase's length, each of my nerve endings lit up like the Fourth of July as desire coursed through my veins. I glanced at Griff, his jaw set tight as he struggled not to follow me over the edge. "Fuck, Blue. Goddamn you squeeze my cock so good."

Before my orgasm could fully wane, Knox suddenly pulled the plug from my backside, leaving me with a sense of loss. But I wasn't left wanting for long. Just as quickly as the plug disappeared, a larger, more blunt object nudged my ass. Knox began to slowly push inside, his lubricated dick breaching me one inch at a time.

"Mmmmm," I groaned around Chase, the sound vibrating along his cock. He closed his eyes, the hand woven into my hair tightening as he guided me along his shaft.

Knox's hands gripped my ass cheeks tightly, pulling them apart to give him better access. I felt each barbell as they slid in, rubbing my walls in an indescribably dirty way. I heard Griff gasp, knowing he could feel the same thing. I peeked up as I continued to suck on Chase's dick, his face the picture of pure pleasure.

Once Knox was fully seated, his balls firmly against my ass cheeks, he paused, giving me a moment to adjust. But I need them to move. Now.

Releasing Chase, I begged them, "Please."

Just one word, but all three of my men knew what I needed. In the next second, they were all fucking my body. Chase gripped my hair, thrusting into my mouth as far as I could take him. Griff began viciously pummeling my pussy, each thrust making my nipples rub against his chest. Knox was sliding in and out of my ass, his movements timed perfectly with Griff's, so I was never left empty.

"Fuck, Larkspur, I'm going to fill that throat," Chase groaned before I felt him thicken on my tongue. His head tipped back, and hot cum spilled down my throat. I swallowed it all down, licking his length clean before he pulled out. He leaned in, kissing me, not giving a shit that I had just swallowed his cum. He moved his fingers back to my clit, pushing me right back to the edge.

Before I knew it, my orgasm hit me like a freight train. My pussy spasmed around Griff's dick, and my whole core clenched with my release. Both the men inside my body hissed at how tightly I was gripping them. I closed my eyes, stars dancing across my lids. I felt like I was floating, like I wasn't even on this plane of fucking existence anymore. All I knew in that moment was the sheer exhilaration coursing through my body at their touch. It was transcendent.

My orgasm set Griff off, his warm release filling me. "Fuck Blue!" he shouted, his thrusts becoming erratic.

Knox tipped over the edge a moment later. "Fuck! Everly!" His voice came out strained, through gritted teeth as he filled my ass. He thrust a few more times before draping himself over my back. Soft kisses trailed down my spine before he pulled out, the emptiness feeling oddly strange. Griff gently lifted me from his body, placing me in the middle of the bed.

Chase appeared next to me, a warm, wet cloth in his hand. He cleaned the cum Knox and Griff had left behind, his touch soft on my already aching core. When he was done, he tossed it into Knox's laundry hamper.

All three guys surrounded me on the bed, Chase and Knox on either side of me, while Griff settled near my head. Each guy had a hand on me, and we lay like that for I don't know how long. I dozed off after a while, but woke when I felt the bed move. Cracking open an eye, I saw Griff and Chase start searching for their clothes, silently moving through the room.

"Sneaking out?" I asked softly.

They both spun around, a playful grin on Chase's face.

"Nah, little Larkspur. We thought you were asleep, so we were gonna go finish cleaning up and head to our own rooms. You stay here, snuggle with Knox. Lord knows his grumpy ass could use it."

The arm Knox had curled around my waist rose in the air, his middle finger flipping them off. Griff and Chase both laughed before giving me sweet kisses good night. Once they were gone, I rolled over, snuggling into Knox's chest. I inhaled his scent, always a mix of cedar and paint. I felt so safe, so secure wrapped up in his arms. Warmth filled my chest, like the feeling you get sitting in front of a roaring fire after spending the day outside in the snow.

He kissed the top of my head, his fingers tracing some sort of pattern along my back. We stayed like that for a long time, neither of us sleeping, just existing in this perfect bubble, a wonderful moment frozen in time.

"Everly?" Knox said my name softly.

"Hmm?"

"Can I show you something?"

I pulled back from his embrace, so I could see him. He looked nervous, the expression immediately forming a knot in my stomach. What if he regretted what we'd all done together? Knox was definitely the most possessive of my guys, but he always seemed more than on board with our group dynamic.

"Uh, yeah, sure," I answered, unease creeping into my gut.

He climbed out of bed, pulling on his black boxer briefs. He picked up his t-shirt from earlier, but instead of putting it on himself, he tugged it over my head before pulling me from the blankets.

"Close your eyes."

He held my gaze until I followed his instructions. Holding my hand, he walked me to the far side of his room where all of his paintings were stored, and I could smell the acrylic as we got closer. I didn't venture over here often; Knox always preferred to watch me paint in my room. I had only seen him work a handful of times, and it was always at his studio. Knox was an amazing artist, but his mother had done a number on his self-confidence.

He left me standing in his t-shirt, the soft material hitting me mid thigh. I clasped my hands in front of myself, nervously shifting my weight from foot to foot. I could hear Knox rummaging around for a few moments before flipping on a lamp. Even with my eyes closed, I could see the brightness through my lids. He quickly adjusted the lamp, swiveling the light away from my face.

Finished with whatever he was doing, Knox moved to stand behind me, his hard chest pressed against my back.

"Okay, open."

A beautiful shock gripped me as my eyes fluttered open.

Laid out against the wall was painting after painting, the stunning pieces highlighted by the lamp's glow. As my eyes focused, my breath caught in my throat. My eyes began to water, and I could feel my heart hammering in my chest.

They were paintings, drawings, of me. Me with Griff, him holding me while I laughed. One of Chase carrying me piggyback, a big smile on my face. There was a large painting to the left, a set of eyes staring at me from the canvas, the outline of a man reflected in the deep blue color. And in the middle was a portrait of me, surrounded by blue and purple peonies, done in the same style as the painting of my mom I had shown him all those weeks ago.

I stood frozen, taking in each masterpiece before me. I brought one hand to my mouth as a sob broke through the silence of the room. Knox created these, *for me*. I spun around to face him.

He reached to gently wipe a tear from my cheek. It was such a simple gesture, the act so basic, but still so completely full of love and adoration. A whole new well of tears leaked from my eyes, my brain trying to wrap itself around what Knox had done.

"Oh, little Monet, please don't cry." He pulled me closer, wrapping his arms around me, cinching me to his chest. We stood in the quiet, neither of us moving, just existing like two halves of the same soul that had finally found one another before Knox finally spoke.

"I've never been great with words," he began. "I've always used art to express my feelings. That's what this is, Everly. These paintings, they are an expression of how I feel about you." He paused, pulling back, so I could look into his dark eyes. They pierced my own, seeing straight into the fabric of my soul.

He dragged in a deep breath before continuing. "My art, these canvases. I've poured every emotion I have for you onto them. They are the physical embodiment of my feelings for you."

He whispered the next words, leaning in until his forehead rested against mine, his hand cupping my cheek.

"They are my love for you. I love you more than I have ever found a way to say. I love you, Everly."

A single tear escaped down my cheek as I whispered back to him.

"I love you, too."

Thirty-Seven

Everly

The next few days had been spent doing absolutely nothing, and it had been glorious, the guys and I taking full advantage of having zero to do.

By midweek, I knew we were going to have to venture off campus to do some shopping for the goddamn ball that was rapidly approaching. My dad texted, saying he arranged for an SUV to be dropped off on Wednesday, so we could drive into the nearest town and get what we needed.

I tugged on a pair of ripped skinny jeans, pairing them with a Solis Lake sweatshirt I had purchased at the bookstore a few weeks prior. Being mid-October, the weather was finally starting to cool down, giving me the perfect opportunity to break out some of my hoodies... and steal some of the guys'. Tying on my red Chucks, I ventured out of my room, waiting to see if Evan was ready to go. As I walked, I pulled my long hair into a high ponytail, knocking on his closed door.

It swung open a moment later, Evan standing in the doorway. We looked each other up and down before bursting into a fit of laughter.

Trying to suck in a breath between my giggles, I managed to choke out, "You have to fucking change." I had to hold onto the door frame to keep from doubling over. My brother was standing in front of me, wearing the exact same damn sweatshirt.

He laughed while trying to speak. "Why do I have to change? You go change!"

"Not a chance, bro. I'm pulling the big sister card." I wiped the tears from my eyes before straightening, planting my hands on my hips in a playful show of dominance.

Evan knew better than to argue, so with a dramatic eye roll that would make any thirteen year old girl proud, he huffed back into his bedroom. Yanking the sweatshirt over his head, he quickly pulled on a gray thermal instead. Coming back to where I was standing, he cocked a brow. "Better, your highness?"

"Much." I reached out, circling his arm with my small hand and pulling him into the living room. I tucked my hand in the crook of his arm, escorting him to our front door. He stopped long enough to push his feet into his sneakers before grabbing his keys and wallet from the counter.

Walking down the hall, arm in arm, I felt so grateful for my relationship with Evan. We had grown distant since coming to Solis Lake, and I had to shoulder a lot of that blame. Most of my time was spent with the guys, and I knew I had been ignoring my brother. Being a twin meant having a built-in best friend, and I couldn't have asked for a better one, even with all his annoying habits.

We picked up the guys and made our way out front to the waiting SUV. The driver handed the keys to Griff before teleporting away, and we all climbed inside, Evan up front with Griff and me tucked in the back between Knox and Chase's giant bodies. Both men instantly laid a hand on my petite body; Chase's wrapped around my thigh while Knox slung an arm along the back of the seat, his fingers rubbing the back of my neck.

Griff drove us to the next town over, finding a parking spot in a public lot. The weather was beautiful, a perfect fall day full of crisp air and sunshine. The street was lined with shops and boutiques, people bustling about everywhere, some pushing strollers while others carried shopping bags down the sidewalk.

Chase tossed an arm around my shoulders, directing me to a dress shop halfway down the street. He had been uncharacteristically quiet on the ride over, but a mischievous smile now danced on his lips, and it made me wonder what he was up to. Griff, Knox, and Evan trailed behind us, already talking about where we should go for lunch.

Stepping inside the dress shop, I was immediately assaulted with tulle and lace. Bright shades in every color of the rainbow lined the racks, and I was already done before I'd even stepped foot in a garment.

"Hi there, I'm Ashley. How can I help you?" A pretty sales clerk stepped from behind the counter, making her way over to us. She let her eyes peruse my guys, slowly taking them in from head to toe. Jealousy flared in my chest, and my jaw tensed in irritation. She sashayed to where we were standing, her hips swaying in an almost theatrical way.

"Well, *Ashley*—" I started, but just as I was about to explain to this woman that my men were off limits, Chase cut me off.

"We have an appointment. Everly Blackwell." Appointment? I hadn't made an appointment. I looked to Chase for an explanation, but he refused to meet my eye, that same smirk still on his handsome face. What the fuck?

"Ah, yes. Right this way." She gestured to the back of the shop. We filed through in a single line, Chase at the helm while I followed closely behind him.

A short corridor led to an open, circular room full of mirrors and plush sofas. A tray with six full champagne flutes sat on an upholstered ottoman and a familiar looking green coat was lying nearby. I stared at it for a moment, the overly friendly sales woman forgotten. I knew that jacket...

A door opening behind me pulled me from my thoughts, and when I turned, I couldn't believe my eyes.

"C!!!" I screamed, running to her.

"Eves!!" Celeste screamed at the same time. We met in the middle of the room, throwing our arms around one another.

"How are you here?" I asked, holding her tightly to me.

She pulled back, nodding her head over my shoulder. When I released her to spin around, I was met with three guilty looking men staring at me and my best friend. Chase's small smirk had grown into a full grin, while Knox and Griff both wore broad smiles. Evan stood suspended in as much shock as me, obviously not in on the best friend surprise.

"How did you guys do this?" I questioned, wiping tears from my eyes and striding over to embrace each of them.

"When you were asleep the other night, Chase may or may not have broken into your phone to get Celeste's number. He texted her the next day to set the whole thing up. I called to make the appointment, and Knox, well... he threatened to kill Chase if he blabbed." Griff explained.

"So that's why you were so quiet on the way over!" I playfully swatted his arm.

"You really need to get a better passcode, little Larkspur," he chastised, throwing me a wink.

I couldn't believe they'd managed to arrange this whole thing, with me being none the wiser. Griff, Knox, and Chase all knew how much I had missed Celeste, only able to see her a handful of times during video calls. The fact they took the time to plan such a sweet surprise made my heart swell.

But, while I loved the guys, their fashion knowledge was limited to t-shirts and athletic shorts. I definitely needed my best friend's opinion when it came to shopping, especially for an evening gown.

After Celeste and I squealed for a few more minutes and the guys formally introduced themselves, they each gave me a kiss goodbye before venturing out into town to get tuxes and do a bit of shopping before we met up for lunch later. When I received not one, not two, but three scorching kisses, little Miss How-Can-I-Help-You's eyes nearly bugged out of her head with shock. Good. At least now she knew she didn't stand a chance in hell.

Speaking of shock, my brother had barely said two words, his eyes nearly the size of saucers when Celeste had come out of the dressing room. He gave her a quick hug, both of their cheeks turning pink at the contact before hightailing it out of the shop behind my guys. As far as I knew, neither had spoken about their kiss, but it definitely looked like it was still on their minds.

We made quick work of downing a few glasses of champagne while *Ashley* pulled a multitude of dresses for me to try on. I made my way into the fitting room, slipping into garment after garment. Forty-five minutes later, I still hadn't found a dress, and I was beginning to lose hope that I'd ever find one.

"C.... None of these are working," I whined. It wasn't that the dresses weren't beautiful. It was that they weren't *me.* I was looking for something classic, timeless. I didn't need layers of tulle, beaded bodices, or lace overlays. Sensing my despair, Celeste stepped up beside me on the raised platform, her gaze meeting mine in the mirror.

"You," she said as she guided me off the pedestal. "Take this off, put on that silky robe hanging in your dressing room, and have another glass of champagne. I'm going hunting." And with that she disappeared, making her way to the front of the shop where the dresses were on display.

Following her officially issued best friend orders, I plopped myself down on one of the overstuffed sofas after tightening the tie on my robe. I slowly sipped on my third glass of champagne, the bubbles tickling my nose. I'd need to slow down if I had any hope of meeting the guys later for lunch.

In the quiet of the empty dressing room, thoughts of the ball crept into my mind. I knew the guys were confident in their plan to keep me as far away from Austin as possible, but I was still anxious. He'd kept his distance since his assault in the woods, but I could still feel his disgusting gaze on me whenever he was near.

I was also nervous for my dad to meet my guys. I hadn't told him about them yet, and while the ball seemed like kind of a shitty place to spring that information, I didn't really have a choice. There was no way he wouldn't be able to tell the minute I introduced them all. Fuck. I had a terrible feeling this whole thing was going to be a shit show, inside of a dumpster fire, on board the hot mess express with me as the conductor.

"Okay Eves," Celeste's voice broke through my spiraling thoughts, pulling me back to the task at hand. She had a dress carefully hung over her shoulder, making it impossible for me to see. "I picked out *the* dress. But I want you to close your eyes. I'll help you get it on and then you can look. Deal?"

I raised an eyebrow at my best friend. She wanted me to get dressed in an evening gown, with my eyes closed. Had she met me? Did she not know how uncoordinated I was? We stared at each other for a moment before I finally relented, huffing out a dramatic sigh in defeat.

Doing as she asked, I closed my eyes once we entered the dressing room. She very carefully helped me to step into the dress, which I could tell was made of silk by the way it caressed my skin. It felt decadent, and it hugged my body as she zipped up the back. Taking my hand, she led me back out into the viewing area, assisting me until I was back up on the pedestal that faced the mirrors.

"Okay, now you can look," she said, her voice pitched high with excitement. I opened my eyes, and a small gasp escaped my lips.

It was a midnight blue, strapless gown, with a sweetheart neckline that showed off my ample décolletage. The bodice hugged my upper body, a thin belt wrapping around my waist before the dress flared out slightly at the hip. A long slit ran up the left side, showing off an impressive amount of thigh. Simple, yet elegant.

I could see Celeste behind me in the mirror, her reflection bouncing up and down with excitement. Her hands were threaded together in front of her chest, a bright smile on her face as she awaited my response.

Tears filled my eyes as I ran my hands down the smooth material. Celeste stepped up on the pedestal next to me, her thin arms wrapping around my shoulders. We stared at each other in the mirror, tears glistening in her eyes as well.

"It's perfect. Thank you, C."

"You look stunning," she whispered in my ear, squeezing me tightly. "Those boys aren't going to know what hit them."

"I missed you, C," I whispered back, my arms coming up to meet her embrace.

Thirty-Eight

Everly

I chose a simple pair of nude heels to go with the gown Celeste picked out, along with a gold floral comb that caught my eye at the register. Once I paid for my items, I texted the guys to let them know we were done. Knox replied, telling me they were down the street at the local pizza shop. With my garment bag in tow, Celeste and I strolled down the sidewalk before spotting the restaurant.

As if they could sense me, three pairs of eyes looked my way as I entered. They commandeered a large table in the back corner, several pies on plates, and a pitcher of beer already waiting for us. My stomach rumbled as the mouthwatering smell of pizza hit my nose, reminding me I skipped breakfast this morning in favor of sleeping an extra thirty minutes.

I laid my dress on an open seat before settling on a chair between Griff and Chase. A plate with a slice of pepperoni pizza appeared in front of me, and I dug in hungrily. We laughed and talked as we ate, and I looked around the table. My heart felt so full, being surrounded by the three loves of my life, my best friend, and my brother, I wondered if it would burst from all the joy I was feeling. I looked around the table, and a thought occurred to me, something that could make me even happier.

"Hey," I spoke up, drawing everyone's eyes to me. "Ev, what if you took Celeste to the ball? Dad said we each get a plus one. Knox is going as mine, and Griff is going with Chase. Celeste could be yours, then we could all go together." I felt a sharp sting on my shin as Celeste's foot met my leg. I winced but kept a smile on my face, hoping I could entice Evan to ask my best friend out.

"Uh, well—" my brother started to stammer, the color draining from his panicked expression.

"Jesus fucking christ, Everly, I swear," Celeste muttered under her breath before speaking louder. "It's alright, Evan. Your sister shouldn't have asked like that." She cut a glare at me from across the table before looking back at Evan.

But I could see it in her eyes. She wanted to go so badly as Evan's date. I'd caught her staring at several dresses in the shop that would have looked perfect on her, her fingers stroking the soft material longingly. I pressed on.

"So what do you think, Evan?" I completely ignored Celeste's protests, focusing instead on my brother. I tried to tell him with my gaze how much it would mean to me, how much it would mean to Celeste, if he said yes.

"Everly!" Celeste scolded me before turning to Evan again. "Seriously, Ev, it's fine."

My brother swallowed roughly before looking from me to my best friend. He rubbed his hand on the back of his neck as his mouth opened and closed several times, making him look like a fish out of water, before he finally spoke, his eyes stopping on Celeste.

"Celly," he started, and my heart dropped into my stomach at his tone. He was going to tell her no. What the fuck was wrong with my brother that he couldn't see that Celeste was perfect for him?

"What, Evan? What's your excuse? Hmm? Why can't you take Celeste?" My words came out sharp, angry. I was beyond irritated with my brother, at his disregard for Celeste's feelings, especially when I knew he felt something for her, too.

"I already asked someone," Evan blurted out. His cheeks turned a light pink as the words flew from his mouth.

My jaw hung open in shock. He had already asked someone? When? And how did I not know? Since when did my brother keep things from me?

"Who?" I demanded, my anger seeping into my words.

"Everly, maybe this isn't—" Griff's voice came from next to me, his hand landing on my thigh. I shot him a glare that had him closing his mouth. Knox and Chase sat quietly, watching the drama unfold.

"Who, Evan?" I repeated the question. My brother narrowed his eyes at me in challenge, refusing to answer.

"Evan Thomas... I swear to god, you better tell me right fucking now, before I really lose my shit and drag you out of here by your ear just like Mom."

His eyes softened slightly at the mention of our mom before he sighed heavily, his shoulders sagging.

"Everly..." he started, a look of defeat on his face, his hands scrubbing down his stubbly cheeks.

"Evan, you better..." I was beyond pissed now, ready to make good on my threat of hauling him out of the pizza shop using any means necessary.

"She's just a girl that's in some of my classes, okay?" he finally admitted quietly, his eyes downcast. "We've been hanging out a lot lately."

He raised his eyes, looking at me before sweeping over to look at my guys. "You've been... *busy* lately, so I've been hanging out with her while you've been gone."

My anger dissipated a fraction as guilt began to gnaw at me. I knew I had been spending most of my free time with the guys, but I thought Evan was okay with that. Apparently, I had been wrong. Not wanting to upset anyone any further, I attempted to smooth over the situation I had so epically fucked up.

"Sorry Ev," I murmured, catching his eye, silently asking if we were okay. He gave me a small smile, telling me yes without uttering a word.

"Sorry, C," I repeated my apology, turning to look at my best friend. She nudged my foot under the table with her own, a sad smile on her face.

"It's okay, Eves," she told me. "But next time, maybe ask first before you try to sell me off to your brother for a night, yeah?" Her voice had a teasing tone, telling me I was forgiven. "Besides, I already have plans for Saturday. Got a hot date with a Staunton football player." She shrugged her shoulders nonchalantly. But I could see the heartbreak under her façade and hear the lie in her words. There was no date, and there was no football player.

As we finished eating, the conversation slowly returned to normal, my outburst forgotten.

"So Blue, how did the shopping go?" Griff asked, nodding at my garment bag. Before I could answer, Celeste chimed in.

"It's midnight blue, and she looks fucking gorgeous in it. You boys are going to be walking hard-ons all damn night," she said and chuckled. My brother made a gagging sound as a Cheshire cat grin spread across Chase's face, heat making his green eyes nearly glow. Risking a quick glance at Griff and Knox, I could see the same desire on their faces. My nipples hardened against the fabric of my bra, flashes from the night of my birthday party racing through my mind.

Before I could get too caught up in a sexy trip down memory lane, Celeste checked her watch, announcing that she had to get going. The guys paid, and we all walked back to the parking lot. Celeste's lime green hatchback was parked in the corner of the lot, just out of sight, so I wouldn't spot her upon our arrival. I hugged her for a long time, the guys giving us space and waiting at our car.

When I didn't think Celeste and I had any tears left, we gave each other one final squeeze before she hopped in her car and drove off, making me promise to send her pictures from the ball. I walked back to our SUV, laying my dress in the trunk on top of the guys' suits before climbing in the backseat between Chase and Knox. All the garments were in black bags, not a hint of what they looked like to be had.

I was excited to see all three guys dressed up. I hadn't worn a fancy dress since my high school prom, and that hadn't been nearly as gorgeous as the dress currently sitting behind me. We drove in comfortable quiet back to campus, early 2000s rock music softly playing through the speakers from Knox's phone.

Griff pulled into the student parking lot, and we unloaded our purchases. Dad rented the car through the weekend to take to the ball, not realizing that Chase's dad was sending a limo, so we were stuck with it until Monday. We trudged into Bliss Hall, the guys leaving Evan and I at our door.

Walking inside our suite, we moved silently to our respective bedrooms. I hung my dress in my closet, taking the shoes out and placing them on the floor underneath.

Back in the living room, I waited for Evan to emerge from his room. I was planning to go back to the guys' place, but I needed to make sure my brother and I were okay first.

Evan finally came into the living room, a zip up hoodie on his lanky frame, his shoes still on his feet. If I didn't know any better, I'd say it looked like he was going back out.

"Hey," I called out when I realized he hadn't noticed me sitting on the sofa. He was shoving his wallet and keys in his hoodie pocket when he spun around at my voice.

"Oh, hey, I didn't realize you were still here."

"Yeah, I wanted to, I don't know, see if you wanted to hang out or something." I hated this. I hated not knowing how to talk to my brother, the feeling such a complete one-eighty from this morning. I got up, moving to stand behind the sofa, leaning my ass against it.

"Uh, thanks, but I figured you were gonna be with the guys tonight, so I made plans," he said sheepishly. "I mean, I can cancel, if you want..." His voice trailed off, and I could tell he didn't really want to bail on his date.

"No, no," I waved him off. "We can hang out another time. Wanna get breakfast tomorrow, just you and me?"

"Sure, Eves." He crossed the room, pulling me into a tight hug. He leaned his cheek against the top of my head, and I wrapped my arms around his slim body.

We held each other like that for a minute, a million unspoken things passing between us. He placed a quick kiss to the top of my head before pulling away. As he walked out, I wondered when my brother and I grew so far apart.

Thirty-Nine

Griffin

Our shopping excursion on Wednesday had been a success, with the argument between Everly and Evan being the only dark spot of the day. She came to our place about an hour after we got home and stayed the night, all of us hunkering down in the living room to watch movies. Everly had been quiet, and I knew something must have happened with Evan when we got back, but I didn't press her on it; she'd tell us when she was ready.

Now, it was Saturday, and I was standing in front of my mirror, straightening my black bow tie. After checking the buttons at my cuffs, I tied my shiny, black dress shoes before pulling on my jacket. Slipping a velvet jewelry box into the inside pocket, I walked out to the living room to meet Chase and Knox.

Chase wore a gray suit with a navy blue tie, while Knox sported an all black tux, sans tie, his top button open, allowing his tattoos to peek out.

Chase let out a wolf whistle as I entered, holding a beer in his hand.

"And here comes Daddy Griff, looking sexy as hell!"

I rolled my eyes, Chase's comment drawing a grin to my face. He always had a knack for being able to make me smile. It was part of the reason he was one of my best friends.

Draining the last of his beer, Chase set the empty bottle on the counter before moving toward the door. Knox and I fell in step behind him, moving down the hall as a well-dressed unit. Within seconds, we were in front of Everly's door. I reached forward, knocking on the heavy wood. I could hear heels clicking across the hardwood floor inside before the door swung open.

The air caught in my lungs, and Knox let out an audible gasp.

She was absolute perfection.

Long, dark hair cascaded over her left shoulder, large waves shimmering in the light. She had a subtle, golden flower pinned into the right side, just behind her ear, holding her hair in place.

Her navy dress clung to her body as if it had been made just for her. Her breasts were encased in silk fabric, the tops spilling over just a touch. Midnight blue wrapped around her body, highlighting every sensual curve. As my eyes traveled south, I saw a high slit along her left leg, her smooth, tanned skin exposed in a sexy, yet tasteful, way.

She was the picture of classic beauty, and I couldn't take my eyes off her.

"Holy fuck," I heard Chase mutter, Knox grunting in agreement.

Everly's cheeks turned a rosy pink, and her blue eyes looked down at her dress as she smoothed it with her hands. She brought her gaze back to us, her eyes lined in black makeup and her lips painted a deep, blood red. She looked like an old Hollywood starlet, glamorous and captivating.

"I know it's not anything flashy, but—" she stammered out, the pink on her cheeks deepening as it spread down over her bare neck and collarbone.

Before I could stop myself, I moved to her, placing my hand at the exposed skin on her neck. I pressed my lips to hers, not giving a fuck if I ruined her makeup. I'd gladly wear that red lipstick on my mouth all damn night if it meant I could kiss her. Sweeping my tongue into her mouth, I tasted her minty toothpaste and that thing that was distinctly Everly.

Breaking our kiss before I ripped off her dress and ended our evening before it began, I stepped back. Chase moved into my spot, giving her just as heated of a greeting, followed closely by Knox. By the time we were all finished saying hello, her lips were slightly swollen and lust flared in her blue eyes. Seeing my two friends give my girl such pleasure had me hard in my dress slacks, my erection pressing against my zipper. I didn't bother adjusting myself, wanting my girl to see exactly what she did to me.

"Blue," I said, drawing her attention. "You look beautiful." She was still in Knox's arms, and he spun her, so she faced Chase and I. Knox pulled out the small box he had hidden in his jacket and held it out in front of her.

Everly gasped, her hands coming up to take the box from Knox's fingers. "Open it, baby," he whispered in her ear.

She carefully opened the hinged box, another gasp falling from her mouth. If we weren't careful, we'd end up giving her hiccups.

"Knox, they're beautiful." She lifted the rose gold, diamond teardrop earrings delicately from the velvet interior, placing them in her ears one at a time. "Thank you." She turned to give him a sweet kiss.

Chase tugged her from Knox's arm with one hand, pulling his own box from his pants pocket. He dangled it in front of her face. She smiled, the flush on her cheeks deepening.

"Come on, you know what to do," Chase teased, putting the box into her hands. Following his instructions, she opened her second gift. Everly carefully removed the rose gold, diamond bracelet, and Chase helped secure it around her thin wrist. He lifted her hand to his mouth, leaving a kiss on the sensitive skin where the bracelet now resided.

"My turn," I said, Chase nudging her in my direction. I pulled the rectangular box from my pocket, holding it out to her.

"You guys," she said and sniffled, her eyes wet with unshed tears. "Why are you all giving me gifts? And super beautiful, obviously expensive gifts, at that?"

"Well, because none of us had time to get you something for your birthday, we did a little shopping while you were with Celeste the other day," I explained, still unable to believe the ravishing creature before me was real. "Now, be a good girl and open your last gift," I commanded, my voice dropping to a low growl.

She inhaled sharply, her eyes darkening with desire. She opened the box, running her fingers over the delicate necklace I had picked out. The guys and I decided to coordinate, getting her a matching set with the necklace, earrings, and bracelet as a belated birthday present.

I took the necklace from her, undoing the clasp. She turned in front of me, holding up her hair while I secured the thin chain around her neck. Once it was in place, I pressed my lips to the spot where her shoulder and neck met, feeling her shiver at my touch.

She reached up to touch the diamond that now lay on her sternum, just above where her cleavage began, stroking it delicately.

"Thank you all, so much. It's all beautiful," she said quietly, touching each gift with reverence. "I don't deserve you, the way you love me." The last words were spoken on a whisper. Her back was still to me, and I leaned forward to speak in her ear.

"My sweet Blue, you deserve everything, and we would gladly move heaven and earth to give it to you." I planted one more soft kiss on her neck before stepping away.

Everly grabbed her tiny black purse, which didn't look large enough to hold anything, as she draped a wrap around her shoulders that matched her dark dress. We made our way downstairs carefully, Everly teetering in her heels to where the limo was waiting. She explained on the way down that Evan left shortly before we arrived to pick up his date from her room, but he'd meet us in the parking lot.

Pushing through the doors of the dorm, a sleek black limo came into view. Mr. Stone sent one every year that I'd attended the ball with Chase, and I was grateful for his generosity. Just as we were getting ready to climb in, we heard the doors of Bliss open again. Turning as one, we saw Evan emerge first, dressed in a classic black and white tux, similar to mine.

The person who appeared behind him had the blood draining from my face.

Everly blanched as Morgan stepped through the doorway clad in a skin tight, fire engine red dress that left little to the imagination. I felt Everly tense at my side, knowing this situation was going to quickly spiral out of control.

"Morgan, what the *fuck* do you think you're doing with my brother?" Everly's husky voice had taken on a deadly quality, rage rolling off her in waves.

Anger and shock colored Evan's face. "What the fuck, Everly? What's your problem?"

"What's my problem? My problem is the cheating bitch dressed up like she's your fucking date for the evening," she snapped.

"Don't call her that! What the fuck is wrong with you!" he roared at her, and I could see Knox bristling from her other side at Evan's tone with our girl. Not wanting this shit show to escalate any further, I stepped forward, placing myself between the twins.

"Evan," I started, trying to keep my voice calm when I wanted nothing more than to throttle Morgan where she stood. "Morgan is my ex-girlfriend. Things didn't end... well." I didn't think telling him that I dumped her for fucking anything with a dick while we were together was something that should be shared out in public, so I opted for a more diplomatic approach.

"What the hell is that supposed to mean?" His eyes darted to Morgan, the smirk she had been throwing at Everly quickly morphing into an Oscar worthy pout meant to elicit sympathy from Evan.

"I don't know what he's talking about, E. We dated, but Griffin broke up with me at the beginning of the semester," she answered, leaving out some pretty fucking vital details.

"Yeah, because you slept with half the campus while you were together, you fucking bitch!" Everly's voice echoed through the courtyard, drawing stares from several students walking nearby. Well, there went my plan for subtly.

"Last time I checked, she wasn't the one fucking three different guys, Everly!" Evan roared back. My Blue's face blanched, Evan's words slicing into her like a dagger. She was shaking next to me, her entire body trembling with her hurt and anger. Knox wrapped an arm around her, whispering in her ear as he glared at Evan. I couldn't hear his words as he slowly moved her inch by inch toward the open door of the limo. She stopped just before climbing inside, turning back to her brother, tears in her eyes.

"Don't do this, Ev, please," she begged, her voice strained.

Evan stared at her for a moment, conflict swimming in his eyes, before straightening his suit jacket, his face turning to stone. "We'll take the SUV dad sent. See you at the party." He placed a hand on Morgan's back, ushering her to the student lot where the car was parked. When Evan had turned away, my ex looked over her shoulder at us with a smug smile.

Everly watched them walk away, a look of absolute betrayal on her pretty face. I didn't know what Morgan's game was, but I'd be damned if I let her hurt my Blue girl.

Forty

Chase

Everly was quiet, lost in her head, during the limo ride to the ball. We let her be for a little while, shooting looks at each other the longer she remained silent. I couldn't believe the way Evan had spoken to her, comparing our relationship to Morgan fucking around on Griff. It nearly had me seeing red, and I contemplated beating the shit out of him for how disrespectful he'd been. I kept my cool though, knowing that me losing my temper would only add fuel to an already raging fire. Knox reached out to her first, putting his hand on her knee. He stroked her bare skin softly where it peeked through the slit of her dress, drawing her attention.

"Little Monet, you doing okay? You've barely said two words."

"Honestly, no, I'm not. How could he do this?" she responded. "How could he believe her over me? I'm his sister." Her voice broke on the last words, her tears threatening to spill over. My poor girl was hurting, and I needed to fix it, pronto.

"Hey," I said, gently gripping her chin, turning her to face me. "Larkspur, it'll work itself out, okay? Don't worry about them for tonight. Let us show you a good time. I'll spin you around the dance floor so much you won't know which way is up." I flashed her a flirty grin, and she gave me a small smile in response. It was a tiny victory, but I'd take it.

"Thanks Chase. And you guys too," she said softly, looking at Griff and Knox. Griff, who had taken up one of the spots next to her, laced their fingers together, pulling their joined hands into his lap. He stroked a finger over her knuckles in small, soothing circles, and I wasn't sure if it was meant to calm her or him. I was positive my friend was struggling with what had just gone down, but I had to give him credit. He was holding it together like a motherfucking champ for our girl.

Once we cracked through her initial shock at tonight's turn of events, Everly came alive a bit more, giving us each flirty smiles and soft touches. Personally, I wanted to dive beneath her dress to see if she was wearing any panties, since I hadn't been able to detect a single line. As much as I thought an orgasm might help clear her mind, I didn't know if she was in the right headspace for that kind of activity, so instead I stuck to jokes and stories about Griff and I at my dad's parties from the last few years.

Before too long the limo was pulling up outside of the hotel where my dad's company hosted their annual Autumn Ball. I could see valets scurrying about, helping attendees out of all manner of expensive cars before driving the high priced pieces of machinery to the underground parking garage.

When our car stopped, the door was pulled open. I climbed out first, reaching my hand through the open door to help my Larkspur to her feet. She was so beautiful, her dark hair swept over her freckled shoulder. She placed her small hand, the one that had my bracelet around her wrist, in mine, and I gently pulled her from the vehicle. She straightened up while Griff and Knox stepped out, all of us smoothing our dress clothes from the ride.

Placing my hand on the small of Everly's back, I guided us to the entrance of the hotel where a man in a suit held open the large glass doors. I threw him a nod in thanks as we entered the opulent lobby. We made our way down a short corridor to the ballroom where the actual event was being held, my eyes watching as my Larkspur took in the space.

I had to hand it to my father, he sure as fuck knew how to throw a party. A plethora of fall colored flowers filled the space, small candles on the round tables scattered throughout the room. Navy blue and burnt orange bouquets sat in vases in the middle of each table and along the bar, which was situated to the left of the room. A four person band was tucked into the far right corner, leaving a large spot on the hardwood flooring for dancing. They were playing some sort of waltz while a few couples twirled around. I spotted my father, a Woodford Reserve bourbon—neat, always neat—in his hand. As if I had a bell announcing my arrival, he looked up, eyes locking on mine, waving us over with his free hand.

"Ready to meet my dad, little Larkspur?" I smiled at her nervously. She looped her arm through mine, her hand coming to rest in the crook of my elbow. Flashing me a smile, she answered.

"Lead the way."

We made our way to the bar, Knox and Griff right behind us, all our eyes surveying the room carefully. We all knew to stay on high alert, in case Austin decided to show up and start shit.

"Dad," I said when we reached him, sticking my hand out. He gripped it, giving it a firm shake before letting go to hand me the second bourbon he'd ordered. I tipped my head to him in thanks, taking a sip of the expensive liquor. He said a quick hello to the guys before turning his attention to the beauty on my arm.

"And who do we have here?" my dad asked, a charming smile on his face. Dad could be a hard ass when it came to a lot of things, and sure, he put an immense amount of pressure on my shoulders to take my place at the helm of his company, but Carrick Stone was a good guy underneath it all. Unlike some of the old assholes in this room, I knew my dad wasn't eye fucking Everly, instead admiring her beauty and grace. Holding out his hand, he introduced himself. "I'm Carrick, Chase's father."

Everly's cheeks flushed a light pink as she reached her hand out to his. "Everly Blackwell. It's nice to meet you, Mr. Stone." Her voice came out softly, a demure cadence carrying her words.

"And just how did my son find himself lucky enough to have you on his arm this evening?"

"Everly is my girlfriend," I answered for her, not wanting her to feel put on the spot.

"Girlfriend, you say? I don't think Chase has ever had a girlfriend in his life. You must be quite special, my dear," my father replied, looking at Everly again. The blush on her cheeks started to creep down her neck, and it made me want to kiss the hell out of her. He gave her a genuine smile, and I had never been so grateful for my old man's respect for women. I knew he adored my mom, his eyes never wandering in all their years of their marriage.

"Where's Mom?" I asked, hoping to give Everly a break and steer his attention in a different direction.

"She's out of town. One of the charities she's on the board of was having a big event tonight, so we figured we'd divide and conquer. You'll see her at Thanksgiving." My dad sipped on his bourbon, his eyes moving around the room, silently cataloging all of tonight's guests.

"Blue, would you like to dance?" I heard Griff ask. She glanced at my dad before looking at me, and I gave her a quick nod. I hadn't told my dad that she was dating all of us yet, and this would give me a good opportunity to talk to him one on one. Knox had already wandered off, most likely to keep an eye out for Thorpe. He grabbed a stool at the end of the bar, a bottle of some overpriced beer in his hand.

"Sure, Griff, that sounds fun. Although, be forewarned, I am not responsible if I break your toes with my horrible dancing skills." She took Griff's arm, and he led her out to the dance floor, twirling her around as they walked. Her husky laugh went straight to my dick. I'd have to see about getting us a room for the night upstairs....

"So, how long?" My dad glanced in my direction before nodding to where Griff had Everly foxtrotting. He'd picked up some decent dance moves over the years, coming to events like these with me. The rich trophy wives loved him.

"We started seeing each other at the beginning of the semester. She's incredible, dad," I turned to look at him, hoping he heard the truth and sincerity behind my words. "I love her."

"Mmmm..." he murmured as he sipped his bourbon. "So almost three months, then. But that wasn't what I was asking."

I looked at him, confused. "What do you mean?"

He didn't look at me, just continued to watch Everly dance with Griff. Finally, after almost a minute, he spoke again.

"How long," he started, taking a larger drink this time, "has she been sleeping with your friends?"

I spluttered into my tumbler, bourbon nearly coming out my nose. Grabbing a cocktail napkin from the bar, I wiped my mouth, taking a few seconds to compose myself. I inhaled a deep breath before answering him.

"I know that she's with them." I pushed my shoulders back before I continued. "She's dating all three of us. Has been since the beginning." I steeled myself for whatever harsh words he was going to throw my way about what a terrible decision I was making. But they never came. Dad just continued sipping on his bourbon, watching Everly move across the floor with Griff, her bright smile evidence of how much fun she was having.

Not wanting to argue, I let the subject die. I could bring it up again at a later date, when we weren't surrounded by all the elite of Emporia.

I waited a few more moments before broaching the subject of Everly's father.

"So, Everly's dad actually works for Thorpe & Stone. I guess he's an accountant or something." I glanced at him, his nonreaction to my previous statement making me cautious about bringing up anything to do with Everly.

"What was her last name?" he asked, seeming to be more interested in the conversation now that we were discussing the company.

"Blackwell. She said he was hired over the summer." My father's eyebrows furrowed, a frown taking over his face.

"Son, we haven't hired a new accountant in over two years. We have a full team. Are you sure she said her dad works for me?" The hairs on the back of my neck stood on end, instinct telling me something was wrong. No, not just telling me, fucking announcing it with a goddamn bullhorn.

"Dad, are you sure?" I pressed, answering his question with my own. Even that fucker Austin had confirmed that Mr. Blackwell was a Thorpe & Stone employee. How was it then that my dad, who made it a point to meet every new hire, had no idea who the man was?

Debating how much information to divulge, I carefully worded my next question. "Austin had mentioned her dad working for the company."

My dad snorted. "Maybe Thorpe hired him as his personal accountant, then. Although, I hope for your girl's sake that's not the case."

"What'd you mean?" I asked him, my spidey senses on high alert.

My dad looked around, making sure no one was close enough to hear our conversation. He leaned closer to me, lowering his voice as he explained.

"I have reason to believe that Alaric Thorpe has been embezzling money from the company and has possibly been dealing in dark magic as well."

While I wasn't super surprised by my dad's accusations—Alaric Thorpe was a piece of shit human being, just like his fucking son—I was shocked he was sharing them with me.

"Have you gone to the authorities?" I asked him quietly, already wrestling with how I was going to explain this to Everly. Fuck. I was praying her dad wasn't involved in some shady bullshit. After losing her mom, I don't think she could handle it if something happened to her dad, too.

"I've got some private investigators looking into a few things," he explained cryptically. He downed the rest of his bourbon, his gaze moving to the entrance of the ballroom. As if summoned by our talk, Alaric and Austin Thorpe strolled into the ballroom, looking like the smug bastards I knew they were.

Austin's eyes swept the room, until landing on something that had an evil smile crossing his face. I followed his gaze to the dance floor, directly to where my Larkspur had traded dance partners, she had Knox now moving to the music in perfect unison.

Feeling that deep seated rage begin to bubble toward the surface, I quickly excused myself from my father, striding swiftly over to where that motherfucker stood. His father had already left his side, no doubt to pull some shady shit.

"Don't you dare fucking look at her, you sick cunt," I ground out, my jaw clenched so hard I worried it may snap. I purposely walked right into his line of sight, blocking his view of Everly. He didn't deserve to see her. Bastard didn't even deserve to breathe the same air as her, but since I didn't figure my dad wouldn't appreciate me murdering someone in the middle of his event, this would have to do.

That fucking smile didn't leave his face as he acknowledged me, malice filling his eyes.

"Stone, to what do I owe the pleasure?"

"You motherfucker." I spit the words. "You've got some balls showing up here after what you did to her. You're lucky I don't rip your dick off and shove it down your throat."

"I don't know what you're talking about, Stone. I'm here as the son of one of the owner's of the company, same as you." The words probably sounded innocent, almost pleasant, to anyone else. But I could hear the snarky bite, each syllable laced with venom.

It took every ounce of willpower I had not to knock out his fucking teeth where he stood. But I couldn't protect Everly if I was sitting in a jail cell, so instead I balled up my fists, clenching them tightly at my sides.

"You're so fucked up," I accused, my voice lowering as I stepped toward him. He did have the good sense to tense as I approached, reinforcing the fact he was, in fact, just a sniveling little twat. "You fucking *hurt* her you sick asshole. You fucking threw her against a tree and sexually assaulted her. Then you fucking threatened her dad and Griff. You're a fucking piece of shit."

"I don't know what you're talking about, Chase." He sneered as he said my name, as if it were poison in his mouth. That same vile smirk sat on his face while he attempted to gaslight me. Spoiler alert, it wasn't gonna fucking work. "But if someone did attack and threaten Everly, I'm surprised she told you about it. Apparently she can't follow directions very well. Something I'll have to work on with her."

"What the fuck is that supposed to mean?" I demanded, my rage threatening to burst through the flimsy dam holding it back.

But Austin simply turned and walked away before I could get an answer, and my stomach churned with hate and worry. I needed to talk to the guys and fill them in on what Austin and my dad said. Now.

Spinning around, I tried to locate Everly and Knox on the dance floor, but the crowd had thickened too much to see anything. Spotting the back of Griff's head at the bar, I pushed my way through the throng of people until I reached him.

"Where's Everly?" I asked, my voice taut with anxiety.

"She's sitting at a table with Knox, why? What's wrong?" Worry creased his brow as he started to scan the crowd. As our eyes continued to ping pong around the room, I finally saw Knox, sitting at a table, nursing his beer. As the people around his table shifted, I realized he was sitting alone, Everly nowhere to be seen. *Fuck*.

Forty-One

Knox

Holding Everly in my arms as we moved along the dance floor was like heaven. Admittedly, she was a terrible dancer, but I held her close, guiding her movements with my own. With a rich, southern belle for a mother, I had been subjected to years of dance lessons, forced to attend my fair share of debutante balls, so while I'd deny it til I was blue in the face, I was a damn good ballroom dancer.

Everly let out a small squeal as I twirled her away, then pulled her in tight to my body, my arm looping around her tiny waist.

"You've got some moves, Mr. Montgomery. Who would've thought?" she teased, a beautiful smile lighting up her face. She'd been so upset since her fight with Evan, it made my heart nearly burst to finally see her happy. I was still contemplating wringing her brother's neck the next time I saw him for the way he'd yelled at her.

We continued to waltz across the dance floor for another song before Everly said her feet needed a break. I didn't imagine dancing in four inch heels could be comfortable, so I led her to a table at the side of the room.

"Do you want a drink or anything, little Monet?" I asked, needing a refill after I finished my beer.

She nodded. "A wine, please? Rosé if they have it." Setting her tiny hand on top of mine, she gave me a small squeeze. "Thanks Knoxy." I gave her a playful glare at the nickname. Clearly Chase had been rubbing off on her, but I'd let her call me whatever the fuck she wanted, as long as she let me call her mine.

I leaned over, leaving a soft kiss on her forehead before I got up, taking a few steps toward the bar before I stopped. Turning around, I fixed her with a serious look.

"Do not move from this table, Everly. Got it?"

"I know, Knox, I won't go anywhere." The light-hearted smile that had been there moments ago disappeared, and I cursed myself for scolding her like a child. I strode back to her, crouching and scooping her hands into my own.

"I'm sorry, baby." I looked into her now-sad eyes, the different shades of blue mixing like the paints on my palette. "I didn't mean to bark orders at you."

She leaned toward me, a soft kiss landing on my mouth.

"I get it," she said, leaning back in her chair. "I promise, I won't go anywhere."

"Good girl," I said, my voice low as I kissed the tip of her nose.

Rising up, I made my way to the bar, which was now crowded as fuck. It was going to take forever to get a damn drink. I spotted Griff near the far end, nudging my way through the crowd until I reached him. I could still kind of see Everly at our table, so I felt semi-okay being this far from her.

"Hey man," Griff greeted me, tipping his bottle of beer in my direction. I slapped my palms to the bar top as I stepped up, watching the three bartenders as they mixed martinis and other fancy ass drinks. I was a beer man myself, a fact that drove my mother half out of her mind.

"Honestly, Knox, can't you at least have a civilized drink? A manhattan perhaps? Beer is simply alcohol for people with no class."

I waited what seemed like forever for the bartender to notice me, finally making his way over. I ordered an IPA and Everly's wine, before responding to Griff.

"Hey," I mumbled, my lips finding the cold mouth of my drink. I took a long pull, enjoying the iciness as it slid down my throat.

"Where's Everly?" he asked, looking around.

"She's at our table. Don't worry, she knows not to leave," I explained, before grinning to myself. "I pulled a Daddy Griff, told her not to move, then called her a good girl." I winked at him as he barked out a laugh.

"Very funny, asshole," he said, playfully punching my shoulder.

We stood together, surveying all the rich assholes in the room. Middle aged men with fat wallets and wandering eyes. Plastic surgery enhanced trophy wives hanging off their arms. I knew I came from money, but fuck if I ever became like half the dipshits in this room. I'd rather gouge out my own eyeballs with a stick of charcoal.

Silence fell between us for a moment before Griff spoke again.

"She's good for you, you know?"

I thought on his words, not answering right away. But he was right; Everly *was* good for me. I had smiled more, laughed more, *felt* more since meeting her than I think I had in my entire life.

Before Everly, my art consumed me. I used it as my outlet for everything, pouring every single emotion onto my canvases. Every passive aggressive comment my mother made, each time she outright insulted my work. As much as I liked to give Chase shit, he and Griff were the only things that made the last few years bearable.

But then Everly blew into my life, and everything changed. I felt... complete. They had become my family, with Everly being the glue that would bind us together. I couldn't imagine a life without her.

"She is," I agreed. "She's good for all of us."

He nodded his agreement, taking a sip of his beer. "Same, man. As corny as it sounds, I thought for the longest time that I loved Morgan. But since being with Everly, I really get it now. What it feels like to truly love someone so much that you would do anything for them." He glanced over at me, his cheeks heating a bit with his blush.

I got it though, that feeling he described. I would raze the fucking Earth for Everly. I would give her the sun, the moon, and every single fucking star in the sky if she wanted them. There wasn't a single thing in this universe that I would deny her, ever.

The crowd thickened considerably, and I struggled to see Everly. Unease swirled in my gut when I realized I couldn't see her. I elbowed Griff's arm, grabbing his attention.

"I'm gonna head back to the table. I don't want to leave her alone for too long. You coming?"

"Nah, I'm gonna hang here for a bit. I saw a few guys from last year's party that I want to say hi to. I'll be over in a bit. Keep our girl happy while I'm gone." Griff grinned, and I smiled back easily. I loved hearing my friends refer to Everly as 'our girl.' Because she was.

She was mine.

And Griff's.

And Chase's.

Ours.

My mind wandered to our night together, all of our hands on her perfect fucking body. Maybe I'd ask Chase if we could get a room here tonight...

I weaved my way through the crowd, careful not to spill Everly's wine. By the time I reached the table, I felt like I just ran a fucking gauntlet. I set her glass in front of her before sinking into my chair. Feeling an overwhelming need to touch her—which, let's be honest, was all the fucking time—I slung an arm around the back of chair, lightly running my fingertips over her gorgeous, tanned shoulder. My body relaxed the moment my skin touched hers, as though she was a balm that settled my soul.

We sat that way for a few minutes, my mind lost in the multitude of ways that I loved the girl sitting next to me. I knew, deep in the furthest reaches of my heart, she was it for me. There was no one else that I could ever love as much as I loved Everly Blackwell.

Her sweet voice brought me back to reality, and I turned so I could focus on her words.

"Knox, I need to go freshen up in the ladies room."

"Oh shit, yeah, okay," I said, "I'll walk you." I went to rise from the table, placing my bottle down when her tiny hand landed on my arm.

"It's okay, I can go by myself." She had a bright smile on her face, but I wasn't about to let her waltz around this damn party alone. Especially considering that motherfucker Thorpe could be wandering around.

"Little Monet," I started, narrowing my eyes at her request.

"Knox, seriously, I can take myself to the bathroom. They're just down the hall, and I'm sure there are a ton of women in there, so I won't be alone. Besides, even Austin isn't stupid enough to attack me in a crowded ladies' restroom." While her reasoning seemed solid, doubt gnawed at the back of my mind, telling me something just wasn't right.

I thought about her request, her insistence that she could handle going alone. I didn't want to treat her like an errant child, someone who couldn't do things for herself. I knew she was a fully capable, grown woman, a fact I kept reminding myself as I agreed to her request.

"Fine," I spoke at last. "But Everly, you go straight to the bathroom and straight back here, got it?" She needed to understand that I would hunt her down and spank her ass red if she didn't listen.

Her blue eyes shimmered with hope, the glow of the candles' light making them appear a few shades darker than normal. "You can trust me, Knox."

Forty-Two

Everly

I watched Knox walk to the bar, admiring the way his black dress pants hugged his ass. All three of my guys looked good enough to eat tonight, each dripping with so much sexiness it was a shock my dress hadn't taken itself off my body in a bid to get me naked for them.

They had each been so sweet since our run in with Evan and Morgan back at the academy, trying their hardest to cheer me up. I'd be lying if I said my heart hadn't been ripped out and stomped on by Evan's angry words.

I was still in shock that he chose Morgan over me. My chest ached with the hurt of his betrayal, but I also felt the burn of anger simmering slowly in my veins. Morgan had another thing coming if she thought I was going to give up my brother that easily.

I can only imagine the lies she fed him, what sort of make believe bullshit she peddled to get him into her bed. Jesus. He was going to need every goddamn STD test under the sun. I nearly gagged at the thought.

As if summoned from the pits of hell itself, Morgan plopped herself in the chair next to mine, her tits nearly bouncing out of the top of her halter dress. I looked at her in disgust, wondering what the fuck she wanted.

"Everly," she spoke, her voice invading my eardrums with its same level of annoying shrillness as usual.

"What in the ever loving fuck do you want? If you didn't get the hint back at the dorms, I don't fucking like you, and I don't fucking like that you're here with my brother." I practically growled at her, my hands balled into tight fists that I was struggling not to drive into her make up heavy face. I could feel the crescent shaped marks my nails were leaving on my palms, leaning into the pain to ground myself.

"Well, I do quite like fucking your brother." She grinned a saccharine smile. I nearly lunged out of my seat, ready to rip her tongue right out of her mouth. I was going to beat my brother senseless the next time I saw him. "But that's not why I came over." She inspected her manicure, as if we were old friends just catching up over a glass of wine.

"Spit it out, Morgan. I'm really over your bullshit."

Sighing dramatically, she rolled her eyes before looking at me again.

"Evan wants to talk to you. Alone. He doesn't want your little harem to get all pissy and kick his ass, so he said to ask you to meet him in one of the conference rooms down the hall. I think he said the third one on the left," she finally explained, before finishing up with, "He was kind of hard to understand. His mouth was a little busy, if you know what I mean." She waggled her eyebrows up and down, forcing me to close my eyes and take a deep breath before I killed her in front of all these people. I'd just met Chase's dad; I really didn't want him to see me led out in handcuffs.

"Fine," I was able to grind out. "Tell him I'll meet him there as soon as I can. But if my guys can't come, then neither can you."

Rolling her eyes again, she agreed. "Oh my god, fine. You know, you could just be happy for us. No need to be such a bitch about it. I mean, with how *close* Evan and I are, you and I are practically family."

"Over my dead fucking body." I spit the words at her. I'd be dragging my brother away from this crazy psycho the first chance I got.

"Hmmm...." was her only response, and I swear something flashed in her eyes that almost looked like glee. I glared at her, my mouth in a tight line, a clear indicator I was done with this conversation.

Without another word, Morgan left the table, disappearing into the crowd. I knew if I told any of the guys about Evan's request, they'd immediately shoot me down. But I desperately needed to talk to my brother without them interfering and potentially making the whole situation ten times worse. I knew once I sat down with Evan alone, and away from Morgan, I could talk some sense into him.

I felt guilty, knowing I shouldn't lie to my guys, but I would only be a few minutes, and the risk far outweighed the consequence in my opinion. Better to beg for forgiveness and all that.

Just as I made my decision, Knox returned to the table, a beer in one hand, my wine in the other. I smiled as he set it in front of me, his large frame sliding into the chair next to mine. He draped his arm around the back of my seat, his fingers stroking my shoulder softly. I sat quietly for a minute, working up the nerve I needed to leave the table.

"Knox," I finally spoke, turning to look at him, a big smile plastered on my face, "I need to go freshen up in the ladies room."

"Oh shit, yeah, okay. I'll walk you." He set his beer on the table and started to rise from his chair. I placed a hand on his bicep, halting him.

"It's okay, I can go by myself," I assured him. His eyes narrowed at me.

"Little Monet," he started, but I cut him off, knowing if I was going to get out of here, I needed to do it quickly before he had too much time to ruin my plan.

"Knox, seriously, I can take myself to the bathroom. They're just down the hall, and I'm sure there are a ton of women in there, so I won't be alone." I swallowed roughly, hoping like hell he didn't notice. "Besides, even Austin isn't stupid enough to attack me in a crowded ladies' restroom." I sucked in a breath, holding it in my lungs as I waited for him to answer.

Knox considered for what felt like an eternity before finally settling back into his seat. Relief flooded me, my plan nearly complete.

"Fine," he said, his voice hard and serious. "But, Everly, you go straight to the bathroom and straight back here, got it?" I could see the hesitancy in his eyes, his love for me making him question his decision. It had the guilt in my stomach eating at me in painful bites. Not wanting him to second guess letting me go, I stood as quickly as I could without seeming too overeager. Although, I guessed I could blame it on needing to pee badly.

"You can trust me, Knox," I reassured him, my insides twisting up as the lie flowed from my lips. Grabbing my little black clutch off the table, I made sure my phone was tucked inside.

Sighing heavily, Knox nodded his head. I leaned down, leaving a sweet kiss on his cheek before hightailing it out of the ballroom via a side door.

Once in the hallway, I stopped a man wearing a nametag to ask where the conference rooms were. He gave me a strange look before directing me down a corridor. I quickly made my way to the third door on the left, my nude heels clicking on the marble tile. As I reached for the handle, I prayed that I would only find Evan inside and that Morgan had magically disappeared to some deserted island off the northern coast of Canada.

I pushed down the gold fixture, opening the door into the modern room. A conference table sat in the middle of the space, at least ten swivel chairs around it. I looked around, but I didn't see Evan anywhere. I stepped further into the room, wondering if Morgan had given me the correct information.

A shift in the air had the hairs rising on the back of my neck. I heard the door click shut behind me, the sound like a fucking gunshot in the quiet space. I turned, a scream lodging itself in my throat. Standing between me and the door was the living embodiment of all my fears.

Austin Thorpe.

A sick smile stretched across his thin face, his eyes gleaming with evil intent. Even in a designer suit, he still looked like a fucking creep. His eyes traveled down my body, lingering on my breasts before crawling down my bare thigh. Even though I was mostly covered, I felt naked and exposed under his filthy gaze.

I could feel fear slithering up my spine, wrapping its cold tentacles around me, locking me in place. I was freezing, just like last time. But then Griff's voice filtered into my terrified brain.

"Baby, hiding in your room isn't going to help anything. It's not going to make you feel better. It's not going to take away what he did to you."

"I want you to fight back, so you never feel that powerless, ever again."

Letting his words sink into me, giving me strength, I pushed my shoulders back. Even though I was scared shitless, I wanted him to see that he held no power over me.

"What do you want, Austin?" I willed my voice to remain steady, even though I was shaking like a leaf on the inside. "Actually, you know what? I don't give a fuck. Let me out of this room, or so help me god, I will call Knox right now, and he'll come beat the ever loving fuck out of you. I kept your fucking secret, you sick asshole. Now leave me alone." My rage was quickly building, overtaking the fear that first threatened to take control. "And where the *fuck* is my brother?"

Austin laughed, the sound so malicious it twisted my insides. He took a step closer, and I backed up until my ass hit the table behind me.

"Oh, Evan won't be joining us tonight. Morgan played her part and got you here. She's probably got him in a coat closet somewhere by now, on her knees." He licked his lips, the lewd gesture sending bile up my throat. "Lucky for you, we will be having a few guests join us momentarily. I would have loved to have had you alone again." His eyes flashed with the mention of his assault in the woods. "But alas, tonight I will have to share your attention."

My mind spun at the words coming out of his mouth. I knew when I walked in that Morgan had lied—again, what a shock—but now I was faced with the realization that she'd handed me over to the man responsible for hurting me just a few weeks prior.

"What the hell are you talking about? Who's joi—" My words were cut off when another door, this one tucked away into the corner of the room, opened with a flourish.

A man walked in, and I could tell immediately that he had to be Austin's father. They shared the same disturbing aura, with a promise of cruelty and violence emitted from their very presence. Mr. Thorpe's eyes roved over my body, and I had that same sickening feeling of being exposed once more. I was certain if I had any food in my stomach it wouldn't have stayed there for long.

The very real fear that I was going to be assaulted by a father-son duo set off alarm bells in my brain. I needed to call Knox. Shit, he was probably storming the women's restroom at this very moment, but that was in the hall on the opposite side of the ballroom, too far for him to reach me before something terrible happened.

I contemplated just screaming as loud as I could for help, and when I realized I had no other options, I decided to go for it. Just as I opened my mouth to let out an earth shattering shriek, a third man entered the room. My scream died in my throat as he came into view, all the air leaving my lungs in a single word.

"Dad?"

Forty-Three

Everly

"Everly, sweetheart, what are you doing here?" My dad walked straight to me, wrapping me in his arms. He held me to him, my mind buzzing like there were a million bees inside, all fighting to get out. I clung to his suit jacket, pulling him as close as possible.

Dad is here. He won't let them hurt me.

"Everly, what's going on?" My dad pulled away, and fear and vulnerability crashed into me again, like he would disappear, leaving me alone with the Thorpe men and their disgusting stares. He tried to take a step back, but I refused to release his jacket. He looked at me, a frown forming on his familiar face.

"Sweetheart, tell me what's going on," he tried again, this time his voice coming out a bit more forceful.

"Dad, I—" but before I could get out another word, Mr. Thorpe interjected.

"Why don't we have a seat, James. There are a few things we need to discuss." Austin's dad moved to the head of the table, taking a seat in one of the plush chairs, while his son sat in one to his right. My dad and I moved to the opposite side of the large table, putting a decent amount of space between

Austin and I. If I was being honest, the entire circumference of the Earth could separate us, and it still wouldn't be enough distance.

"Alaric," my dad spoke, looking to Mr. Thorpe, "what is going on? Why is my daughter here?"

I watched a smirk play on Austin's lips, and my stomach clenched. A sick feeling of dread crept through my body, knowing something terrible was about to unfold.

"Well James, we need to discuss the terms of your contract," Mr. Thorpe—*Alaric*—– answered cryptically.

"Alright, but what does Everly have to do with that?" My dad kept shooting glances at Austin, his unease with the situation becoming more and more apparent on his face. The sick fuck across the table just continued to grin.

"James, when you signed your contract, becoming my employee, one of the stipulations of your employment was that you would, essentially, owe a favor of my choosing. Do you remember that?" Alaric questioned, his voice eerily calm.

"Umm, yes, I think I remember that portion. But I thought that had to do with my acquisition of additional pow—" my dad began to respond, but Alaric held up a hand, cutting him off.

"The contract reads," he spoke as he snapped his fingers, a document appearing on the table before him. "Mr. James Blackwell, upon entering into a binding contract with Mr. Alaric Thorpe, agrees to the above stated terms of employment, compensation, and other *benefits,* on the condition that he maintains a satisfactory level of performance within the duties of his job. Mr. Blackwell further agrees that he will be beholden to Mr. Thorpe for a future request of Mr. Thorpe's choosing. Mr. Blackwell may not deny this request, or his *termination* will be effective immediately."

My dad sat silently, waiting for Alaric to explain further. After another thirty seconds had passed, I could see my dad fidgeting, his bushy eyebrows drawn together in confusion. "I still don't understand—"

Mr. Thorpe didn't let my dad finish. He turned his attention to me, his eyes glancing over the exposed skin of my breasts. I wished I had my wrap to cover myself, or better yet, a biohazard suit.

"Everly, did you know that I knew your mother?"

His question hit me out of left field, alarm bells blaring in my head. Deciding I needed to proceed with caution until we knew what he wanted, I responded carefully.

"Umm, no, Mr. Thorpe, I didn't. How did you know her?"

"Funny you should ask. James, do you want to explain to your daughter how you stole the love of my life, or shall I?"

My jaw nearly hit the table as it hung open in shock. What in the hell was this man talking about? My parents had been college sweethearts, married for nearly twenty-five years when my mom died.

She had been a beautiful woman, and I had no doubt she dated before she met my dad, but he was it for her. She had been head over heels in love with my father my entire life. Evan and I used to get so grossed out when we'd catch them making out in the kitchen like a pair of horny teenagers, yelling at them to get a room. I remembered a conversation my mom and I once had about their relationship.

Dad ran out to grab a few things from the store for dinner, leaving mom and I to start prepping the ingredients we had on hand. I'd been teasing her about the fact they couldn't keep their hands off each other, when she turned to me, smiling.

"I love your dad so much, Everly." Her words were so genuine and sincere, a soft smile on her face. "I think I've loved your dad since the moment I met

341

him. He hasn't always been perfect, and lord knows we've had our fair share of arguments, but through it all, I'm so happy I get to be his."

I considered her words carefully before responding.

"Mom?" I questioned. "Do you think there's someone like that out there for everyone?"

She set down the knife she'd been using to peel potatoes to grip my hand instead. She cupped my cheek, her sweet smile aimed at me.

"Oh my little artist, I hope you find someone who completes you the way your father completes me. The missing half of your soul. That you get to experience a love so deep, it steals your breath. That your heart hammers in your chest when they walk into a room. Someone who makes you laugh and holds you when you cry. I hope you're lucky enough to find someone the way I found your father. Besides you and your brother, he is my everything."

Shaking myself out of the memory, I looked to my dad. He was staring slack jawed at Mr. Thorpe, completely perplexed by his accusation.

"Rick, what on Earth are you talking about? Maggie was your friend. We were all friends. You never dated," my dad answered him finally.

My dad had been friends with Alaric Thorpe? That was certainly news to me. Not once in my twenty one years on this Earth had either of my parents mentioned Alaric Thorpe, let alone that they'd been friends. What in the actual fuck was going on? I kept my mouth shut, waiting to see what Mr. Thorpe would say next.

His face hardened, anger flashing in his eyes as he turned his gaze to my dad.

"You stole her right out from underneath me, James. She was mine, but you weaseled your way in and took her from me!" By the last word he was nearly shouting, his face turning a mottled red with his rage. His chest heaved several times before he brought his breathing back under control. Smoothing a hand over his slicked back salt and pepper hair, he took one last breath before he pressed on.

"Now, however, I intend to right the wrongs of the past. As I stated before, per your contract, you are indebted to me for one favor of my choosing, no exceptions. The time has come for me to collect."

His words sent a chill up my spine as I looked across the table at Austin. He was staring at me, like I was a piece of meat sitting atop a silver platter. His eyes danced with a brutality that had me absolutely terrified for whatever was about to happen.

A long moment of silence stretched across the room before my dad finally spoke again.

"What is it you want, Rick?"

Mr. Thorpe sat back in his chair, his fingertips pressed together in front of his chest. A sinister grin slowly crept up his mouth, and he turned his eyes to me.

"Your daughter," he stated simply.

The words flowed out of his mouth like he was giving his dinner order to a waiter at a restaurant, and not just casually blowing up my entire life.

"Excuse me? What do you mean my daughter?" my dad spluttered. I probably should have been yelling, screaming, doing something, *anything*. But I sat, frozen, unable to move. I was trying to drag air into my lungs, but it felt like nothing was happening with each inhale.

"My apologies. I guess I should have been more specific," Thorpe sneered before glancing at Austin. "I want Everly, for Austin. I think they'll make a fine pair, don't you?"

No no no no...

"No," the whisper just barely made it past my lips. My vision was growing dark along the edges, and my head was spinning. I tried to take a deep breath, but it was like my lungs just wouldn't expand.

Blood rushed in my ears, so loud I could barely hear my dad yelling at Mr. Thorpe. I closed my eyes, willing this all to be some sort of nightmare. That I'd wake up, snuggled in bed with my guys, wrapped up in their love for me.

A touch on my arm jostled me from my thoughts, and I was finally able to suck in a lungful of air, relief surging through me. But it was short lived.

Austin had quietly moved around the table, slinking into the seat next to mine. His callous, cold eyes looked at my body, and I jerked away on instinct.

"Now, pet, don't be like that. Didn't you hear my dad? You belong to me now." He reached out to stroke a finger down my cheek. It would have been a sweet and delicate gesture from one of my guys, but coming from Austin, the act made me want to take a cheese grater to my face. Bile rose in my throat, and I was half tempted to spew it on him, Exorcist style.

"Don't. Fucking. Touch. Me," I growled at him. "I am not, and will never be *yours*. Get that through your thick fucking skull you wannabe rapist piece of shit."

"Pet, that's not very nice," he replied, his tone that of an adult scolding a child for taking the last cookie. "We'll have to work on that behavior once you're with me full time."

Not even able to formulate a response to his insanity, I turned to my dad. Where I expected to see anger, rage, indignation, I instead was met with resignation. Sadness. Defeat.

"Dad, he can't be serious. Austin is a psychopath. He attacked me a few weeks ago!" I gripped his arm tightly in my hand, pleading with him to tell me this was some sick joke. "Daddy? Tell me this isn't true. Please." My voice broke on the last word when I realized my dad was refusing to meet my eye.

Mr. Thorpe answered for him.

"I assure you my darling, I am completely serious. And your father is well aware of the consequences if he chooses not to honor our agreement."

I squeezed my dad's arm again, willing him to look at me. When he finally raised his eyes to mine, they were full of tears, regret and guilt swimming in his blue orbs.

"Daddy, please," I whispered, begging him not to do this. "Just quit. You can find another job. I can quit school, I'll work. But please, please don't make me go with him."

"Everly, darling. It's not that simple. Your father can't simply quit his job. The consequences of breaching our contract are immediate termination," Thorpe explained smugly.

"Then fucking fire him!" I roared. I would slit my own wrists before being bound to Austin fucking Thorpe for the rest of my life.

"Everly, they won't fire me." Tears streamed down his face now, and I knew I missed something.

"He just said they'd terminate you if you break this stupid fucking contract!" I all but screamed the words at him.

Thorpe answered again, a completely depraved smile on his face. His next words stole the breath from my lungs in a violent grab.

"And we will. The cost for your father's failure," he explained, his grin becoming predatory, "is his life."

To be continued....

Acknowledgments

So about that cliffhanger... Please don't hate me! Ever Dark: Solis Lake Academy Book Two will be coming out soon and will pick right up with Everly and the guys dealing with that crazy ending!

Writing Ever Blue was truly a journey I never thought I would take. I have laughed, cried, and fallen in love alongside each character and I hope you did, too. So much of who I am was poured into this story; my love of rock music, art (although admittedly I'm a terrible painter), and squirrels seeped onto the pages, bringing small pieces of myself into my story and to all of you. And don't worry, you'll be seeing Onyx again soon....

To my husband, who has always encouraged me to follow my dreams, has stuck by my side through thick and thin, and tolerates my personal brand of crazy. Remember baby, we'll be the last ones dancing, in a faceless crowd.

To my writing ride or die, Lauren, I don't think I could have ever done this without you. Thank you for always being there to bounce ideas around, send me silly videos, and for allowing me to be a part of your writing. I'll be forever grateful that fate brought us together!

To all the GLS: you know who you are! Thank you for all the words of wisdom and support as I wrote this book. And for all the peen pics! Maree Rose, this book would literally not exist without you! Thank you for creating such a beautiful cover and for helping me navigate all of my formatting issues!

Lastly, to my readers, thank you for taking a chance on a brand new author. For reading my words and giving me the opportunity to share Everly's story with you. I love each and every one of you.

K.D. is a country girl, born and raised in the backwoods of western New York. She has two kids and is married to her college sweetheart. She is a former teacher and now spends her time writing and organizing the lives of others. K.D. is a die-hard Buffalo Bills fan and may or may not have named one of her characters after a certain tight end. She loves rock candy (a necessary staple while in the writing cave) and espresso martinis. The X Ambassadors are always on her play list, as well as a healthy dose of early 2000's rock.

Made in the USA
Columbia, SC
16 September 2024

41879024R00196